Praise for

*Pioneering*
**Sarah Goodwin**

'*Shearsby's writing will give you goosebumps*'
**Amanda Cassidy**

'*The master of villainy, the author of bar-raising*'
**AJ Law**

'*Nicky is adept at creating an incredibly dark, surreal atmosphere*'
**@Calmstitchread**

# THE LOST RAVEN

## NICKY SHEARSBY

SRL PUBLISHING

SRL Publishing Ltd
London
www.srlpublishing.co.uk

First published worldwide by SRL Publishing in 2024
This paperback edition first published 2025

Copyright © NICKY SHEARSBY 2024

The author has reserved their right to be identified as the author of this work which has been asserted by them in accordance with the Copyright, Designs, and Patents Act 1988.

ISBN: 978-1-915073-38-9

1 3 5 7 9 10 8 6 4 2

This book is sold subject to the condition that it shall not, by way of trade or otherwise, be reproduced or transmitted in any form or by any means, electronic, mechanical, photocopying or otherwise, without the prior permission of the publishers.

SRL Publishing and Pen Nib logo are registered trademarks owned by SRL Publishing Ltd.

This book is a work of fiction. Names, characters, places, and incidents are either a product of the author's imagination or are used fictitiously. Any resemblance to actual people, living or dead, events or locales, is entirely coincidental.

A CIP catalogue record for this book is available from the British Library

SRL Publishing is a Climate Positive publisher offsetting more carbon emissions than it emits.

Nicky Shearsby titles

## **The Flanigan Files**

*#1, Beyond the Veil*
*#2, The Lost Raven*

## **Other titles**
*To the Bitter End*
*Green Monsters*
*Black Widow*
*Darkridge Hollow*

# One

## *Angela*

A trail of white fog from my unsteady breath indicates I'm alive, yet I can barely feel the icy breeze that nips my skin, a sense of awareness as unobtainable as my sense of belonging. I've found myself in the middle of an isolated street. How that's happened I'm not sure, but the early hours denote a false illusion that all is calm, despite an irritating clack of stilettos against uneven paving demonstrating otherwise. In fact, nothing about this moment confirms I wouldn't be better off *dead*. Nobody would notice. I doubt anyone would care.

I was attending a party a few hours ago but I don't remember much about it now, my memory sporadic, hazy. All I know is I woke up a short while ago with a vile taste of sick in my mouth and a headache that feels as if my skull has imploded. I was barely able to move, my body throbbing in places I know could *not* have been caused by the consumption of alcohol alone. I was in a bed not my own, and I didn't recognise my surroundings—shadowy grey walls, heavy bedding, male body odour, thick, like soup. I wasn't wearing any underwear.

I stare at my wrists, angry bruises already forming, grip marks around my skin. In this light, it's difficult to tell if my imagination isn't to blame, yet my hips ache too. I'm not imagining *that*. I take a moment, a breath. Despite not wanting to go to the party, I was there anyway, grinning like a demented freak, pretending to be having fun, raising a half-empty glass towards anyone who might show me enough attention to guide me through the evening unscathed. The music was too loud, my dress too short, most of the men in attendance consumed by beer goggles that heightened their attraction to me for the wrong reasons. As it is, I now feel oddly strange, as if something happened without my consent, although I'm too incensed to conclude what. I wish I'd stayed at home.

I don't realise I'm crying until I can no longer see where I'm walking. Tears burn my eyes, stinging my sinuses, thoughts I can't control pounding metaphoric fists against my skull. I remove my shoes and throw them into the road, slamming hard against the tarmac breaking a heel. I don't care. I want to claw at my face, scream aloud, race into the path of an oncoming vehicle. Instead, I shiver because I don't have a coat, my handbag dangling from my trembling shoulder.

I lean over and vomit on the kerbside, a sudden staleness hitting me from nowhere. My privates are throbbing and there's bruising around my inner thighs that, until now, I've tried to ignore. I pull myself into a standing position, my spinning head ensuring I almost stagger backwards in protest. I don't wish to acknowledge the obvious, don't *want* to believe it's true. I manage to take several steps before it hits me, the balls of my feet taking the impact of unforgiving stones that elevates my heartbeat.

*I think I've been raped.*

\*\*\*

I can't keep walking, my legs refuse to cooperate, so I slide to the ground and sob. I *should* go to the police, report the crime, but I don't remember what happened. I don't even know if there *is* a crime to report. It will probably make things worse anyway, my past dealings with such people not something I want to think about right now. If I *was* attacked, surely I'd remember? I'd have fought back, kicked out, done *something* to prevent the unwanted attention? Anything would be better than what I'm left now to deal with, by myself. Alone.

A passing stranger attempts to speak to me but I don't hear them, too busy dealing with the carnage in my head, no time to worry about what's going on in theirs. When I feel a hand on my shoulder, everything becomes too much and I clamber to my feet and run. Stones and debris bite into my skin but I don't care, can hardly feel it, more important things on my mind. I race along the street, only stopping to lean against a lamppost when I'm out of breath. I already feel out of my mind.

I'm desperately trying to think back, yet nothing logical is coming to mind. I have just left the house of a friend, *his* party I attended, the very reason I am in this street now because of an invite I should have declined. Yet again, can I even call Liam Goodman a friend? No. Probably not. He is an acquaintance, nothing more. A colleague. We've worked together at The Royal Eastcliff Hospital for the last three years, spending the occasional lunch break together, sharing a joke, my job as an A&E receptionist ensuring nothing gets past me. I can't dwell on the fact that it was *his* bedroom I woke up in, unable to recall how I got there. I merely

*The Lost Raven*

wanted to support him, celebrate his promotion, my needs set aside for the evening to pander to his. I can't imagine he'd hurt me. I'm sure he's not that kind of person.

I suck in a lungful of air. Who am I kidding? Of course he wants more from me. Men always do. I didn't believe it mattered until now, a possibility jumping into my mind I'm not comfortable considering, the idea he'd willingly *attack* me something I can't easily disregard. Has he grown tired of waiting, taking matters into his own hands, taking advantage?

Ice is forming now, clinging to the surrounding trees, nothing to keep away the cold air that chills my bones. My bare feet ache, the freezing pavement readily rubbing blisters into my numb skin. I stumble around until I find myself in the middle of Eastcliff town centre, watching from a distance two young women leaving a club: chatting, giggling. Adjusting their clothing, checking hair and makeup in mirrors that double as mobile phones. I don't know why I'm here, I barely know what I'm doing, yet I can clearly see what they can't. *I see danger.* I see what will happen if they're not mindful to watch each other's backs, stay alert. Keep safe.

I wish I understood the male species but the sad truth is I don't. Most of them assume they can do what they want without consequence, acting without remorse, women nothing more than a target of their impossible lust. I used to believe that, if I could remove myself from all thoughts of men, I might stand a chance of a normal life. My lesbian phase lasted an entire summer, two fumbled attempts behind me, a woman's touch something I assumed would help my mindset and ease my suffering. It didn't. It merely confirmed I'm *not* a lesbian.

I am, in fact, nothing now but a lost soul who doesn't find women sexually attractive yet equally can't abide the touch of a man. It isn't something I dwell on. I despise how testosterone is used carelessly for selfish gain, a pointed, phallic symbol of everything I loathe about the male species, the *thing* in their trousers a sad consequence of who they are. Their thoughts are never on anything other than sex, the monsters between their legs to blame for that.

I lick my lips. The copious amount of wine I drank earlier is seemingly unable to quench my insatiable thoughts, an unsupported quest for answers leaving my entire body quivering. I ignore several sideways glances from Friday night revellers heading home, musing over *my* intentions, *my* motives. It doesn't matter. I'm silently pondering how to protect my fellow females from a pain they don't yet know is coming—like a stalker, lying in wait, wondering how and when I can make my move. I'm a coiled spring, my mind set only on saving all women who can't appreciate how much they *need* saving, these innocents forever the subject of unfettered attention. My heart is pumping, my eyes wild, irritation prickling violently.

I observe with silent frustration as an intoxicated male leans towards a potential victim, wilfully absorbed in cleavage that has been lustfully placed on display. The woman is attracting the wrong type of attention, laughing, tilting her head to reveal bare flesh, a shoulder, a leg, her heart beating swiftly in exposed neck veins that await the vampire's attack. To any outsider, this is a mutual interaction, two willing adults connecting in conversation— innocent, normal, *consensual*. Yet, I see nothing but monstrous consequences that will leave this poor thing naked, exposed and trembling with fear she will never dislodge no matter how much therapy is thrown her way. *I know*. I've been there, worn the t-shirt, still have it hanging as a painful reminder in the back of my goddamn wardrobe.

Aside from Liam (who I'm now unexpectedly uncertain

about), most men disgust me. I can't help the way I feel about that. I hate how they behave, how they look at *women*, each one assuming every female desires their attention. If she doesn't reciprocate, they assume her gay, a *real* man able to show a woman what she's missing. Even gay men seek the same attention, often sleeping with those they meet on a whim, one-night stands deemed normal. But gay men pose no danger to women of course, their endless lust shared with each other instead of females who can't defend themselves from the nightmare of heightened arousal. Everyone is looking for sex, it seems—everyone but *me*.

'Are you okay?' someone asks, aiming a concerned face towards me that I don't immediately acknowledge. I stop dead in my tracks, my heartbeat quickening. I can't think, can't respond, this night triggering something in me I'm not even aware exists. A consistent thud of music is keeping pace with my heart, surrounding laughter engulfing my senses.

'Can I buy you a drink?' he queries. I don't know what the time is but it's assumedly still early enough for the alcohol he now wants to ply me with, still dark enough to disguise his motives.

I almost miss the question, my focus set on a woman applying lipstick, smoothing her hair, straightening her dress.

'You okay?'

The same voice is growing louder and I turn to see a male, approximately thirty, potentially older, although I can't tell in this light. He is smiling, beer-goggled eyes and rosy cheeks confirming he's already consumed too much.

'I'm fine,' I mutter as politely as I can, stepping to one side, his proximity too close. His aftershave is overwhelming, a muted blend of musk and sweat that makes me feel sick.

'Let me buy you that drink?' he repeats. Louder, in case I missed him the first time.

'No. Thank you.' I'm still trying to be polite. He should be grateful.

'You look lost.' He won't leave me alone, won't take the hint, closing the gap I've readily created between us. 'I'm Lee.' He holds a steady hand towards mine, a simple gesture, nothing more. He probably believes he's a nice guy. I know better.

'I'm fine,' I repeat, louder, firmer, in case *he* didn't hear *me* the first time. I try not to snap, try not to glare at him in disgust. The last thing I need is to engage in anything that might accidentally pass for conversation.

'Do *you* have a name?' he asks flatly, taking in my unkempt appearance, my bare feet.

I'm not about to tell him, not about to express the profound hatred I've held my entire life for the male species. I can guess what he wants, of course, yet I give no smile of encouragement to lead him on, tears already burning the edges of my eyes, blinking back a pain I'm unable to control. Recent events are catching up with me, the party still vivid, my body still sore. It was a mistake coming here.

'Leave me alone.' I'm biting my lip so hard I can taste blood.

'Sorry, I didn't mean to offend you.' Lee steps away, wounded now, his hands raised defensively. He looks disappointed. 'Can I make sure you get home safely?' He looks at me as if he assumes I need saving, yet all I want is for him to turn his attention to something else, *anything* other than me.

'No!' I spit the word towards him as if he's strangling me with it. 'I'll be fine.' I need to leave. *Now*.

I break into an unsteady jog, a gust of wind taking me by surprise, whipping the edge of my dress around my exposed legs.

'Are you *sure* you're okay? Can I *call* someone for you?' Lee is behind me, his voice raised, troubled.

'People like *you* make me sick,' I scream loudly, causing attention I don't need, spitting out words I don't want in my head. So far he has done *nothing* to warrant my wrath, yet here I am offering it anyway.

'What did I do wrong?' Lee doesn't know, doesn't see what he is. Why won't he leave me alone?

'You're all the same. Delusional. Twisted. You're all *freaks*.' I can't help the words that catch the back of my throat as I yell into the darkness. I turn around, the guy already at my back now, his presence shocking, overbearing. He's a sexual predator, nothing more, a symbol of everything I despise. I'm panicking, annoyed by my decision to come here instead of going home, frustrated by my inability to think straight. The darkened street is imposing, strangers either too drunk or too far away to notice, no aid coming my way. I glance around, uncertain, nothing of my brain intact.

'I'm sorry if I upset you.' Lee is still talking, holding large hands towards mine as if he assumes I need his help. Yet, his body language is telling its own story, intent on trouble. I believe he's going to *attack* me. I can't help it, can't take the risk. Not again. I reach into my bag, grappling wildly for my phone, the bloody thing eluding me as my trembling fingers probe against a torn seam. I'm still crying. I can't help *that* either.

When Lee steps into my personal space, I see nothing beyond the opportunity for him to *rape* me, my mind unravelling swiftly. I won't allow that to happen, I can't. Liam's touch still too painful, his imposing scent still tickling my nostrils. I stumble backwards, fumbling inside my bag for something, *anything* I can use as a weapon, momentarily shocked when I pull out a knife. I don't recall putting such an item into my bag, no idea where it came from.

Lee doesn't initially react when I stab him, neither of us registering what I've done until I see the blood, my blade plunged deep into his belly. He staggers backwards, his face contorted, shock setting in.

*Jesus Christ. What the hell?*

He should have stayed away, heeded my warning. Instead, he drops to his knees like a ragdoll, both hands pressed against his gut as angry blood spills between his fingers. He doesn't speak, probably can't, isn't yet able to register what's unfolding. His once-flushed cheeks have already turned pale. He falls to the ground, his unstable legs unable to keep him upright.

I take this as my cue to leave, racing along the street as if I'm being chased, away from unaware strangers and imminent detection. I can't bring myself to turn around or acknowledge my actions, already halfway home when it hits me, my thoughts stopping me in my tracks.

*I just killed someone.*

# Two

## *Angela*

I run until my legs ache, until my bare feet are blistered, sore, unwilling to propel me forward another step. I stop, forcing air into my overwrought lungs, all logic and pride gone. I stare at my hands. There is no blood but I see crimson red, all the same, trickling over my palms, between my fingers. I can barely keep them steady, pointedly scolding me for what I've done. I can't even bring myself to look at my reflection in a nearby shop window for fear of what I might see, nothing but a hollow demon staring back, searching frantically for something I will never find.

My sanity has escaped me in a single impossible action, clawing my neck, tearing my throat, silencing an insatiable need for clarity over a situation I can never now change. I hear nothing beyond my failing heartbeat, the town behind me already falling silent—as if watching, judging. It takes some doing but I eventually find my mobile phone lodged inside a torn seam of my bag, barely able to hold it steady long enough to check the time. I almost don't believe it's four o'clock in the morning. How did it get so late?

Panic is rising in my chest but nothing I do seems to ease its increasing wrath. If I'm not careful it will devour me whole, nothing left but ash that would have once been my skin and bone. I find spontaneous combustion oddly fascinating, though I don't know why such a thought has popped into my head. It's hardly appropriate. Perhaps because it matches how I feel. Forgotten, lost, my bones crumbling to dust beneath the weight of my sins. As it is, I can barely catch my breath, feeling as if *I'm* the one who's been subjected to a brutal stabbing and not the poor bastard I've left for dead in the street. *Shit*. What the *hell* have I done?

I can't go home. My home is too familiar, a ready meal left in the microwave no doubt causing a stench by now along with perfume I earlier spilt on the carpet. Instead, I glance skyward, hoping for a glimpse of a passing raven, nothing left to sedate my fragile mindset aside from the hope of their presence. I wish I could fly. If I could, I'd have flown away by now, my body locating freedom my mind never will, escaping my private hell once and for all. I adore ravens, always have. Those beautiful birds the one creature on this entire planet that possess the power to calm my mood, my home full of reminders—feathers, pictures, books.

I have a sudden urge to climb higher, to gain a better vantage point and locate my Arcadian companions before penance finds me. It holds the potential to calm my emotions and bring back much-needed clarity to my evening. Besides, I need to work out my next move. I notice a nearby multi-storey car park, nothing left to lose, climbing concrete steps until I can go no further. Yet, it isn't until I step into the thin air above that I begin to sob, my brain finally succumbing to the harsh reality of my situation.

Mascara has dried on my skin. I can tell by the tautness of my cheeks, my face no doubt pale and drawn. It usually *is* when I'm stressed. I probably look like shit. I didn't dare look in a mirror before leaving Liam's house, couldn't bring myself to check. Instead, I slowly opened his bedroom door, the music downstairs still thumping, his guests unaware of what was unfolding above. I had tiptoed out of his back door, unsure where I was going, unconvinced I wanted answers to questions I wasn't yet ready to ask. My shoes were grasped in my trembling hands, tears rolling down my cheeks, my hair like a bird's nest, my throat as dry as toast. I didn't make a sound, couldn't. My embarrassment displayed openly to anyone who might find me like *that*. I didn't want to know where Liam was.

Now, I honestly just want to scream, pound the concrete beneath me, cry into the night. How has my evening turned out like *this*? Then it hits me. What did I do with the *knife*? I frantically tip the contents of my handbag across the empty car park in frustration, exposing a bared soul that is surely now doomed. *Nothing*. Shit. There are fingerprints on that knife. *My* fingerprints. Why was I even in possession of a knife?

I should probably confirm at this stage that I have bipolar disorder. An unfortunate factor of my condition is that I sometimes do things without warning, my mental health forever suspending me in limbo, my own personal hell to placate. Maybe I subconsciously picked it up in Liam's kitchen, just in case. My brain on autopilot, my unconscious thoughts in control.

I peer into the void, the darkness ready to engulf me, the black sky not enough to cover my deluded actions. It's still out there somewhere, ready to cut me open for what I've done, a simple unsuspecting discovery only a matter of time. Did I leave it on the ground or sticking out of Lee's body? *Jesus*. It doesn't bear thinking about. He was on his back when I left him, blood seeping into the cracks of the pavement, the guy easily able to identify me if he lives to tell the tale. I'm panicking, my throat tightening with each ridiculous breath I take. I need to calm down, nothing I can do now able to change what's already done.

I slump to the ground, my knees buckling under my chin, my lips chattering with fear. The surface below me is cruelly hard and unfeeling against my body, as if mocking my recent actions, my failing thoughts. All I wanted was to protect women from the same fate I've experienced. Now that fate has taken control, it seems, making me do things I never assumed myself capable. My failing mindset was hell-bent on causing chaos, reaching its own conclusions, imagining impossible ideas I genuinely can't bear to consider. It took less than a second to bring the guy to his knees, his flesh at my whim, his entire life in my hands.

I cast off my thoughts with a scoff, clambering to my feet in an attempt to throw aside painful emotions I can't abide in my head. He might not even *be* dead. Yet, if he is alive I'm definitely screwed, the guy easily able to identify me if asked. I don't exactly blend in. I'm barely five foot four, my long blonde hair always drawing attention, blue eyes that sparkle green when I laugh, freckles often viewed as cute. I'm *not* cute. I see nothing but an invitation for pain, a calling card I was given at birth to ensure men can abuse me at will. I cover them with makeup. It saves a lot of hassle.

Feeling sick, I shakily make my way over to the ledge and lean my head against railings purposefully erected to prevent unwanted jumpers from taking their lives. *Oh, the irony.* I've spent many evenings up here, my feet dangling over the edge, watching a vague sea view in the distance,

## The Lost Raven

dreaming of a far better place than this. I now can't get close, can't sit where I need to be, a thin layer of metallic mesh holding me back, laughing, taunting.

I reach my fingertips through the gaps and tug, the panel rattling loudly, my judgment clouded by suffering. I can't help it when I scream into the clouded sky, bellowing towards a heaven I'm not convinced exists. My fingers hurt but I don't care, the sharp edges drawing blood, my shouting unnoticed. I force the metal as hard as I can, my strength given over to the object in my grasp, to my frustration, my pain. I hate my life. *I hate my life!*

I scream into the void, not caring who might hear. It happens to be true. What is this all for anyway? *Life.* Why do I keep going around the same loop of relentless shit, my existence designed purely to keep me suspended over an abyss of *nothing*?

A screw dislodges as if answering my call, freeing a section of the panel from its rusted fixings. I take it as a sign, a higher power responding, the ravens proclaiming hope I never expected to find. I gasp as the metal comes loose in my hands, rattling in the breeze, providing an unfathomable opportunity for me to slip through. My fingers are bloodied but I feel nothing as I prise a section upwards, bending the mesh enough to crawl out to the ledge beyond. It takes some effort, but I'm on a mission, nowhere left to go now but down, nothing of my thoughts intact.

My dress pops a seam as I crawl through the gap, a cool breeze lifting the edges, cooling my skin. I'm vulnerable, no underwear to protect my modesty, no protection from certain death that awaits me below. All I require is silence. No more drama, no more pain, no more impossible thoughts of men consuming me in the dark. I allow my feet to dangle over the edge, nothing but fresh air between my body and the ground. It would take no longer than a second to slip over the side, to slip away to some other place.

I wish I could confirm that suicide isn't on my mind but that would be a lie. Thoughts of suicide rarely leave me, the idea consuming me now as if I've been planning it for a while, no detail left unchecked, nothing on my mind but death. I glance across to the rooftops below, understanding how the ravens must feel, away from the relentless drama that comes with humanity, their lives far simpler than the raged souls who live down *there*.

I close my eyes, tears still falling, my eyelids swollen, sore. *Why am I crying?* Have I not welcomed this moment in my dreams, when the painful throb of my brain allows a possibility that I might, one day, end it all? This is, in fact, the one thing I've considered for years. I've never told anyone, of course, my reasons kept private, my pain mine to endure alone. I stare into oblivion—everything so small, tiny cars, tiny people, none of them aware of my pathetic existence so high above this town.

It would be easy to jump. Fast. After all, I feel nothing but pain anyway so a little more won't matter. I don't want to continue like this, don't need tonight's ordeal in my head. I take a breath. How long will it take my body to hit the ground? How far will I fall before my brain registers what I've done? It will be too late by then to change my mind and nothing will matter after that. I'm cold, exposed, yet I feel little beyond a fundamental desire to raise my arms into the air and fly away.

I close my eyes, imagining the majestic flap of a raven's wings, unencumbered, free, the "Corvus Corax" powerful, beautiful. He drifts silently through the clouds above me, watching, waiting, his heartbeat strong. I often imagine what it would be like to be a raven—sturdy neck, dense beard of shaggy throat feathers, bright glossy eyes. I close my own, a patter of talons distinctively close now, large

## The Lost Raven

claws clipping over the concrete ledge towards me. My friend's call is loud, prominent, a throaty gurgling croak, much deeper than his common crow cousin. I want to call out to him, respond, acknowledge, but I dare not open my eyes for fear of losing this precious moment. He's so close. I can almost touch him.

Fresh tears sting my face and when I finally dare to look, my friend the raven is seated next to me, his black eyes piercing mine. I smile. He seems to smile back. He isn't *really* here, of course, yet I'm grateful that my mind has temporarily removed some of my burdens, this single moment of escapism the only thing I need. He yells at me, flapping his large wings, the two of us locked in this impossible, *incredible* moment. He assumes I'm in the wrong place, wondering why I've climbed so high. I reach out. I only want to touch him, to feel the warmth of his body, but he jumps away from my grasping fingertips, leaving nothing but struggling air between us. When he takes flight I want to flap my arms in response and follow. I want him to lead the way, lead me to freedom, take me to a place I can finally call home.

I look down. A single black feather has settled on my lap. I pick it up and run my fingers across its surface. It's so beautiful, so soft. I believe it's a sign, a symbol of *forgiveness* when I can never forgive myself. I release a tiny yelp, unsurprised by how my voice is snatched away on the breeze as if I'd never opened my mouth at all. Taking a breath I prepare for take off, clambering to my feet, my throbbing bare soles ready to leave this earthly ground forever. I close my eyes, an odd calm creeping over me.

I can do this.
*I can fly.*

# Three

## *Newton*

I was in the middle of a dream when my buzzing phone woke me up. It wasn't ideal, yet DCI Paul Mannering's disgruntled voice and unwelcome background noise were enough to confirm the encroaching chaos before I'd even planted my feet on the bedroom carpet. I was enjoying a well-needed lie-in, my rare day off holding the potential to placate my brain and rationalise my impossible thinking into some kind of semi-passable order.

'Newt? You there?' My friend's mannerisms as always, a stressed undertone, denoting he was not enjoying his morning as much as I previously assumed *I* might.

'Good morning to you, too,' I muttered, stifling a yawn, padding into the kitchen across several cold floor tiles, the heating not yet on, my bare feet as now numb as my brain.

'Yeah, sorry, morning.' Paul returned my mutterings with his own, the man forever distracted, a distant angry horn confirming he was already deep in police business, my day racing to catch up.

'Where *are* you?' I was asking but wasn't exactly interested, his phone call made to extract information he assumed I'd provide without question. I was pouring coffee. Under normal circumstances such a simple indulgence would have woken me up. My friend's requirements holding the power to flesh my depleted ego, wake *him* up. However, it wasn't yet five o'clock in the morning. I was in no mood for chitchat.

'Freeman House Car Park,' Paul responded, flatly, unaware he had already put me in a bad mood. A forceful breeze snatching most of his words into the air. 'How quickly can you get here?'

'Why?' I took a sip of hot black liquid, grateful for the soothing warmth, only realising I'd forgotten to add sugar when a bitter taste hit my tongue.

'I need you to talk someone off a roof,' he confirmed. 'I have two officers up there at the moment but the young lady is having none of it. I know you've dealt with this type of thing before.' He paused. 'I wouldn't ask if it wasn't urgent.' I could hear the passive aggression in his voice, the words he wasn't using. *"You'll be doing me a favour."* I always seemed to owe him one.

I added sugar to my mug with a sigh, glad Paul ignored my reaction. Freeman House Car Park was a couple of streets from my flat. I could get there on foot, no need to take my car. It was probably just as well. The way my old Volkswagen Beetle was performing lately, I could do without the stress. I glanced out of the window. A light frost had coated everything in a thin veneer of white, a low fog drifting lazily across the glass. I wondered how desperate a person would need to be to end up on a rooftop in *this* weather.

'Didn't the council put metal panels around the edges to

stop people trying to jump?' It made the place look unsightly but at least it saved lives.

'They did, but she somehow managed to get onto the ledge anyway. Keeps saying she can *fly*.'

Paul's words saddened me. Suicide consumes a person, taking them beyond rational consideration, reasonable thinking. The concept that this young lady believed she could *fly* told me she wanted an escape, not death. A way to deal with something her mind couldn't. It wasn't a comfort. 'Do we know who she is?'

'Not yet.'

'How did *you* get involved?' Suicide attempts were usually dealt with by uniformed police, not CID.

'We were just passing when I noticed her out on the ledge. We couldn't exactly leave her up there, could we?'

'We?'

'Myself and DI Avery.'

It made me smile how Paul always used formal titles whenever he was in the midst of police duties, turning from relaxed friend to highly professional detective. It was how he dealt with things, got the job done. I imagined the roll of Tony's eyes, a shake of an exhausted head.

'Where were you going at *this* time of the morning?' It seemed early, even for Paul.

'To a stabbing in town that I've now had to allocate to DS Baker. Actually, I need to get off the phone and see how she's doing. Any more questions?'

'Not that I can think of.' I hoped Alice was okay. She deserved the occasional weekend off, too. The poor woman just as much at Paul's beck and call as I was. It was a shame that *crime* rarely took a break.

'Good. Then shall I see you shortly?'

'Okay, fine.' I breathed, taking a large gulp of much-needed coffee. 'Give me ten minutes.'

*The Lost Raven*

\*\*\*

My haste saw me burn the back of my throat with coffee while searching for a clean item of clothing, my housekeeping failures met with unrequired frustration. I subsequently ventured into the morning air dressed in a crinkled shirt, a tank top that had acquired an odd-looking stain, shoes that needed cleaning. It was Saturday morning, my supposed day off, my day set aside for relaxing, marking essays, eating crap. Instead, I was now heading towards the unknown: Paul and his team of disgruntled officers already waiting, radios in hand and a mental health team on standby. Between us, we had witnessed many suicide attempts, many deaths, this day nothing new, but it never got easier, never felt any less troublesome to deal with.

Paul looked tired, as always. His frustrated expression something I'd grown oddly accustomed to in recent months. He nodded when he saw me, thankfully ignoring my hastily assembled appearance, merely glad I was willing to help.

'Thank you,' he muttered, his own jacket doing nothing to stave off the incoming cold, the thing pulled tightly around his neck. He was shivering.

I glanced towards a young woman standing bare footed on a high ledge, the dress she was wearing wholly inappropriate for the occasion by the way she, too, was trembling. She was crying, yelling, expressing to officers already with her to leave her alone. Twice she looked as if she was going to jump, nowhere else to go but down, her potential actions creating a fresh wave of panic from everyone.

'What makes you think *I* can talk her down?' I was staring skyward, craning my neck, unsure my presence would be enough. Freeman House Car Park had no lift, jagged concrete steps my only way up, urine and filth my only unfortunate companions.

'Because that's what you *do*.' Paul didn't look at me, too busy waiting for me to deal with the situation so he could get on with his day in peace, more pressing matters to attend.

I smothered a sigh, unwilling to comment, instead heading inside the building, eager to help. I was grateful he didn't see me running out of steam halfway up, forced to puff and pant the rest of the way hunched forward like an old man. I needed to get fitter, start jogging, join a gym. My sister-in-law, Stephanie, had joked about my health for a while, confirming my podgy belly and flabby arms. I hoped this young woman hadn't decided to jump by the time I reached her. I was unconvinced that, in my haste, I wouldn't join her on a potential swift route down.

'Dr Newton?' A male uniformed officer was waiting for me as I reached the top step, the morning breeze far cooler up here, icy and unwelcome. It took my breath.

'It's Dr Flanigan, actually,' I corrected, still panting, the coffee I'd earlier consumed not yet enough to wake me up. I was often referred to by my first name, *Newton* seemingly only remembered as the guy who'd discovered gravity.

'Sorry,' he muttered, a rosy flush appearing on his cheeks. 'My colleague has been speaking with the young lady.' He shook his head, changing the subject. 'But she's refusing to budge. I'm not sure how much help you'll be at this stage.'

I nodded, knowing what he meant. Anyone considering suicide does not hang around; excuse the expression. They venture high for a reason, wanting a way out, nothing and no one preventing their ultimate goal. Yet, I assumed if she *was* going to jump, she would have done so by now, the fact

## The Lost Raven

she was still on that ledge confirming she needed help, not a coffin. Several police officers had gathered below us, flashing lights adding nothing to this young woman's troubled mindset, *or* mine. This attention something she probably didn't need in her day.

'Do we know her name?' I asked, not anticipating the blast of cold air that almost took my balance. *Shit*. I glanced towards the ledge, impressed the fragile thing was retaining hers.

'She isn't saying much,' the officer confirmed, shaking his head, directing me towards the chaos. 'Just keeps saying she can fly.'

From this position, the young lady appeared near frozen to the bone, the fresh autumnal weather hardly appropriate for her outfit. She was trembling, goose-bumped skin exposed, arms outstretched, no shoes. A female officer was currently reaching her head through the damaged panelling, her pleas disregarded. I assumed her words were being carried away on the morning wind, this location hardly conducive for a rational conversation. She looked grateful when she noticed my approach, stepping back into the safety of the car park.

'Are you the psychologist?' she asked, looking as out of breath as I was, her hair lifted in places, cheeks flushed.

I nodded. 'What do we know?'

'Hardly anything. She won't speak to me.' The constable shrugged, her limited training not exactly helpful in situations like these.

'Did you get her *name*?' I asked again, keen to establish a basic form of communication. I wondered what *had* been said to this poor girl that had resulted in nothing but fresh air and a cold chill.

The female officer shook her head, nothing on her expression telling me she wasn't glad for the respite I was about to provide.

Taking a handkerchief from my pocket to protect my hands, I peeled open the mesh as wide as it would go, catching my hair on the damaged wire in the process. A gush of wind whipped past my cheek, making me momentarily grab the ledge. I glanced at the officers behind me, knowing what they were thinking, knowing they were waiting for me to take control so they didn't have to.

'Hi there,' I called out. 'Do you mind if I join you?'

The young woman was standing with her head down, her makeup-streaked face and runny nose confirming her volatile state of mind. She didn't acknowledge me, didn't want anyone's help. She didn't look that old. Highlighted blond hair spiralled down her back, ruffled, as if she had just got out of bed.

I slid my legs along the cold ledge, holding on with both hands, my knuckles white. I hoped she wouldn't notice, accidentally glancing towards the ground below, closing my eyes in protest. It was a long way down, my legs still throbbing from the effort it took to get up here. I had never been good with heights.

When the young lady finally looked my way, she seemed shocked to see me, her private world the only space that existed until now. I was careful to retain a safe distance, of course, my legs left dangling over the edge because there was nowhere else to place them, my buttocks clenched tight in protest to the swaying panels behind me. There was no way I was letting go. I may have been holding my breath. Paul and his team were hovering below, tiny dots in the distance, the uniforms of several police officers reflecting flashing lights of their imposing vehicles. At least it wasn't raining.

'My name's Newton. Newton Flanigan,' I confirmed loudly, grateful to be in close enough proximity now to be heard over the dewy air. 'It's cold up here.' I was stating the obvious, merely trying to engage the girl, gingerly turning up the collar of my jacket for effect. 'You must be freezing?' I had only been here a few minutes and I already was. All I wanted was an acknowledgement, for her to appreciate the position she was putting us *both* in, and a coffee. I considered removing my jacket and handing it to her. She looked as if she needed it. Yet, I was unsure what such a proclamation would achieve. She might lose her footing and slip, this day reaching an unsatisfactory conclusion, tipping the balance of Paul's frustration completely. She didn't reply. I wondered what she was thinking. By the look on her face, nothing good.

Instead, we sat on that ledge for a good ten minutes, silence that would have otherwise driven me insane sliced into by a biting wind that hurt my ears. I was taught long ago that silence often allows the other person some well-needed space. You don't have to fill every gap with chatter, instead allow them the time they need to consider their emotions, their actions. It is a rule I still follow to this very day, designed to convey a non-judgmental position, providing a notion that conversation is *optional* and therefore unforced. Eventually, when the stillness becomes too heavy, it triggers a discussion that might not otherwise occur, setting up an opening for potential therapy. After all, this is *their* time, *their* rules.

It wasn't helpful that I was freezing to death, a sharp chill nipping my ears, penetrating my soul. I needed to hurry things along, no coffee up here to keep me alert, no ticking clock to help pass the time. The girl was holding a black feather in her tiny white hands, its glossy surface at odds with the paleness of her trembling fingertips.

'That's nice,' I stated. I was attempting to reach her on a level she might appreciate, already tired of the silence, that simple object no doubt holding a meaning I was yet to understand. A small bag sat next to her, no bigger than a purse, covered in sparkling gems, the sort usually reserved for parties, nightclubs, weddings. She was dressed as if she had recently left one, her evening ending in unconfirmed chaos I was not about to highlight. It no doubt contained her mobile phone, keys, lipstick, girly things. She wasn't wearing shoes, did not have a coat. I wondered about her life, who might be missing her, the type of friends who would allow a young woman to leave a party alone.

'I've never really liked birds,' I continued, unconcerned that I was speaking more to myself than my newly acquired companion. It was a lie, of course. I had nothing against them. I was merely trying to distract the moment, provoke a reaction.

The female turned to face me, for the first time allowing cold eyes to meet mine, narrowing defensively. I'd hit a nerve. Good. I smiled, continuing as if this was a normal day for me, this high ledge somewhere I often contemplated my thoughts. I tried not to shiver, tried not to allow my teeth to clatter together in protest. It wasn't easy.

'The way they fly around, no fear of falling from the sky,' I chided. 'It isn't something *I'd* want to do.'

'You know *nothing*,' she spat, stroking the feather as if she needed its limited protection to stave off my unwanted words. At least she was talking to me.

'Then why don't you explain it?' The one thing I knew about suicide was that those considering it were either serious or wanted help they felt they might not otherwise find. They either ended things amid insurmountable pain, no one aware of their actions until it was too late, or they sat on rooftops, thinking, waiting for someone to notice. I assumed this young lady fell into the latter category. She would be dead by now, otherwise.

## The Lost Raven

'Why don't you *fuck off?*' she spat. Emotion. Good. Emotional people are usually willing to vocalise their feelings, even if it's to do nothing other than lash out.

'Dirty, disgusting things, aren't they, *birds?*' I was glancing blankly towards a dark grey sky, the pale sun barely peeking over the horizon. I was staring at nothing in particular, clinging to cold metal as if my life depended on it, hoping this young woman wouldn't notice how absolutely *terrified* I was. 'They shit from a great height, leave feathers and filth all over the place and make other people clean up after them.' I shuddered, pretending to be repulsed. I needed a reaction, anything to distract her mind from death.

'I disagree,' she muttered, sobbing quietly now. 'I love how *free* they are.' If nothing else, she was willing to give me that much. *Bingo.*

'I can understand that,' I sighed casually, stretching my legs out in front of me in an attempt to avoid cramp, scratching my cheek, the upside of my actions making me appear relaxed. I wasn't. 'Birds don't have walls to cage them. No rules. No constraints. Especially *ravens.*' I didn't look at her, instead kept my eyes focused ahead, staring towards low passing clouds, not daring to look down in case I fell or noticed the perpetually disgruntled features of my good friend below, Detective Chief Inspector Paul Mannering never one to mince his words. I didn't want him to see my ashen skin or wide eyes. He was probably wondering what was taking so long.

The young lady sighed, dropping unsteadily to the ledge beside me, dropping her guard, no fear of slipping, falling to her death. She dangled her legs over the edge, mimicking mine, kicking goose-bumped skin into the morning air. I was grateful she was sitting down, at least, unable to prevent the relieved sigh that left my lips.

'How did you know this is a raven feather?' she asked, her interest piqued, my mouth automatically curling into a smile. She was holding it aloft, examining it, turning it over, pointing it my way.

I didn't. But it was black, fairly large and thankfully I had a nephew who never stopped talking about them. It was a lucky guess. 'My nephew loves ravens,' I replied truthfully. Timothy was on my mind now, my brother's youngest son the brightest in his class. My sister-in-law Stephanie and her boys lived close enough to The Tower of London for Timothy to take a keen interest, that famous home of the ravens unwittingly becoming Tim's obsession from a young age. He knew each of their names, how far they could travel for food if they had to, the lengths they will go to find a mate. He even dressed up as one for an entire week until Steph was forced to take action. He needed a bath. I smiled at my memories, glad I had some to keep me company. It was more than I could say about this poor young thing. What was her story? What had led to this impossible moment? I glanced her way. I didn't even know her name.

# Four

## *Newton*

'I love Ravens,' a soft voice emerged from my right-hand side.

'I bet you wish you could fly away.' It wasn't a question. The girl had already confirmed she *could*. I was merely continuing the conversation no one had yet engaged her in.

'I guess.' She was crying again.

'I know how you feel.' Why I said such a thing, I have no idea. I didn't know *anything* beyond wanting to get off this rooftop. I was trying to empathise with her emotions, that's all. It seemed to fit the moment. Nothing else would suffice. I certainly didn't want to fly. *Ever*. There have only ever been two people in my life who have tried to get me on a plane. My brother: our family trip to Spain ending up with my head down the toilet and a missed flight. And a girl I was dating who'd arranged a weekend trip to Paris as a surprise. Imagine *her* surprise when I refused to go through the airport doors. Needless to say that relationship didn't last long.

'*You?* What the *fuck* do you know about my feelings?' My companion scoffed, shaking her tear-stained head in defiance. She was still shivering, her chattering teeth now joining the commotion, joining mine.

'I probably know more than you realise,' I stated, a little too confidently, attempting a smile, momentarily glad for Tim's incessant bird chatter and my impossible failings. I promised to thank him later for the vital snippets of information he had unwittingly provided. He would be pleased to know he held the power to save someone's life. 'I can tell you the names of all seven ravens in The Tower of London but I don't yet know your name.' I smiled, hoping she would appreciate I was no threat, praying she wouldn't grow tired of my words and jump.

The young woman turned away from me and shook her head. I tried not to take it personally.

'So, how *far* do you think a bird can fly?' I was impressed I'd thought of such a question, asked with nothing more in mind than to initiate a casual conversation. I already knew, of course, Tim's statistics forever lodged in my head. That's what happens when you don't have kids of your own. Other people's take over.

The young lady displayed a flicker of emotion, a gesture that could almost pass for a smile. 'Wild ravens can fly up to a hundred miles in a single day.' She sounded pleased to confirm it, her *death* seemingly not as important as the daily habits of wild birds.

'Wow, that's impressive,' I confirmed, a genuine smile on my own face, the first time today I was able to display something other than exhaustion. 'Although, I'd struggle to *drive* that far without several cups of coffee in my system, at least two toilet visits planned ahead of time, and a bag of sugary sweets in my possession before I could even *think* about getting to my destination.' I thought again about Stephanie and the boys stuck in London without me, my monthly visits nowhere near enough to ensure my continued support. I *never* drove to London, a train journey safer, faster. I wished my brother Isaac could see how well his boys were doing, his absence not enough to slow the passing of time. It wasn't something I needed to dwell on.

I swear the young lady laughed. It was a tiny but genuine gesture, heartfelt. I turned to see her tear-streaked features looking at me, red and swollen, her mind blatantly troubled. Her eyes were blank, yet her mouth was willing to show something of her personality, something I wasn't expecting. *Hope.*

'I'm Angela,' she confirmed, finally willing to give me her name. 'Angela Healy.'

*Progress.*

'It's very nice to meet you, Angela.' I held a hand towards her, hoping she would reach back. She didn't. Her skin was prickled with goosebumps, a warm blanket needed to prevent hyperthermia, a hot drink needed to comfort *me*. I didn't know her story, couldn't understand her pain, but she was oddly willing to allow a glimmer of hope that I might potentially help her, at some point. That was something. I was grateful.

'What are you *doing* up here?' It was an honest question and one that required an answer before I either lost my grip or the respect of the police, whichever came first. I could sense their twitching legs, chattering teeth, radios that never stayed silent. They probably wanted a coffee, a warm room. We all did.

Angela glared at me as if she'd forgotten her unfathomed reasons for today's interruptions, the very fact I'd asked forcing an unwanted consideration she didn't want to share. She shook her head, a silent scoff emerging that I understood more than she knew. I'd unwittingly brought her back to the present moment. To a place she probably did not want to be.

'You *can* talk to me,' I stated, unable to help my casual remark. It was, after all, why I was here. I needed to know what she was thinking, what had happened to bring her to this moment, how I could help make things better. We couldn't speak properly until I understood her motives, her reasons. I tried to force a smile but my facial muscles ached, the icy wind setting my jaw into an uncomfortable position. My teeth were still chattering.

'You're not interested in talking to *me*.' Angela didn't look my way, instead continued to entertain herself with the feather in her grasp.

'I wouldn't be here if I didn't.' I could think of far better places, my bed still calling. I was, in fact, only here at *all* because Paul had asked me, got me out of bed, woke me up.

'You just want to tick boxes.'

She was right. Boxes needed to be ticked, as always, but her life was on the line and that was more important, no matter what legalities, bureaucracy, and my brain demanded.

'You don't like authority do you?' I whispered, glancing behind us, those officers standing now by the car park exit, chatting quietly, wishing I'd hurry up. I got the feeling Angela didn't like *anyone*.

Angela scoffed. 'How would you know *what* I like?'

I shrugged, my casual passing comment meant only to aid a two-way conversation. She probably wouldn't appreciate a response.

'I'd rather talk to the ravens,' she confirmed flatly.

Ah yes, the ravens. I wondered how long it would be before our attention was returned to those birds. What was it about them that made her hold their lives in a far higher regard than her own? I got the impression they meant more to her than people did. I swallowed, glad this conversation was giving the poor girl something to focus on other than *death*.

'Do they talk to you often?' I couldn't help asking. I sounded like a typical psychologist. *Do the voices talk to you often? Do they tell you to do things?* I tried not to dwell.

Angela tutted, shaking her head. 'Of *course* they do.' She rolled her eyes skyward as if I was an idiot, no doubt hoping one would pass overhead and confirm her remark.

'Tim will be thrilled to learn that I've been talking to a fellow raven enthusiast.' I sounded like a proud father who attends school assemblies, wanting other parents to acknowledge their child's nondescript achievements without question.

'Tim?'

'My nephew.'

Angela furrowed her brow, still unwilling to look my way for more than a fleeting second. She hung her head, staring instead towards the ground. She wasn't holding onto anything other than that feather, wasn't concerned by the height or my words, the breeze buffing her tiny body around like a ragdoll, her hands cupped in her lap.

'So, why *ravens*?' I wasn't interested in the answer but if my query kept her alive I was happy to indulge her fantasies, no matter how short-lived this conversation might be.

'Because ravens are the most intelligent of *all* birds.' I could see she had a real affinity with them. I'd openly scoffed at my nephew, laughed at his enthusiasm, rolled *my* eyes. Until now, that was. Now I was eternally grateful for Timothy Lucas Flanigan and his seemingly mindless chatter.

'My nephew would probably agree with you.' It was true. I swallowed a sudden urge to laugh.

Angela nodded. 'He sounds like a bright kid.'

*He is.* I should tell him more often. I glanced skyward, momentarily forgetting my place, my position, almost losing my balance to the torment of my own thoughts. I could no longer feel my legs.

'If the ravens *could* speak to you, what do you think they would say?' I tried not to notice the wobble that had formed in my voice, the tremble that had developed in my hand. My nephews were on my mind now, Steph, Isaac.

'They *do* speak to me. All the time.'

'And what do they say?' *Careful Newton.*

'They tell me to fly away. That I deserve to be free.' I assumed Angela had heard them many times.

'Is *that* why you're here?' I took a deep breath that threatened to knock me sideways. 'Because you're trying to find your freedom?'

Angela nodded. She'd stopped trembling.

'Because I can't imagine you'd be here for any *other* reason.' It was a blatant statement, made to dislodge the idea of suicide from her mind once and for all. I couldn't help it. I was cold.

Angela closed her eyes, nothing to say about that, though I didn't miss the tear that trickled along her cheek.

'But if the ravens *are* intelligent,' I continued, 'would they not also tell you that you can't fly? You don't have wings.' I didn't mean to sound condescending.

'I'm not a *fucking* idiot,' Angela snapped, curling her legs beneath her chin. She began rocking backwards and forwards, nothing of a potential fall on her mind, the ground below of no concern. I almost reached over to grab her, glad I didn't, needing to retain a safe distance. She might have reacted badly, pulled me over with her, provoking a terrible outcome for the both of us.

'Sorry, I just meant—'

## The Lost Raven

'What? What exactly *did* you mean?' Angela snapped again, narrowing her eyes, turning to directly face me for the first time since we'd met. Nothing in her expression confirmed she was thinking anything good, nothing to suggest she didn't hate my guts. 'Why are you even here? I don't need anyone's help, especially *yours*.'

I was making progress and now I'd messed it up, putting us right back where we'd started. *Well done, Newton.*

'My apologies.' I glanced her way, needing to bring this conversation back on track, calm an increasingly difficult situation. 'Now who's being the idiot?' I rolled my eyes towards the clouds, ignoring the shivering officers behind us hell-bent on listening to my every word. 'Typical *bloody* Newton Flanigan.' I shook my head, purposefully chastising my stupidity for Angela's benefit, ensuring she knew how frustrated I was with myself. I was hoping to make her laugh, that's all, my words capable of disrupting her pain, calm her down.

'I *hate* people,' Angela muttered, adding 'especially men,' low enough so I almost missed it.

'Yeah, tell me about it. Men, hey?' I scoffed loudly, fully prepared to join her in her mission to dislodge the male species from the face of the earth, this conversation whatever Angela wanted it to be. It didn't matter that I *was* one. To this young woman, such a fact was unimportant.

I was offered a sideways, almost nondescript, glance. I couldn't read what the poor thing was thinking. It was probably just as well.

'Do you want to talk about it?' It was a direct question. I was freezing and I needed coffee.

Angela shook her head.

'Okay, that's fair enough.' I shivered, that action involuntary, not for Angela's benefit. It was late November, a chill readily creeping around the edges of the mornings, the sun barely making it above the horizon, autumn firmly in place. At least the earlier mist had cleared. 'I don't know about you, but I could use a hot drink.'

'No one's stopping you.'

'I can't leave you out here.'

'Why?'

'Because my boss would have my guts for garters.'

She glared at me condescendingly, uninterested in my problems.

'You see that guy down there?' I pointed to Paul. He was currently pacing up and down, no doubt bored, frustrated, control being something he didn't like to lose before his morning cup of tea. 'The one with the oversized belly and balding head that he doesn't realise is *this* visible from above?' I thought I heard a snigger. I didn't look. I couldn't help tilting my head to get a better look at my friend below, age creeping in fast. I'm sure Paul wasn't aware how much hair he was losing and I wasn't about to tell him. He would blame stress, the job, his age, *me*. 'He's my boss.'

He wasn't, of course. He was a colleague, a friend. A police officer who asked for my help when he needed a second opinion, valued viewpoints something I was happy to provide without measure, a man I trusted with my life. Angela didn't need to know the details. I was merely continuing the illusion that I was incompetent, a firm eye kept on my abilities, the officers behind us sent as chaperones. 'You might not be able to tell from up here, but he's not impressed with my performance at the moment.'

'Why?' I'm sure a smile tugged at Angela's lips.

I swallowed. 'I probably shouldn't be telling you this, but the last person I tried to talk off a ledge ended up in a body bag.' I reenacted a falling body with an outstretched hand, my mouth pulled tightly into a fake grimace, producing a splattering sound that looked as if I was about to throw up. 'I don't want to get fired. I've only been in the job a couple of months.'

Angela sniggered again, unable to control her unfortunate amusement. I'm sure it was the way I told the story and not because she believed some other poor sod had committed suicide on my watch. I couldn't imagine she was *that* insensitive.

'Christ, you're really bad at this shrink shit, aren't you?' She couldn't hide her disgust in what she assumed she now knew about me, my little lie something I was merely hoping would work in my favour.

'I guess,' I smiled, still hoping to win her affection. I wasn't *that* bad. 'You'd be helping me so much if you could come down with me.' I glanced behind, lowering my voice, pretending my next statement was for Angela's ears only. It didn't matter if the officers behind us overheard. They might not have known me well enough to trust my judgment or how well I usually dealt with moments like these, but Paul did. 'Who's going to stop you coming back later? Trying to fly again? You'll have no more distractions once everyone's gone.' I'd give myself a medal for effort, ten out of ten for quick thinking. My heart was in my throat, the idea that I'd accidentally given the poor thing permission to kill herself, *not* something I wanted in my head.

Angela glanced behind me in response, my unfathomed words seeming to sink in. Neither officer had heard our chat, they were probably no longer listening judging by the disinterested expressions they aimed into the air.

'They'll want to lock me away.' Angela sounded worried.

'Why? You haven't done anything wrong, have you?' I'd never heard of anyone being locked away for trying to take their *own* life. Someone else's, maybe, but not their own. Angela needed help she wouldn't find up here.

'Haven't I?' I'm sure I heard a confession in her voice. I ignored it. Instead, I laughed, wanting to diffuse this impossible situation.

'I'm sure your raven friends would want you to live another day.'

She looked at me, something behind her cold eyes telling me I'd misjudged her. 'They *are* my friends,' she confirmed sadly. She was shivering again, the magnitude of this moment obvious.

'Then allow them to guide you, Angela. You don't *want* to kill yourself. Not today.' I was going along with her theatrics now, nowhere else for me to be.

Angela didn't reply.

'I can't prevent you from jumping to your death. You can do *that* anytime you like.' I pointed a trembling finger over the ledge, the ground below us too encumbered for me to consider that Angela might take me up on the idea. 'But if you do, you'll be left with the knowledge that I had to deal with my boss because of yet *another* suicide victim I was unable to save.' I sucked in a lungful of air, my words holding the potential to become Angela's last if I wasn't careful. I still wasn't aware of just how vulnerable she was, still didn't know why she was in this position. 'The idea of being evicted from my flat a *month* after I moved there isn't something I want to think of either, if I'm honest. And let's not get into my wife's response when I go home tonight and tell her that, despite freezing to death on a rooftop ledge trying to talk you down, you still jumped anyway.' I pulled a funny face. 'You don't want to do *that* to me, do you? She might never forgive me.'

'I guess not.'

I could see Angela was a good person, deep inside, no matter what had happened to convince her she had no other way out. She didn't need to know I wasn't married. At least, not anymore. 'There *are* people you can talk to.'

'They never helped me before. Why would they now?' She was shaking, my words nothing but frustrated noise she probably couldn't abide.

'Before?' I asked before I could stop myself, unconcerned I might overstep her boundaries. I was usually careful how I dealt with vulnerable people, my brain apparently too cold now to worry. Angela was obviously dealing with a lot she hadn't yet shared with me.

She flinched.

'Maybe *I* can help?'

'I thought you said you were *shit* at your job?'

'*You* said that, not me.' I laughed. It was inappropriate. It might have been true.

'What was the last guy's problem anyway?'

'The one who jumped?' I almost forgot I'd invented him.

Angela nodded.

I needed to think fast. 'I guess he saw no way forward. Didn't assume anyone would support him, didn't appreciate that he wasn't alone.' I glanced skyward again, heavy rain clouds forming. 'But I suppose he didn't have the *ravens* to look after him.' I closed my eyes, trying to visualise Angela's viewpoint.

When I looked at her again I saw something I hadn't noticed before. She was *frightened*. Whatever life had thrown her way had taken a toll I couldn't begin to comprehend. She needed support, understanding, someone to unburden her thoughts and help process painful events I presumed she hadn't yet dealt with. I held out my hand, unable to keep it steady, hoping she wouldn't notice, hoping she would reach out and take it. I wasn't expecting much, yet she leant over and grabbed my palm, her icy fingers wrapping around mine. I guided her gently backwards, inching towards that unfortunate gap, safety suddenly too far away. I wouldn't be happy until we were on the other side, excuse the expression, away from sheer drops and icy winds. Whatever happened after today, we would deal with it together.

# Five

## *Angela*

Why am I allowing a stranger to talk me down? He doesn't know me *or* appreciate what I've been through. In fact, the guy looks *fucking* terrified. I stare at him sideways, a light breeze tugging his hair, a faint scent of aftershave wafting my way I suspect isn't fresh. The last thing I need is someone else's death on my conscience, should he fall, his mistake made due to a fundamental lack of self-awareness. I'd be done for manslaughter, as well as murder. A perfect end to my pathetic existence. *How ironic.* The idiot doesn't even know what he's doing, has practically confirmed so himself. Why can't they all leave me alone?

He's holding my hand as if his life depends on saving mine and yet he's trembling, probably from the cold, but it might be from stress, I can't tell. Until now I've barely felt the breeze, my thoughts too fragile, my mind in a dark place no one should ever endure. It matters little that my dress is inappropriate for the current weather conditions, although reality is beginning to set in, the way I look obviously creating a first impression I didn't anticipate I'd make. I hope there's no blood on it that I've failed to notice, Lee's predicament something I can't dwell on at the moment. As it is, I either jump or freeze to death. Both would result in the same outcome. I glance over the ledge, almost believing my crazy considerations, almost lunging into the void.

'You okay?' the guy's voice is snatched into the air. He sounds cold, tired. I'm unconvinced he can't see the poisonous thoughts swarming my head, merely waiting for his moment to pounce.

I nod. I can't show my vulnerabilities, can't express my problems. I have no idea what will happen now or how I expect to get out of the shit I've unwittingly created without answering questions I've no answers to. My feet hurt from this morning's unfortunate incident, blisters already formed from an unforgiving pavement. I've only just noticed how dirty my soles are. I don't know why I've allowed him inside my head, under my skin, the power to talk me down entirely unexpected. Instead of ending my life, strangers will want to discuss my problems, each assuming they hold the ability to help me, as if they can fix those broken pieces I've never learned to accept. Everyone believes they have the answers. *If only.*

We shuffle along the ledge, inch by painful inch, the firm grip he has on me something I haven't anticipated. Is he hoping to save me, or himself? I glance down, a dense grassy area below filled with faces hell-bent on preventing my death. Do I *want* to die? No. Do I see any other way out? Absolutely not.

'Just a little further.' The guy is sliding backwards, his tank top more at home in a classroom than a rooftop, his hair looking as if he just got out of bed. I look a terrible state too, of course. I'm not deluded. But I didn't expect it would

## The Lost Raven

matter today. Why would I care what I look like when I'm dead? I wish he would hurry up. I'd be back through that gap by now if he would just get out of my way. I glance skyward, the ground not something I'll be saying hello to any time soon, the ravens already moved on to better things.

As it is, the outside world feels strange, as if I've slipped into a parallel universe, everything muffled and slow. Logically I know it's nothing more than the shit show continually spinning my head out of balance, but it isn't helpful. I ignore several sideways glances from strangers in uniform, maintaining a safe enough distance to protect my assumed personal space. It might sound crazy, but I often believe that if someone were to come too close, they'd end up inside my head and be trapped in there with me forever. My mind isn't a nice place to be when I'm having a bad day, today being the worst I've experienced in a while. It's the reason I haven't maintained a relationship. I don't need to drag someone else into my chaos.

It takes some doing, but eventually we make it to the supposed safety of the car park where a tinfoil blanket is draped around my shoulders by an awaiting policewoman. Like me, she is shivering. She thinks I haven't noticed. I don't want it, but it covers my modesty, preventing unwanted attention I don't have the energy to expel. The last thing I want is to admit my vulnerabilities, my *crime*, standing here with no underwear, no shoes. Instead, I allow myself to be guided downwards, the silence too much, a guiding arm around my shoulders, that annoying *shrink* guy hovering behind. He is busy speaking to a male police officer who hasn't once acknowledged my existence. I wonder if these men feel sorry for me or fancy me, like the idea of more than a passing glance, annoyed we're not alone.

The policewoman is speaking but I'm not listening, my

dark thoughts far too overpowering, today's unplanned mission a failure. Maybe I should have thrown myself over the edge anyway. Left them to deal with the aftermath. Why should I care?

'Miss?'

I glance up, cool words I can't understand left floating in the frosty air. I don't wish to appear skittish or troubled so I attempt a smile. For some reason my face hurts. 'Sorry?'

'I said, we would like to take you to the hospital to get you checked out.' The female officer is speaking to me as if my existence is irrelevant, her day merely designed to tick boxes. I see no compassion in her eyes.

'No!' I stagger backwards. There's no way I'm enduring that shit. I've been there before, many times. They can piss off and leave me alone.

'It's okay. No one wants to see anything happen to you—'

'What would *you* care? You don't know me.' I'm yelling at the poor woman, my frustration apparent. I can't help it. What if they lock me away, drug me, tell me things I don't want to hear? I'm sick of people assuming they know everything, can fix *everything*.

That tank top wearing shrink bloke steps in, attempting to calm a situation he can't possibly understand. 'It's okay,' he states, his unpolished shoes clattering down several stone steps towards me. 'I'll deal with this.' The female police officer has already stepped away, already bored of my unwanted, irritating company. What exactly does he think he can *deal* with? I very much doubt he has the ability to deal with his *own* shit.

'Are you okay, Angela?' he asks. He oddly sounds as if he cares.

I nod, nothing else for me to say. I'd forgotten I told him my name and hearing it now is upsetting. Inside I'm

## The Lost Raven

screaming. I just want them all to leave me alone. Is that too much to ask? 'I don't *need* to go to the hospital.' Even my voice no longer sounds like mine.

'I appreciate that.' Shrink Bloke steps towards me as if his presence is of no consequence, forcing me to take an automatic step back. 'But a few moments ago you were standing on the ledge of an eighty-foot building, threatening to throw yourself off. They just want to check you over, make sure you're not suffering from hypothermia or anything equally distressing.' He smiles. I don't return the gesture.

What he's failed to confirm is that they want to ensure I won't try anything like that again, that my suicidal tendencies aren't going to cause further problems. My actions equate to taxpayers' money being spent on cleaning up any chaos I leave behind, ambulance services, cleaning crews, coffins. Yet, none of them *care* if I kill myself. Not really. Why would they? They don't know me.

'I'm fine,' I state coldly. My teeth are clenched tight.

'Clearly, you're *not*.' This guy isn't backing down.

I step backwards, ready to run, considering racing into the middle of the road, into the path of an oncoming vehicle. I need to end this thing once and for all. I've taken up too much valuable time today. Time I haven't anticipated. Time I don't have.

'Angela, you don't have to be afraid. You don't have to do this alone.' He is smiling again. It makes him look funny, as if smiling isn't something he's accustomed to.

I *am* alone. Do these people not understand that? What do they want from me? I think about last night and what Liam has begun. I can still feel him touching me, breathing heavily, sliding his hands where they have no business being. I can still see the look on Lee's face.

'*No!* Please. Don't let them take me to hospital.' I sound

desperate. I can't help it. They'll want to examine me. They'll find out what happened. They'll *see* what Liam did, only a matter of time before they uncover what *I* did.

'Why are you afraid?'

I can't tell him. I can't tell *anyone*. Not now, not ever. I can deal with this thing alone, as always. I shake my head, unsure where I go from here, wishing I'd never let him talk me off that roof. I'm crying, my eyes blurred with frustration, my throat crackling with words I will never say aloud.

The stranger steps forward, holding a warm hand towards mine. 'Nobody's going to make you do anything you don't want. But you were up there a while and it's cold out here. Everyone just wants to make sure you're okay.'

*And wholly unstable.* Don't forget that.

'But they'll want to *talk* to me.' I'm muttering. I can't help it. They'll ask why I was up there in the first place. They'll probe, just like before, aiming accusations my way. They'll say I'm a liar. I can't go through that again. I can't go to jail.

'You don't have to tell them anything you don't feel comfortable with.' He sounds as if he's about to arrest me. 'I can come with you. I'll tell them I'm your counsellor.'

I almost want to smile, glad I'm unable to pull off such an expression, forcing myself to look down instead. My counsellor? *Seriously?* As if I haven't seen enough of those in my time. Yet, my feet are dirty, my toes blue, my goose-bumped legs already peppered in stubble from the relentless cold. I dread to think what my face must look like. They're bound to assume me unstable. They won't be wrong.

I want to like this guy, really I do, but all I see are alternate motives, ideas only men possess. I nod anyway, my neck muscles doing the talking my mouth can't,

## The Lost Raven

allowing a now uncertain policewoman to guide me towards an awaiting ambulance. I glance behind to ensure Shrink Bloke is following, oddly glad when he climbs into the back and sits down next to me.

I endure unrequited chatter from strangers, unsure what to say in response as they assess my temperature, take readings, sticking needles into my veins that hurt. How can I put into words the forces that drove me to almost end my life? This was never just about Liam Goodman, my unfeigned imagination left now to wander off somewhere without me. It isn't as if I haven't been here before, suicide a word I became familiar with at the age of sixteen. I won't go into details. All I know is I'm *not* about to endure another psychical examination. I'm not going through that humiliation again.

\*\*\*

I don't want to go to the hospital, yet here I am, going anyway. I know everyone who works in A&E and I'm unsure how I'll handle their reaction when they find out what I did, judging me for an event I had no control over, falling over each other to obtain gossip. I don't think I can deal with that today.

I press my palms into my pulsating forehead, an icy chill numbing my skin as the ambulance doors swing open. I don't know where Liam is or what he's thinking but I can still feel his breath against my neck, the way he touched me not something I want to recall. He doesn't know about my past or what I've been through. He didn't ask and I was *never* going to explain. Yet, I've been told my bipolar comes from the trauma I sustained many years ago, that time in my life long gone now, of course, although still raw, painful. It waits in the dark to devour me when no one is looking.

When a ramp is lowered I consider running. I'm about to be subjected to unwanted probing, questions and faces I don't wish to acknowledge, in limbo, nothing recognisable of the person they assume I am. I can't let them witness the real Angela Healy. I don't think they'll like what they see. Despite this, I allow myself to be guided into the building, perturbed that Shrink Bloke doesn't leave my side, not even to obtain the coffee he's confirmed several times he needs. I admit I find his presence comforting, though. I don't know why. He looks like someone's grandad. I'm sure he can't be that old.

'Please get yourself a cup of coffee,' I command. I'm not going anywhere and I'm *not* asking twice. This is the warmest I've felt for hours and I'm oddly okay with that.

'I'm okay.'

'You look tired.'

'Thank you.'

I ignore his sarcasm. 'Well, get *me* one then.'

He smiles, his eyes crinkling in the corners. I sense he might be a good man. Do they exist? 'Coffee?' He sounds far too enthusiastic.

'Hot chocolate.' I try to smile yet my mouth doesn't comply, my lips too sore to move. Besides, smiling would imply I don't care what I did to Lee. I wonder where he is, if he's here, in surgery, the hospital saving his life. Either that or they're currently telling his family he's dead. I don't want to think about either.

Shrink Bloke leaves my cubicle to get me a drink I don't want, my only requirement being for him to leave me alone to assess an impossible situation I've found myself in. I ignore several shocked requests for information, those around me keen to know how I am, what happened, why I'm here. I offer no rational answers, of course, unable to accept my position or acknowledge what happened. I'm

*The Lost Raven*

assessed by the department's head consultant, Dr Andrew Hansley, who, although doesn't usually have much to do with me, looks at me now with an awkward stare.

Andrew was at the party. He *saw* me, yet thankfully hasn't said anything about that. I'm not sure it's a good thing, not sure I want to recall how drunk I was. I've been given a pair of jogging bottoms to cover my modesty, pumps that feel alien on my feet after being barefooted so long. I'm wearing Shrink Bloke's jacket, my mish-mashed outfit a collection of hastily gathered items that no doubt make me look insane. I don't even notice I'm still clutching my raven feather until he returns with two polystyrene cups and points it out.

'Wouldn't that be safer in your bag?' Shrink Bloke questions, placing a hot cup on a nearby table, pointing to my hand, my fingers numb with the continued exertion it has taken to maintain a grip. He's sipping coffee, the strong aroma making me feel sick.

I haven't noticed how firmly I've been holding it, threatening to crush its delicate spine with my trembling fingers. This feather has become a lifeline, a thread to a different world now keeping me alive. He's right, of course, yet if I lost it, I don't know what I'd do. *I need it.* I nod, searching for my bag, glad when he hands it to me. He hasn't asked questions, hasn't probed. Not like the staff who've all been quizzing me for the last twenty minutes, no words I utter sounding sane. As it is, my bag becomes the thing I now cling to, clutching it to my trembling body, my mobile phone confirming several missed calls that have all gone unnoticed.

'Can I call someone for you?' Shrink Bloke asks.

I shake my head. How should I respond? No one will understand. I doubt any of them will care. I can't tell him I have no family, my mother's life cut short long ago, my friends mostly tied to a job I'm not even sure I like. Instead, we sit for a while in silence. I know he is allowing me the time he assumes I need to process events, but I'm sure he has better things to do. He doesn't want to be inside my head. Not today. I should probably stop calling him *Shrink Bloke*. It's hardly a kind gesture of gratitude.

When Andrew Hansley appears around a curtain I've requested remain drawn, he has a worried look on his face and I'm glad I can't read what he's thinking. He smiles but I sense he does not mean to appear so casual. A nurse is with him. She looks equally troubled. I can't look at either of them.

'Angela, are you able to clarify your recent whereabouts, please?' He is holding a clipboard. I sense a note of arrogance in his tone, an air of unrequired authority. He gives Shrink Bloke – *Newton* – a sharp look I can't discern.

I glance up, recent events too vivid, yet distant, as if I dreamt the entire thing. I shake my head, nothing else to do with it. 'I was up on a roof.' I'm almost embarrassed to confirm it, my words nothing but strained that Andrew is fully aware of. I hope he doesn't know about Lee.

'I mean, before then?'

*Before I killed a man?*

'I was at a party.' Andrew already knows this, too, of course. He saw me there. I'm surprised he managed to get up for work, the guy ever ready for what life throws his way. 'Why?' My voice sounds strange, strangled. What does he know that I don't?

'Because we found gamma hydroxybutyric acid in your bloodstream, Angela. Do you know how you came to have such a substance in your body?'

I can't speak. GHB? Does he mean the *date rape* drug? *What the hell?* Andrew glances at Newton, both men

## *The Lost Raven*

unappreciative of events I wasn't planning on confirming, looking at *me* now as if I took that shit on purpose. I open my mouth, yet no words emerge. I no longer know what I'm thinking, my brain numb, exposed. The only thing going around my head is the painful confirmation that Liam *raped* me. I wasn't wrong, wasn't dreaming, and now it seems, he drugged me to make the job easier. No wonder everything feels so hazy. No wonder I was able to stab a man in cold blood.

# Six

## *Newton*

It probably wasn't a good idea to go to the hospital with Angela. I didn't know her *or* her history. All I knew is, I couldn't leave her alone to deal with whatever had brought about this unfathomed moment in her life, unable to rationalise how *anyone* could struggle with mental illness. It was Paul's fault I was unavoidably involved, today meant to be my day off. It was irrelevant I had nowhere important to be, nothing else to focus my attention. I couldn't, of course, appreciate what she'd been through, the reasons for ending her life still unconfirmed. It is a fragile thing, the human mind, easily tipped, easily damaged.

GHB is not a substance any rational person would willingly ingest if they knew what was good for them. As a depressant, it acts on the central nervous system, able to comatose someone when used in combination with other drugs or alcohol. The fact Angela had it in her bloodstream was concerning and although she hadn't confirmed it, I

## The Lost Raven

couldn't help wondering if this was another failed suicide attempt. Finding herself on a roof may have been a last resort, a final option that would see no way out but down.

It didn't help that the A&E consultant was a man I knew well. Andrew Hansley and I had studied together at university, had once considered each other good friends. It was an unfortunate state of affairs that meant I hadn't seen him in years, had almost forgotten what he looked like. His presence brought up painful memories of my own failed marriage, the fact he became a highly regarded hospital doctor whilst I became a psychologist due more to my wife's sudden departure than a loss of interest in medicine. I was now thinking about Kate, time relentlessly slipping forward in a painful hurry.

Andy seemed as surprised to see me as I was to see him, the look on his face matching my own. Yet he didn't mention our connection whilst in Angela's company, retaining a professionalism I'd always admired. He asked about the drugs in her system but she gave nothing conclusive aside from a shocked expression I noted clearly. Instead, she remained silently perched on the edge of a hospital bed, clutching her bag, unwilling to acknowledge those around her who only wanted to help.

'Angela? Are you all right?' I leant across the bed towards her. She tilted her head but didn't see me, her eyes blank. I wished I knew what she was thinking.

No answer.

Andy sighed, giving me a knowing look before leaving us to our privacy, nothing more he could add, a swift nod of his head confirming he didn't wish to say anything else. He'd probably already said too much. Angela didn't respond, heavy tears perched in saddened eyes that saw nothing but unforgiving pain.

'Are you sure you won't talk to me?' I asked once we

were alone.

Still nothing.

I didn't want to crowd the poor thing, we barely knew each other, so I made my excuses and took a stroll along a cool corridor, glad of the unassuming blandness, grateful to have been given time to assess my thoughts. I needed another coffee, anyway. Affording myself a much-needed respite from the morning's impossible events.

'Newton Flanigan, as I live and breathe.' I turned to see my old friend grinning at me, an expression he wasn't able to express until now planted firmly on an exasperated face

'Andy. How are you?' We embraced, our handshake firm. I wasn't sure if I was pleased to see him or shocked by his presence. He hadn't changed, still as charismatic as ever.

'It's been far too long, my friend.' Andy patted my arm, still laughing, glancing over his shoulder, aiming yet another inappropriate grin at nothing in particular. 'What are you doing here and how do you know Angela?' His questions came thick and fast, as if we'd parted company only yesterday, delving directly into our once assumed comfortable accord.

I stared at him blankly, any response I might offer potentially unwanted. 'I live here now,' I confirmed, the last ten years of my life slipping by in a void of uncertainty.

Andy didn't need to know how I felt about that. It honestly didn't feel that long. After my brother passed away, the sea air merely helped clear my mind of the clutter that had become my daily existence. I needed an escape, some place to avoid reality and a blinding pain I still struggled to dislodge. I'd climbed into my car and drove, no clear destination in mind, no concern of where I was heading. The ends of the earth wouldn't have been far enough. As it was, my journey ended with a blinding sea view and Eastcliff subsequently became my home. Right now, it didn't matter about me. I was more interested to know what Andy was doing here. The last time we spoke, he was engrained in London life, ambitious, planning his future. I didn't assume he'd end up here.

'And Steph? I heard she's got kids now?' Andy was grinning, the idea that my sister-in-law was a mother, seemingly surprised him.

'Yeah, they're great.' I felt a pang of sadness dart across my chest, my words holding a coldness I didn't know how to sedate. I missed them, my phone calls and visits never quite enough. Andy didn't mention Isaac, didn't offer condolences for his passing. He had never met my nephews, had already left our lives before they were born.

'You still haven't told me how you know Angela?' Andy was smiling, keen for information.

'I talked her off a roof.' I didn't want to confirm it, automatically lowering my voice as I spoke. It happened to be true. There was nothing else for me to say that wouldn't have left a gaping hole in this conversation, no matter what I concluded.

'*Seriously?*' Andy looked at me as if he was impressed by my abilities.

I nodded.

'She okay?' He licked his lips, unsure how to respond to my unexpected revelation. 'I mean, obviously I know *why* she was brought in, but she hasn't said much and I don't want to push it.' He paused. 'But to be honest, I never saw *that* coming.' He glanced around as if he didn't want Angela's vulnerabilities open to debate. It isn't a comfort to appreciate that serious mental health issues all too often reside inside the minds of those we see nothing amiss with until it's too late. 'I still don't know how *you're* involved with Angela Healy?' He spoke Angela's name as if she was someone he admired, assumed incapable of dark thoughts,

## Nicky Shearsby

his world so very different to mine.

'I work with the police.' I didn't confirm that my friend was a DCI and therefore expected me to be on tap whenever he required assistance.

'You didn't go back into medicine then? After—' Andy didn't finish his sentence but I knew what he wanted to say. *After Kate left.* I still couldn't believe it had been so long.

'No. Psychology.'

Andy laughed, raising his clean-shaven chin to the ceiling in response to the joke he assumed I'd made. 'So you ended up a doctor, anyway, despite *everything*. Typical Newton.'

I had no idea what he meant by that. I didn't ask.

Andy glanced around, changing the subject, growing serious. 'To be honest, Newt, we're all worried about Angela. She *works* here. We consider her a friend.'

Angela's reluctance to come here now made sense. She should have told me she was on the hospital payroll. 'I take it she hasn't mentioned *anything* to you about how she's been feeling?' I couldn't imagine she hadn't confided in *someone* about her mental health. Aren't women meant to lap that shit up? It's usually men who don't talk.

Andy shook his head. 'She keeps mostly to herself, although I think she's fairly close to one of the other girls on reception. Rosie.' He paused, lowering his voice. 'We'd like to keep her in overnight if she'll agree. To *monitor* her.' He was whispering, motioning me towards a window so we could speak in private.

'I take it you want *me* to help with that?'

Andy nodded. 'We've done some preliminary checks and *psychically* she seems okay, but unfortunately the mental health assessment team are already involved and I'm not sure how she's going to take the news.'

'Why?' What did *he* know that I didn't?

## The Lost Raven

'Angela has bipolar disorder. And she can be a bit... *psychotic*.' Andy paused. 'She doesn't like to tell many people. Doesn't even know I'm aware of her condition. She's usually fine as long as she takes her medication and looks after herself.'

I understood bipolar, had seen it many times. I nodded, knowing what he wanted from me. I'd deal with it. I sighed, leaving my old friend to his busy schedule, a passing nurse offering him a folder and a smile.

'We must catch up some time, Newt,' he called after me, already halfway along the corridor, already glad to have rid himself of my company, our brief encounter over. I raised my hand in response, aiming a wayward thumb into the air. He was a good friend once and I wondered what had changed. Life, probably.

\*\*\*

I hovered for a while next to a plastic plant that looked as if a reckless child had been carelessly yanking its leaves, looking through large windows to the increasing bustle beyond. My coffee was lukewarm and when my phone rang, I was glad of the distraction.

'Everything okay?' Paul's contumacious tone was unbefitting of the moment. He sounded as if he was at the station, a telephone ringing in the background.

'I'm still at the hospital.' I wasn't even sure how long I'd been here.

'How's the girl doing?'

'Not sure.' I got the impression she *wanted* to speak yet didn't know where to begin. I didn't confirm it. 'They found GHB in her bloodstream.'

'*What?*'

'She hasn't said how. Hasn't said much of anything, to

be honest.' I wasn't sure it was even a police issue, didn't want Paul jumping to conclusions. I probably shouldn't have mentioned it.

'Was she drugged or did she willingly take the stuff?'

I shrugged. Paul couldn't see. 'I haven't had a chance to speak to her about it yet.' Wasn't sure how I could.

'Does she want to press charges against anyone?'

'I honestly don't know.' Paul was annoying me now. 'Give me a chance to do my job and I'll let you know.' He must have noticed my frustration because he changed the subject.

'Okay. Anyway, I just called to thank you for your help this morning.'

'That's fine. I was glad I *could*.' It was true. Angela might be dead now if I hadn't. I didn't confirm it.

'I guess it's in the hands of the hospital and the mental health team now, so you can probably get going.' He no doubt assumed I'd want to. Angela wasn't my patient, not my problem. As far as Paul was concerned, I'd done my job.

'I might stick around for a while. Make sure she's okay.'

'She's not your responsibility.'

'I know, but everyone deserves a break, Paul, someone to care. Honestly, I'm happy to stay.'

'Ever the psychologist, hey?'

'You know me.'

'I do. That's the problem.' Paul paused, before adding, 'don't get too involved.'

'She's suicidal. I want to help if I can.'

Paul didn't respond. I ignored the silence but knew what he was thinking. I was still recovering from the last police case I'd helped with, from the last person I assumed I could save, the near fatal stab wound I'd endured at the hand of a madman something I didn't assume would ever leave my thoughts. I rolled my eyes, unsure I wanted Paul

*The Lost Raven*

to elaborate on injuries sustained because I got too close to a psychopath. I didn't need the reminder, didn't need the unfounded confirmation that convicted serial killer *David Mallory* was still taking up unwanted space in my head. None of us appreciated how dangerous he was, especially me. My abdomen still ached if I twisted awkwardly.

'Well, you have my number if you need me,' I concluded. I wanted to get off the phone, this conversation too much.

'Yeah, I do, Newt. In more ways than one.'

I ignored what he meant by that. Instead, I took a breath and picked my coffee from the windowsill, the liquid now cold. I didn't mind. Coffee was coffee at the end of the day, and the way I felt, I wouldn't taste it anyway. I walked along the corridor with the single intention of turning my attention to a young woman I'd only met that morning, a woman struggling, seemingly no one around her to appreciate the obvious pain she was in.

\*\*\*

I peeled open Angela's cubicle curtain to find her curled against the far wall, everything around her alien and frightening. She was trembling. I don't think she saw me, don't think she cared, too busy clinging to an inanimate object for comfort she probably believed she might not find in real life.

'Are you okay?' It was an honest question.

Angela didn't reply.

'You didn't tell me you *worked* here.' I was attempting to keep our chat light, nothing heavy to weigh her down or pull her over the edge.

She shrugged.

'Is there anything you need?' I wanted to help if she'd

let me. I was a good listener, my biggest asset according to Paul, as well as my biggest failure according to a police interview with David Mallory. I took a seat on a plastic chair, wincing at the perpetual ache in my belly, careful to maintain a safe distance. I didn't want to overstep the mark. She didn't know me, didn't trust me. Not yet.

'I just want to go home,' Angela confirmed, her voice so small I barely heard.

'I know. But they want to do some assessments first.'

'What kind of assessments?' She shot me a cold look. She was still trembling.

'Nothing invasive, I promise. Just to confirm you're okay.' I couldn't tell her they wanted to assess her mind, probably needing to check she was on the right level of medication for her bipolar. I was keen to discuss the drugs in her system, still unsure how to broach the subject of GHB.

'I can't stay here.' Angela was scrunched into a tight ball, her feet pulled under her chin. She was dressed now in jogging bottoms that looked too big, her dress passing as a top. An old pair of pumps completed the outfit. She could keep my jacket.

'It's okay. No one is going to force you to do *anything* you're not comfortable with.' It was the second time today I'd confirmed it, yet I was unsure my words rang true. She was found on a rooftop, ready and willing to jump to her death, GHB in her bloodstream and troubling mental health issues unknown to many. I wasn't surprised she couldn't talk about it. 'But they won't be happy to let you go without a plan in place and the knowledge you have friends or family who can take care of—'

'No!' she screamed, jumping to her feet. She rounded the bed, shaking off my words, her eyes wild, terrified.

'What are you afraid of, Angela?' I got to my own, only wanting to help.

## The Lost Raven

'Nothing. I have to go.' Angela didn't look as if she knew what to do, hovering at the end of the bed clutching her bag. 'I have to go,' she repeated, her unsteady legs aimed towards the exit.

I turned to raise the alarm but Angela rushed passed me into the corridor, almost knocking me off my feet. 'Angela, wait,' I called out, nowhere else to go but after her. I'd never forgive myself if something happened, ignoring several concerned calls from surrounding staff, each as worried as I was. Despite calling her name, she didn't turn around, didn't acknowledge me, too busy making her escape.

I followed her outside, watching my jacket disappear towards the bay beyond the hospital car park. Angela was still shivering, despite my best efforts, my garment too big for her anyway, swamping her tiny frame. I headed down a set of sand-covered steps onto a narrow coastal path in pursuit, navigating a bend, crashing into an oncoming dog walker in my haste, no sense of direction, no concept of safety. I apologised, of course, avoiding a sheer drop that tipped violently into the ocean below, out of breath by the time I made it onto a narrow stretch of shingled beach.

I'd forgotten how beautiful this beach was. I should come here more often, clear the cobwebs, feel the sand between my toes, ignite old memories. There is something special about this part of Eastcliff, eerie even, the entire area breathtaking in the summer with its wildlife, bees, butterflies, honeysuckle, whilst at the same time wholly inaccessible in winter. Today was threatening to become one of those days, already much colder now, the earlier mist giving way to a light drizzle that made me shudder. Thick salty air took my breath, the entire place set amid a backdrop of wild blue and gold. Angela was standing in the swell, her bare feet and trembling lips near frozen, her borrowed pumps grasped in her hands, my jacket pulled firmly around her. I couldn't assume she wasn't considering drowning herself, her mind too far gone for me to believe I could ever *really* help her at all.

# Seven

## *Angela*

A simple affirmation was given to me by a well-meaning psychiatrist several years ago after a therapy session ended badly, a diagnosis of bipolar provided because the woman was unsure what else to label me with. I think about that affirmation occasionally, when life becomes too much, when nothing in my head makes sense. I can't now, in fact, get those words out of my brain as I race across the hospital car park towards the bay, nowhere else to go, nothing left to do but run.

*My name is Angela Healy and I am not defined by my actions.*

I repeat the sentence, over and over, attempting to convince myself I believe what I'm saying, my voice too fragile to battle the oncoming breeze. Yet, no matter how many times I repeat these words, they never help — probably because I don't appreciate what they stand for. Aren't we *all* defined by our actions? Doesn't everything we ever do in life provoke who we ultimately become?

My mobile is ringing, vibrating constantly in my bag, the person on the other end desperate for attention. It had better not be Liam. I can barely bring myself to think about him right now let alone speak to him. He won't want to hear what I have to say, won't want to suffer my wrath. I thought I could trust him. Now I'm genuinely not sure what to believe. I guess if it all gets too much, I can race into the sea and drown myself.

I close my eyes, my feet twisting and stumbling over unyielding pebbles and shells that hurt my ankles and bring tears to my already swollen eyes. If I had a match, I would light myself on fire and end my suffering once and for all. What would it feel like to combust spontaneously? Would it hurt? Would I be *capable* of feeling any further pain than what I'm already enduring? I visualise my body turning black, then white, nothing left but ash to identify me, a patch of dust on the shoreline, a tooth, a filling, a lock of hair. I've been somewhat sporadic with my meds lately. I can't help it. Sometimes I forget to take them, other days I can't be bothered. Some days I take them and *still* have an episode so I honestly can't win no matter what I do. I can't change how my brain works, can't alter who I am.

Some people with bipolar might be okay for a week or two before they notice any behavioural changes, but with me, it doesn't take long, twenty-four hours oddly all I need for severe anxiety to set in. A tight knot has already embedded itself in my stomach, paranoid delusions closing in fast. I don't remember the last time I took my medication. All I know is that bipolar grips me in the depths of the night and pats me on the back during the day. It ensures I'm able to laugh and scream at the same time, my friend, my enemy, pushing me to do things I shouldn't, laughing when I don't, scolding me when I do.

## The Lost Raven

Thankfully this beach is quiet today, too cold for a stroll, too late in the season for tourists. Eastcliff's main stretch is further along the coast, around the bay, an imposing seafront peppered with restaurants, bars, ice cream stands, arcades. I'm glad I'm alone, unconvinced I can deal with more shit from strangers today. I might punch someone. I've already stabbed a man. I'm crying. I can't help it. If my phone doesn't stop buzzing, I swear it's going in the sea.

I can hear someone calling my name but I'm too incensed to deal with my imagination today, in no mood for the psychosis that creeps up on me when I'm not watching. I'm merely thankful to have escaped that overbearing hospital, requiring a moment to think, to process what I've been through. How do I have *GHB* in my system? I turn, noticing some old guy stumbling down the steps onto the beach. I don't know what he's doing. As long as he stays away from me, I don't care.

I yank my buzzing mobile phone from my bag, ready to scream, the screen displaying an incoming call from my friend Rosie. I consider rejecting it, still hoping those memories of last night aren't real. Yet, in fairness, she's probably worried about me, wondering why I disappeared so suddenly, unaware I didn't leave Liam's house until the early hours of this morning.

*'What!?'* I can't help but snap. I'm cold, dressed in someone else's clothing including a jacket that smells like old sweat and Old Spice aftershave. I look like a victim of some unfortunate event.

'Where the hell have you been? I've been trying to call you for ages.' Rosie sounds irritated, as always, her muffled voice filling the morning air, cutting me like a knife. Just because she's twice my age, it does not give her the right to act like my mum.

'I'm fine,' I lie, unsure what else to say.

'Where are you?'

'At home.' I have no idea why I can't just tell her the truth.

*Liam raped me. I spent a few hours unconscious in his bed, then got up in the early hours of this morning and accidentally killed some guy before I tried to kill myself. I was at the hospital for a while. Currently have GHB in my bloodstream. How are you?*

'You sound as if you're outside.'

Why would she care? She wouldn't know my whereabouts unless she's already been to my flat and therefore knows I'm not at home. I wouldn't be surprised. After confiding in her about my bipolar a few months ago, she's since taken it upon herself to *stalk* me, to ensure I'm okay, to keep an eye on me, keeping me on a metaphoric track.

'I needed some air.' I take a breath. 'What do you want?' I don't mean to sound annoyed. It isn't Rosie's fault.

There's an awkward pause and I assume my phone has lost connection, but the call duration is still counting the seconds on my screen so I know she's still there. 'Actually, do you have a minute? I really need to talk to you.' She sounds almost as stressed as me.

'Can it wait?'

Another pause. 'Of, course. Ignore me.' Rosie attempts a laugh that doesn't sound convincing. 'What time did you leave the party? I didn't see much of you after ten.'

No matter what is going on in Rosie's life, she's oddly always willing to drop everything for others, her needs less important than everyone else's. The oldest of our group, she's taken on the role of Mother, looking after the rest of the A&E staff as if they are her family, her clan. I usually like it, should now be grateful for the continued support, yet today isn't one of those days and I honestly don't know how

*The Lost Raven*

to respond. How do I tell my friend I was left to rot half-naked beneath a ruffled duvet and several unattended coats? That I was *raped*?

'I don't know.' I can't help the lies that leave my mouth, the morning air stealing my voice, my sanity. I'm oddly sore below, although it might be my imagination, I can't tell, a lingering emotion from old wounds that never really healed—just my overriding paranoia.

'Are you okay? You sound funny?'

'I'm fine,' I repeat, biting my bottom lip, staring towards the crashing waves, wishing I had the guts to…

'Are you on the beach?' Rosie's voice is beginning to irritate me now, her continued accusations hanging.

'No. Why?'

'Because I can hear the ocean in the background.' A seagull takes that precise moment to squawk, leaving Rosie in no doubt as to my current location, my lies crashing against her like waves. 'Angela, are you *sure* you're okay?'

My friend is only trying to help, of course, but I'm beyond redemption. I close my eyes, close to tears again, no intention of answering her stupid questions, my name still being called in the distance. I turn around to see that the guy previously stumbling across the beach a few minutes earlier is, in fact, that tank top-wearing Shrink Bloke, *Newton*. He's jogging towards me, a demented grin on his face, his hand raised in the air. *What the hell does he want now?*

'Gotta go.' I hang up to the sound of Rosie's worried protests, her voice raised.

'You're a hard one to track down,' he yells against an incoming sea breeze, out of breath, his hair flopping wildly in protest. He looks cold. I still have his jacket. He's not getting it back.

'What do you want?' I can't help the annoyed tone that emerges on cue, my face contorting into a painful grimace.

Why can't these people leave me alone to figure out my own shit in peace?

'I wanted to check you're okay.'

'Why?'

'It's kind of my job.' He smiles but I can't return it, my face unwilling to acknowledge a damned thing, such simple expressions impossible today. I'm not his patient *or* his friend. My needs have nothing to do with him.

'I just want to be left alone.' I can't say that any clearer. I wish he would listen.

'I don't think that's a good idea, Angela.' The guy is shivering now, the fresh sea air biting into his skin.

I shrug. Who cares what he thinks? I turn, ready to leave, still searching for much-needed solace I won't now find. I just need some space to breathe.

'The hospital hasn't finished assessing you.'

'Assessing me for *what?*'

'Angela, you tried to *kill* yourself.'

I can't tell him that I didn't try hard enough because I'm still alive. I shrug again, glad I'm able to keep my mouth shut about the reasons bringing me here in the first place. It will do me no favours to confirm what really happened, such revelations potentially making me far more vulnerable than I'm currently prepared to admit.

'Why are you bothered about me?' I raise frustrated hands towards him, shocked by how much they tremble.

'Because everyone needs someone to care.'

I can't help but glare at him. What does *he* know about caring? Is this a ploy to get my unwanted attention? I know guys like him. Guys like *Liam fucking Goodman*.

'Nobody cares. Nobody *ever* cares.' I haven't meant to express such words aloud. It makes me look weak and I'm tired of feeling as if I don't matter in a world that doesn't understand who I am. I'm angry, frustrated with life as a

## The Lost Raven

whole. It's hardly Newton's fault.

'What makes you believe no one cares?'

*Because I've been here before, seen it all and worn the t-shirt. Nobody gives a shit about anyone. Full stop. The end.*

I ignore the fact that Rosie was only seconds earlier calling to check on me, convinced she wouldn't care about me if she knew everything. I bite my tongue, unable to say such things. I can't speak, can't open my mouth for fear of what might spill out, my emotions left to run amok. He can turn around and sod off.

'Sounds as if you could use a friendly ear.'

The guy means well, I'll give him that, yet I laugh, a strained, frustrated chuckle that emerges from the back of my throat like bile, no better than a strangled grunt. 'And I suppose you're the perfect person to give me one?' I don't mean to sound so irritated.

'Why not?' He's standing with his hands in his trouser pockets, a pair of glasses wedged untidily in his hair. He looks like a schoolteacher. Smells like one, too. All coffee breath and stale odours he's probably unaware exist.

'Because I don't need *anyone*.' I refrain from adding "especially someone like you", instead bite my bottom lip until it hurts. I'm final in my statement, demanding in my mannerisms, automatically turning around to escape before I burst into yet more tears and express my true emotional vulnerabilities. The only thing on my mind is to leave this beach and this man behind, to find a place where I won't be disturbed. The breeze has died down a little now although heavy clouds still linger, drops of rain spotting over my skin. Several seagulls catch my attention along with the crunch of shoes across shingle.

'Surely you have *someone* you can speak to, Angela.' Shrink Bloke is still talking, still assuming I'm listening.

'I don't need anyone's help.' I wish that were true. He

doesn't need to know my thoughts on the subject. I'm still walking, my back to him, several seagulls keeping time with my footsteps.

When he touches my arm it makes me flinch. I'm sure he means nothing by it and I turn to see his hands held aloft, a simple step backwards saying more than words ever could. 'It's okay. I'm not going to hurt you.' He looks surprised, shocked by my overreaction.

I haven't meant to respond so violently, my behaviour not usually so volatile. But this morning is still on my mind, my fear of men as strong now as it was when I was four years old, when I was forced to do things no child ever should. It can't be helped, of course, yet I can *never* tell anyone about that. Nobody helped me then and they won't help me now. I swallow, my lips dry, my throat a mass of unpronounceable syllables I'm sure will throttle me at some point today. I hope he hasn't seen something I wasn't intending on displaying so readily.

'Why do you have GHB in your system?'

I shake my head, Liam strong in my mind, Lee's face looming, the wine I consumed a few hours earlier seemingly laced with poison that provoked our downfall.

'You can talk to me.'

'Leave me alone. Please.' I'm failing to hold back my tears. I wish he'd go away. I catch something in his eyes. It looks like pity. I don't need *that* either.

'I'm sorry if I've offended you.'

I glance his way, my eyes unable to linger too long for fear of what I might see. He *appears* sorry. That should count for something. I can't respond.

'I guess sometimes we just have to do what's right for us.' Shrink Bloke shrugs, throwing a casual remark into the equation I don't initially understand.

'I don't know. Do we?' I roll my eyes towards several

*The Lost Raven*

grey clouds. For a moment I swear I see a raven overhead.

'Indeed. Sod everyone else.' He smiles, kicking shingle with his foot.

'Including you?' I can't help asking, can't help my sarcasm.

'Probably,' he confirms flatly. His smile looks genuine, his casual actions accidentally easing the tension that has gripped my stiffened shoulders for hours.

'And how *exactly* do you expect me to do that?' I fold defensive arms across my chest. My head hurts and I'm sick of feeling angry. It's exhausting.

'By taking back control.' The man is nodding, believing words he doesn't realise have the power to control *me*. He means well, I'm sure, but I don't know how he assumes I can do such a thing. How can *I*, Angela Healy, ever take back control of my life?

He reaches into his trouser pocket, still smiling, still trembling in the cold air, the rain falling heavier now. 'Take this. You can call me anytime, day or night. You're *not* alone. I promise.' He hands me a business card, the words "Doctor Newton Flanigan, Clinical Psychologist" printed on one side along with his email address and telephone number. He holds the card towards me for several unbearable seconds, waiting for me to take it. I don't want it, can't bring myself to touch it. Eventually, he leans forward and tucks it inside his jacket pocket, the decision made for me, familiarity for his own possession something I don't fully appreciate. 'Anytime,' he concludes firmly, looking at me with sympathies I don't need.

I can't speak, don't know what to say, so instead, I turn around and run. I race up the steps towards salvation, out onto the road, avoiding the hospital car park for fear of being accosted by so-called mental health experts. The Royal Eastcliff Hospital has a wonderful view over the bay, its location designed purposefully facing the east coast to promote assumed health and wellbeing benefits. I don't give a shit if I never see it again. I don't, in fact, care if I see *anything* again.

*My name is Angela Healy and I am not defined by my actions.*

# Eight

## *Newton*

By the time I'd made it back up the steps from the beach, Angela was gone. In her distressed state she was probably unaware that her borrowed pumps were soaked, her hair a tangled mess, eyes and cheeks black from makeup left to dry. She hadn't noticed, and I wasn't about to tell her. I hadn't indulged in my usual morning shower either, no time to look in a mirror before leaving my flat. *Christ* knows what I must look like. I still hadn't properly woken up, more coffee required to achieve that end, my disorganised brain requiring far more than I would ever find out here. I hoped by giving her my card she would call if she needed me, my intention purely to offer a friendly ear, some advice. I'd never forgive myself if she did something stupid, unable to accept the fact that a further attempt on her life might end entirely differently.

I considered calling Paul but thought better of it, nothing more he could do about this unfortunate situation than me. It was out of our hands. Instead, I took a steady walk home along the bracing cliff tops, ignoring the rain, hoping to find clarity I was unsure I'd locate elsewhere, a chance to clear my head, wake up. I was thinking of my brother, Isaac, as usual, in my own world, my thoughts forever lodged in the past.

I was, in fact, daydreaming when I entered my street, not expecting the entire area to be crammed with neighbours, each one fretful, concerned, a thin veil of evaporating smoke streaming from my open front door. *Shit*. There was a fire engine outside, the crew finished now, packing away their equipment, the continued looks they gave me matching those of several locals hovering behind us. They were chatting, reaching conclusions, discussing unwanted assumptions. I raced towards the chaos, anxiety reflected across every face, my disgruntled upstairs neighbour Kenneth hovering, looking frantic. He was holding a handkerchief over his mouth, his cheeks flushed, out of breath.

'Where the *hell* have you been?' he asked anxiously as I raced towards him, the old man's features as knotted and stressed as ever. 'I've left you dozens of messages.'

I pulled my mobile from my pocket, too late to notice it was out of power, my needs perpetually far less important than those of strangers, it seemed. I glanced behind him, dreading what I was about to see. 'What happened?'

Ken handed me a melted saucepan. 'You're lucky I was in. Things could have been far worse.'

I glanced at the damaged pan in my grasp, unable to recall setting it on my stove. My existence, as usual, taking a backseat to the demands of the police. I didn't function well without coffee, but this was too much, even for me, five o'clock in the morning hardly a time for conducive, rational thinking. It would have taken less than an hour to boil dry

## The Lost Raven

and catch fire. I would have been at the hospital by then, oblivious. *Shit*. I would have been wholly disappointed if I was planning on boiling an egg. *I didn't have any.*

As it was, I was grateful my neighbour had the forethought of mind to come downstairs and check, a spare key thankfully left under my doormat for such profound emergencies. Ken had been alerted by my screaming smoke alarm, the fire crew currently still inside my home, heavy boots and trailing hosepipes littering my hallway floor. The smoke had been intense, apparently, a choking fog of black billowing into the street. It wasn't a comfort.

Although the fire had been extinguished a while ago, I wasn't allowed to enter my home until it was confirmed safe to do so, a fire inspector required to check the cause and any untoward intentions. Thankfully, the only intention was my breakfast, my kitchen sustaining relatively little damage, thanks to Ken, most of it due to smoke. I was lucky, *apparently*. My hob and splash back had taken the brunt of the flames, the swift actions of my ageing neighbour bringing what could have been a total disaster under control. I was left to deal with a thick patch of black along an entire side of my kitchen, several scorched cupboard doors requiring attention. Tea towels were in the sink, burnt, unusable, every surface dripping with water. I rolled my eyes before dumping my damaged saucepan into the sink to join the rest of the mess, heading outside to thank my quick-thinking neighbour.

'I don't suppose a *thank you* will cut it?' I was standing outside Ken's front door, my embarrassment obvious, a bottle of brandy I was saving for a special occasion the one thing I hoped would appease him. I ignored several hovering neighbours behind me, a feigned grin stretched across my flustered cheeks, nothing more to add to this morning's mayhem aside from the potential peace offering in my grasp.

'You really *should* slow down, you know, Newton,' Ken said, stepping to one side to allow me entry into a home that smelled far better than mine, the unopened bottle in my hand the only thing he noticed. He reached forward, taking it from me without a word of thanks. 'I've noticed you coming home at all hours, stressed out, looking as if you haven't slept in weeks.'

I wasn't about to confirm that I didn't always sleep well, my mind too busy to concern myself with such unimportant actions, my days too encumbered for me to notice. Today was one of them.

Ken's home formed the bulk of what would have once been a large Victorian property, the place split now in two. It overlooked a row of parking spaces that everyone argued about, forever jostling for position, my old Volkswagen Beetle often caught in the chaos. My basement flat was directly below, the converted space at one time housing servants, sculleries, storerooms, a kitchen supporting the grand house above. I liked it. It was tucked away below street level, a retaining wall and several weed-ridden steps the only things I saw from my lounge window. I could close my front door and pretend the world above didn't exist. Until today, that was. Now the entire neighbourhood was talking about *stupid* Newton Flanigan and his continued inability to think straight.

'Why are you *always* in a hurry?' Ken continued his assessment of my life as if we were old friends, heading into his kitchen. He opened the brandy, taking two glasses from a cupboard that he laid carefully on the countertop.

'An unfortunate factor of my existence, I'm afraid, Ken,' I concluded. It was true. Every day was spent rushing from place to place, moment to moment. I was no different to anyone else. We're all just trying our best. Ken scoffed. I tried not to notice.

I'm ashamed to admit that I'd only been inside Ken's flat twice—once to collect a parcel he kindly took in for me, and now. Yet I remembered his kitchen well, I had ironically always liked it, with its large open plan layout and bi-fold doors that led to a well-tended garden. It was the type you see featured in magazines, converted Victorian properties seemingly popular with everyone these days. I didn't exactly have a garden, my outside space nothing more than a forgotten, barely used courtyard tucked behind a now warped kitchen door. It was coated in weeds and moss, enclosed by high walls leading to an alleyway that *nobody* used. It would have once stored sacks of coal for the family upstairs, crates of milk, vegetables, wood. Now it housed my wheelie bins and anything I couldn't fit inside them. I'm sure there were boxes out there from bookshelves I was still to erect, always something else to occupy my time.

Ken ignored the fact I hadn't yet put his mind at ease and instead poured a large brandy that he handed to me. I took it with a nod, not wishing to appear rude, although I'd prefer a coffee.

'Where's that sister-in-law of yours, anyway? Why doesn't she help you out more? You need someone to look out for you, Newton.'

'Stephanie lives in London, Ken,' I reminded him, taking a sip of strong-smelling liquid that had lived at the back of my cupboard for a while, its texture sliding down my throat, burning slightly. I tried not to cough. 'And she's got the boys to look after. She can't be travelling here to check on me.' It was, in fact, the other way around. *I* was the one consistently checking in on them, the last decade unforgiving, my monthly visits never enough.

'So you're telling me there's *nobody* who can look out for you?' Ken looked disgruntled by the idea I was alone in life.

Just like *him*.

I stared at my neighbour. As long as I'd known him, Ken had never smiled, never looked happy. I assumed the death of his wife was to blame for that, triggering a permanently low mood, his sullen attitude towards everything equated to loneliness and isolation. I could understand that.

'I guess not.' Why did I sound so downtrodden? I was perplexed to conclude that I didn't have friends or family to call on aside from Paul, our relationship held together by police work and necessity. I didn't want to think about my ex-wife. It had been years since I'd spoken to Kate. She was irrelevant in the scheme of things despite my flat being dotted with the occasional item we'd bought together, gathering dust, negative energy, *despite* Andrew Hansley bringing her into my thoughts.

Ken took a breath, shaking his head. 'You young 'uns. Always running around. You need to find a balance, Newton, or one of these days you'll come home to a smouldering shell where your flat used to be. You were lucky I was at home otherwise both of us would have been in a hotel room tonight.'

I offered Ken a thin smile. He was right. It was the second time I'd almost burned the place down, the first seeing me race outside at ten o'clock in the evening with a flaming police folder in my possession and expletives on my lips. *Get a few candles,* Stephanie had said. *They'll brighten up the place and help calm you down.* Well, I wasn't calm that evening, I can tell you.

'And I'm very appreciative, Ken.' I raised a shimmering crystal glass towards a neighbour I was ashamed to admit I'd rarely spoken to until today, drinking the contents in a single gulp, embarrassed it had taken a *fire* for me to hold a conversation with the man. I thanked him again for his help and left him to his brandy, grateful for his swift actions and barking dog. Albert was chewing a bone in the corner of the kitchen, barely noticing I existed, hardly caring. I wasn't planning on telling Stephanie what had happened. She'd only worry. I probably wouldn't tell Paul either. I didn't need the lecture.

\*\*\*

It took three gruelling hours for me to wipe down several charred surfaces that had once passed as my kitchen, checking my slow-charging mobile phone every few minutes for any potential messages or calls from Angela. There were none. My breakfast bar was coated in thick sludgy ash, water on the floor no matter how many times I mopped it, personal belongings fit only now for the bin.

I thought back to this morning, autopilot an unfortunate side effect of a "morning" brain I've become all too familiar with. I've lost count how many times I've found socks in the fridge and toast in my shower tray. I'm sure it isn't dementia but I doubt I'll *ever* confide in anyone about my frequent spells of absentmindedness, my brain too busy to focus on *anything* without the coffee I've become dependent on. To make matters worse, I had Angela Healy on my mind, the poor girl suffering far more than me, anything I might have accidentally subjected myself to in the past, nothing compared to the private hell she was already in. At least *I* wasn't suicidal. Well, not anymore.

I opened every window I possessed, allowing an icy breeze to drift through my space to quell the stench of burnt kitchen. It was a necessity, nothing more, a way for me to throw off the morning's trauma. I thought about Ken's four-bedroomed home above me, too big for him now, marble work surfaces and brass taps no consolation to a wife long dead and kids long fled the nest. Maybe my kitchen deserved a redesign? I hadn't done much with the place since moving in, hadn't thought much about it until now. Yet, after using up several bottles of bleach and bin liners I left piled against my back door, I concluded a lick of paint and new saucepans would suffice, for now. It wasn't as bad as first appearances would have me believe, thankfully, and I was grateful to Ken and the fire crew who'd saved my home. We were all alive, that was something. I should be more careful, probably *should* see a doctor.

# Nine

## Angela

I get home in a panic, out of breath, feeling as if I'm going to be sick. The party is still lodged in my thoughts, the smell of Liam's bedroom still on my mind, and, to make matters worse, I now have Lee's face permanently implanted in my head. I kick a pair of discarded boots across my hallway floor, perfectly placed for my rising temper, my outstretched foot swiping wildly, my frustration unmoving.

I despise the dress I'm wearing, someone else's jogging bottoms and pumps doing nothing for my appearance, including the jacket I *conveniently* forgot to hand back to Newton. I look ridiculous. I take it off and fling it on the floor in temper, nothing but a reminder of my recent endeavours. It tells me everything I don't want to know about the life I don't want to live, my every action resulting in disaster. Why did he give me his card, and what did he think it would achieve? Does he believe I'll actually call him? I remind myself to throw it in the bin when I get a chance, digging it out of the pocket he earlier placed it in. There is some kind of sweet attached to it, a toffee I think, although it's covered in fluff and dust and I really can't say for sure what it is. I stuff the offending item back inside the pocket, tossing his card across my coffee table. All I want is a shower, a hot drink and a damned good cry. I might, in fact, drown myself while I'm there.

I didn't set out to kill myself *or* anyone else, yet who will believe that now? Suicide is a concept that hovers in the back of my mind, that's all, no actual *intention* of doing anything about it. That was, of course, until I found myself up on that ledge, nowhere else to be, the very idea of death taking shape without me. I can't go back. I can't change it. In an ideal world, I would go to the police, tell them everything, confess, the hospital easily able to confirm the drugs in my bloodstream, if questioned. I'm still dressed in the same clothes, Liam's DNA still on my skin. I glance down, knowing that Lee now lingers there, too. I don't live in an ideal world do I—mine not an ideal situation.

I head into the bathroom and strip naked, barely able to look at my reflection in the mirror. I have a bruise on my left breast that hurts when I press it, more around my wrists that look as if I've been held down by force, and a circular graze on my thigh which upon closer inspection, might actually be teeth marks. *Jesus.* Injuries that didn't exist before the party mock me, showcasing what happened in my unwitting absence, my inability to say *no* something I can never now change. My once styled hair has frizzed, my eyes a sunken reflection of the night's ordeal—barely any makeup, just a pale face that has subsequently done something incredibly *stupid*.

I spend too long curled inside the shower tray crying, attempting to wash every trace of those men from my body, raw emotion washing over me in waves. I'm a victim of circumstance, nothing more, always have been, probably always will be—a *stupid*, pathetic victim. My name should, in fact, be Angela *Victim* Healy. Good for nothing, good for no one—hateful, despicable, weak. I should take my medication but I can't get up, the idea of getting dressed too much like hard work. I'll stay here for now, unconcerned by the torrents of rapidly cooling water racing into the plughole, my goose-bumped body left to its own failing devices. It's all I deserve.

My mobile is vibrating, on silent because I don't want to be disturbed. If it's Rosie, she can go away. I don't want to talk to her, don't need her drama right now. If it's Liam, I won't be responsible for my actions. I endure several agonising moments of distinct vibrations before I relent and turn off my now cold shower, wrapping a towel around my body, my hair leaving a trail of water behind me as I head into the lounge.

I pick up my phone. Newton's business card still rests where I tossed it, mocking me, a sugary stain still on the surface, his apparent offer of help given in jest. I pick that up too, turn it over, deliberately curling the edges within my trembling grip. I silently curse the guy, none of his earlier words hitting their mark. What would happen if I were to call him *now?* What would he say if I told him what I'd done? Would he still be willing to help me? Will he still see the unassuming victim I was on that rooftop, or the *killer* I've become?

I stand uneasily in my lounge, my body trembling, staring at seven missed calls; four from Rosie, one from Andrew, two from Liam. How *dare* he contact me after what he did? He was meant to be my friend, yet the idea now makes my skin go cold. I want to scream at him, tell him exactly what I think, but I'm unsure I'll say anything good, unconvinced I can stand more pain today. Instead, I leave my phone where it is and head into the bedroom to dress, yanking a pair of jeans from the hanger so forcefully it snaps in half and hits me on the shin. I slump to the floor, tears engulfing me, my entire body shaking and convulsing wildly.

Nobody knows about my past. I don't speak about it often, the traumas of my childhood something I'll take to my grave, if I have to. In fact, the only evidence of what happened back then now rests in an ageing police file along with several hospital records and a few handwritten notes taken from misguided social workers. My mum is dead, my dad thankfully rotting in a prison cell, the passing of time removing those haunting memories from everyone else but me. Yet, Liam Goodman has singlehandedly brought everything to the surface, reminding me of who I am. How dare he. *How dare he!*

I don't want to remember the party, but I have nothing else to focus on, my mind a jumbled collection of broken pieces I'll never reassemble. I was sitting on Liam's sofa, pretending to be okay, sinking into cushions I knew would never protect me. I wasn't okay, obviously, but nobody cared, not really. All too busy to notice, entertained elsewhere, dancing, laughing. Those who *did* show me attention were given their marching orders, a flee in their ear the only thing they were getting from me last night.

I vaguely recall my so-called *friend* carrying me upstairs, lying me on his bed, talking softly. I was drunk, attempting to forget a life I didn't want to admit was mine, desperate for peace I know I'll never find. I felt woozy, slurring my words, the room spinning. Now I'm not sure what to think. I sit on the edge of my bed, eyes screwed shut, water still running down my back in protest to memories I haven't yet processed.

I remember him lifting my pathetic body into the air as

## The Lost Raven

if I was made of paper, expressing his intentions to move me somewhere more comfortable. It made me giggle because I felt as if I was flying—like a raven. He carried me into the hallway, past a kitchen crammed with chattering humans and half-eaten sausage rolls, up the stairs, along the landing to his bedroom. He apologised as he manoeuvred me into his room, his strong arms cupping my body with ease, removing me from the noise of his guests below. I'd liked it, to begin with, enjoyed the feeling of disconnection.

I don't, however, recall him removing my underwear. I was mortified I couldn't find them when I woke up, and, even now, everything is fuzzy. I lie on my bed, recalling how he laid me on *his*, the duvet pulled back, several guests' coats slid to one side in haste. He removed my shoes. I remember nodding, I think, but the room felt strange, as if I wasn't really *there*. He slipped off the bolero I'd chosen to match my dress, unhooking each arm, pressing me on my back. He was speaking but I could barely hear him, far happier in my slumber. I didn't notice him peeling off my underwear, probably too far gone by then to realise.

I stare at my ceiling, a sudden memory slapping my cheeks. Something touched me, I couldn't tell what, but it was warm and probed between my legs. I think I may have tried to swat the air with my arms but the bloody things wouldn't move. I guess they don't when you're asleep. I couldn't even speak. I assumed it was nothing, just something that had fallen from his pocket, a mobile phone, a dream. Liam's breathing had changed too, although I didn't appreciate why until I woke up, violated and sore.

I don't *want* it to be real, of course, don't want to believe such things about the man I assumed my friend. It takes a lot for me to trust a person and until this morning I'd assumed him gay. I don't know why. It seems stupid now. Maybe it was wishful thinking because I wanted to feel safe in his company, wanting that impossible moment to be nothing but delusions caused by depression, alcohol, prescription drugs. Yet his breath *had* deepened, I'm sure of that, his tongue probing mine, my hair pulled away from my face to gain access to my lips, my ears, cheeks.

I don't want to know what happened after that. I must have slipped into an unconscious state, my mind unwilling to linger further on events it didn't need to dwell on, thoughts of my so-called *friend* something I'm still not ready to acknowledge. When did our relationship tip towards something else, something he assumed he could take without permission?

I'm still crying when I venture back into my lounge, my faded jeans paired now with an old vest top, my hair towel dried and pulled into a ponytail because I can think of nothing else to do with it. Several damp ends drip across my shoulders in defiance, but I don't notice. I can hardly bring myself to look in the mirror. My cheeks are ashen, eye sockets red and bulging with unrelenting pain. I can't believe how men have the power to make me feel so despondent. They do what they want, when they want, no repercussions to their actions, no shame or remorse. If I ever see Liam Goodman again, I'll probably kill him too. He'll end up like Lee, just another statistic of my failing mind. *What a bastard!*

# Ten

## *Angela*

I don't recall falling asleep but I wake up on my lounge carpet an hour later to the sound of my mobile phone vibrating loudly. It's Liam. I endure several seconds of agonising hell before I relent and answer, barely plucking the courage to acknowledge his existence.

'You've got some nerve,' I snap, more words ready to leave my lips than I've anticipated. My heart is pounding, my throat tight with ideas I haven't yet expressed.

'Angela, hey. I've been trying to get hold of you for hours. Are you okay? You were gone when I went back to my room to check in on you.' He laughs, a thought popping into his head I honestly don't need in mine.

'Are you serious?' *What the hell?* How dare he act so casually.

'Why? What's wrong?' He seems momentarily taken aback, unnerved, his throaty voice painful against my ear.

'What's *wrong*? Are you joking?' I can't believe what I'm

hearing. Surely he can't be that stupid, can't be so *vain* to think I'd go along with his delusions so readily? It was his fault I stabbed a man, still unconvinced I haven't killed him. I'm still waiting for the police to knock my door.

'I don't understand.' There's a wobble in his voice, something that tells me he hasn't expected my response.

'What's not to understand?'

There's a moment of silence, a lingering sliver of time where everything seems to stop. My heart is beating in my throat, my breathing unsteady.

'Liam?'

I can hear his breath so I know he's still there. I wonder what he's thinking. Nothing good. I want to drag him through the phone and throttle him, scream in his face, beat him to a pulp.

'What did I do to upset you?' He sounds hurt.

'*You bastard.*' I can't help the poison that leaves my lips. How *dare* he behave so casually? How can he put this on *me?*

'Angela, what on earth is wrong with you?' His tone has changed, his irritation increasing. *Wow!* The nerve of the guy.

'*Me?* Are you serious?'

'What have I done?'

I'm dumbfounded, unable to speak, barely able to breathe. I was practically comatose when he attacked me, on his bed, unable to move, unable to say *no*—drugged so he could fuck me while he assumed I slept. What did he *do?* Is this guy deranged?

'I hate you, you *fucking* arsehole.'

'Ang, come on? Seriously, how am I meant to respond to that?'

Liam doesn't realise I was semi-awake when he raped me, unable to move, unable to stop him. He was on top of me, inside me, grunting away, just another conquest to add to the others I don't wish to consider. Does he get a kick out of hurting women, weakening them so he can do what he wants? He assumes his drugs worked, no doubt, my mumbled grunts just part of a sick, twisted game. I want to scream. I want to *kill* him.

'I *know* what you did,' I spit into my phone, unable to control myself. I barely recognise my own voice. Yes, the night is still hazy and I'm unsure I want to remember everything, but I know enough, have enough memories in my head to fill in the gaps.

'You got drunk. I put you to bed. Fucking hell, Angela, I won't bother next time if you're going to behave like this.'

I take a sharp breath, thin air catching my throat, making me gag. 'You absolute *bastard*,' I scream again, slamming my phone so hard against the wall that it smashes, the back dislodging, the screen and case cracking. I'm crying again. I can't help it. How can Liam be so blasé? I can't sit back and allow him to treat me like this, no repercussions, no remorse. I won't put up with it. I grab my car keys and head into the evening, leaving my phone in pieces on the floor.

\*\*\*

It takes around ten minutes to get across town to Liam's house, retracing a journey I took on foot this very morning. Those once isolated streets now feel so long ago, my aggravated driving heightening my disorderly emotions. He has no idea how he's made me feel, this day still too raw and painful for me to make sense of. No idea what I'm going to say or how I'll react when I look into his twisted, condescending eyes.

I park along the street, unwilling to get too close to his

house for fear of what I'll do. Windows I might smash, profanities I'll no doubt scream towards unwitting neighbours should they get too close to me. I almost turn back, the concept of being here again so soon too much to process. I left this place in a hurry, this morning still fresh in my thoughts, semi-naked, traumatised, no idea what I was doing. Nothing has changed.

I endure several painful minutes sitting in my car, tears streaming down my face, thumping aching fists against my steering wheel before turning the same aggravated attention towards his front door. I'm furious, trembling, frustration aimed blindly into the air. I see nothing but a heavy red mist in front of me, almost battering the door down when no immediate acknowledgement is offered. I don't mean to draw attention, don't intend to alert his neighbours.

'Are you okay?' a woman pokes her head out of her front door, her concern misplaced, a barking dog in the background doing nothing for my failing state of mind. She's mid-fifties, old enough to keep her nose out of other people's business, the look she gives me making my temper worse.

'Where *is* he?' I yell. 'Where's Liam?'

'He left, my love. A few minutes ago.' The woman offers a smile but sees the look on my face and changes her mind.

'Where's he gone?' I'm panicking, nothing else to do, nowhere left to aim my anger other than towards a stranger who has done me no harm.

'Oh, I didn't speak directly to him, I'm afraid. I just saw him from my kitchen window getting into his car.' She looks at me with sympathies that make me want to cry. I can barely look at her. 'Are you okay?' she continues. 'Do you want to come inside for a moment? You look terrible.' She obviously feels sorry for me, can see something I can't. It doesn't help. I don't care how I look.

*The Lost Raven*

I shake my head, my temper and frustration increasing, nothing this woman can do to help me now. 'No, thank you,' I mutter, in tears again, nothing I can do about that. I glance her way. I'm sure we've never met. I'd have remembered if we had. She probably assumes me Liam's friend, her neighbour an innocent she believes she knows well. I can't tell her the truth. She'll never sleep again, will never look at Liam the same way.

With nothing more to add, I turn around and head along Liam's path, his missing car something I only now notice. How pathetic. I wanted to see his face when I confronted him, see the look in his eyes when he denies what he's done. Did he call me to *mock* me? To taunt me? I consider calling Newton but think better of it. He'll see right through anything I might tell him, any lies I offer dissolving with a single disgruntled look. I can't have anyone in my business. Not today. I'm too vulnerable.

I get home exhausted, my car collecting a dent I don't remember producing, calling Rosie because I have no one else to call, my single intention to locate Liam.

'You sound odd. What's wrong?' It's the first thing she asks, as if I'm under investigation, her relentless quest for knowledge wholly unrequited. She sounds as downtrodden as me.

'Nothing.' I don't care that I sound angry.

'Something's wrong. I can tell.'

Nothing's wrong, Rosie.' I wish she'd shut up and let me talk.

'You okay?'

'Of course.' I'm not convinced my voice is steady, the lie barely leaving my mouth before I realise how stupid it sounds. *I'm not okay*. I haven't been okay for a very long time.

A pause. 'Are you busy, Angela? I *really* need to talk to

you.'

'Can it wait? I've got a few things to do and I'm running late.'

I honestly don't mean to sound rude but right now I don't care what Rosie wants to talk about. I'm on a mission, my only aim to find Liam, punch him in the face, yell, knee him in the bollocks—whatever comes first. What I'm really doing is trying not to sob, sitting cross-legged on my lounge floor with a box of tissues in one hand, my damaged mobile phone in the other, trying to quell tears I can't prevent whilst keeping my voice as steady as my traumatised throat will allow. My earlier conversation with Liam ended in disaster, his disappearance proof that he's now hiding away, waiting for the fallout, terrified of what's to come.

'Do you know where Liam is?' I almost bite my lip as I say his name, the sound of it alien on my tongue.

'He's gone to London.'

'Why?' *What have I missed now?*

'He's got that nursing conference thing next week don't forget, something to do with his promotion to senior staff nurse. Honestly, Angela, your memory is *terrible* these days.' It sounds as if Rosie is being sick, her words emerging in sporadic bursts that leave her breathless, her voice trailing in and out as if she's struggling to maintain our conversation. 'To be honest, he was a bit annoyed when I spoke to him earlier. Told me he was getting away at the right time.'

'You spoke to him?'

'Yeah.'

'When?'

'A couple of hours ago. I needed some advice.' Rosie pauses, something in her tone I don't like, can't appreciate. 'Angela, please, I *need* to talk to you about something important.'

## The Lost Raven

I'd forgotten about that conference, yet I still believe he's avoiding me *deliberately*. I find it convenient he chose last night to *rape* me, an entire week ahead now to avoid facing the consequence of his actions. Did he tell Rosie we were together last night? Did he assume it was mutual? Is *that* why she's behaving so oddly now?

I leave a lingering moment between the two of us, contemplating my reply. I can't tell her what he's done. Not yet. She'll make everything worse. She'll call the police, forcing me to tell them what happened. They'll want to do an internal examination, ask questions. No, thank you. I'm not going through that again. I might say more than I want, confirm my *own* guilt.

'You still there? Ang?'

'Yeah. I'm here.' My hands are trembling. I can't help it. I feel sick.

'I *need* to tell you something.' Rosie sounds sad, *her* troubles set to overshadow mine if I'm not careful.

I scoff. I don't need anyone else's drama. Not today. My head is full enough as it is. 'Can we talk tomorrow please, Rosie? I'm bushed.' It's a lie, of course, but I don't care. I end the call quickly in case I change my mind, unwilling to allow my friend the chance to confirm something I'm not yet ready to hear. I can't think about anything right now.

I don't realise I'm calling Newton until I hear his unfiltered voice in my ear, the day taking a toll, my mind unravelling fast. I panic, screeching a random apology into the air before hanging up. *Jesus Christ.* What the *hell* is wrong with me?

# Eleven

## *Newton*

The smell in my flat was overwhelming, the early evening engulfed by relentless Netflix dramas I wasn't interested in watching. My television was subsequently left to entertain itself instead of me, my brain disintegrating along with a kitchen that had become a heady blend of bleach and burnt charcoal, semi-scrubbed cupboards abandoned due to a lack of enthusiasm. Despite having the windows open for most of the afternoon, a heavy smell still lingered, my flat now as cold on the inside as it was out. Eventually, boredom set it and I headed out for a walk.

I was silently berating myself for the choices I'd made when my phone rang, the last twenty-four hours no better than any other. I didn't recognise the number, answering it to a high-pitched apology and a dialling tone that stopped me in my tracks.

*Angela?*

Her voice had a wobble, mine something she obviously

## The Lost Raven

wasn't ready to acknowledge, any thoughts of reaching out gone now, it seemed. I attempted to call her back but it went straight to voicemail, the upbeat recorded message that met my ears inappropriately calm for this moment. I considered leaving a message, but what would I say? Angela's problems made my burnt surfaces seem mundane in comparison. I didn't assume I could say anything over a telephone that would help.

I'd dealt with suicide and depression, of course, today nothing new, but it never got easier to put myself in the shoes of someone so vulnerable, their fragile minds easily triggered. Appreciating this without accidentally tipping them over that proverbial edge is almost impossible. It's ridiculous, but I feel helpless when I can't see things through to a satisfying conclusion, confirming all is well with those I meet along the way. Paul often jokes that I'm a control freak, but it's not true. I just care about people, especially those who are misunderstood.

Inevitably, I found myself outside Angela's flat, nowhere else to be, nothing else required of my attention to distract a perplexedly overactive mind. The hospital had already confirmed her address, assuming me part of her support network, my profession and connection with the police enough to solidify any involvement. It ensured this unexpected diversion, a fresh cup of coffee in my system the only thing helping maintain focus.

I grasped my mobile phone in my hand, glancing every few seconds at the screen in case I somehow missed another call, every potential message important. I called her number, rang her buzzer, hoping for a chat, nothing more, my heart firmly in my throat. All I wanted was confirmation she was okay, to provide a heartfelt apology for not doing much when I'd promised I would. I couldn't dwell on anything else.

*Nothing.*

I hung around for several frustrating minutes before calling Paul, pacing up and down a dilapidated pathway, kicking stones into weeds that grew around a seemingly forgotten entrance.

'Everything okay?' He sounded as if he was speaking inside a toilet cubicle.

'Yeah. I just wondered if you'd heard anything about that young woman from this morning?' I glanced towards Angela's building, wondering if she could see me through her window.

'The jumper?'

She hadn't jumped, thankfully, in the end. I closed my eyes. 'Correct. Angela Healy.'

'No. Should I have?'

'She called me not long ago. Sounded a bit—'

'Christ Newt, what the hell did you give her your number for?'

'I thought it might help.' I was unappreciative of Paul's lecture, this moment not the time for relentless irritation.

'And did it?' His sarcasm was oozing through the phone, his tone as condescending as ever. I didn't enjoy being chastised so openly by a man I considered a friend.

'That's why I'm asking if you've heard anything. I'm outside her flat at the moment.' I swallowed, biting my lip, knowing what he'd say about *that*.

'Jesus, with no authority?' Paul might have been inside a toilet, actually, an unexpected flushing in the background along with a door springing shut setting my teeth on edge. I know the guy multitasks a lot, but that was too much, even for him.

'I think my capacity as a psychologist qualifies—'

'No, Newt. It does *not*.' Paul cut me off for a second time. 'You're a professional. Start acting it.' He was probably right.

'Well, can we get a warrant or something then, to gain access to her flat?' I was staring towards several upstairs windows, wondering which ones belonged to Angela, genuinely worried she might do something stupid. I couldn't tell Paul.

'No we damned well *can't* get a bloody warrant, and you have no reason to even *be* at her property. She's done nothing wrong.' Paul was no doubt rolling his eyes, veins popping at the side of his skull. I was glad I couldn't see.

'Yeah, but I'm not here in the capacity of a police officer, am I,' I muttered sarcastically. In fact, I wasn't here to confirm *any* wrongdoing aside from preventing the poor girl from ending her life. Surely that was important?

'All the more reason to leave her alone.' I knew what Paul was thinking. He didn't have to confirm it. She was vulnerable enough without my interference, her mindset and ultimate actions firmly out of my hands. A mental assessment team would deal with it now. It had nothing to do with us.

'But what if she's dead?' I bit my lip again, not wanting to think about that. For a moment I thought I saw a curtain twitch. I couldn't be sure.

There was a pause, something that sounded like a door closing, a zip. 'Stop playing God. Please, Newt. Go home. I'm sure she's fine.'

\*\*\*

I headed home as instructed, nothing else to do, my card metaphorically stamped. Yet, I couldn't get that poor girl out of my head. She wouldn't have called unless she was desperate, her strangled vocals still in my ears as I unlocked my front door. Her vague expression would no doubt end up in my dreams tonight, the mud I'd now trailed across my hallway floor merely adding to my chaotic life.

I wasn't about to ignore Angela's obvious cry for help, no matter what Paul instructed. When several more attempts to call her went unheeded, I logged onto my laptop, glad it wasn't anywhere near the fire, thankful I was as terrible at putting things away as I was at cleaning them. I remembered my password on the second try, keying Angela's name into a search bar that took forever to return any results. All I wanted was to uncover enough of her life to confirm she had at least one person who would be there for her during this difficult time. I ignored the state of my semi-cleaned kitchen, sitting on the one barstool that had escaped today's fire, kicking my dirt-coated shoes into a corner, nothing else to do whilst I waited for the screen to load.

She was on Facebook but her account was inaccessible unless I sent a friend request, which I wasn't about to do. I didn't assume she'd appreciate *that*. I had no idea how to use Snapchat. Instagram looked slightly more promising, her account public, plenty of selfies and outlandish nights out with friends to scroll through. She didn't *look* suicidal. In fact, there was nothing to raise immediate concern. I told myself I was worrying over nothing, my impatience for a slow-loading computer giving me a headache. When my phone rang, the distraction was almost appreciated. Paul.

'Hey, how're things?' I breathed, getting to my feet, needing air. It didn't matter that I had to kick my back door twice before it would open, another casualty of today that needed addressing. 'Sorry about earlier.' I wasn't sure exactly *what* I was apologising for, but it usually calmed a potential mood shift between the two of us.

'Don't worry about it. How are *you*?' It was kind of him to ask. It sounded as if he was driving, his voice constantly

## The Lost Raven

moving in and out, his mobile phone probably resting on the dashboard. At least he was no longer in the toilet.

'It's been one of those days.' I traced a finger across an ash covered chopping board, considering throwing it in the bin. It wasn't pleasant. 'Where *are* you?'

'We're just heading to an alleged rape incident. I have DS Baker with me if you want to say hi.' I couldn't see him but I could tell he was smiling, grinning towards his mobile with an all-knowing glint I'd grown oddly accustomed to seeing. He enjoyed winding me up about Alice, badly timed banter just another part of his day.

'Hi Alice,' I muttered, knowing I'd be on loudspeaker. It explained the constant interference. Paul knew I liked her. It made my cheeks flush.

'Hey, Newt.' Alice's soft vocals filled my ears, like birdsong, turning my legs to jelly. I instantly leant against the doorframe. One day I might actually tell her how I feel. One day.

Paul's team dealt with a lot, from murder to rape and everything between, always something new to deal with. I was only ever asked to help when a suspect needed assessing or if a fragile person required mental evaluation. I didn't assume my services fitted the criteria for rape, Alice Baker far more experienced in that field than me. I didn't envy her having to deal with that. Not for all the money in the world.

'Sorry to call you unannounced,' Paul continued. It didn't usually bother him. 'But I felt bad about earlier and I wanted to reconfirm how grateful I was for your help this morning.'

Did Paul Mannering just apologise?

'The hospital confirmed they're dealing with that young girl, so it's under control. You don't have to worry about it anymore.'

*It?* He'd made Angela sound like a statistic instead of a human. I wanted to tell him my thoughts, enquire about this latest case, but knew better. I didn't need another argument, another lecture. Criminal investigation was none of my business unless directly asked to assist.

'No problem. Glad I could help.' I *was* glad, although I wished I could have done more. I could still see that poor girl's face as she ran from the beach, her mind filled with suffering I couldn't yet understand. 'Anything else I can help you with?'

'I don't think so. We're just heading across town to interview the female victim. Unless her attacker turns out to be a serial killer or a psychopath, I probably won't need you tonight.' He was jesting of course, but it was hardly appropriate, especially in front of Alice. Paul's sense of humour was not always welcomed, not always understood. He meant well. She must have given him a funny look because he changed the subject. 'Anyway, so yeah, have a good one.'

'You too,' I managed to reply before he hung up. I hadn't even said goodbye to Alice. I glanced at my laptop, Angela Healy's smiling face looking up at me from a flickering screen. I hope we *all* have a good one.

# Twelve

## *Angela*

I sit in my lounge, listening for any potential noise outside. For several minutes someone was ringing my buzzer, yet there was no way I could acknowledge who it was. I could barely move in case I drew unwanted attention, one twitch of my curtains enough to alert my caller to my desperate position. As much as I *want* to speak to Liam, need to confront him, I can't have him showing up uninvited. Rosie said he's gone to London, but what if that's a ruse? I can't be alone with him. The very idea gives me a shudder. I can't have *anyone* knowing I'm at home right now.

Eventually, whoever was outside left, allowing me time to assess my hellish situation. I stare at my mobile phone, several missed calls from a number I don't have stored in my contacts, assuming they must be from Newton. I momentarily wonder if a brand-new phone would afford me a brand-new number and therefore a brand-new reason to expel the people from my life I no longer want to endure. I'm being unkind, I know. Rosie isn't a bad person and under normal circumstances, she might be a good friend. A friend when I *need* one. Unfortunately, she doesn't appreciate how difficult it is for me to let people in, my head not a place you'd want to linger for long. Besides, how can I tell her my secrets? I have no idea what she would say if she knew about my life beyond bipolar, the poor woman only aware of my mental health because of an episode at work a few months ago. Would she believe what Liam did or understand what I suffered at the unforgiving hand of my monstrous father?

I take Newton's business card in my hand, glancing at its contents briefly before tossing it across the room, the guy's calming voice still lingering in my mind. I don't like the man. He creeps me out. All men do, to be honest, it's nothing new, hardly *his* fault. I don't understand why he would want to help me. No one else ever has. Why should I assume this man is any different to the rest? Why the hell did I call him?

The party has been coming back to me in fragmented snippets, sometimes forcefully, painfully, Liam's actions unforgivable. I try not to linger too long on Lee. Is he okay? *Is he dead?* I haven't found anything on the local news about the stabbing and so I try not to overthink what I can't change, too many people called "Lee" on social media for me to narrow any potential search. I barely remember what he looked like, wasn't really paying attention.

As it is, DNA evidence now resides in the corner of my bathroom, my green party dress covered in the sweat and saliva of two men, evidence of unforgivable crimes I'm still hoping aren't real. I glare at my reflection in the mirror. I look thinner than I remember, a lack of appetite something I can't help. I haven't eaten well lately, not since my depression worsened and my medication failed to placate me. Now, suddenly I'm starving, as if the day has ignited

## The Lost Raven

something insatiable in my belly that I'm wholly unable to settle.

I head into the kitchen and turn out my cupboards one by one, tearing open a pack of digestive biscuits that I devour, no better than a starving dog, the resulting empty packet offering no consolation to the way I feel. I'm crying, slumped like a ragdoll on my cold floor, too vulnerable to move, crumbs and betrayal covering my skin. I don't know why I'm behaving this way. I don't even like digestive biscuits. I open the fridge and dig trembling fingers into a tub of margarine, behaving like an unsatisfied feral animal. It's the only item I have in my fridge that doesn't require cooking, gulping down the buttery mixture as if my life depends on it. I don't care how I look, salty tears and saliva along for the ride, my emotions in turmoil.

Despite an unrelenting pain that squeezes my lungs and makes me gag for air, I'm forced to concede that for the first time in my life, I *took control*. I emerged the victor over a man who would have caused irreparable harm if left to his own devices. In the time it took to plunge a blade into his belly, Lee became nothing but a slab of flesh I was able to inhibit with ease. I release a slow breath, his unexpected demise permanently on my mind, my chest rising and falling with the magnitude of an event I can never undo. I have butter around my mouth, crumbs in my hair, dried mascara under my eyes. Yet, all I know is I halted him in his tracks, prevented his unwanted gaze thrust upon other women, stopped him hurting someone else. Surely that has to be a good thing? In that moment, I was powerful, almighty, my actions all-consuming. *He had no control over me.*

A savage emotion begins to rise in my belly and I suddenly want to laugh. My thoughts are racing, the idea of triumphing over a man twice my size strong now in my head. I still don't know where the knife came from, but it became an extension of my emotions, an implement of my unwitting desire. For a brief moment, I was able to aim my suffering towards someone else, inflicting agony elsewhere. Lee didn't even see it coming. I scoff, taking a moment to catch my failing breath.

I can still see his twisted features if I close my eyes, the way he fell to the ground at my feet, the look he gave me something I will never forget. *It was so easy.* I glance at my hands, my margarine coated fingers oddly making me feel sick, yet all I see is angry red blood. Both palms are steady, as if my brain is finally registering what I am, what I've *done*, past events to blame, this night merely the beginning of an unimaginable change in the life of Angela Healy.

I'm not exactly ugly, but I *don't* feel attractive, not like other women, not like those on TV or in magazines. For me to pass as adequate, I require a false confidence that comes in the form of hair extensions, lip gloss, padded bras, high heels, anything to invite an impossible idea of perfection. I cover my freckles because they make me feel like the little girl who bore the brunt of an evil man, heavy foundation and concealer able to pretend she doesn't exist. I've lost count how many times I've stared at my hair in the mirror, forcing everything I have inside not to chop the whole lot off, my frustration taken out on a hairbrush that has done nothing to me. I'd only regret it anyway and I regret enough as it is. I don't need more shit adding to my existence, too many questions still lingering that I have no honest answers to.

My feelings come from a dark past, my outer appearance ill-matching my inner turbulence. I can't help how I feel, the person I see in the mirror still that little girl who was hurt time and time again, a father who didn't love her how genuine parents should. I've worked hard to throw

## The Lost Raven

off my memories, yet they are as fresh now as they were the day my dad got drunk and molested me. *It was our secret*, he said. I was to tell no one. He told me that no grown-up would believe me and I'd be a naughty girl who'd be punished if I didn't do as I was told. He promised me the earth, that only *special* daddies loved their daughters enough to show affection in such a way. I believed him for a while, our private moments meant only for the two of us, our dirty secret protected. That was, of course, until it became a regular thing, my childhood disappearing with my innocence, two painful minutes all it took to lose far more than my sanity. I was just four years old. What kind of sick bastard does that to a kid?

For as long as I remember my emotions have consumed me. It doesn't help, but now something new is taking shape deep in the pit of my stomach. I begin to laugh, tears of confusion streaming down my cheeks, my vision blurred by what I can never undo. I begin flinging myself around in circles, hysterical, unhindered, unencumbered by feelings I've never been able to address until now. I'm having a manic episode, I know. I haven't endured one this bad for a while, yet I didn't anticipate how this day would unfold, didn't expect to feel like this.

I stop mid-twirl, a savage collection of ideas springing from nowhere. I race into my lounge, still laughing, my heart still pumping, flinging open my laptop in search of something so simple, it seems almost inconceivable. I probably shouldn't consider searching online for GHB, but nothing I've done over the last few hours has felt rational so why should I stop now? It isn't a substance I assumed I'd have to purchase, never thought I'd *want* to. Yet, it was in my system last night and if Liam got hold of it, so can I.

I trawl through page after page of nonsense, talking to myself because there's no one else in the room, eventually finding someone on Facebook who claims to have what I need, for a fee, obviously. The guy is masquerading as a "fish tank cleaning expert", a cover, in case anyone should ask, although apparently he does clean fish tanks as well, should I need *that* service. I don't, but good for him.

The solution he uses turns into GHB in the bloodstream. I want to laugh. What was the guy doing when he discovered *that?* I visualise him halfway through a deep clean before passing out, breathing in vapours that consumed his entire body, no doubt giving him a headache when he awoke. He probably got a kick out of it. He doesn't care what I want the offending item for, only that I'm prepared to pay well for it, and after parting with almost two hundred bloody quid, I receive a confirmation of my order via text. *Shit.* That was too easy.

I don't have time to overthink my decision, my typing fingers doing most of the thinking for me, my racing brain merely along for the ride. I'm curious, nothing more, wanting to see the effect such a substance might have on someone else, any unsuspecting males that show me attention soon to get more than they bargain far. Tonight has triggered something in my head I can't settle down, unable to silence its now screaming voice. I haven't been this hyped for months and although my decision-making may appear slightly weird to any unsuspecting onlooker, it's merely my way of trying to *feel* something aside from constant bitterness, resentment, pain. I can't help it. I can't help who I am.

Eventually, exhaustion overwhelms me and I curl my body beneath my duvet, sleep prickling the edges of my eyes. It's been a long day. I watch the moon creep across the sky through the gap in my hastily drawn curtains for over an hour before I finally drift off to sleep. There's a smile on my lips, a devilish plan in my head. It's probably just as well

## The Lost Raven

no one can see me like this. I doubt anyone would understand what I'm planning to do.

# Thirteen

## *Newton*

I twisted Angela's nonsensical telephone call around my head for an hour whilst making another half-hearted attempt to clean my kitchen. It was futile, my attention continually pulled back to a case that wasn't even mine, events of the day as strong as the perpetual smell of bleach. I drank several cups of coffee, eventually emerging semi-satisfied from a room that could now pass as adequate. I ignored the unsalvageable areas, the splashback and my hob bearing most of the damage, cupboard doors that had blistered and peeled, my blackened ceiling.

When the doorbell rang, I was glad of the distraction, a few moments all I needed to reclaim my rapidly failing sanity. It was getting late, my evening slipping by in a bleach-filled blur, not expecting to open my front door to the sight of my old friend, Andrew Hansley, hovering on the bottom step, a bottle of wine in his hand and a grin on his flustered face.

## The Lost Raven

'Andy?' It was the second time I'd seen him today, the last fifteen years disappearing in a flurry of familiarity. In fact, the way he smiled at me assumed such a time frame had never occurred.

'Hope you don't mind me turning up like this?' Andy queried, holding the wine bottle towards me as if, despite the time and distance, we'd remained firm friends. I glanced at him uneasily, unsure why he was here. How did he know where I lived and what had brought him to my home? I hadn't seen him since our university days, so much happening since then, so many memories I'd long since tried to dislodge.

'No,' I stammered, suddenly aware I was being unnecessarily awkward. 'Of course not.' I stood to one side, allowing my old friend to step into my flat, glad my kitchen no longer looked like a scene from a forgotten horror film. It didn't help that the smell of bleach overwhelmed the place, a hint of barbequed plastic continually wafting through the stagnant air.

'Christ, what's that smell?' Andy was quick to pick up on my recent misfortune, a dilemma I was hoping to spare anyone else. He stuck out his tongue, wrinkling his nose, pulling a face that said it all. Same old Andrew—still as blasé as ever.

'I had a bit of kitchen trouble.' I was embarrassed to confirm, my efforts to clean the place seemingly not as satisfying as I'd hoped.

Andy raised an eyebrow and headed straight for my kitchen, my statement all he needed to instigate a full investigation. I could hear him whistling through his teeth before I'd even closed my front door.

'Shit, Newt. You can say that again.' He stood in the doorway assessing the carnage, unable to divert his eyes from the obvious damage that required more work than I'd acknowledged. No one *ever* saw inside my home, therefore I was prepared to let it go, until now. Now I was mortified. 'Who invited the arsonist for dinner?' Andy was tracing an index finger along my blistered cupboard door fronts, tracking wild eyes across every unkempt surface I owned.

'It was an accident. Nothing that won't be dealt with in due course.' I was frustrated enough as it was, disgruntled now by this never-ending day and events I had no control over. I wanted him out of this room before I did something regretful. 'Can I get you a tea? Coffee?'

Andy held his wine bottle towards me. 'Or a couple of glasses?'

I nodded, taking two glasses from a cupboard that was luckily nowhere near the vicinity of the fire. They were clean enough but I wiped them anyway.

'So, what brings you here?' I didn't confirm we hadn't seen or spoken to each other in fifteen years, our parting lingering in my distant memory. I wanted to ask what had happened for him to assume he could turn up unannounced, uninvited.

It was strange. After five years of solid friendship, things had come to an abrupt end, a single text message the only thing I received. He needed some time out, apparently, having secured a temporary training position somewhere in the North of England, although he never said where. I called him as soon as I could but his number had already been disconnected. I never saw him again. Now the guy was standing in my kitchen as if no time had passed between that moment and this. I didn't mean to sound so blunt. I was tired. It had been a long day.

Andy paused, looking at me as if he wasn't sure how to reply. 'I guess when I saw you this morning it put a few things into perspective.'

'Oh? How?' I poured him a glass of wine that he took

## The Lost Raven

with a nod of thanks, glad it was the cheap sort, the type with a screw lid. I didn't own a bottle opener. I was suspicious of him. I'm not sure why.

'Life's short, Newt. When I saw you looking after Angela, I felt bad we'd lost contact. You're a good man.' Andy was drinking his wine as if it was water, gulping the red liquid the way a vampire devours blood. I didn't *lose* contact with Andy, Andy *cut* contact with me. To this day I didn't understand why.

'Why *did* you leave so abruptly?' I couldn't help the pointed questions, couldn't help how I felt. Andy had left a wound that had taken a while to heal, not many friends in my life at that time, very few remaining now. His sudden disappearance had led me to assume I'd done something wrong. It would be nice to know what.

'Christ, I don't know, Newt. A lot of water has passed under the bridge since then. I guess it was just nice to see a friendly face again.' He was still smiling but something had changed. Time perhaps, and the inevitable shift that comes with age.

'A friendly face?' I raised my eyebrows, still waiting for a valid explanation.

'You always had one,' Andy nodded uneasily, his apparent joke failing to resonate.

I nodded, still unsure of his words, nothing I could do about my suspicious mind other than wait for it to subside. I concluded I'd been in the mind game too long, very little surprising me these days. It didn't help that I knew Andy well, knew how he operated, how he thought. He wanted something. Something he obviously assumed I had. I guided my old friend into my lounge, equally embarrassed by the state of that room too, but for a different reason. Books, half-written papers, and unassembled bookshelves were dotted around, forgotten, uncared for, gathering dust—just like the rest of this place. Andy lowered himself onto an armchair and sighed, his eyes blank, his tone unmoving. He didn't seem to notice the mess I'd surrounded myself with.

'Cut the shit, Andy. I know you better than that.' *Bloody hell.* I hadn't meant to blurt it out so readily, hadn't meant to react so sharply. I sat down, sliding several unmarked assignments to one side of my sofa, knowing I only had tomorrow to sort them out before they needed to be handed back to my students on Monday morning. It seemed there was more resentment in me than I'd realised.

Andy laughed, taking a large gulp of wine, draining the glass. 'I forgot. You always *could* see right through me.' He was chuckling, amused by my curt response, thoughts of an old friendship making an unexpected appearance.

I didn't smile, didn't reply. I was still waiting for the punch line.

'Remind me again how you came to be with Angela?' Andy's tone had shifted, my old friend sounding slightly agitated now, his eyes darting briefly towards a photograph of my brother behind me. I tried not to acknowledge the sharp movement his head made or the sudden twitch in his jaw. I wasn't expecting our conversation to turn so readily to the stranger I barely knew, this morning's event something I was still struggling to process. I shook my head, shaking off distant thoughts of Isaac, instead focusing once again on Angela Healy.

'The police called me in to speak to a young lady who was on the roof of a multi storey car park.' I wasn't convinced I was helping *anyone* by openly confirming what had happened, as if I was soiling the poor girl's troubled experience by mentioning it. 'They were concerned she might jump.'

'So you and Angela don't actually *know* each other?' Andy was looking at me as if he wasn't sure what to make

*The Lost Raven*

of our non-existent relationship, more concerned by how I knew the girl than the troubling circumstances surrounding our brief introduction.

'No. I was just glad I was able to help.'

Andy nodded, seemingly glad I'd put his mind at ease. 'So, is that what you do now then? Work with the police?'

*Jesus.* Why all the questions? He still hadn't answered mine. 'Sometimes. When they need me.' I didn't see how my line of work was relevant, couldn't understand why this conversation was becoming all about me. Yet, I assumed he wanted to know his work colleague was okay, that she was in safe hands. 'Do you know how she's doing?' I shouldn't have asked. It was none of my business. I bit down on my bottom lip, Paul's recent irritation still in my head.

'Oh, yeah, she's fine, thank you for asking.' Andy shifted in his chair, avoiding making eye contact with me. He didn't sound convincing.

'So, how are things with *you?*' I needed to change the subject, my mind forever assessing others, assuming everyone was hiding their emotions.

Andy placed his unwanted glass on the table, reaching for a book I hadn't yet started reading. It was called, "The Mind of a Killer," the only item in this entire place I could relate to.

'To be honest with you, Newt, it felt like a sign that I ran into you this morning.'

'Oh?' I knew his visit wasn't casual. With Andy, nothing ever was.

Andy nodded, an expression on his face I couldn't read. 'Have you eaten?' He suddenly shot out of my chair, bored of flicking through my book, his turn now to change the subject.

I hadn't eaten all day. It hadn't even crossed my mind. In fact, I felt a bit sick because of the perpetual stench of bleach. I shook my head.

'Dinner? On me?' Andy was grinning.

'Now?'

'Why not?'

I glanced at the clock. It was almost nine thirty. 'It's a bit late—'

'Jeez, Newt, I'm not suggesting The Ritz.'

'I have a lot of work to be getting on with...'

'Pish posh, that can wait. We need a catch-up.' Andy was already heading for the door, fresh enthusiasm unwavering. I glanced around, momentarily grateful I wouldn't have to cobble something together tonight. I wasn't looking forward to spending any more time in my kitchen and I had been contemplating a takeaway, anyway.

'Okay, sure.' I grabbed my keys, checking twice that I'd left nothing switched on that could potentially burn the place down in my unwitting absence.

'I heard about Isaac.' Andy suddenly stopped in my hallway, his words unexpected, his back to me. He didn't turn around. 'I'm so sorry.' I understood why he'd been staring at that old photograph now. He probably knew it would upset me to recount that day. He was right.

I hung my head, allowing a moment of silence to linger before reaching for a jacket I was momentarily mortified to discover was still in Angela Healy's possession.

So was I.

# Fourteen

## *Newton*

I found myself standing outside *The Royal Grill* restaurant, a scent of over seasoned steak and garlic filling my nostrils. My ex-wife Kate and I had spent our first date in a restaurant similar to this one, memories I didn't anticipate would hurt after all this time. She was forty minutes late, the woman oblivious to my spinning nerves and tapping foot. She didn't seem to care, didn't apologise. I should have known *then* our relationship was doomed.

I didn't mention it to Andy. He didn't need to concern himself with past events neither of us could change. It was irrelevant now anyway. He hadn't asked about her, had barely commented on my brother. I assumed he already knew the two of us were divorced, no doubt made aware of my wife's departure long ago—a painful truth we were never coming back from. The three of us used to be good friends, our university days filled with a lust for life that comes around only once. As it was, fifteen years separated that fun-loving, easy-going guy from the man I subsequently became. Fifteen years of nothing but work, my evenings now spent assessing police case files and marking essays instead of having fun. I couldn't dwell. As Andy had so eloquently put it, it was all water under the bridge anyway.

'I'm starving.' Andy was oblivious to my hidden thoughts, already looking at the menu, dissecting each course as if he was a condemned man about to consume his last meal.

A waiter came over and placed a water jug and two glasses on the table in front of us, the look on his face telling me he just wanted to go home. There were no other diners here aside from us. I smiled as I poured myself a glass, hoping he hadn't noticed the tremble that had formed in my hand.

'What's all this about Andy?' I couldn't help asking. I was thinking about Kate again.

Andy took a breath, laying the menu on the table. 'Actually, Newt, I need to ask you a favour.' His cheeks had reddened, his eyes darting everywhere but on me.

*A favour?* This should be good. I sighed, biting my bottom lip to stop myself expressing how I really felt, his needs coming first, as always. 'Is everything okay?'

Andy shook his head. 'Not really.' He took a moment to compose himself, words he hadn't yet shared teetering on uncertain lips. 'But you might be the one person who can change that.' He still wasn't looking at me.

'Anything for an old pal.' *Shit*. Why did I have to say that? I was unconsciously slipping into old patterns, our much earlier days seeing me accommodating my friend's actions more than I should, Kate's laughter now filling my head. Aside from the constant wants of the Eastcliff police, my students, my nephews and sister-in-law, I hadn't felt *needed* by another human being for a while and didn't expect Andrew Hansley to need me now. It was an alien emotion, a foreign concept. I was along for an uncomfortable ride.

'Really?' Andy's face had lit up. 'It's nothing major.'

I took a breath, unsure what I was letting myself in for. *Christ, Newton.* 'Shoot.' I shrugged casually, taking a much-needed gulp of lemon-infused water that almost choked me.

'Oh, Christ, where do I begin?' Andy shifted in his seat, wiping something from his mouth with a napkin I didn't notice him eating. 'I've been having some trouble at home.'

'With your wife?' I shouldn't have been so presumptuous.

'I'm not married.'

*That* didn't surprise me. 'Sorry, I didn't mean to—'

'My neighbour made a complaint about me,' Andy cut in sharply, pulling himself upright, the mention of a potential wife hitting a raw nerve.

'*You?* A revered doctor?' I wanted to laugh. Andrew Hansley was popular with *everyone*. It made him good with his patients, his bedside manner far better than mine. I'd always admired that.

'Okay, yeah, you made your point.' He glanced towards the floor, unaccustomed to being placed in such an uncomfortable position, embarrassed by my sarcasm. In his haste, he'd probably forgotten how close we used to be, the banter we'd openly shared. In Andy's company, I was sarcastic. Always had been.

'It was meant as a joke.' I didn't mean to step on a nerve. What wasn't he telling me? My friend's face had turned bright red.

'We're all human, Newt.' He didn't sound impressed by my failed attempt at an apology.

I pressed my lips together, wishing I'd kept my mouth shut. I picked up the menu, averting my eyes, keen to focus on something else.

'She told my landlord I've been harassing her.' He glanced my way briefly before amusing himself with a stain on the table, spitting words towards me as if they were laughable. 'It's a goddamn lie, *obviously*, but the bloody woman can be very persuasive and I've been asked to leave my flat.'

'Your neighbour got you *evicted?*' Was I hearing this correctly? I assumed he would be living in an expensive apartment in some equally expensive area, the penthouse probably. Evictions didn't happen to people like Andy.

He nodded.

I glanced across the table towards a man I used to admire, wished at one time I could be more like, had secretly envied. *Harassment?* 'That doesn't sound like something you'd do.' I furrowed my brow. It didn't, in fact, sound like Andy at all.

'Of course it isn't something I'd *do*, but my landlord fancies the stupid bitch and he's sucking up to her so he can get into her knickers.' Andy was leaning towards me, his voice purposefully low, the idea of being overheard not something he relished. He still couldn't bring himself to make eye contact.

'Why would she accuse you of harassment?' It didn't make sense.

'How the fuck should I know?' Andy had unexpectedly raised his voice, triggering attention from a passing waiter. He sighed, glaring at his hands in frustration.

I swallowed, slightly embarrassed for the man. 'So, how can *I* help?' I almost didn't want to know, didn't need the idea in my head of *any* man being nice to a woman purely with an end goal of having sex with her.

Andy licked his lips. 'I need a place to stay. Just for a couple of nights until I find somewhere more permanent.'

## The Lost Raven

He was finally looking at me now, staring at my face as if he couldn't believe he was asking. Neither could I.

I took a sip of water to quench a thirst that had come from nowhere. 'Well, I guess you could —'

'Thank you, thank you. Jesus, Newt. I was worried you'd say no.' Andy was smiling keenly, a look of relief evident on his flushed face. He picked up his menu, eagerly scanning the contents.

I hadn't exactly said *yes*, yet. 'Well, I do have a spare room. It'll need a clean, fresh linen on the bed, but —'

'Don't worry. You won't even know I'm there.' Andy was grinning, glancing over his shoulder in search of the waiter to take our order. *Shit.* How on earth did I just agree to a houseguest? I preferred my own company whenever possible, which was most of the time. *Bloody hell.*

\*\*\*

By the time we got back to my flat, Andy was drunk, the small bar we'd found ourselves in once the restaurant had closed, keeping my friend entertained until they'd kicked us out, too. I was subsequently forced to drive his car because he was in no condition to do so, too intoxicated to appreciate my own fears of being pulled over by the police. Ever since I'd known him, my old friend had a penchant for trouble; shit always following him around without apology.

'I *love* you, Newt,' he slurred into my ear as I manhandled him out of the passenger seat. He planted wet lips on my cheek, his hot breath a rancid mixture of booze and garlic-infused steak. I pulled away. *Jesus.* 'You're the best friend anyone could have.' He was crying, prodding my chest with an unsteady fingertip, taking deep sobs into the evening air before he began singing.

I glanced towards Ken's bedroom window, hoping he

was asleep and therefore wouldn't hear the kerfuffle outside, praying I wasn't disturbing yet more neighbours. The last thing anyone needed was further hassle from me today, enough of my shit already aimed their way. Thankfully it only took a few moments to get Andy through my front door, grateful I lived in the basement. There was no way I was getting him up a flight of stairs anytime soon, needing to make several attempts to guide him down six dilapidated steps to my front door. I was exhausted.

'Newton?'

'Yes, Andy.'

'I love you.'

'So you said.'

'You're a good friend.'

'Yep. I know.'

'Do you find Angela Healy attractive?'

I glared at him, unsure where the question had come from. 'Me? No. Why?' Why on earth would he ask *that*? It had never crossed my mind. For the last two hours, I hadn't even thought of her. Now I felt guilty.

'Because *I* do. I think she's the most beautiful creature I've ever seen. But she doesn't know it.' Andy was crying again. 'That's why I was surprised to see her at the hospital in such a state. I worry about her, you know.' He patted my shoulder. 'I'm glad you were there for her. She's a good girl. She *needs* me. She just doesn't appreciate it yet.' He bent forward and for a moment I thought he was going to be sick. Luckily he managed to compose himself. 'We're just friends but I would like to take our relationship to the next level. I think she might be up for it. If I asked nicely.'

'Then why don't you?' I was wondering if I should get Andy a bucket, contemplating the idea he might not make it to the bathroom during the night. The way he was currently behaving, I doubt he'd notice. I steered him into my lounge

## The Lost Raven

where I placed him temporarily across my sofa, the man still clinging to my shirt.

'Because she might say *no*.' Andy was sniffing the air, a stench of booze strong on his breath.

'She might say *yes*.' The only thing I wanted right then was for this man to lie down, sleep it off. Why do people always have to make relationships sound so complicated? I paused, my actions no different. Detective Sergeant Alice Baker didn't know I liked *her*, either.

I prised Andy's spaghetti grip from my body and headed into my spare room, mortified by the state of that room too, clearing a path to the bed whilst retrieving clean sheets from my airing cupboard. I *never* used this room. It was currently left as a dumping ground. Even during the rare occasions when Peter and Timothy came for the weekend, we wouldn't use *this* room, both boys far happier sprawled across my bed watching television until they fell asleep. I usually ended up on the sofa, uncomfortable. I didn't mind. I missed those days.

It had been a while since the boys were last here and thinking about them made me sad. I considered asking Steph if they could stay soon. It might do me some good. Yet, they might assume themselves too old for a sleep over with their Uncle Newton. Peter was fourteen already, too busy being a teenager to care about poor unloved me. Tim might be more willing, eleven still young enough to appreciate the attention I could give him. It gave me something positive to think about. That was, of course, once Andy had moved on.

By the time I made it back into my lounge, he was asleep, snoring like a pig, his body stretched across my cushions, slobbering. I removed his shoes and placed a blanket over him, leaving a bucket by the side of the chair, just in case.

# Fifteen

## *Angela*

I endure a sleepless night, thinking impossible things, feeling unthinking emotions. I haven't exactly been given a delivery schedule for the *item* I ordered last night in a hurry, and I don't for a second assume the driver will care what he's transporting. I find myself hovering by the window, nothing better to do, my mind a tangled collection of thoughts I can't unravel. I've asked for urgent shipping, my newly acquired Facebook "friend" confirming he can do a same-day delivery, even on a Sunday, so that's no problem, as long as I'm willing to pay. I guess if *Amazon* can do it, this guy can.

As it is, I didn't sleep well, my head filled with nonsense I still can't assess. I miss several calls from Rosie, messages that, at first glance, seem to denote a genuine concern for my health. She wants to talk, yet I assume she's prying, nothing more, gleaning information to make *her* life appear better than mine. Besides, how can I tell her what I've been through? How can I explain what Liam did, what *I* ultimately ended up doing? I deliberately ignore calls from

Newton, my annoyance increasing further when he leaves me a message.

*I hope you're okay*, he says. *I'm always available if you need to talk.* There's a painfully long pause before he hangs up, as if he wants to say more, yet doesn't know what. I consider calling him back but I don't know what to say either, still embarrassed by the limited time we've already spent together and the call I made last night in haste. I can think of a million words to describe myself. "Okay" is not one of them.

My "delivery" takes all morning to arrive and I've wasted it pacing up and down, barely able to eat, vaguely able to watch TV, the news channel only adding to my frustration. I'm constantly checking my damaged mobile phone for an update on Lee, needing confirmation I'm not going mad, that *none* of it happened—anything to offer a different conclusion. When my door buzzer finally rings, I race downstairs to the front entrance and practically snatch my parcel from the unsuspecting driver. I don't concern myself with the look he gives me as I slam the door in his face. He doesn't seem a legitimate delivery driver anyway. I don't assume he'll require a signature.

I sit on my bed, my heart in my throat, staring at a box that looks too small and unassuming to *ever* cause any lasting damage. Eventually, I tear it open to reveal the drugs I ordered, a tiny bottle wrapped inside several layers of toilet paper. There are no instructions, no receipt, nothing to tie this item back to the guy on Facebook.

Now what? *Shit.* I haven't thought this through. I hold the bottle towards the light, my trembling hand sloshing the substance around the container, unsure what I'm even looking at, unconvinced I can do this, whatever *this* is. I contemplate my choices, lost in thought. It isn't too late. I can tip the contents down the sink, do something else with my day. Yet, that won't change how I feel, won't dislodge the pain I now can't get out of my head.

# Sixteen

## *Newton*

I didn't sleep a wink, continually listening for signs of choking in the next room, alcohol-induced vomit something I've seen people die from, unfortunately. I lost count of how many times I got out of bed to check Andy was okay, clean sheets mocking me every time I walked past my unused spare room, my sofa bearing the brunt of a grown man's discomfort. I spent the morning camped out in my room for fear of waking him up, daylight fully surrounding the edges of my closed curtains before I finally heard him in the kitchen.

'Sleep well?' I didn't mean the sarcasm, didn't mean to imply anything untoward. *I* hadn't, thanks to him.

'My mouth feels like my throat's been cut,' Andy muttered, searching my charred cupboards for a mug, leaving several doors wide open. The cold tap was running. I turned it off.

'What do you expect?' I sounded like I was speaking to

one of my students, my face pulled into an aggravated knot, arms folded across my chest. I couldn't help it. My head throbbed with all the thinking it had been forced to endure, my old friend to blame for that, too. I switched on my coffee machine, listening to the mechanic's spring to life, glad this vital part of my day hadn't been damaged in the fire. I wasn't sure how I would have coped with such a painful loss.

'You got anything for a headache?' Andy was rubbing his head, unable to look at me, his squinting eyes telling their own story. I pointed to a cupboard in the corner, allowing my friend the freedom of rummaging through my first aid box before finding a tub of Aspirin that he placed on the countertop. 'I'm sorry about last night,' he said, once his tongue was no longer stuck to the roof of his mouth.

'Are you *sure* everything's okay?' I was pouring coffee. 'You mentioned Angela Healy a lot last night.' I probably shouldn't have mentioned her. It was none of my business.

Andy glanced across the room as if I'd caught him doing something he shouldn't, his pale cheeks flushing wildly. 'Shit, what did I say?'

I laughed, rarely surprised by how drinking always seems to lead to memory failure in the cold light of day. I'd been there myself. Many times. 'Well, you told me you *liked* her.' I raised my eyebrows. 'Several times.' In fact, by the time we'd arrived home, he'd declared his *love* for her too, but he'd also told me he loved *me*, so it certainly wasn't worth confirming.

'God, *did* I?' It was probably my imagination but I'm sure the man was on the verge of tears, or throwing up, something on his mind he wasn't saying. I tried not to notice. He took a sip of water, seemingly glad when I handed him a large mug of black coffee, passing me his glass in return so I could pour the unwanted liquid down

*The Lost Raven*

the sink. 'I'm sorry if I made a fool of myself,' he added, struggling to open an Aspirin bottle.

'Do you want to talk about it?'

'Not much to talk about.' Andy turned to face the kitchen window, nothing much to see beyond the glass other than his own dulled reflection.

'When did you start drinking?' I wasn't accusing him of alcoholism, I'm sure it was due to stress. The fact we'd not seen each other for a long time, bad timing, nothing more.

'What do you mean?' Andy was enjoying his coffee, waking up a little now, looking slightly less hung over than he did a moment ago. Over-the-counter drugs could be thanked for that, or my unfettered words. He didn't turn around.

'I mean, I know you've always *liked* a drink. We all did back in the day. But you seemed to be putting it away like I haven't seen you do in a while.' I wasn't in any position to comment. I hadn't seen him do *anything* for a while. I couldn't ask what was really bothering him, he wouldn't have told me. But he was in my home. I recollected our younger days, nights out always ending with our heads down the toilet, swearing off alcohol for life until the following week when we'd do it all over again. But something about Andy's drinking seemed different. I couldn't put my finger on why.

'You don't want to know about my problems.' My friend looked momentarily saddened that I'd reminded him.

'Try me.'

'It's nothing.'

It was obviously *something*.

'Andy?'

Andy sighed and turned to face me, sitting at a barstool that still bore a thin layer of ash from yesterday's misdemeanour. I joined him on the one that *hadn't* escaped the fire, a melted plastic seat now digging into my backside. I probably should have thrown it outside. The smell of bleach had infused with a residual burnt hue that would no doubt remain in this room until I redecorated or *moved*, seeping into every corner of my flat, reminding me I'm an idiot. My laptop was still open, the screen black now, last night's search for Angela Healy still readily available. I closed the lid and slid it to one side. I didn't need Andy to see her smiling face looking up at us, didn't need his sarcasm. He wouldn't appreciate my unwarranted worry over a woman I barely knew. He might take offence, presume something that didn't exist.

'Things have been getting on top of me recently, that's all.' Andy didn't seem happy to confirm it, didn't seem comfortable expressing his private business aloud.

'You? Andrew Hansley? The guy who is rattled by nothing and no one?' I took a swig of coffee. I didn't mean to sound blasé. I was unaccustomed to Andy's shifting mannerisms, nothing more, such a change in persona unexpected after fifteen years of dusting down the pedestal I'd kept him on.

'Yeah. *That* guy.' Andy was looking at his steaming mug as if he wasn't convinced such a person now existed, the fact that I was a psychologist and therefore should know better than to make jokes, failing to resonate. He found the fridge, poured milk into his mug, cursing when he realised it had soured.

'I'm a good listener.' My voice had softened, my mouth turning into a worried frown. I couldn't make light of a situation that was obviously troubling him. After all, this was what I did. I sat. I listened. I evaluated. I'd probably spent too much time around Paul, his sarcasm rubbing off.

'That's the reason I'm here, Newt. Because you *are* a good listener.' He paused, offering me an honest smile I

## The Lost Raven

wasn't expecting. 'And you were always a good friend, too. I haven't had one of those for a while.' Andy poured his ruined coffee down the sink, folding his arms across to his chest as if he couldn't breathe.

I realised in that moment why he'd turned up unannounced, my doorstep the one place I didn't expect to see him. *Ever*. He assumed I could save him, fix him, help with whatever was going on in his life he felt he couldn't deal with alone. I'd always looked up to the man, held him in high regard. We were more than friends. Brother's, he'd once confirmed. Yet, the way he hunched forward in front of me now was far removed from the man I once called a friend. He looked almost broken. I didn't assume I had the right to ask why. I couldn't recall us parting on bad terms, thankfully, more a case of life sending us in different directions. It was fitting we both now lived in Eastcliff, having hankered after the bright lights and fast pace of big cities for so long, laughed about it, made plans.

'Well, I'm always happy to help,' I confirmed. It was the second time I'd said that in as many days. I should have it inscribed on my headstone.

*Newton Flanigan. Always happy to help.*

\*\*\*

Andy sent me out for milk, then spent the day drinking my coffee, lying across my sofa and enjoying his own company far more than he was enjoying mine. It was a shame that, since his arrival, we'd touched on nothing of our shared past, nothing that might *matter*. In fact, I struggled to recall when things had changed. I guess life gets in the way when you're busy. I decided that marking my student's essays would distract me from my guest, at least putting me on schedule for once, my week now one step ahead of where it would have been if left to my own devices. Yet, the day was slipping by without me, nothing happening that might lift my mood, nothing to do but play host to my unexpected visitor. Instead of calling Stephanie to check on her and the kids, Andy and I ate a takeaway meal on my lounge rug, the pizza mostly left untouched in the box because neither of us were hungry.

For a while we skirted the edge of conversation, avoiding the reason for Andy's visit, my sofa sustaining a stain I tried to ignore. We touched on the subject of his landlord, our university days, Angela Healy, but nothing was mentioned about his eviction, that so-called harassment accusation festering like a scab waiting to be picked. Instead, Andy watched television whilst I grappled with my student's assignments, commenting several times how implausible he thought my working as a university professor was.

'Springfalls University? Seriously? You?'

'Yep.'

'*Professor* Flanigan?'

'That's me.'

'Why?'

'Because it's just around the corner.' Convenience had become my middle name. It wasn't the only reason, of course, but Andy didn't need the details.

'But you *hate* kids.'

'I don't hate kids.'

'You hated school.'

'Everyone hates school.'

'A university is a *school*.'

'It's a further education institution and a place most people aspire to attend.' I rolled my eyes, noticing that the ceiling in this room hadn't exactly escaped smoke damage either.

## The Lost Raven

'*Institution,*' Andy scoffed. 'You got that right.'

I glanced towards the back of Andy's head, a gentle shudder of his shoulders confirming his private amusement. 'Well, *you* should know all about universities and institutions. You're the big shot doctor.' Seven years in the making followed by a decade of building a highly regarded career.

Andy fell silent. I couldn't help thinking I'd said the wrong thing.

'Yeah that may be true, Newt, but if I had my time again I'd do something different. Something fun.' He was no longer cracking jokes.

I couldn't understand Andy's low mood. He was the best in our class, the brightest of our group, the one destined for greatness.

You don't find your job fun?' I wanted to add, 'anymore' but refrained. Maybe he never did.

'Do you?'

'I *love* what I do.' It was true. Despite outward appearances assuming otherwise, continued stress, police pressure, a fire-damaged flat.

'But *you* didn't complete your studies in medicine to become a medical doctor.' Andy sounded frustrated that I'd departed early, leaving him to complete the training without me. 'Wasn't that always the plan, Newt? To work in London together in some prestigious hospital? Make our fortune?'

Did my old friend begrudge me my change of direction? 'I went into psychology,' I confirmed. 'That still makes me a doctor. A doctor of the mind.' I was proud of my achievements, my graduate degree in medicine more than enough to aid with police enquires, where they needed it, to understand the workings of the human body. I had a Master's degree in psychology now, too. I didn't mention it to Andy. 'Besides, there's more to life than money.'

'But why?'
'Why what?'
'Why did you drop out?'

I didn't see myself as a dropout, instead taking some time to assess what I really wanted from life. Psychology was a natural progression for me, medicine merely a starting point in my journey, an unexpected string to my bow. I saw how hard Isaac was working in the city, the stress his job put on him and his young family. I didn't want that kind of life. The fact that I'd lost *my* wife in the process was irrelevant, the stress it put on me in the end, unimportant.

'I went into psychology. It was hardly dropping out.' Andy was putting me in a bad mood.

Andy took a breath. 'So what makes *psychology* so amazing?'

I laid my pencil on the table and leant back in my dining chair. 'Because I like dissecting people, understanding how they think.' It was true. I enjoyed the satisfaction I got from a job well done. I was smiling, the stress worthwhile when placed into perspective.

Andy turned around and glared at me. He didn't say anything. I wanted to dissect *him* but I didn't know where to begin. I wanted to ask when he'd last spoken to Angela, her nonsensical phone call still lingering in my mind. He told me she was doing all right, yet I didn't get that impression, his eyes saying something his mouth wasn't. I wanted to query what had happened with his neighbour, dissect *their* relationship, uncover why she would have made such a claim against a man usually so professional and astute. He'd claimed it was a mistake, an error, nothing he'd done to upset a woman he barely knew. I wanted to dissect my friend's emotions, uncover *his* truth. I didn't buy his act, his blatant mannerisms. I knew him too well.

*The Lost Raven*

'How long have you known Angela?' I was changing the subject, glad I was sitting far enough away for my question to sound casual, annoying music from the television setting my teeth on edge.

'About a year, give or take,' Andy called out flatly, not even bothering to turn my way or turn down the volume. He was laughing, seemingly glad that whatever was troubling him earlier was keeping a temporary distance.

'And she was *definitely* okay when you spoke to her yesterday? After she left the hospital, I mean?' I still wasn't convinced Andy was telling the truth.

'Yeah, I went round to her house. We had a good chat.'

'She lives in a flat.'

'You know what I mean.' He sat upright, muting the television. *Hallelujah*. 'Why are you so concerned about her?' He was looking at me now, eyes narrowed.

'You actually saw her yesterday? After she left the hospital?'

'Yeah. She said she wasn't proud of the way she'd behaved, wished she could take it back. Told me not to worry about her, that she was dealing with things in her own way.' Andy unmuted the volume again, turning his attention back to the television.

'She actually *said* that?' I couldn't help raising my voice. I'm not sure it wasn't in frustration rather than a response to the aggravating noise he was subjecting me to.

'Yes. She did.' Andy glanced across his shoulder towards my dining table, his eyes aimed more towards the ceiling than me. 'Why are you so interested in how Angela is? I thought you said you didn't know her?' His face had changed, his eyes darker somehow, denser, guarded. The profile of his face was knotted, as if he was waiting for a declaration, for me to confess I'd been having some illicit affair with the girl, was secretly in love with her.

'Because Angela Healy was suicidal yesterday, Andy. It seems a little odd she recovered so quickly.' I was tapping my pencil across a sheet of paper, annoying myself in the process and oddly wanting to throw it at him. I wanted to unplug the television, force my friend to explain himself, tell me what was going on. Andy knew more than he was saying.

'You know *women*,' he chided, laughing at some joke I must have missed.

I stared at his head. Andy had readily confessed he liked the girl, confirming it during a drunken stupor whilst crying into my shoulder, smearing snot and saliva on my shirt. Yet, he didn't seem overly concerned that only yesterday the poor thing had tried to end her life. I wasn't convinced he'd spoken to Angela at all. I don't know why. If he had, he would have heard what I heard in her voice when she called me, hanging up too fast for me to do anything other than worry. He claimed he was being evicted, his neighbour causing chaos he was a victim of, yet I was sure there was more to the story, more he wasn't sharing.

No. Apparently, I didn't know women at all.

# Seventeen

## *Angela*

I can't sit around doing nothing. These four walls are closing in on me and the last thing I need is more time to *think*. Instead, I head into the bathroom for a much-needed shower, a change of clothing holding the power to lift my mood. In fact, this evening has the potential to change a lot of things and I need to look good, the idea that something is about to change me not a concept I'm able to shake from my declining thoughts. I take a taxi to nearby Shelby, terrified of going back into Eastcliff in case someone recognises me, a bustling club the one place I can potentially aim my attention for a few hours whilst remaining undetected. The last thing I need is to inadvertently highlight what I did to Lee, still no idea if I killed the idiot, still unwilling to acknowledge my actions. I don't want to find myself inside a police cell answering questions no one will understand.

The music is loud, my clothing louder, the makeup I've carefully applied setting a tone I know will draw attention.

Don't get me wrong, I don't want male attention, but tonight I *need* it. It's a means to an end, nothing more, nothing left to do but see this thing through to its inevitable conclusion. I press my bag against me, the handle draped across my chest to prevent someone from stealing it, adding to my frustration, ruining my plan. I'm gripping my bottle of poison through a section of thin leather, constantly checking it's still there, other items I've collated for my mission also inside, ready, waiting — like me.

I did not intend to stab Lee and, although there's nothing I can do about that now, I've thought of nothing else since. I can still see the look in his eyes, the way he stared right through me, shock setting in on his trembling lips. Tonight I have set myself a test, nothing more. A vague idea swilling around my brain of what it might be like to *feel* something other than repulsion for my own existence, to force an acknowledgement of what men have already done to me. The concept that I took *control* has now become my constant companion. It was a fleeting moment, I know, but I can't help confirming I liked it, can't help how that's changed my perception, my mood.

I order a glass of wine and find a dimly lit corner in which to hide, observe my surroundings, survey my prey. I'm a majestic raven, a hunter, my piercing eyes ever watchful, ready to strike, plucking my chosen victim from this location with ease. And, like a raven, I'll use my voice and body to allure, feathers preened and erect to communicate my impossible desires beyond anything these savage men will ever see coming.

I need to keep a clear head. I can't get drunk. Not tonight. I glance around, my wandering eyes fixed on every male here. Who am I looking for? Certainly not a *weak* man. I won't feel powerful enough over someone like that. No. I need a stud, a man who can hold his own in a fight, if

## The Lost Raven

needed. Someone who can defend himself against an unexpected attack. A "have-a-go-hero", if you like. I'm doing this for all the women out there who feel the way I do, for every female who finds herself on the wrong side of unwanted male attention.

I smile, impressed I look seductive enough to draw attention, my hair and makeup on point, the very dress I wore to Liam's party now readily inviting interest I'd recently deemed disgusting, high heels the perfect weapons of seduction. I never assumed I'd wear this dress again, a favourite of mine until now. Yet, it's part of tonight's test, that's all, forcing myself to face the very demon I know I've already become. *I know men.* I know what they enjoy, what they want, how they think. Looking the way I do now, it won't take long to find what I'm looking for. I feel a bit sick, actually. I need to calm down.

I'm a juddering collection of nerves, my body unwilling to settle down, my trembling hands barely able to hold my drink steady, each passing moment instilling fear into my icy veins. I've never done *anything* like this before and I'm not confident I know what I'm doing now. My knees are jolting violently up and down, unsettled and restless, a ball of sick sitting in the back of my throat. I stand up and head towards the bar, needing to shake off my nerves, my fears. Sitting still is doing nothing for my unhinged state of mind and I need something to do other than *think*. When a male smiles my way, I take it as a sign, the perfect opportunity to pounce.

I lick my lips and smile back, automatically sliding next to him with my head tilted sideways as if I'm interested, wetting glossy lips with a probing tongue to appear as willing as he assumes me to be. I push my freshly styled hair over my shoulders, exposing my cleavage, my neck. He glances down, likes what he sees, unable to hide his excitement. He's tall, muscular, his hair little more than stubble purposefully shaved from his head. I don't know why. He looks like a bouncer, an exquisite candidate for my *experiment*.

'Can I buy you a drink, darling?' he asks, already intoxicated.

I nod, accidentally narrowing my eyes in response before realising my error, the term *darling* irritating every inch of my being. 'A Cosmopolitan, please,' I respond curtly, physically shaking, hoping he won't notice. Less than twenty-four hours ago I was unintentionally drawing attention from Lee, my ultimate actions borne from terror, shock. Tonight, I *know* what I'm doing, despite a false confidence I probably don't deserve. If alcohol aids my mission, so be it.

The guy nods, his eyes studying the body I've deliberately placed on display, a keen hand hovering against my lower back. Until now I haven't thought much beyond an insane desire to take control over a man I'd never assume willing, my tiny frame usually unable to overpower *anyone*. Yet, I haven't anticipated how close such a man would need to be, haven't expected to feel so exposed. How am I meant to slip drugs into his drink without detection? How am I meant to go through this without being sick? My smile slips, my brow furrowing. Every time he glances my way with an openly creepy grin, mine is forced back in place. He orders a beer, his pint glass wide, the liquid therefore exposed. I stare at his glass as he speaks, not listening to anything he says, my cleavage thankfully keeping his attention away from my vengeful eyes.

He's a soldier, apparently, on leave of absence for reasons I don't absorb. *I don't care.* He tells me about his training and the tours he's completed, as if I want to know, bragging, laying it on thick, making himself out to be

## The Lost Raven

something he's not. I'm not impressed. I swallow, forcing another grin. This isn't going to be as easy as I've assumed, the solace of my flat so very different to the reality of this night. One hand is permanently resting on the rim of his glass, the other around my waist, the slow gulps he takes only adding to my rage. I can't just lean over and pour the liquid into his drink whilst slapping his hand out of the way. "Will you excuse me for a moment while I pop this into your drink."

Instead, I do the unthinkable. I lean closer, pretending his words have made an impact, his presence and chatter appealing. I can't abide his aftershave and his unruly chest hair makes me want to tear it from his skin. I can smell something on his breath. Curry, I think. I can't be sure. I'm giggling, but it's for effect, I assure you. I don't mean it. It is a ruse. Nothing more.

'Why don't we finish our drinks and head somewhere a little quieter?' I ask loudly towards his outstretched ear. He'll *know* what I mean by that, no need to confirm the intentions he assumes I'm offering. I haven't even asked his name.

He smiles and picks up his drink. Although I feel sick by the thought of it, I reach up and kiss his lips, sliding my tongue into his mouth to distract him, pressing my breasts against his arm. It does the trick. He leaves his glass on the bar and reaches for my bottom, pulling me close, kissing me forcefully. *Fucking hell.* I *hate* men.

With no time to think, I pour the entire contents of my little amber bottle into his glass, impressed I'm able to do so with one hand, the lid already loosened whilst he was busy talking to my *chest*. I hope no one has witnessed what I've done. I complete my task, my intruder busy, his lips pressed firmly over mine. My face is turned his way, a swelling in his trousers telling me *all* I need to know. My plan is working.

I watch carefully as the offending liquid swirls, mixing with his beer, ready for action. I hope to Christ he doesn't taste it. Yet again, too many people are raped with the stuff every day, myself included. It can't have a taste otherwise the bastards wouldn't get away with it. *I* didn't taste it. I was oblivious, taken advantage of with ease. I feel suddenly unwell, wanting to pull away from my intruder, but I can't take the chance that my mission might be thwarted, so I allow him the time he needs to fumble over my body before I casually step away. After all, it isn't the first time I've been forced to allow a man's hands to wander, my eyes closed, my breath held so firmly I thought I'd die.

I smile, wanting to vomit, taking a gulp of alcohol that suddenly tastes like poison, my memories serving only as a painful reminder of a past I wish I could leave behind. My actions have the added benefit of looking as if I'm keen to leave, keen for more of the attention he's affording me, eager to get him alone. He sees this as an invitation, a smile spread across his stupid face as he picks up his now-drugged beer and downs it in one go. *Yes, perfect.* I can't help grinning in response as froth coats his wetted lips.

'Ready?' he asks probingly, anticipating his evening is about to get interesting.

I nod, leaving my cocktail mostly untouched on the bar. He won't mind. He assumes he's about to be paid in full for his affections, something far more valuable heading his way. I almost throw up as we head towards the exit, too late now to change my mind, this night already set in motion. I still have no idea what I'm going to do. I just *need* to get him alone. I'll figure it out as I go. He's still kissing me, rubbing keen fingers across my dress, eager to know what lies beneath. I can feel his growing anticipation, can feel it pressed against my leg.

## The Lost Raven

We stumble into the evening air, my fake laughter and drunken appearance merely a lie to keep him on side. It's just turned eleven thirty now, plenty of time for me to enjoy my moment of power before I locate a taxi and go home. I have a feeling that, after tonight, I'll have earned some much-required sleep that has eluded me for some time. I roll knowing eyes towards several disinterested people who stare at us and smile, my shoulder hooked beneath his sweaty armpit in an attempt to keep him upright. I'm aiding him, nothing more, yet I might have miscalculated how heavy he is, how difficult he is to manoeuvre.

I mutter something about how much he's had to drink, laughing at the *state* of him as we disappear around the side of the building, away from potential prying eyes and unwanted witnesses. I manhandle my newly acquired *victim* into a narrow space that leads nowhere but to a collection of dustbins. Aside from drug users and rats, I doubt anyone will notice us here. Not until much later, and by then I'll be long gone.

'You're... lovely,' he slurs, his words slowing now, the guy sounding less coherent with every struggling breath he takes.

He's giggling, losing his footing, succumbing to my unwitting actions and gravity, slumping to the ground with a thud. He reaches a free hand towards my leg before he closes his eyes and passes out. I wasn't anticipating it to work *that* fast, wasn't expecting it to be so easy. I think back to last night and vomit. Now what? What the *fuck* do I do now?

# Eighteen

## *Angela*

I'm staring at this stranger as if I hate him, yet I've never (until this evening) set eyes on him before in my life. It makes this moment easier to process because in my mind I imagine he's Liam and can do to him what he did to me. I want Liam to suffer, therefore *this* wretch will suffer in his place. I kneel by his side, momentarily grateful for the quiet that has fallen, a light breeze cooling my skin, calming my mood. Heavy music is still drumming in the background, of course, but it's far enough away to afford me some space, no longer aware of distant chatter. My breath is shallow, my lungs struggling, yet I contemplate what I am about to do with ease, nothing to do but go with the flow of shit I've already created. After all, I can't waste two hundred quid. I don't have that kind of money to throw around.

My victim's body is taut, several tattoos lining his chest, a dog, a crown, something on his shoulder I can't identify from this angle. He groans when I unzip his trousers and I

*The Lost Raven*

struggle to slide them from his heavy body, inching the tight material from his bulky frame. He isn't wearing any underwear and I'm shocked by how I react to his semi-naked form, the earlier swelling in his trousers nothing more now than a sleeping *slug* that makes me laugh. I turn my head from side to side, assessing the "weapon" that from this position appears wholly irrelevant, weak. Seeing it lying between his legs makes me want to vomit. How can men hold such power whilst possessing something so *pathetic*?

Bipolar controls my life. I wish it didn't. Yet, every part of me is constrained by drugs I unfortunately haven't been taking. I am unaware of my actions when I'm off my medication, easily distracted and agitated if I don't get my own way. It isn't pleasant, not always fun for those around me. That might be the reason they're currently stored in my cupboard. I don't want to rationalise my life anymore.

I think about Rosie and how she often bares the brunt of my frustration, the poor woman not always aware of my suffering. What would she say if she knew I'm staring at a stranger's flaccid penis, unable to get the ridiculous idea out my head that it might grow teeth and bite me? I expect it to come to life at any second, yell at me, lunge towards my leg and attack. I'm psychotic, I know, creating visions that don't exist. It doesn't help that I *know* I'm deluded, doesn't take away the feeling of dread. I consider taking a picture for social media, another humiliation, another act of the power I now hold over him. Yet, I repulse myself by such a thought so instead, I take a deep breath, tears ready to fall.

I don't remember putting a dildo in my bag, but I reach in and pull it out anyway, wanting to laugh at what it represents. I bought the thing online a few years ago whilst trying to "rediscover" myself, attempting to rebuild a tainted life after my father went to prison. I thought it was all over, assumed I'd be okay. However, it has been sitting unused in my underwear drawer ever since because I can't bring myself to feel *anything* other than repulsion for what it represents, my lesbian phase ending in nothing but frustration that has ultimately exasperated my declining mental health.

I've been raped many times in my life. Firstly as a child, too young to understand, then as a teenager, the same man to blame. Now as a woman, I'm taking back control that was brutally taken from me long ago, Liam's party bringing it all back to the surface in a single, selfish act. I deserve this moment. I deserve to feel something other than my own repulsed anger.

I kick this stranger in the ribs before struggling to roll his heavy body onto his front, my mission clear. I want him to feel what I've felt, my life nothing to those men who assumed me unworthy of anything else. It doesn't matter that I might become the very thing I always claimed to hate. It's too late to change my mind now. I take a moment, the instrument in my hand large, unfeeling, although it might be normal sized, I honestly don't know. I've nothing to go on, nothing to compare it to, no man in my life willing to show me true affection. I jab unfeeling silicone between his buttocks, trying to locate his anus, my thoughts on nothing but revenge and the pain I want to inflict. He grunts and I remember all the times when *I* grunted, my muffled outbursts enough to seemingly turn them on and make them fuck me harder.

I'm crying. I've only just realised, my open bag lying unassumingly at my feet. It doesn't help that I see no pain on his sleeping face, nothing that tells me I actually *have* the control I crave. I slap his face to provoke a reaction, angry when he responds with a muffled sigh. I'm growing increasingly irritated as I jab my phallic object inside him

## The Lost Raven

sharply, simulating with aggravated force what I've experienced many times before. I want to scream, yell, confirm how much I *hate* him. But I won't be speaking to this guy. I don't even know him. It's my father I hate, my father I want to scream at, my own flesh and blood the one person I wish I'd taken revenge on long before now. This guy isn't even moving, sleeping like a baby, smacking warm lips against an unassuming tongue, probably dreaming of somewhere far nicer than here. He isn't aware what I'm doing.

I reach into my bag and take out a knife, still wondering what happened to the one I used on Lee. It isn't a large knife, just a paring blade I keep in my kitchen drawer for peeling vegetables. However, it's sharp, sharp enough. It will do the job. I roll him onto his back, bored now of trying to rape him, staring for a few unfathomable seconds at his still flaccid penis. I don't want to touch it but I take it in hand and slice the blade into his flesh, tugging the base, pulling it taught. Blood spits across my arm but I keep cutting, not stopping until I have the offending item in my hand, severed, unusable, unable to *ever* cause pain again.

He begins to stir, my actions too much, *his* pain obviously overwhelming. I can't allow him to wake up. He'll identify me, describe me to the police, should they ask, which they will. Without thinking, without hesitation, I slice open his throat, wanting to scream into the night as I watch in shock the blackened blood that spills to the ground around us. He chokes unconsciously, his penis still in my trembling grasp, my heartbeat the strongest it's ever been. Repulsed, I toss it onto his naked belly where it lands with a thud and remains unmoving, like him. He's dead. And I am officially a killer.

***

A nasty taste of bile hits the back of my tongue, the bitter texture too much. I'm staring at a dead man, a strong smell of blood engulfing me, the feel of his fleshy penis still tickling my palm, mocking my unthinkable actions. It took little over a moment to kill him, ensuring I *was* all-powerful, all-knowing. Now, I feel disgusted, no one to turn to that can help me, no way to change what I've done.

I pull my mobile from my bag but think better of it. Who the *fuck* am I going to call? Not Rosie or Liam. Definitely not Andrew up-his-own-arse Hansley. Although he's always been polite, casual, we don't *know* each other, have barely spoken in the year I've known him. To be honest, I don't really like him and until yesterday we'd never spent any length of time in each other's company. I didn't mean to become his unwitting patient. I haven't seen him since I raced out of that cubicle. I don't know if I can face him again, my troubles too personal to share with the likes of him.

I'm not sure I can leave a mutilated body to be discovered by some unsuspecting idiot, yet I can't move it, can't hide the crime I've committed. The guy is too heavy anyway, my earlier strength vanishing now along with a confidence I didn't possess in the first place. I still don't know his name, destined to find out soon enough on the news. I have a cigarette lighter in my handbag, an item left over from a habit I managed to kick a while ago. Without thinking, I flick the ignition, aiming a flickering flame towards his trousers, an orange glow erupting around his ankles, creeping along his legs.

If I burn him, there'll be no evidence to connect me to this crime, no way for the police to uncover my deadly deed. I want him to combust, turning rapidly to ash and dust, nothing left to identify. I know it's possible. I've seen the evidence, the proof sitting in books in my flat. I watch, waiting for his body to become engulfed by the heat, knowing I'm potentially drawing attention as the flames creep higher. Yet, I've inexplicitly miscalculated how long it takes to burn a human body, an accelerator needed for swift results. There *are* flames, of course, licking at his ankles, yet he resists my efforts, his clothing burning slowly. *Shit.* I step away, racing into the darkness, nothing for me to do but leave him to his fate, a bloodied knife firmly in my possession.

\*\*\*

I'm less than a mile away from the club when I collapse, unable to propel my legs any further. Newton pops into my mind again. He does that a lot, I don't know why. I remember his offer of *help*, the last call I made to him done out of panic that doesn't now come close to the way I feel. I dial his number, the soft purr in my ear too quiet, my struggling breath too loud. I'm covered in blood, my bare legs mocking me, warm liquid dripping over my knees, my ankles. My shoes are no doubt leaving a trail, my criminal activities soon to be exposed.

I'm about to hang up when he answers, the casual *hello?* he aims my way too calm, his tone relaxed, unaware of the mad woman on the other end of the phone. His evening was probably uneventful until now. I almost don't believe what I've done, almost can't breathe. What am I meant to say? I open my mouth, close it. I'm still crying, the sting of acidic tears preventing rational words from emerging. Newton is speaking but I can't reply. I've made a mistake. I wanted to hear a friendly voice. Now I can't believe how stupid I am, can't even move.

'Angela?' He no doubt assumes I'm suicidal again, that

ridiculous rooftop event stronger in *his* mind than mine. 'Are you okay?'

I shake my head, knowing he can't see me, can't appreciate the state I'm in. I can still feel that appendage in my grip, the way it wobbled like jelly as I cut it free from its unassuming owner.

'I'm a terrible person,' I find myself muttering, my eyes closed, my head throbbing. I feel as if I'm being strangled.

'You're not terrible, Angela. Just depressed, and obviously suffering more than you're willing to say.'

Newton is trying to be nice, yet I'm way beyond depressed, way beyond saving. I *am* suffering, though. He's right about that. He assumes I'm suicidal and yet I've done something far crazier, something I can never correct. I can't offer anything of value, can barely catch my breath. Instead, I hang up and race into the night. It's almost midnight now, a few people still ambling around, able to witness my unhinged existence if they look hard enough.

I keep away from the main streets, out of sight, skulking around in alleyways and stealing someone's washing from a clothesline that looks as if it's been there a while. I don't care. I'm temporarily grateful for the comfort of a pair of jeans that fit loosely around my trembling legs, a t-shirt covering my shame. I discard my bloodstained dress at the bottom of a skip, nothing else to do with it, hoping nobody will find it there, a landfill site the only place it's destined to spend eternity now. I liked that dress, too. It's a shame it brought nothing but pain.

I sit in a bus shelter waiting for the last bus of the day to take me home. I need to appear calm, forcing down gulps of poisonous air in quick succession, panic never a good look on me. Every time I close my eyes I feel something watching, in the darkness, waiting. I'm clutching a bag that now houses a murder weapon and a used dildo, both

## The Lost Raven

covered in someone else's blood. I can't think too long about my empty bottle, no label to convict me, should anyone check. Yet, *anyone* looking at me can see what I am, what I've done. There's no going back for me now. My life is well and truly over.

# Nineteen

## *Newton*

I was almost glad when Andy retired to his room with a supposed headache. It was just after nine o'clock. He hadn't said much to me all evening aside from confirming he was on an early shift, a six o'clock start. I was grateful for the solace, to be honest. A few hours without his company oddly appealing. I could indulge in some reading, another coffee, a nap.

I left Angela a couple of messages that might have sounded desperate. I was worried about her, sitting for almost an hour with my mobile on my lap, willing it to ring, hoping she was okay. Then at just before midnight she called, although the line was terrible and I could barely make out what she was saying. She sounded out of breath, as if she was running, crying into her phone, nothing else to do. She didn't stay on the line for long, was gone by the time I'd found my shoes, shaking off thoughts of burnt kitchens and screaming ravens. I called her back, of course, but her phone went straight to voicemail. It was a further forty minutes before mine rang again. I was still in my armchair, my shoes still on my feet, still thinking of a girl I barely knew.

'Sorry to call you so late.' Paul's distinct voice echoed along a windy line, sounding stressed, as always. I often wondered if a different career would be beneficial to his health. It would certainly help mine.

'Everything okay?' I sat upright, the light from my mobile phone stinging my eyes.

'Any chance you can get over to Lux in Shelby?'

'The nightclub?'

'The very same.'

'Now?' I was half asleep.

'No, next week, Newt. Of course, *now*.' Paul sounded irritated.

I rolled my eyes. I didn't assume he was asking me to join him for a drink at this hour. Stress wasn't one of Paul's friends.

'What happened?'

'The usual. Another sick bastard on the loose.'

'Care to elaborate?'

'I'll fill you in when you get here.' Paul hung up, leaving the dialling tone in my ear and an ache behind my eyes that had nothing to do with lack of sleep or unwanted guests.

I stood in my lounge listening to the sound of snoring from my spare room, staring at Andy's car key on my coffee table. As much as I loved my ageing Volkswagen Beetle, it was just that. *Ageing*. I'd ignored a continued knocking from the engine bay for a while and it now saw me question the idea of driving into the night, the risk of breaking down a real possibility. Andy wouldn't mind if I borrowed his for an hour or two. I'd be back before he needed it and if all else failed, he could order a taxi. He owed me that much, at least. The fact that I was uninsured to drive the thing was irrelevant. Paul *needed* me. This was mitigating circumstances. Nothing else mattered.

\*\*\*

The drive to Shelby was quiet compared to the chaos that met me outside Lux nightclub. It was one o'clock in the morning yet the place was buzzing with activity, flashes of blue streaking across a busy street from several police cars blocking the road. I parked Andy's car some distance away and walked, a fresh sea breeze at least waking me up. A crowd had gathered, craning their necks to see what was happening, their mouths and teeth chattering, shivering in the early morning air, some too drunk to notice, most too excited by the unfolding scene to care.

'He's with me.' Paul's familiar tone boomed along the pavement as a uniformed police officer halted my approach. The guy nodded, lifting a length of tape to allow me inside a cordoned zone, my friend's face set in a twisted knot that made him look old. 'Thanks for coming,' he continued, his words aimed ahead instead of towards me, no time to exchange pleasantries, more important things to deal with.

I still had Andy on my mind, a hastily written note the only thing I left him before leaving my flat. *Borrowed your car. Won't be long.* I didn't want the guy to wake up and notice it was gone and assuming someone had stolen it. I'd had enough stress this weekend as it was. I was still waiting for Angela to call me back, still expecting her to do something *stupid*.

'You okay?' Paul noticed my silence, glancing momentarily over his shoulder, our footsteps in sync.

'Yeah.' I wasn't convinced by my response.

'You seem distracted.'

## *The Lost Raven*

'An old friend turned up.'

'Oh dear.' Paul stopped walking, turned to face me. He had his hands in his pockets, the collar on his coat turned up to stave off an incoming breeze. He looked cold.

I nodded. 'I left him sleeping off a *hangover*.' I didn't realise how frustrated I was until then.

'Ah.'

'Ah, what?'

'I take it the guy's taken over your space?' Paul knew how much I valued my private space, my time my own for a reason. I liked living alone.

'You *could* say that.'

'Well if you need a handy copper, let me know. I know someone who can boot him out for you if he gets too much.' Paul tapped his nose, offering a brief smile. I knew what he meant, grateful for the friendship *he* now afforded me.

I nodded. 'No problem.' Obviously that wouldn't be necessary. I was just glad for the fresh air, thankful to get out of my flat. Andy wasn't a bad soul. I just wasn't expecting him to turn up on my doorstep. 'So what are we dealing with?'

I knew it would be bad, of course, my expertise only required when the murder scene in question didn't add up. I assumed it *would* be a murder scene, a team of forensic experts already filling the space, several white paper suits mulling around in the dark. Paul led us along a narrow alleyway behind the now-closed nightclub where forensic pathologist, Bernard Taylor, greeted us. He handed me a pair of paper slippers and surgical gloves. We nodded our greetings. It was a shame our time together was limited to unwitting incidents like these.

Paul was already standing next to the remains of a white male, around the age of thirty from what I could tell, although he was covered in blood and what was left of his trousers seemed to be bunched around his ankles. I tried not to stand downwind, tried not to look too closely.

Bernard took a breath. 'This fellow was found just after midnight. Someone tried to set him on fire.' He raised an eyebrow, his thoughts not yet fully expressed.

'Why would they do that?' The idea of burning someone wasn't something I wanted to consider. Fire *terrified* me. It was a shame I'd already dealt with it once this weekend.

'Probably to try and cover *that*.' Bernard knelt at the victim's side, aiming a flashlight towards the charred corpse.

All I could see was blood, his semi-naked form oddly unrecognisable in this light. A smell of rusted iron and barbequed meat hit my nostrils, overwhelming, disgusting. Several evidence bags had already been collected, details collated for later viewing, plastic numbers scattered around, highlighting potential important areas.

'What am I looking at?' I couldn't help narrowing my eyes, holding my breath as I spoke. It didn't help that it was dark and I didn't have my glasses.

'Well for starters, his throat was cut.' Bernard pointed towards a bloodied neck that shone bleakly against his torchlight.

'And…?' Whenever Bernard said "for starters" there was always more.

'*And*, someone decided to cut off his penis.'

*Shit*. I couldn't bring myself to look. I hadn't noticed, didn't want the image in my head. I took a breath, needing a moment to gather my thoughts.

'Do you know if his throat was cut first or…' I pointed a wayward finger towards his nether region, glad that in the dark no one could see the horrified look my face had formed. Mutilations were never easy to look at, no matter how many times I witnessed the results, the cruelty of human beings never failing to alarm me. Thankfully the darkness was keeping my imagination at bay, encroaching shadows preventing a clear image.

'Not sure, yet. I'll know more once I get him back to the lab.' Bernard's words weren't comforting. 'Although massive blood loss suggests he was *alive* whilst he was being mutilated. There's something for you to mull over.'

I shuddered. Bernard noticed.

'Was he aware of…' I couldn't finish my sentence. The idea of being burnt was unpleasant enough, the concept that he was *aware* of having no dick, unthinkable. I hoped the killer had cut his throat first, spared him the misery. He'd have been oblivious by then, dead, no awareness of the humiliation that would keep the rest of us awake tonight.

'Again, hard to say for certain. I *can* confirm the killer probably wanted to cover their tracks by burning the body. Luckily someone noticed and put the fire out.'

I raised my eyebrows. '*Luckily?*'

There was nothing lucky about what had happened to this poor sod. I glanced at his ankles, charred soot where his ankles used to be, his legs black, unrecognisable.

Neither Paul nor Bernard responded.

'Motive?' I wanted to believe this was a random attack. Wrong place, wrong time.

'That's why *you're* here,' Paul chipped in.

*Of course.*

'We found this,' Paul said, handing me an evidence bag.

'What is it?' I took the bag from him, holding the contents against the light of a nearby streetlamp. A feather. It had blood on it.

'It was jammed between his legs,' Bernard confirmed, no emotion on his masked face to express his feelings.

I winced. 'When you say jammed, do you mean…?'

'Yep. Proudly erected where his manhood used to be.'

I didn't need that image in my head either. Did he *have* to say the word "erected"? 'Could it have been the wind?' The feather was large, black, I think, although in this light it was difficult to tell.

'Possible, but highly unlikely.' Bernard got to his feet, all three of us hovering over the body on the ground.

'Why?'

'Because unless a freak gust blew it directly over his crotch before getting wedged down there, I doubt it innocently fell from a passing bird. More likely to have been placed there deliberately.'

'Like a calling card?' My words were unexpected. Both men turned to look at me.

Bernard nodded. Paul was biting his lip. I was contemplating throwing up.

'Why the hell would someone place it *there*?' Paul couldn't help asking. I knew what he was thinking.

'Same reason they cut off his penis, I suppose,' Bernard confirmed. The man needed a strong stomach to do his job, a lack of emotion required, a lack of *anything* needed to casually discuss such things without vomiting.

'For revenge, or to humiliate?' Paul looked my way, knowing it was my job to assess a motive.

'Or both?' I added.

Photographs had already been taken, images I would need to mull over later, with a coffee, studying the potential reasons for such vile actions. I turned the bagged feather over, recognising it as a crow or *raven*, my nephew Tim popping into my head along with a conversation I'd recently shared on a car park roof.

'Are crows common around here?' Paul asked, reading my thoughts.

'I think it's from a raven.' I was almost certain of that now, *my* turn to become the expert. 'Did you know there are

*The Lost Raven*

approximately eight thousand breeding pairs in the UK?' I was oddly proud I knew that fact, Tim's passion suddenly lodged in my head.

Paul furrowed his brow as if I'd lost the plot, his friend the "twitcher" a person he never knew existed until now. I couldn't overthink it. He probably secretly already thought of me as a *twit*, this new revelation just another part of his day.

'Crow, raven, what's the difference?' he stated, his eyebrows raised. I ignored the sarcasm.

I had nothing to say about that.

Instead, I handed Paul the evidence bag, trying not to notice the blood, ignoring the amused look my friend was now giving me.

'Maybe we should dub the killer "The Raven Rapist",' Paul chided, handing the bag to Bernard.

'Why?' What was I missing now?

Bernard took a breath. 'Because the poor bastard appeared to have been *raped* before he was killed.' He glanced towards Paul, a brief nod aimed flatly my way.

*Shit.*

'How do you know it happened *before* death?' I was trying not to hold my breath. Hadn't this man suffered enough?

'Because of the damage caused, the blood loss, the bruising. You don't tend to see that in dead tissue.' He looked at me. 'Want me to show you?'

'*No!*' I didn't mean to yell.

No one spoke, a few painful moments passing before any of us could move.

We'd each dealt with rape before, of course, yet it never got easier, never made me feel any safer walking the streets because I was a *man*. Rape is seen as a problem only women encounter, but it isn't always true. This poor sod was evidence of that. I hoped he didn't suffer. It wasn't a concept I wanted in my head. I wasn't looking forward to seeing the photographs.

'How did you get on with your case from yesterday?' I was addressing Paul, Bernard still privately amused by my reaction judging by the expression I assumed existed beneath his mask. I could tell by the way his eyes crinkled in the corners, the little chuckles that occasionally left his lips. Paul's rape case was a stupid thing to remember, none of my business, my question unimportant to this moment. I was trying to change the subject, failing miserably.

Paul sighed. 'Oh, you know. The usual.'

He turned, leaving me to assess the body and consider the type of killer who would do something this savage to a fellow human being. I didn't hang around long, didn't need Bernard's blatant amusement aimed my way. I almost stepped in vomit located near the body, provoking a further chuckle I also didn't acknowledge. Needless to say, I wouldn't be getting any sleep tonight.

# Twenty

## *Angela*

I have no idea how I got home but I woke up on my living room floor, fully dressed, blood on my shoes and vomit in my hair. It's the second time in as many days I've found myself in stranger's clothing, the poor girl who used to answer to the name of Angela Healy steadily disappearing between the cracks of a life. It matches my mood, my emotions, the way I've been failing to deal with things forever beyond my limited control. I don't *feel* like me anymore. I'm ashamed to admit it. I barely recognise the person I've become.

I try to think, yet I'm unable to recall getting on the bus let alone getting home, lingering memories still fuzzy in my head. This entire evening is wrong, impossible. Did I speak to the bus driver? Did I say anything stupid? *Shit.* A ticket is wedged in the side pocket of a pair of jeans I stole in a hurry, all the confirmation I need that my trip home actually occurred, although no memory of the journey remains. Perhaps I blanked it out, unwilling to play along with the evening's unmitigated events? I wish I could blank it *all* out.

I get to my feet and head into the kitchen, nothing on my mind aside from a cup of tea and my wayward thoughts. It's still dark outside, my ticking clock confirming it hasn't yet turned three. I must have passed out shortly after turning the key in the lock, the familiarity of my personal space enough to remove me from unwanted reality. I'm exhausted, the evening too much to deal with, not even aware I'm burning myself on the hot kettle until a searing pain shoots across my hand.

I reel backwards, the sudden intrusion intense, an angry whelk forming across my palm. It has an unexpected impact of waking me up, although a stranger's burning body is the only thing I see. *Jesus.* I close my eyes. Surely that couldn't have happened? I must have been dreaming. Maybe I didn't leave my flat at all and my visions are nothing but an unruly imagination brought about by a lack of medication, zero enthusiasm for life, anything that might provoke a much-needed reality check. Yet, every time I take a breath I smell his aftershave, his bloodied penis imprinted into my palm, boiling steam readily burning its phallic shape into my flesh.

I vomit into my kitchen sink, the sullied memory of his burning flesh and exposed body parts hitting me in the face like treacle. I *actually* cut off his penis.

*What the hell is wrong with me?*

How was I able to do such a vile thing without any thought of consequence or remorse? I don't remember much about it, if I'm honest, overriding anger the reason I was unable to stop until the thing was severed and in my grasp.

I can't blame the booze. Not tonight. Aside from a relatively untouched Cosmopolitan left on an unassuming bar and a few sips of wine I barely tasted, I haven't been drinking. I was determined to remain sober in order to keep a steady head. It makes my current situation all the more terrifying, my reality all the more worrying. I stare at my hands, a sudden urge to scrub them clean jumping into my mind, my brain screaming at me to tear the skin from my arms in case traces of his DNA still linger.

I run the hot tap, attempting to wash away anything incriminating, scrubbing my hands and arms raw with a scouring pad I use to clean saucepans. I no longer feel my own burns that have already turned an angry deep red, whelks forming to mock me, pain that in my heightened state I barely feel. Even when my hands bleed I still can't stop, acidic tears allowed uncensored freedom along with blood-soaked water that cascades down the plughole. I'm dirty, disgusting, wrong. I *deserve* to suffer. There's nothing more to be said about that.

I'm ashamed of how I behaved, mortified for luring a guy whose name I didn't dare ask into an alleyway with an intention I don't dare appreciate. I can't help the thoughts that race through my brain, can't prevent the vivid recollection of what I've done.

*Did I intend to kill him?*
Yes, I did. It is most regrettable.
*But why?*
Because he's a scumbag. All men are. They all deserve to have their penis's cut off and their dignity removed.
*So, do they all deserve to die?*
Yes. Yes, they do.

I yell freely into the silence of my assumed private space, no one to hear me, no one to care. *What the hell has happened to me?* I slump onto the kitchen floor and cry until I can't imagine any more tears escaping, nothing left to produce them. I have no energy to get up, no emotions to sedate my wild imagination beyond the agony of desperation that comes from nowhere. My throat hurts from screaming. I honestly don't know what more I can do.

My mobile is ringing again, still in an incriminating bag I left in my hallway. I take a breath, remembering the knife. Scrambling to my feet, I race into the hall, scrabbling around for the murder weapon, my ringing mobile lighting up the inside of my bag like Blackpool illuminations. Luckily the knife is exactly where I left it, at the bottom, covered in drying blood, my recently scrubbed hands once again succumbing to the agony of my painful reality. I drop the blade onto the floor, no consideration for the incriminating evidence I'm spreading around my home. If I was hoping to delude myself that I was dreaming, such thoughts have been firmly removed from my head.

I turn on the TV, wanting to know if they've found the guy, whoever he is, unconvinced I want to know his name, almost throwing up again when the club I attended earlier comes into full view of a shaky camera. A sullen faced reporter is standing some feet from the very alleyway I might never get out of my mind, the street cordoned off by police. I turn up the volume.

'...body of a young man, found in the early hours of this morning, seemingly raped with his throat cut and genitals removed. The police have yet to identify him, but he is a white male, late twenties to mid thirties, partially burned...'

I can't breathe, can't think, forced to stare blankly at an event happening inside a TV screen I *know* can't be real. Yet the incident is readily being confirmed, my callous act openly described to a soon to be enlightened public, my calloused hands the executioner. *Rape?* I vaguely remember holding my dildo, scarcely recall wanting to hurt him. Yet, I gave up, I'm sure I did, no enthusiasm to undertake such a vile act, no desire for *that*. As it is, the entire evening is now a blank, my memory serving only to mock me from afar. If I raped him, does that make me as bad as the man I've tried

*The Lost Raven*

for years to dislodge? Why does the newsreader have to make the incident sound so bad? Why does she have to look so *traumatised*?

'...police are taking this very seriously and have already dubbed the perpetrator "The Raven Rapist" because of a large black raven feather found with the body. Further details have yet to be...'

I take in a lungful of air, automatically glaring at my bag. A *raven* feather? Surely they can't mean *my* raven feather? The very feather I'd clutched to my chest so hard I thought it would break? I vaguely remember putting it in my bag for safekeeping but I haven't thought of it since, my time in the hospital seemingly so long ago now. I open the clasp, peering inside, my probing eyes wild, sore. I'm hoping I'm wrong, of course, yet unsurprisingly it's gone. My fingerprints are on that feather, the fact that I had it in my possession several hours earlier easily confirmed by a *shrink*.

I take an unsteady breath, unable to contemplate the ridiculous ideas now filling my mind. The police don't have my fingerprints on file, so I'm probably worrying about nothing, nothing for them to link back to me. It's a coincidence, that's all. I don't understand why they're linking a feather to this crime anyway. It makes no sense. I don't remember taking it with me, do *not* recall seeing it. Why do they assume it's connected? What the fuck did I do?

A scratching at my window catches my attention, a tree branch, of course, nothing else, only the breeze to blame. But I feel as if the ravens are outside, waiting, laughing, speaking to me through the glass. It's my imagination, I know. It doesn't help.

*You left one of our feathers at the scene. Are you completely stupid?*

I didn't mean it. It must have fallen from my bag.

*Why did you take it with you?*

I didn't realise I still had it in there. I wasn't exactly thinking straight.

*You don't say.*

Please don't be angry.

*Why would we be angry?*

Because I'm an idiot.

*You're famous now.*

Am I?

*Yes. You are The Raven Rapist.*

It should be fitting that my love of ravens would one day afford an elevated status, yet I can think of nothing above the noise in my head. I can no longer unravel reality from my own perplexed stupidity, sitting glued to the TV in a vague attempt to locate my sanity, my thoughts a knot of tangled string I'll never unravel. I flick channels constantly, hoping to find more news coverage and learn anything of interest about the impossible actions that have led to this impossible moment, *anything* about The Raven Rapist I don't yet know.

I don't remember using my dildo. I must have been in a terrible headspace to do *that*. I remember holding it, remember having disgusting thoughts I now don't want to recall. I can barely bring myself to check my bag for the evidence I'm unconvinced I left behind, blood I shed, pain I inflicted. My curtains are closed. I'm glad. I imagine the ravens outside, tapping the glass, mocking me, rolling their eyes in frustration. I swear I can hear them downstairs yelling, ringing my buzzer, spitting tiny stones against my closed window from their opinionated beaks as they fly by. I place trembling hands over my ears, unable to abide the noise they're making.

## The Lost Raven

*The Raven Rapist* sounds like a name the police would give a serial killer, someone capable of repetitive action, not a silly young woman wholly incapable of repetitive *thinking*. Yet I like the way it sounds, the way it flows from the mouth of the newsreader who has already confirmed it. I struggle to my feet and stand in the middle of my lounge, those three little words spilling from my own like nectar.

'The... Raven... Rapist... The. Raven. Rapist. *I am* The Raven Rapist.'

I laugh. I can't help it, although my voice sounds somewhat alien, strangled. *Me.* Angela Healy. Twenty-four years old, bipolar, oddly suicidal, frustrated by the entire world and fifty percent of the adult population, forgotten and discarded by those who were meant to love me. I offer a fleeting glance towards my mobile, knowing Newton has tried calling again. I wish he would leave me alone. I need time to think. A smile forms on my mouth, from where I don't know, but I like how it feels, my suffering temporarily placated. For a moment, nothing else exists, that simple title providing an unexpected concept of overriding power. I stare at my sore hands, palms trembling yet capable of far more than I understood until now. I don't know what I did with the feather, am still unsure how it's connected, but one simple fact remains.

I *am* The Raven Rapist.

*My name is Angela Healey and I am not defined by my actions.*

# Twenty-One

## *Newton*

Although still technically the middle of the night, the Eastcliff CID incident room was increasingly busy, the coffee machine working overtime alongside the minds of everyone who'd been called in at such an ungodly hour. This was hardly the Monday morning start I'd anticipated, my weekend passing in a haze of frustration that had ultimately led nowhere. We had a dead man with no genitals on our hands, his slashed throat and burnt legs enough to kick-start Paul's team into action, many blurred eyes awaiting further instruction. Alice handed me a cup of coffee and a smile, a simple gesture that saw me blushing long after she'd walked away. I almost drank it in one go, ready to blame the night, the cold, the crime scene I'd just attended.

I stood in front of a whiteboard purposefully positioned for the investigation, images taken not yet two hours earlier staring intently from freshly printed paper, the ink still drying. The body was male, mutilated, *raped*. Was he a victim of some random attack or was it premeditated? Did he know his killer? The guy was well built, able to defend himself in a fight, yet there were no reports of any fight breaking out. Did that mean he was somehow rendered unconscious and therefore unable to fight at all? I paced back and forth as Paul issued instructions and cups of tea. Why would someone be angry enough to instigate such a horrific attack?

The police had already taken CCTV footage from the nightclub, all nearby surrounding businesses shortly required to provide any recordings they had. They'd taken statements from those in attendance, bouncers, bar staff, *anyone* who might have seen the guy, remembered him. Was he alone or with friends, and if so, what did they see?

'Okay everyone, listen up.' Paul was addressing the room, his unshaven features confirming that, like everyone else, his private life had been disturbed in order to assess the brutal murder scene we'd just left. By the stern look on his face, nobody was getting any sleep tonight. 'We now have a name for our victim. Thirty-year-old, Corporal Mark Jenkins, currently based at Northcote Barracks, just outside Digsby.'

'Army?' someone at the back of the room asked, a hand raised in the air.

'Correct.'

'So capable of looking after himself?'

We all knew what was meant by *that* question. Paul took a breath, several of his team already muttering under theirs, no officer here willing to assume the guy was easy to overpower. He didn't look the type, his Army status enough to assume his supposed safety.

'Under normal circumstances, yes,' Paul confirmed to the group, knowing what everyone was thinking. The guy was six foot tall, muscular, lean. How could he have been attacked so easily, his throat cut, brutally raped from what early indications implied, his penis removed, the guy subsequently set on fire. It wasn't a pleasant image, the photographs on display not for comfortable viewing. 'Mark was out with a group of friends before leaving the club with a female at around eleven thirty. Nobody thought anything untoward about that until he was found dead a short while later.'

'So we need to find the woman he was with?'

'Obviously.'

Paul continued talking whilst I scanned the images peppering the incident board. Mark was well toned, tattoos lining his chest, a dog, a crown, another that looked as if it had been partially removed at some point, a girl's name no doubt, something he didn't want reminding of. His head was shaven, yet his features remained unaffected by the evening, as if he'd fallen asleep, not a hint of suffering on his face.

'There's a partial shoe print next to the body, but it appears to be from a stiletto, so we're assuming it came from either the woman he was with or a passerby.' Paul scoffed, glancing at the board behind him before resting his eyes on me. That might explain the vomit I almost stepped in. I didn't mention it. 'We'll know more when we've gone through all available CCTV footage.'

'Probably just a nosy, drunk woman,' someone laughed. A few others joined in.

'Or a drunk *tranny*,' someone else pitched in. 'It isn't just *women* who wear women's clothes these days you know.' More laughter erupted.

'Okay, enough!' Paul yelled, the evening's findings still fresh in his thoughts, Mark's body not yet cold in the morgue. He slammed his fist against the whiteboard.

Everyone fell silent. 'This is *serious*. A preliminary search of the area has uncovered a woman's dress, found in a nearby skip, covered in blood.' Paul pinned an image to the board of a green party dress now tinged with red, spread flat on a plastic sheet. I thought for a split second I recognised it, lack of sleep blending my recent days together.

A couple of officers grunted a vague acknowledgement that the crime scene would have probably been contaminated before the police arrived.

'Do we know if the blood on the dress belongs to the victim?' Alice asked, reading my mind. At least someone was being professional.

'We won't know much until the results come back from the lab,' Paul replied, 'but we can't, at this stage, rule out the consideration that the stiletto print and the dress aren't connected.'

Alice nodded her understanding. I was still looking at the dress. Someone muttered something else about transgenders and the idea that a man dressed as a woman might be to blame.

'If it was the same dress worn by whoever he left with, then somebody went home *naked*.' More laughter. 'If he was drunk, he might not have noticed he'd pulled the *wrong* type of female,' the same officer yelled.

Paul ignored the comments, as did I. Nobody could say at this stage if Mark was straight, gay, or somewhere in between, if he enjoyed the company of transgenders or if this speculation was even relevant.

I tapped the photograph of the dress. 'Where did you say this was found?' I queried. My paper coffee cup was empty and I was absentmindedly chewing the rim.

'About half a mile from the club, in a skip behind Tesco.' Paul looked exhausted. Everyone did.

'Nothing else?'

'Not that we know of. Why?'

'I think I recognise it.'

'How?'

'I think it's Angela's.'

'Who?'

'Angela *Healy*.' I glanced towards my friend, hoping he'd remember her. It was only two days ago. He was the one who'd called me, got me out of bed, sent me to the top of a car park in an icy breeze.

'The jumper?' Paul sounded as if he'd already forgotten all about her. I tried not to roll my eyes.

'I think she was wearing it at the time.' Or something similar. I tried to think back, my memory keen to fail me, eager to laugh in my face. 'I only remember because it was vivid green with gold glitter piping along the front that looked as if she'd been zipped into it backwards. And it was short. Too short.' I sounded like someone's dad. I couldn't believe Paul had forgotten.

He stared at me, confusion planted across his cheeks.

'Angela called me.' I was still staring at the image.

'When?'

I glanced at the clock. 'Must have been around four hours ago. Not long before you called *me*, actually. She sounded panicked. Do you think she was there? Do you think she *saw* something?' I didn't like the idea but I had to ask. She wasn't in a good place as it was, her thoughts troubling enough without having something like *this* in her head.

Paul pulled a face. 'I guess anything's worth a shot at this stage. We need witnesses. She might be a key one.'

I pulled my mobile from my trouser pocket. 'Should I call her?'

Paul shook his head. 'I have a better idea.' He grabbed his jacket, giving me an awkward sideways glance. 'Where's

## The Lost Raven

*yours*?' I never usually left home without it, the one I was wearing now worn purely out of urgency. It was Andy's actually, as mine was missing. Maybe Angela would give it back if I asked nicely.

\*\*\*

I wasn't surprised the lights were out when we pulled up outside Angela's flat. It was four o'clock in the morning. Where else was she going to be other than in bed? As we made our way towards the entrance we noticed a woman sitting on the doorstep, her head in her hands, feet tucked tightly beneath her trembling body. It wasn't Angela. The poor thing looked near frozen to death, despite the coat she was wearing. She sprang to her feet when she saw us and sprinted along the street.

'Hey!' Paul called out. 'Don't I know you?' He seemed unconcerned he might wake the neighbours, a dog already alerted to the noise.

'What was that about?'

'I'm sure it's nothing,' he replied, although his face had knotted, his eyes narrowing in sharp response to the stranger disappearing along the pavement.

'Who is she?' I couldn't help asking. She seemed almost as vulnerable as Angela, almost twice her age.

'It looked like the woman Alice and I interviewed on Saturday.'

'The rape allegation?'

Paul nodded, ringing Angela's buzzer, glancing periodically along the darkened street, his thoughts twisting violently.

'Go away.' A blurry voice echoed through the intercom, interrupting any thoughts I might offer. Angela sounded even more fragile now than she had the day we met.

'It's the police. I need to speak with Angela Healy, please.' Paul raised his voice so he'd be heard through the crackling speaker.

There was a moment of silence, a pause before she answered. 'What do you want?'

'I'm Detective Chief Inspector Mannering. I'm here with my colleague, Doctor Newton Flanigan. Can we have a moment of your time please, miss?'

'Shrink Bloke?' Angela sounded surprised.

*Shrink Bloke?* Nice.

Paul muffled a chuckle, not daring to look at me in case he burst into unwanted laughter. 'Can you open the door please, Miss Healy? I'd much rather we speak face to face.'

A further moment of silence, then a click as the door unlocked. Paul pushed it open, allowing me to step into the building ahead of him. 'Come on, *Shrink Bloke*.'

I ignored that.

Paul was still trying to muffle his amusement as we made our way to the top floor, composing himself when he saw Angela already waiting on the landing. She was dressed in pyjamas, trembling, her mousy features unreadable, her hands red and sore. She'd been crying.

'Sorry for the inconvenience, Miss Healy.' Paul took his identity badge from his pocket and held it out so Angela could see. 'But we have a couple of questions we'd like to ask you.'

Angela looked as if she'd been caught in a set of approaching headlights. She smoothed hair that looked as if she'd been recently plugged into an electrical socket, her movements jittery, as if she'd consumed too much coffee. I could use one myself, come to think of it.

'Come in,' she muttered, stepping into her flat, grabbing a jacket from a hook in the hallway that she quickly stuffed behind a plant pot. *My jacket.* I pretended not to notice.

## The Lost Raven

'What do you want?'

'I'm sorry to call at such an inconvenient hour, but we were wondering if you recognise the item in this photograph?' Paul held an image of the green dress towards her, a piece of folded paper as unassuming as I imagined Angela's response would be. What if I had this wrong? Would it tip her further towards the edge of her already failing existence? What if such a confrontation did nothing but bring back terrible memories she might not appreciate being raised?

Angela took a moment to absorb the contents, glancing hastily towards me as if she knew all too well what I was thinking. 'No,' she shook her head, pushing a strand of hair from her face. She looked nervous, wringing trembling hands together that she quickly placed behind her back.

'Did you go out at all earlier this evening, Miss Healy?' Paul was surveying the hallway floor, scanning prying eyes across several pairs of shoes, no doubt hoping to locate one with a bloodied footprint.

'No.'

'So you haven't left your flat for any reason?'

'No.'

I half expected her to add, "comment" to the end of each response. She couldn't have sounded guiltier if she tried. I glanced around, her hallway nothing more than a tiny space littered with rubbish and discarded clothing. Angela didn't look much better. When was the last time the poor girl slept?

Paul folded his sheet of paper and placed it back inside his pocket. 'Do you know a gentleman called Mark Jenkins?'

'Who?'

Paul pulled a photograph of our victim from his pocket, an innocent smiling image the police had managed to retrieve from his social media pages. I wasn't even sure if his family had been told. He looked nothing like his picture now.

Angela glared at the image, hesitating, the confused look on her face telling me everything I needed to know. She *knew* him. Paul looked at me as if he was glad I'd taken him from his busy schedule, glad I'd raised suspicion.

'Do you know him?' Paul was still holding the image in front of her.

'Why would I?' Angela was fidgeting, shifting from foot to foot.

'You haven't met him by chance?'

'No.'

'Have *never* spoken to him, even in passing?'

'No.'

'Okay.' Paul looked at me. 'Well, thank you for your time, Miss Healy. I'm sorry to have bothered you.' He turned sharply, heading towards the front door. Angela took a deep breath, openly glad we were leaving, continually glancing over her shoulder towards her front room. I couldn't see why. Maybe she was embarrassed by her housecleaning failures. I knew the feeling.

'Oh, just one more thing before I forget.' Paul paused, offering Angela a smile that, to anyone else, might have looked innocent. Angela's eyes widened, she looked terrified. 'Would you be able to come down to the station when you're free and provide a DNA sample? It's purely so we can confirm the dress in this photograph isn't yours and eliminate you from our enquiries.' Paul smiled, trying to appear relaxed, not wanting Angela to assume she was under suspicion at this stage.

'Why do you think that dress belongs to me?'

Paul glanced my way. I swallowed.

'My fault,' I pitched in. 'It looks remarkably like the one you wore on Saturday morning.' I could feel my cheeks glowing red.

'For God's sake, I don't own Topshop, you know. It could be *anyone's*.' Angela folded trembling arms across her chest, her sudden outburst a contradiction to her earlier quietness.

'Are you now confirming you *do* own a dress like it?' Paul was hovering in the doorway.

Angela hesitated. 'Yes. No. Not anymore.' Another pause. 'I threw it away.'

'Why?'

She didn't respond.

'Where?'

No answer.

'In a skip?'

Angela swallowed. We both noticed the shock on her face. Paul had his answer.

'So you'll come to the station when you're free?' Paul smiled again.

'Sure. No problem.' She glanced around, trying to return Paul's smile but it looked as if she was struggling to get her lips to work.

'Thank you.' Paul's tone was too relaxed for my liking. 'No rush. Any time will do. As long as it's today.' He stepped onto the landing, leaving me to say our goodbyes, apologise on his behalf, exactly how he knew I would. 'By the way, did you know that someone was on your doorstep when we arrived?' He was already halfway down the staircase.

Angela shrugged. 'I'm not the only one living in this building. It was probably one of the neighbours.'

Paul nodded vaguely and turned to leave, disappearing down the stairs, out of view. He didn't contradict her.

'Why do the police want my DNA?' Angela whispered once Paul was out of earshot, looking at me now as if she expected me to save her. *Oh, the irony.*

'I'm sorry about that.' I *was* sorry. 'It's just not the type of dress you'd forget easily.' I'd *never* forget it, would probably never get the image of her wearing it out of my head. She'd looked so fragile, so vulnerable, so alone. She didn't need to know.

Angela stared at me but didn't reply, didn't confirm or disregard my comment. I wanted to ask if she was okay, if there was anything she wanted, anything she wanted to *tell* me. Instead, I smiled weakly, stepping onto her landing. 'I'm always available, any time, day or night if you want to talk.' I knew she did. She'd already called me. Twice.

***

'Why didn't you question Angela further?' I was sitting in Paul's passenger seat, the first flicker of dawn threatening to appear over the horizon. He was well within his right to bring her in, if he chose to do so, demand an explanation, her DNA. I was rarely wrong about these things, my instincts always serving me well. We both knew that dress belonged to Angela, and we'd both witnessed her slinging my jacket behind a potted plant. Why didn't he probe more?

'She looked terrified. I wasn't about to wade in with both feet. How would that have made me look?'

'Why not, you usually do.'

Paul tutted. 'Firstly, if she's as fragile as you say she is, Newt, I don't want to be the one to tip her over the edge. I don't want *that* on my conscience, thank you very much. Secondly, as I said, she looked scared of something. We don't know her involvement yet, if any. If she's hiding something or protecting someone, she'll slip up. We'll find out. If she knows who Mark Jenkins is, we'll know soon enough.' He glanced my way, knowing Alice was already searching through CCTV footage from the club. 'You know how this works.'

'You mean you want *me* to do some digging?'

Paul smiled. 'Well, what else do we pay you for?'

I raised my eyebrows, an automatic response. 'Why do you think that woman was outside Angela's property at this time of the morning?' If it was a coincidence I couldn't yet tell, so tired I could barely tell the time.

'No idea.' Paul was manoeuvring his car into the police station car park. 'Her name is Rosie O'Connor. Forty-one years old. Looked as terrified this morning as she did when we spoke to her about the alleged rape on Saturday. I might need to find out more about her and if she knows Angela Healy.'

I was staring at my friend, trying to figure out his thoughts. He didn't notice.

'Why did Miss Healy have your jacket?' he asked, turning off the engine.

'Because I leant it to her.' I was embarrassed now.

'Then *why* did she stuff it behind a plant pot?'

I sighed, glad he'd noticed that. 'Now *that's* the million-dollar question.'

Paul patted me on the back as we climbed into the morning air, leaving me to my thoughts as I ambled across the car park to collect Andy's car, calling him in case he was already out of bed and hadn't yet noticed my hastily written note. He was drinking my coffee by the sounds of it, my machine grinding away in the background.

'Don't worry about the car, it doesn't matter,' he muttered absently, a wayward yawn escaping his mouth that kick-started my own in response. 'Everything okay?'

I glanced towards the station, Paul already through the door, already anticipating another long day of unrewarding brick walls and bureaucracy. 'Of course,' I lied. 'You?'

Despite my frustration, the man was still my friend. He sounded depressed.

'Yeah. It's just that…'

I took a breath, ready for more revelations.

'Am I okay to stay a bit longer? A couple of weeks maybe? Definitely no more than a month.'

I should have known I wouldn't be enjoying his company for just a few nights. Yet, what kind of friend would I be if I didn't offer him a place to stay, a sanctuary when he needed one?

'Sure,' I confirmed when I really wanted to say *no, go away*. 'Stay as long as you need.'

I got off the phone, swore, and immediately called Stephanie. It didn't matter that it was still early and she'd still be in bed, the boys not yet up for school. I needed a friendly ear, someone who wouldn't mind if I had a good moan. Heaven knows I needed one.

# Twenty-Two

## *Angela*

*Shit, shit and shit with knobs on.*

What the *fuck* was Shrink Bloke doing with the police, at my flat, standing in my hallway as if they were on a casual day out? I couldn't help slamming my front door behind them as they left, bolting it top and bottom in case they changed their minds and returned, a warrant the only thing needed to unravel *everything*. There is still evidence lurking inside these walls I haven't disposed of, blood behind my fingernails I haven't washed off.

I take a breath, glad they're gone, grateful they didn't feel a sudden urge to search the place and ruin it all. I watch as they drive away, peering through my trembling curtains, holding my breath. I can't believe they've already found my dress, a request for my DNA something I didn't expect so soon. *What the hell?* I need to defer attention from me, stop the panic that's bubbling in my gut. My dress is covered in that guy's blood, only a matter of time before they match it to his body, my DNA something I won't be able to deny. I can't believe they showed me a picture of him.

I don't want to but I call Newton, waiting as long as I dare before dialling his number, hoping he's alone so we can talk in private. I need to know why he pointed wagging fingers my way, what they know that I don't.

'Angela? Are you okay?' The idiot sounds genuinely concerned for me.

I don't know where to begin. I wish this weekend had never happened, wish I hadn't got carried away.

'Angela? Are you there?'

'Why did you bring the police to my home?' I can't believe how quiet my voice is.

A sigh. It sounds as if he's driving. It's still fairly earlier, still too early for breakfast, too early to think straight. 'I was worried something had happened to you.'

'Why?'

'Because of your dress.' There's a pause. 'The one you were wearing the other day.' We both know to which day he's referring.

'It's not *my* dress.' It's not true. I deliberately altered my dress to include a fake gold zip that outlines the entire thing front to back. It was, in fact, my favourite part about it, the reason I am distressed that it was so readily discarded. I can't decide if Newton is concerned for me, or if he's *onto* me. Nothing makes sense.

'Well, that's easily dealt with. All the police need is a sample of your DNA and they can eliminate you from their enquiries.'

But my DNA *is* on that dress. All over it, in fact, including fingerprints and other bodily fluids I don't wish to think about. Neither can I knowingly confirm I didn't wet myself with hyped anxiety, a damp patch potentially still drying. It's not the first time it's happened during a stressful event.

'What if I refuse?' I'm practically whispering into my phone in case someone overhears.

'It wouldn't be wise.'

'But this has *nothing* to do with me.' I slump to the carpet, nowhere else to go, my legs buckling beneath me.

'Then why would you refuse?' I visualise his granddad smirk, a roll of tired eyes, hair flopping in the breeze.

Good question. I close my eyes, needing to share something I've promised myself I'll tell no one. 'Because the dress I wore that day was the one I was *raped* in.' The words are out of my mouth before I can stop them. *Shit*. No going back now.

'You were *raped?*' I hear a set of brakes, as if he's pulling hastily over to the side of a road. I hope he doesn't crash.

'Yes.' *Stop it, Angela, just stop it.*

'When?'

'Friday night.'

'Is that the reason you were up on that roof?' he sounds as if it's all slotting into place for him.

I can't speak. I release a muffled sob into the air, allowing Newton to hear the magnitude of my pain for the first time.

'Oh my goodness, Angela, why didn't you tell anyone?'

'Because I didn't want anyone to know.' I still don't, still can't believe I'm telling *him*.

'You could have talked to me. I can help.'

'No one can help.' I bite my tongue, wishing I'd just shut up, willing myself to hang up before I hang *myself*. I had nowhere else to go but down, my plight still not confirmed. I still feel as if I'm falling. 'I'm okay.' I don't know how to avoid providing my bodily fluids to the police.

'Do you mind telling me what happened?'

'I don't want to talk about it.'

'But you ended up on a rooftop at five o'clock in the morning.'

'All I remember is waking up in one of the bedrooms.'

'Whose bedroom?'

I can't tell him.

'Angela?'

'Just a party.'

'Where?'

'Does it matter?'

'Of course, it matters. Why don't I speak to the police-'

'*No!*'

A sigh. 'What did you do with your dress?'

*Shit.* I can't tell him. 'I gave it to a charity shop.' *Liar.*

'You didn't put it in a skip?'

'No.'

'You sure?'

I don't respond. I feel as if I'm being strangled, my lies steadily poisoning me.

'Angela?'

'I'm not sure about *anything* anymore. I honestly don't know where all the blood came from.' *Another lie.*

Newton is quiet and for a moment I believe he's hung up. 'So the dress found in the skip *is* yours?' he says eventually.

*Fuck.* 'Yes.' I don't mean to say that aloud, whimpering now, tears falling.

'And so your DNA will be on it.' He's whispering, worried someone might overhear him.

'Yes.'

Actually, all the evidence you need to convict me of murder is still on the bloody thing. Why did I wear it again? Because I'm a cocky, stupid, bitch. I thought by wearing it, I could prove a point, take back control, demand respect.

'Please don't allow them to take my DNA.'

## The Lost Raven

'I can't do that, Angela.'

'Why?'

Newton takes a breath I'm not sure isn't about to seal my fate. 'Because, unless you explain your recent attack, the police won't understand why your DNA is on the dress. They need to take your DNA. By any means necessary.'

Silence.

'So you still need to come into the station, I'm afraid,' he continues. 'You'll need to explain what happened, tell them what you've just told me.'

I really haven't thought this through. *Shit*. I pull the phone away from my mouth and muffle a scream, unable to believe the crap I keep getting myself into.

'I didn't have *anything* to do with any crimes, I promise.' I'm in tears, lies pouring from my lips like water from a leaking tap. I said "crimes". I hope he hasn't noticed.

'Do you *know* the man who attacked you?'

*Yes, I do.*

'No.' I want to believe my confirmation, want to block it all out. If I told him about Liam, the police would do nothing. He'll get away with it, just like my father did, a stupid mistake the only reason he ultimately ended up in prison.

'Did Mark Jenkins attack you, Angela?'

I can see Newton is trying to add two and two together to find a reasonable conclusion, trying to understand why the guy ended up dead. But he couldn't have this more wrong if he tried.

'I don't know *anyone* called Mark Jenkins.' Saying his name aloud isn't helping. It makes me feel sick. I'm glad Newton can't see. I *do* know him. *I killed him.*

He takes a moment before speaking again. 'Why don't you arrange to go to the police station later today? I can meet you there if you-'

'*No!* Please don't make me tell them what happened.' I'm clutching at straws. I can't help it. 'Please, I'm begging you. This needs to stay between the two of us. Promise me.' I'm a terrible liar, my face giving me away every time, learning to hide my problems behind a mask everyone assumes is reticence.

'What are you afraid of?'

More Silence.

'Are you still there?'

I nod, vaguely releasing a response that sounds like a strangled cat.

'It's okay. Nobody is going to make you do anything you don't want to do.' It is the second time he's said this to me. I don't believe him. 'Angela, why did you put your dress in a skip?'

'Because I wanted it gone.' *Shit, Angela shut up*. I clamp my hand over my mouth, too late.

'And the blood?'

'Nothing to do with me.' Newton is strangling me through the phone, his cold hands reaching towards my throat. I'm struggling to breathe.

'Were you in Shelby last night?'

'*No!*' The hole I'm digging is large enough to bury me if I'm not careful. Bury everyone around me.

'Why are you lying?'

'I'm not.'

'The police *will* find out what happened. It's in your best interest to tell the truth.'

I can't speak, can't think, can no longer continue this conversation. I hang up before I say anything that will seal my pathetic fate forever.

\*\*\*

*The Lost Raven*

I pace until my feet ache and the sun begins to creep through the gaps in my still-closed curtains, ignoring several calls from Rosie until her persistence forces me to relent and answer. She sounds like *shit*.

'I've been trying to call you.' Her irritated voice vibrates against my ear, making me roll tired eyes towards the ceiling.

How do I begin to tell her the hell I've been through? 'Sorry.' I can't be bothered to offer anything more than that right now. It's been a long night and I'm exhausted.

'You okay?'

'Yep. All good.' I can barely speak.

'I came to see you last night.'

'When?' I stop pacing and stare at my window, my drawn curtains no protection from the outside world.

'It was late. I couldn't sleep.'

'Why?'

Silence.

'Rosie?'

'I saw the police outside.'

'When?'

'Around four.'

'What the hell were you doing outside at *that* time?'

'I told you, I couldn't sleep.'

That explains the noises I heard. I can't tell her I thought she was a *raven*. I don't assume she will appreciate that. I feel bad now.

'Did you throw stones at my window?'

'Yeah. Sorry. I was trying to get your attention.'

'Did the police see you?' I'm worried she told them something about me.

'Yeah, but I ran off. Didn't want to deal with any more shit.'

'Bloody hell, Rosie, it was four in the fucking morning.

What the hell were you doing walking the street at that time?'

'Sorry.' My friend's turn now to apologise. 'What did they want?'

The question hits me hard. I can't tell her. 'Can this wait? I have a headache and I'm not sure you want to be in my company right now.' It's true. I need sleep and the last thing I need is to explain my unexpected involvement with the police.

'Okay.' A pause. 'Sorry to have bothered you.' Rosie hangs up abruptly. I ignore the sarcasm in her tone, the hurt behind her words. I'm honestly too tired to care.

\*\*\*

I spend the day pretending to be unwell so I don't have to go to work and face anyone, throwing a flu virus and my bipolar disorder into the mix as the reason I'm sick, keeping my flat door locked and bolted. I'm determined to avoid the police and everyone I know for as long as possible, assuming they'll be back at some point, probably with an arrest warrant, the idea of barricading myself inside, a very real possibility. They will expose my pain, my lies.

I order a takeaway because I have no energy to cook, unable to get out of my pyjamas or brush my hair. It isn't ideal, depression not something I endure by choice. I spend too long stalking Liam on social media, hating what he's unwittingly turned me into, what he did to me still painfully real, the man unaware of the consequences his actions have triggered. I don't know what I'm planning to do when I see him again. All I know is nothing good is heading his way, nothing I can dislodge from my already poisoned brain about the punishment I'm planning to inflict.

I keep the news channel on in the background, unable to

## The Lost Raven

turn off my TV in case I miss something, greeted occasionally with non-descript updates of The Raven Rapist. It's an impressive name and the more I hear it, the more I like it. I love ravens, always have, devouring everything I can about them, my once innocent adoration for these birds steadily becoming an obsession. Every time someone mentions The Raven Rapist, be it on TV or social media, something inside tingles. I don't know why.

Newton calls me a few times, leaving messages I don't wish to acknowledge. I shouldn't have told him about the rape, the guy already assuming I'm a mental case. I'm too deep inside my head now to acknowledge the outside world anyway, manic episodes coming thick and fast. I've been trying to subdue them, of course, yet the last one ended with a giant raven standing in the corner of my bedroom telling to me commit more murders or forever suffer the consequences. Eventually, these four walls and my hallucinations become too much and I pull on a pair of boots and Newton's jacket, heading into the afternoon air, my single intention to spend time with *real* ravens. I'm still dressed in my pyjamas.

It's cool outside and the breeze is bracing, a shocking yet welcome relief from the stifling atmosphere of my flat. I trudge along the main road, past Sainsbury's that I never shop at because it's too expensive, down a side street towards a patch of woodlands I'm grateful exist. I want to be alone, my thoughts and my birds the only company I need. It doesn't matter that relentless chatter about The Raven Rapist has triggered the need to find more feathers, the *real* reason for today's mission bubbling violently in my mind. I can't get the weekend out of my head, two men potentially dead because of my actions. I stop in the street, something on my mind I can't sedate. For the first time in my life, *I* held all the power. I loved it. What the hell does that say about me?

I head away from the bustling town, along a narrow track where cars are allowed to park as long as they don't leave unwanted litter, a disused CCTV camera hanging from an old tree to try and combat anti-social behaviour. Yet, the only people who venture here are dog walkers and *me*. My boots pad along the softened ground dusted with leaves of brown and orange that crunch underfoot. I take a breath, absorbing a familiar fragrance of pinecones and earthy moss from nearby conifer trees, a pungent aroma of autumn carried on the breeze. If I could, I'd move here permanently, but I like running taps and electricity too much. It probably wouldn't work long term.

I scan the ground for raven feathers, gathering the best specimens I can find, placing them carefully in my pocket so I don't crush them. Eastcliff has unwittingly formed the perfect habitat for these beautiful birds, its rocky coastline and densely wooded areas idyllic. They prefer forests, of course, and Chestermill Woods, set on the outskirts of Shelby, is the perfect location. But it's not a drive I want to endure today, grateful for the few breeding pairs that live here. I can hear them overhead, although I can't see them. It doesn't matter. The Raven Rapist knows they're close, and it's all she cares about.

# Twenty-Three

## *Newton*

For the rest of that day I thought of nothing but Angela Healy, checking my mobile regularly in case she'd left a message, losing track of the messages I left her. The Raven Rapist was now permanently on the lips of every Eastcliff resident, the media drawing whatever information they could glean from the local police in order to produce a fresh angle to their stories. Even Andy messaged me about what had happened, poor Mark Jenkins an unwitting subject of unexpected attention.

I got home from the university after an exhausting day of relentless teenage chatter, not expecting to walk through my front door to a smell of fresh paint, my lounge cleaner than I'd ever seen it. Bookshelves I'd been meaning to erect for months were now lining the far wall, awaiting further instruction, already housing books usually stacked on the floor. Cushions had been plumped, my dining table wiped clean. The place was spotless.

'Hope you don't mind,' Andy called out as I kicked off my shoes in the hallway. He was busy clearing away packaging material, flattening boxes, chasing polystyrene pieces around the floor with a dustpan and brush. 'I wanted to thank you for letting me stay.' He glanced around, his handy work something I'd have never achieved if left to my own devices.

'You honestly didn't have to do this,' I spluttered, feeling suddenly guilty for harbouring thoughts of resentment about a friend who needed nothing but help.

'It was no bother.' Andy grinned, scooping cardboard into his arms. 'Happy to help.'

That phrase. *Happy to help*. I used it myself all the time, yet until now I didn't appreciate its meaning. I smiled, heading into the kitchen to find the walls and ceiling scrubbed, cupboard doors replaced where needed, repainted where viable, a new stainless steel splash-back and hob in situ, more discarded packaging resting against a brand new back door.

'Again, no biggie, Newt,' Andy called out as he disappeared outside loaded with cardboard. 'What are friends for?'

I was at a loss for words, my spare bedroom nowhere near good enough to warrant such a kind gesture. I felt guilty for being secretly frustrated by the space Andy was unwittingly taking up in my life, my home constantly swamped by wet towels and empty mugs. I preferred my own company, my home no longer my sanctuary. Now I felt terrible for thoughts I'd been having in private. My friend needed a place to stay. I should be more supportive. After all, wouldn't *I* want help if I were in trouble?

'I'll pay you back,' I yelled.

'You already have.'

## The Lost Raven

\*\*\*

It was nice to be in a flat that didn't look as if a tramp lived there, the only smell of bleach now in my bathroom, my burnt surfaces all gone. Andy bought us dinner along with a new jar of coffee beans, the grin he gave me barely leaving his face for an entire hour. For a while, things didn't seem so terrible. I might get used to the idea, might ask him to stay forever. The following morning saw me smiling for the first time in days, a good night sleep enough to confirm my houseguest was nowhere near as annoying as I'd expected.

As it was, I headed to the police station in a relatively good mood, my first lecture of the day not due to start for a couple of hours. I needed to ask questions, catch Alice before her day became too much for the likes of me, no chance to talk if I didn't grab her whilst I could. She'd recently dealt with Rosie O'Connor, rape something I wasn't prepared to ignore, Angela's confession still on my mind. The police still required a DNA sample to eliminate her from an equally tragic and gruesome attack, the blood on a dress they didn't yet know was hers, potentially belonging to Mark Jenkins. I hadn't told Paul about Angela's confirmation, still hoping to protect her from the inevitable. I stood next to the coffee machine, frustrated by a slow-moving system and slow-moving mechanics, peeling the edge from a paper cup threatening to crumple in my grip.

'You okay, Newt?' Alice's warm smile greeted me as she drifted through the incident room door, several files in her possession, her glossy hair tied back to reveal glowing cheeks and beautiful eyes. Why she had such a profound effect on me, I had no idea. I'd spent my evening going through The Raven Rapist case, the fact that such a nickname was already circulating among the local press, not impressing Paul. It was his fault anyway, a throwaway comment, a dismissible phrase that had stuck. Such prolific names were usually only given to serial offenders, not the low-life chancer we were currently dealing with.

'Actually, I was hoping to have a quick chat with you if you don't mind.' I stood to attention, unable to disguise my blushes, unable to assume Alice hadn't noticed. I'd blame the coffee, if she asked, and the fact that Andy's unexpected thoughtfulness was playing on my mind. I didn't know how I could repay him, didn't assume she'd want to know my private business. Instead, I smoothed my hair, trying to straighten my crinkled shirt, wondering why I didn't own an iron.

'Well aren't I the lucky girl,' Alice laughed, still walking, oblivious to the thoughts I couldn't help having about her.

I smiled, licking dry lips, no immediate reply jumping to mind. Instead, I laughed, nothing else to do. *Christ alive, Newton, get a grip.* 'I need some information on that alleged rape incident from a few days ago.' I was attempting to sound professional, probably failing. Alice didn't notice.

'Which one?'

'The one you attended with Paul on Saturday.' It wasn't comforting to consider this type of crime happening often. I hoped there was only *one* rape incident that day.

'Oh, yeah. Poor thing looked terrified.' The look on Alice's face told me she'd seen far too many sexual assaults, wished things could be different, knowing, of course, it never would.

I shouldn't have asked but I needed an opinion on Rosie O'Connor. I didn't assume Paul would offer one, and I hoped to appeal to Alice's softer side, seeing as she was a woman. I still had the image of Rosie racing along the street at four o'clock in the morning.

'Can you help me?' I forced a smile.

'That's not exactly your line of work-'

*The Lost Raven*

'I know,' I cut in. 'I just want to check a couple of things, if you're okay to help. It's a theory I'm working on about The Raven Rapist case.' It was true.

'Didn't The Raven Rapist attack a *man*?' Alice looked at me as if there was nothing unusual in rape against women, the fact that attacks on men were far less reported and therefore more uncomfortable to acknowledge. Such a sad truth was hardly worthy of investigation, barely worthy of my time.

'I know. It's just that I'm working on an angle.' I didn't confirm it wasn't The Raven Rapist that was bothering me, but Angela Healy, the fact that the very same female who'd recently reported an attack had been outside her flat a few hours after a raped dead male was found. I couldn't get it out of my mind. My close involvement with Paul and his team ensured I was privy to such information if they deemed it important enough for me to double-check events, scan files, provide a second opinion.

Alice picked up the coffee I'd poured her in anticipation, taking a sip. She sat at her desk, placing a lipstick, her handbag and a box of tissues next to her computer. It provided an insight into who she was, what she was like, what made her tick. I liked it. She was busy tapping a keyboard, unaware of the thoughts I harboured when she didn't notice me glancing her way from the corner of my eyes.

'Rosie O'Connor reported the rape after a party she'd attended with work colleagues, although she stated she wasn't able to recall all the details.'

'Why not?'

Alice sighed. 'The police doctor performed a preliminary examination, took samples, the usual. She was found to have a substance called gamma-hydroxybutyric acid in her bloodstream.'

'What?' My attention was caught. It was the second time GHB had been found. I didn't believe for one second it was a coincidence.

Alice glanced my way. 'Gamma hydrox-'

'I know what it is. *When* was the party?' I sounded more frustrated than I intended.

Alice clicked more keys. 'Friday night. Unfortunately, Rosie has been unable to name her attacker, although it's not surprising she doesn't remember anything.' Alice didn't sound happy to be sharing this.

'Where was the party?'

More clicking of keys. 'Clayton Road.'

Clayton Road was three streets from Paul's house. He had teenage daughters. I dreaded to think what he'd think of such goings on so close to home. 'Did the police go to the property?'

'Do you think we don't know how to do our job, Newt?' I thought I caught a flicker of irritation flutter across Alice's face but it disappeared the moment it presented itself, making me question my thoughts, my sanity.

'Sorry,' I muttered. 'Do we know anything else?'

'Only that she works at The Royal Eastcliff Hospital as a receptionist for the Accident and Emergency department and has never had any prior involvement with the police.' Alice looked at me, wondering what I was thinking, no doubt pondering how these unsubstantiated facts could support any supposed theory I was having about The Raven Rapist.

'She *does* know Angela Healy.' I was whispering, talking mostly to myself.

'Sorry?'

'Do we have a guest list for the party?' I couldn't help finding it coincidental that Rosie O'Connor was raped the same evening as Angela, although I couldn't confirm they'd attended the *same* party. Not yet.

Alice looked at me, a blank expression confirming she had no idea why I was asking. She nodded. 'Yeah, I think so. Why?'

'Angela and Rosie both work in the same hospital department. It stands to reason that they know each other.' It at least explained Rosie's presence outside Angela's flat. I was talking aloud, batting information around the room that wasn't yet straight in my head.

'Angela?'

'The woman who tried to jump from a multi-storey car park.'

'What does the Rosie O'Connor case have to do with an unconnected suicide attempt?'

I took a moment to think. Angela told me about her attack in private, had begged me not to share the information with anyone, *especially* the police. Yet, I needed Alice's opinion. After all, it was why we were having this conversation in the first place.

'Angela told me she was also raped on Friday evening.' Even as I spoke I knew I'd betrayed a trust.

'She confirmed this?'

'Yes.'

'Reported it?'

'Not yet.'

Alice sighed. 'Then it's purely speculative, Newt. Nothing we can do to tie the incidents together, if that's what you're thinking.'

I was. It wasn't helpful. Women are attacked all the time. It's an unfortunate truth. It would probably make *me* suicidal too.

'Unless Angela Healy comes forward with evidence from clothing she wore at the time of her attack, we can't accuse the same guy. Whoever *he* might be.' Alice was right, as always, any evidence that might have been on her body, long gone by now.

'Actually, we *do* have her dress.'

'*What?* How?' Alice's puzzled features were beginning to concern me. I wanted to reach forward and smooth her furrowed brow. I didn't.

'It was found in a skip.'

Alice raised her eyebrows. 'The Raven Rapist case?'

I nodded. 'Hence the theory I'm working on.'

'You know this for sure?'

Another nod. 'I'd like to see the guest list. Our rapist might be on it.'

Alice gave me a knowing look. I wondered if we were both thinking the same thing.

'Was Mark Jenkins at that party? Did he rape those women? Was *that* why he ended up dead in such a vile way?' I was speaking aloud, throwing ideas around, hoping for a breakthrough I wasn't sure I'd get. It wasn't ideal that I was convicting the poor sod of something so horrific, no evidence to prove what was done to *him* wasn't a potential revenge attack made by someone who knew what *he'd* done.

Alice now understood the angle I was working, the way my mind was operating. 'I'll check the list, get onto the lab, see if we can get any matches from Rosie's clothing and the green dress.' Alice looked impressed with the connection I'd made.

'Do we know whose blood was on it yet?' I was chewing my bottom lip absently, a piece of skin peeling around the edge. I hadn't noticed.

'Not yet, but I bet you ten quid it belongs to Mark Jenkins.' Alice leant back in her chair.

'My thoughts exactly.' I was steadily becoming convinced the two incidents were linked, Alice now thankfully joining my thoughts, joining the dots. It was too

*The Lost Raven*

much of a coincidence. Both women worked in the same hospital, were attacked on the same night, potentially at the same party. It stood to reason their attacker would be the same person, someone who would have known them both.

'Do we know anything else about the party?'

Alice tapped her keyboard again. 'Yes. It was being held for a nurse called Liam Goodman for a promotion he's recently been given.'

I tapped my fingers against her desk as she tapped her keyboard. 'I wonder if Angela knows what happened to Rosie.' The poor thing hadn't yet reported what had happened to her, still unable to come to terms with such an unimaginable event. I assumed the police were already questioning everyone who attended, collating alibis, verifying movements. 'Did CCTV bring up anything from outside Lux nightclub?' I assumed it would have.

'Unfortunately, no. That drew a blank. The main camera that shows the front entrance was damaged last week along with two further camera's inside the club by an ex-employee looking for a promotion he didn't get. The owner is currently waiting for replacements.'

'What about nearby cameras?'

'The only footage we have was taken from a car hire company at the end of the street, but it isn't clear enough to pin point anything concrete.' Alice didn't sound happy to confirm it.

Paul came into the office then, interrupting our discussion. 'Are you looking for a promotion or something, Newt?' He tried to laugh but it was still fairly early, my friend not yet woken up, not had his morning tea. I ignored his sarcasm, tried not to smile at his inappropriate timing.

'Do you have much on this morning?' I asked. I'd finished my coffee now, already pouring myself and Alice a second cup, a wild thought popping into my head. I poured

Paul a tea at the same time, needing to keep him on my good side.

Paul shook a tired-looking head. 'No. Thought I'd kick back all day and watch telly.'

*Funny.*

I offered him a sarcastic smile, handing him a piping hot tea that he took with a grin.

'Do you have time to go and see someone with me? It would look better if you're there.' I could defer my morning lecture. No one would mind. Aside from a couple of hardworking students, most of them probably wouldn't notice.

'Who exactly are we seeing?'

'Rosie O'Connor.'

Paul raised his eyebrows. 'Why?'

'Humour me.'

Alice smiled, turning her attention to her computer, leaving Paul and I to our non-descript conversation.

Paul took a swig of his tea. 'Okay, fine. But you'll be doing something for *me* later.'

'What?'

'Haven't decided yet. I'll let you know.'

# Twenty-Four

## *Newton*

On first impressions, Rosie O'Connor appeared just an average middle-aged woman, her home a three-storey townhouse with a neatly presented front garden, trimmed lawn, potted plants by the front door and a welcome mat underfoot. I almost dropped my guard, almost assumed this visit might be easy. That was until she opened her front door, the dense darkness behind her confirming the obvious fear the poor woman was currently living in—curtains drawn front and back, last night's uneaten dinner abandoned judging by the smell wafting towards us.

'Hello again, Ms O'Connor,' Paul offered his kindest smile, his hands clasped together in front of him. 'I'm sorry to disturb you, but I have a few more questions if that's okay?'

Rosie nodded disgruntledly and stepped inside the property, leaving the front door open for us. A cat saw its chance, shooting through the gap, taking off along the garden path.

'Is it okay for the cat to—'

'She's okay. I forgot to let her out.' Rosie didn't look back, simply wandered into the kitchen where she stood by the sink, waiting.

'How are you?' Paul was trying to sympathise with the woman, yet I could see how nervous he was in the way he was clicking his tongue across his teeth.

'How do you *think* I am?' Rosie replied snippily. Paul didn't respond. I assumed it was Alice who'd previously done all the talking, his last visit made under uncomfortable circumstances. Rosie looked terrible, bags under her eyes where she hadn't slept, hair not brushed, her face pale, gaunt. She was trembling.

'Hello Rosie,' I pitched in, needing to put the poor thing out of her misery, Paul's attendance purely to appease me. We were standing in her dimly lit kitchen, a heady smell of rotting food lingering in the air.

Rosie glanced my way, seemingly having forgotten I was there.

'I'm Doctor Newton Flanigan. I was hoping to ask you a few—'

'I don't want any more examinations.' Rosie shuffled backwards sharply, clutching her arms around an oversized jumper in defence of words she assumed I was about to say.

'It's okay, I'm not that type of doctor.' I thought of Andy, about the traumas he must see daily, unwilling patients he'd no doubt been forced to deal with over the years.

'Oh.' Rosie relinquished the grip she had on herself. 'Can I get you a cup of tea or—'

'No. Thank you,' Paul chipped in. 'We shouldn't need to take up too much of your time.' He was waiting for me to hurry up, get to the point, still no idea what my intentions

## The Lost Raven

were or why we were there.

I took the hint. 'How well do you know Angela Healy?' I asked, coffee on my mind now, my throat dry.

'She's a friend. A colleague. Well, a friend *and* a colleague. We work together at the hospital.' Rosie was looking at me as if my question was unnecessary, stupid. So was Paul.

'Is that why you were outside her flat the other night?'

Rosie looked confused.

'You ran away from us.' I didn't want to highlight any potentially painful memories but I needed to confirm it.

'Oh, I'm sorry about that.' Rosie's legs faltered a little and she leant against the countertop, holding onto the edge in case she fell. 'I didn't mean to run.' I could tell she didn't want to think about it. 'I just wanted to see Angela. I wanted to talk to her about what had happened to me. I needed a friend.'

I could understand that.

'Do you know that Angela was also raped?' I didn't mean to blurt it out, didn't mean to sound so blunt.

'*What?*' Rosie sprang upright. So did Paul. He glared at me, unsure where I'd retrieved such information, no doubt wondering why I hadn't mentioned it beforehand. I probably shouldn't have said such a thing aloud, breaking Angela's trust so easily, yet I needed to know if the incidents were linked. I owed it to Angela and, now it seemed, to Rosie too.

'She hasn't mentioned this to you?' I didn't assume for one second she would. She'd barely confided in *me*.

'No. When did it happen?' Rosie was struggling to speak, struggling to breathe.

'I believe it was the night of the party. Friday evening.' Angela's rooftop escapades now made sense. 'Although she hasn't reported it yet.' I think I was addressing Paul but I couldn't be sure, glancing between the two, needing them to understand my motives, my theories. We all knew the police could do *nothing* unless she came forward, foolproof evidence required to build a case. 'I'm wondering if you can verify your whereabouts again. I appreciate it's probably not something you want to think about right now.'

'I already told the police everything I know.'

'And I'm so sorry to have to ask you again.' I was. I didn't like asking personal questions. I could have taken the information from her statement but I couldn't gauge her emotions from a sheet of paper.

Rosie nodded. 'It's okay.' She lowered herself onto a barstool. 'But I can't believe Angela hasn't told me. We usually tell each other *everything*.' She closed her eyes, painful memories swimming behind eyelids I was glad I couldn't see. 'We were celebrating Liam's promotion.'

'Liam Goodman?' I queried. Paul glared at me. He was the detective, yet here I was, seemingly privy to more information than him. I didn't look his way.

'Yes. He's the senior staff nurse. Or at least, he is *now*.' Rosie smiled, her feature's momentarily softening. 'It was a rare night off for those who attended, although it consisted of mostly his close friends and family.'

'What happened? If you don't mind talking me through it.' I was taking mental notes, the way she was picking at a thread on the sleeve of her jumper, her lip continually quivering.

Paul glanced at me sideways, silently willing caution in such delicate matters.

'I'm very sorry to make you relive it again,' I confirmed softly. 'But it's my job to assess the emotional state of—'

'I'm sure Rosie just wants to get on with her day in peace,' Paul pitched in, still waiting for me to hurry up so we could leave. I could tell he didn't appreciate me

## *The Lost Raven*

confirming Rosie's emotional mindset, unwilling to allow anything else to cloud her day.

I smothered a sigh. 'I promise we won't take up much of your time.'

Rosie nodded. 'I got to the party not long after Angela. I'd just finished a shift, so came straight from the hospital. She was on Liam's sofa, drinking. I didn't want to disturb her.'

'Why?'

'She has bipolar. She suffers from terrible anxiety and can be quite argumentative if she's having a bad episode.' Rosie paused. 'Especially when she's been drinking.'

I offered Rosie a blank look.

'To Angela, *her way* is the only way and if people can't see that then it's them who need help, not her.' I got the impression that Rosie had been on the wrong end of Angela's manic episodes before. I didn't ask. Instead I nodded, allowing her to continue. 'I went into the kitchen to get a drink. Got talking to a couple of people. It was a good party. Everyone was enjoying themselves.'

'Who's everyone?'

'Andy, Claire, a few others from the hospital. It's weird because I didn't see Angela again that night. I wasn't feeling very well, so Andy offered to drive me home.'

'And who is Andy?'

'The A&E consultant, Andrew Hansley.'

I felt the little hairs on the back of my neck prickle. It was ridiculous. Andy worked in A&E. It stood to reason that he would have been at the party if he could. I should have asked him, should have realised *he* might have been able to aid my mission directly.

'And did Andy drive you home?' My voice had formed a wobble. I'm not sure why. I'd driven his car myself *twice* last weekend. I don't know why that mattered.

'No. He got sidetracked by something so I got a lift back with Claire.'

I almost sighed audibly.

'Claire Simmons is one of the A&E nurses. We've already spoken to her,' Paul confirmed, in case I was wondering. He was looking at me, contemplating how much longer I was planning to be.

'She's a good soul. Always looks out for everyone,' Rosie added.

'And she took you *straight* home?'

Rosie nodded.

'What happened after you got there?' I was biting my lip. So was Paul.

'That's just it, I can't remember. It's like I told the female police officer the other night. I remember *getting* home but I woke up on my bathroom floor around six o'clock, naked, with bruises on my wrists and inner thighs.' She pulled the sleeves of her jumper over her hands before closing her eyes, not wanting us to see her injuries, not wishing to think back. I felt bad for making her relive the trauma.

'So you knew you'd been—'

'Of course, I *knew*. My body didn't feel right. I was sore...down *there*, and it hurt to pee. A woman knows her own body.' She paused. 'I called the police a few hours later. They came out and took my clothes, did an examination. The usual.' She could barely bring herself to look at Paul now, or me.

'Why did you wait so long before calling the police?' It was already early Saturday evening before Paul called to tell me he was on his way to an alleged rape with Alice. The poor thing must have suffered all day, alone.

Rosie shook her head. 'I was afraid to admit what had happened.'

I nodded. I didn't know how to respond to that.

## The Lost Raven

'But you say you have *no* memory of what happened between leaving the party and waking up on your bathroom floor?'

'No. As I said, I wasn't feeling very well, so I came home. Apparently, I had GHB in my bloodstream.' She glared at me, seemingly seeing me for the first time since my arrival. 'I don't want to assume someone at the party drugged me, but—' She looked as if she was going to throw up, as if she couldn't imagine someone sick enough to do that *or* follow her home. 'What happened to Angela?'

I wasn't sure I should say. It wasn't my place and she'd confided in me to remain silent. Yet, I'd already confirmed the attack and if Rosie remembered something, it might help. Angela had the same drug in her system. I didn't know if I should confirm that either. How could I tell her friend the incident had driven her to attempt suicide?

'Apparently, she woke up in one of the bedrooms.' I didn't know whose, hadn't yet extracted that information. We had no way of checking unless Angela cooperated. I didn't assume Rosie would appreciate the connection.

'You're saying someone at the party attacked her?' I could see Rosie didn't want to comprehend such a thing, didn't want such terrible thoughts in her head about the people she knew.

'How many guests knew you'd be home alone?'

Rosie glared at me. 'Everyone, I guess.'

It wasn't helpful.

'And did you see anyone leave the party around the same time as you? Do you think your friend Claire might have seen something?'

Rosie shook her head.

'And you're certain you didn't see Angela before you left?'

'I saw Liam talking to her at one point. I think he got her

a drink.'

Paul nodded. I knew what he was thinking. Liam Goodman was probably already on his list of people to speak to, eliminate from enquiries.

'Do you know a man called Mark Jenkins?' I took a breath, the reason for my visit coming into fruition.

Rosie furrowed her brow. 'Who's that?' She genuinely looked as if she had no idea who I was talking about, the local news obviously something the poor woman hadn't concerned herself with. I almost sighed audibly. I was hoping she'd know him, could help narrow my thoughts a little further.

Paul glared at me. He didn't know where I was going with this. I didn't look at him.

'Do you think Angela might know him?' I was clutching at straws, nothing else to do.

'She's never mentioned anyone called Mark Jenkins. He's certainly no one who would have been at the party and I don't think he works at the hospital.'

'Thank you, Rosie,' Paul pitched in, cutting off my train of thought. 'That's all we need for now.' He grabbed my arm and steered me into the hallway swiftly, almost giving me whiplash. 'What the *hell* are you doing?' he spat as he practically marched me outside, Rosie's cat still loitering by the front door, waiting for attention.

*What had I done now?*

'Detective?' Rosie called from behind us, no time for me to ask.

Paul turned, offering the woman a blank smile, his hand still gripping my arm.

'Do you think this Mark Jenkins had something to do with the attacks?' She was serious and Paul gave me one of his looks. The type that told me I was in big trouble.

Paul shook his head. 'I can't confirm that, no. He's

## The Lost Raven

nothing for you to worry about. Thank you for your time, Ms O'Connor.'

I glanced at my friend, unable to confirm she had a point. We didn't know much about Mark Jenkins or what he might have been capable of. Why was a dress worn by Angela Healey the night she was attacked discarded in a skip mere streets from where his brutally mutilated body was found? How could Paul not confirm that the guy *might* have been involved, that his death could have occurred as revenge for rapes no one had yet substantiated?

Paul made our excuses and left Rosie to once again ponder her trauma alone. I wasn't sure which was worse. Knowing someone had attacked her, or the fact that we didn't know who. Mark Jenkins' injuries could have been a coincidence *or* a direct link to both rapes. He could, of course, be innocent, just some poor sap in the wrong place at the wrong time, nothing to do with any of this. I wasn't sure I liked the way my theories were going as I climbed into Paul's car.

'Why the *hell* didn't you tell me about Angela Healy?' Paul did not sound happy.

'Because I only just found out.' I glanced his way. He was already driving away from Rosie's property, his face contorting in grim acceptance. 'Sorry.'

'And *please* do not mention the names of my murder victims to anyone else. It isn't helpful.'

'Sorry.'

'The only thing we currently know about Mark Jenkins is that he was a soldier. We haven't confirmed his movements over the weekend and I haven't yet divulged his identity to the press. This is a murder investigation, Newton.'

*Newton?* Christ, I really *was* in trouble.

'We can't go randomly connecting what happened to

him to *any* other crimes unless we have a valid reason to do so.'

'Sorry.'

'And if you say *sorry* one more time, I'll cut off your tongue.' Paul's cheeks were bright red, his forehead throbbing.

I sighed. Loudly.

'Angela Healy isn't your responsibility.' Paul was glancing between my disgruntled features and the road ahead, uncertain which one he was finding the most annoying.

'I know. But I hate to see people suffer.' It was true. I didn't even kill flies if I could steer them out of an open window.

'As much as I value your opinion, sometimes you can be a complete idiot.'

I stared out of the window. '*You* didn't have to sit with the poor girl on that rooftop. *You* didn't see the fear in her eyes.' I couldn't get it out of my head. It didn't matter what Paul thought of me. Angela deserved better.

# Twenty-Five

## *Angela*

I spread my newly acquired raven feathers across my lounge carpet, stroking each one, giddy on the power I don't deserve. I repeat the same phrase in my head for a while, smiling wildly, my thoughts distorted.

*I am The Raven Rapist.*

I don't know where the name came from but I'm fully appreciative of it, all the same, thankful to whoever invented the phrase in the first place. It gives me an edge I won't otherwise possess, a feeling I couldn't otherwise appreciate. Until a few days ago, I was *nobody*. Just Angela Healy from Eastcliff, twenty-four years old, single, painfully mistrusting of men, merely trying to get through the fragments of what's left of my tainted life the best I can. Yet, because of a recent incident I can never change, I've become far more important than I ever thought I'd be.

I watch the news constantly, checking my mobile, my laptop, flicking TV channels for anything of interest. I want to discover if the police are any closer to arresting me, any closer to confirming my involvement. I can't assume they won't, at some point, a request for my DNA already made. I can't hide forever, only a matter of time before the net closes in. Yet, I've only killed one person that I know of, *two* if Lee died. I haven't found anything newsworthy about him, so I assume they haven't connected the incidents. I can't dwell on that. It was an accident. I'm hardly a serial killer. Yet, the way they talk makes it sound as if they are looking for a *lunatic*.

They've confirmed the identity of Mark Jenkins now, constant news coverage showing the same photograph of him in his army uniform, his mug shot almost as prolific as Myra Hindley. I vaguely recall him telling me about his job, yet I wasn't listening, nothing he had to say worthy of my attention. The guy lived with his mum and dad. Had a dog called Pete. *What a stupid name for a dog.* I oddly don't feel responsible for what happened to him because if he'd kept his lustful thoughts to himself, he might not have ended up *dead*.

Although bipolar is a complex condition, most people with it can get by in life relatively well as long as they take their medication and keep stress to a minimum. Yet, for me, things are never that simple. I've lived with experiences very few people could process, forced to deal with shit no one ever should. Because of that, my condition has become somewhat warped over time, ensuring I'm often psychotic, chaotic, deluded in both my thinking and the actions I ultimately take. Nothing usually escalates beyond my drunken misfortune, punching someone in the face if they get too close, a kick in the testicles if they get too rowdy. No one ever presses charges, none of them see me as a threat. Not until now. This is potentially why I feel so overwhelmed.

## The Lost Raven

When my phone rings I almost ignore it, assuming it will be Rosie or Newton, *again*. However, I don't recognise the number, a landline, so I answer, my curiosity misplaced, nothing more.

'Miss Healy?' A distant voice hits my ear, a crackling line irritated by a painfully slow female vocal that sounds as if she's speaking inside a cupboard.

'Yes?' I mutter, rising to my feet, wondering if I should hang up and run, anticipating a police officer at the end of this call, my time up, my short-lived fame over.

'I'm sorry to call you under such circumstances,' the voice continues, unaware of my racing thoughts. 'I'm calling from Colhurst Prison. I'm dismayed to convey the sad news that your father passed away an hour ago and I was given your details as next of kin—'

For a moment I'm stunned. It was made abundantly clear to *everyone* that I was never to have contact with the man again. Yet, someone is calling me, confirming he's dead. I can't breathe, yet it isn't grief I'm feeling. How am I still listed as the man's next of kin? My instincts tell me to ask how he died, but I honestly don't care. I hope he suffered, painfully, choking his last breath in his cold cell, left alone to rot. I hope someone killed him, made him suffer as he made me suffer.

'Miss Healy, are you still there?' The voice sounds concerned now, worried for my wellbeing, believing that such terrible news has come as a shock.

'I'm here,' I breathe shallowly, berating myself for holding this conversation without screaming, no strength left to discuss the man I despise. I close my eyes, the momentary darkness allowing my father's features to loom towards me from the shadows, exactly how he used to. 'How did he die?'

'He was diagnosed with testicular cancer last year. Did

nobody tell you?'

Testicular cancer? *Wow.* I almost laugh at the irony. I'm crying. The voice on the end of the phone assumes I'm upset, shocked, grieving. I'm not. I'm devastated I've left things too long, no way for me to ever confront the man now. Anger, repulsion and hatred have kept me going, the idea that I might one day become strong enough to request a visit, all I had left. Now I have nothing. I *am* nothing.

Every emotion I've forced to the depths of my being bubbles to the surface and I release a yell that comes from nowhere. I hang up, unable to listen to any more words, pressing my hands over my ears, unwilling to acknowledge my thoughts, my turmoil. I always believed I'd confront him one day, tell him how much I detest him, observe the look on his face when he sees how strong I became, despite his best efforts. Now I can *never* do that, eight years too long a gap for me to change the past. It doesn't help that I've been off my medication for two weeks and it's beginning to take a toll on my already damaged brain.

I sit and stare at my laptop for an hour before I cave in and order more drugs, a demonic grin planted across my confused face, raw tears mocking my emotions. The guy on Facebook is surprised I'm back so soon. He doesn't care, of course, merely glad to be paid for his efforts. Besides, if I'm going to prison, I might as well have some fun.

\*\*\*

I'm in a strange mood now, my emotions made worse by news I never expected to receive. I'd always visualised my brutish father murdered in his sleep, the hands of some criminal who *loathes* "kiddy fiddlers" around his demented throat. As it is, my manic mood has ensured I can no longer see those metaphoric hands choking the last breath from the man's pathetic corpse, in the end *cancer* becoming the very murderer I'd dreamt of.

I amble around my flat waiting for my delivery, frustration building, my temper rising, an eagerness to go out on the prowl keeping me alert. After all, if the police are looking for a killer, I may as well put on a show. They are no doubt looking for a man, my tiny frame easily blending into a crowd. I'm just a *woman*, nothing more, incapable of hurting the brutish thugs I've already laid savage claim to. They won't look my way, won't see me for what I've unwittingly become. I might hang around this time, see how the police handle yet another brutal murder on their doorstep. And brutal it *will* be. Men are easy to target, easy to trap, and now my father is dead I need a way to dissipate my emotions, dissolve the fears I've carried so long. It's an odd feeling. I will have no issues attracting my next victim.

\*\*\*

I feel strangely confident as I head into Eastcliff, my hometown far more knowledgeable and familiar than Shelby. I'm dressed to impress, *wanting* to attract attention, hoping to do so with ease. The guy I choose is tall, dark-haired, a tattoo on his neck that, in this dimly lit bar, I'm unable to see clearly. I smile, he smiles back, a raven feather, my dildo, a bottle of death, and an eager knife all I need to conclude tonight's encounter.

Just like Mark Jenkins, whose name has welded itself to my brain, this guy is full-on, his wandering hands unwanted, his attention set one way. I take a breath, biting my bottom lip as he leans towards me, whispering in my ear. I want to scream, run, grab him around the throat and squeeze as hard as I can. Yet I stand my ground, my mission simple, *all* men deserving of what's coming to this one tonight, his life set to end before this evening is over.

I sense a case of déjà vu as he and I head outside, his hands lingering over my trembling body, onlookers smiling casually. He's on a promise, they assume. They couldn't be more wrong about that. I'm nervous, more so than before, grateful for the anger that floods my body, already numbed by alcohol and shock, my companion wholly unaware of the drugs I've poured into his drink. I feel nothing beyond the concept of revenge, rage my one true ally, tonight's actions resulting from my prior treatment, my father's death, the male species the reason for my uncontrolled wrath.

This guy is not a big drinker, unfortunately, and I hope the taste of lemonade is enough to disguise my heinous crime, every sip he consumes sending my brain into overdrive. I can't have him realise what I've done before I have time to *do* it. Luckily, it takes hardly any time for him to waver, stumbling around as if he's drunk, complaining of a headache. We barely make it into a nearby car park before he passes out, almost collapsing on top of me. I stare down at him, hating everything he stands for, everything he is. Methodically, calculatedly, I peel away his clothing, leaving him naked, vulnerable, exposed.

They readily named me The Raven Rapist because of a crime no one anticipated I'd commit yet, when I killed Mark Jenkins, the instruments I used were chosen at random, designed to satisfy an inner gratification I'm still not able to understand. I didn't *intend* to leave behind my precious feather, didn't *want* to become a killer. I wanted to hurt him, of course, anger the reason for the carnage I ultimately left behind. I didn't, however, mean to become so prolific, didn't mean to start this thing.

I felt nothing but desperation, no sense of the power that men have always held over me. Even the sight of blood as I cut off his penis didn't initially bother me, only

## *The Lost Raven*

registering with my brain in those frantic moments after he was dead. Tonight I've drunk enough wine to take off the edge, such an unassuming substance easily able to sedate my emotions from what I'm about to do. Tonight, I plan to take things to a whole new level. Bring on The Raven Rapist.

\*\*\*

When I'm done, my dark-haired beauty is lying in a pool of his own blood, his ruptured anus something I would have, at one time, baulked at, disgusted by the thought of it. Tonight, however, I'm too angry to care, acting on impulse, something deep inside now dead. It's my father I hate, of course, my actions resulting because of him, what *he* did to *me*. Yet, I'm unable to slice off this guy's penis, unfortunately, such an act apparently not so easy to achieve the second time around. I take it in hand, ready, but I vomit mid-way through, leaving the thing partially severed.

It's a shame. I'd readily visualised his testicles joining the chaos that would become his devastated torso, the insides popped out like marbles, stamping on both before leaving the scene with a cold, misjudged laugh. It was my *dad* I was thinking of at the time, of course, not this wretch, the walls of my flat cocooning my thoughts, protecting my fantasies.

As it is, I can't even *look* at the appendage between his legs, instead leave him with a slashed throat and a raven feather jammed deep inside his bloodied mouth, his body engulfed in flames. It's my newly found calling card, apparently, a symbolic reference to the painful agony I hope my father died in, and it unexpectedly makes me smile. I *never* anticipated the power the media and the police have given me, nationwide publicity escalating my pathetic life to a whole new level.

When they find this man's body, they will know who is responsible.

The Raven Rapist *will* have her day.

# Twenty-Six

## *Newton*

I found Andy in my kitchen attempting to cook breakfast, wreaking havoc, several eggshells discarded on the countertop alongside a pack of bacon I was saving for the weekend. The only burnt smell lingering now was a distinct whiff of overdone toast. Despite my friend's best efforts, I couldn't stomach one of his infamous toasted sandwiches, so I grabbed a coffee and left him to it, ignoring several frantic suggestions for me to sit down, relax. It was his way of continuing his gratitude campaign, no doubt, and I *was* thankful, despite my current mood claiming otherwise. I closed the front door to the sound of Andy's disappointed mutterings, a greasy breakfast not something I needed at eight o'clock in the morning. I didn't mean to appear ungrateful. I was tired. My first cup of coffee hadn't yet hit its mark, my brain still waking up.

I needed to drop some files into the police station before heading to the university, therefore allowing plenty of time for that second cup of coffee. The traffic was quiet, thankfully, getting across town with no issues, nothing adding to my rising stress levels.

'Good, you're here.' Paul clapped his hands together as I walked through the station door, as if he'd been waiting for me, hovering in reception for my imminent arrival.

'I'm just dropping off a few bits.' I glanced around, wondering if my friend was addressing someone else. He wasn't.

'Didn't Alice call you?'

I checked my phone. She had. I hadn't noticed.

Paul shook his head. 'I'm calling in that *favour* you owe me.' I gave him a blank look. 'For my assistance yesterday with Rosie O'Connor.'

'Now? I'm literally on my way to the university.'

'No, you're not. I need you *here* this morning.'

'Who said?'

'*Me*. I'm the DCI in an important murder investigation.' Paul performed a miniature bow as if denoting himself more important than anything else I or the university might assume worthy.

'But the—'

'No.'

'I'll get into trouble.'

'No you won't.'

'How so?'

'Because your day off has already been sanctioned.'

'By who?'

'Alice called them on your behalf. She can be very persuasive when she wants.' Paul grinned at me, narrowing his eyes. I knew what he meant.

'What's the favour?'

'I'd like you to assist Bernard with the postmortem on Mark Jenkins.'

## The Lost Raven

'*What?* Why me?' It was the last thing I needed, Andy's breakfast suddenly far more appealing.

'Because it might help us understand more about the type of murderer who would do something so disgusting to another human being.'

'I can look at photographs to achieve that.' I *always* worked from photographs, two-dimensional images and police files more than able to help me assess the sort of person capable of murder. It was enough that I often saw the scenes up close, first-hand encounters with the dead left where they fell. The last thing I needed was a close encounter with a mortuary slab.

'You won't *actually* be chopping the guy up, just going through Bernard's findings and reporting back to me.'

'Why can't *you* go?' He usually did, when time afforded him the unfortunate privilege. I'd lost count how many postmortems he'd attended over the years. Paul was hands-on. It's probably why we got on so well.

'Because another call just came in and I'm needed elsewhere.' He glanced at his watch, keen to get going.

'Another murder?'

Paul nodded.

'Same M.O.?'

Another nod.

*Shit.*

\*\*\*

The one thing I've never adapted well to is the smell of a pathology lab. Aside from the obvious aroma of dead bodies, there is a toxic blend of chemicals that linger on every surface, penetrating every inch of space, infusing your hair, clothes, skin.

'Ah, Newton.' Bernard greeted me at the door, already

dressed in wellington boots, scrubs, apron, mask, gloves. 'Paul mentioned you'd be attending today.' He didn't shake my hand.

I nodded, still unsure *why* I was here, still uncomfortable with the idea. I was led into a brightly lit space where a body was laid on a stainless-steel platform awaiting attention, a tag on a greyed toe the only thing to identify him by.

'How do you *stand* that smell?' I couldn't help asking as Bernard handed me a pair of gloves, one hand already covering my nose. I didn't mean to sound rude. I wasn't planning on touching anything, wasn't intending to get that close.

'You get used to it,' he laughed, heading towards a thin sheet covering Mark Jenkins' naked form, picking up a scalpel that he pointed towards the light. He probably wanted to ensure it was sterile, of course, but to me it looked as if he was being over dramatic. I didn't say anything.

'I have to admit, though, Newton, the smell of blood and human tissue remains with you for days after an autopsy.' Bernard shuddered for effect, making me pull a face in response. 'But over the years I've found I no longer think about it. My only requirement is to determine the cause of death.' He was so matter-of-fact, so cold. He probably needed to be. I couldn't help wincing as he peeled the sheet from Mark's body, the man's damaged features now on full display.

I'd seen death, of course, many times, baulked at it often. Yet the sight of a dead body when laid on a mortuary slab was something I'd only been exposed to once, adding yet another dimension to the concept of human mortality. It was the day I'd identified my brother, poor Stephanie far too traumatised to do it herself. He'd been covered like this, too, his head and shoulders unveiled to reveal injuries thankfully limited to a collision with an oncoming bus. Yet, it was an image I'd never forget. I wasn't fully anticipating the greyed features of the body in front of me now, his blank expression, the sight of this mutilated male enough to almost see me race from the room.

There was a deep, uneven wound where his throat had been cut, several attempts required to achieve death, by the looks of it, blood blackened and dried around the area, congealed now—a failed attempt to clot. I could barely look at his genitals, nothing there but a circle of angry bruising where his penis should have been. His skin was ashen, his tattoos the only colour left on his pale skin, his lower legs charred by fire, flesh burned away, bone exposed. I'm glad I didn't throw up. I'm sure Bernard wouldn't have appreciated that.

Bernard must have noticed the look on my face but thankfully didn't say anything. Instead, he took great pleasure in explaining the tools of his trade, talking me through each procedure, every requirement. A large bone saw, several scalpels, scissors, rib shears, and a pair of toothed forceps were laid out on a table next to us, although to me they looked like butcher's tools, the type used to hack animal carcasses into sections. He swiftly set about creating a Y incision across Mark's body from his sternum to his groin, cracking open the man's ribcage like a slab of raw meat.

'You're not squeamish are you?' he joked as his working hands exposed several internal organs.

'Do you always have to cut them like that?' It looked cruel, like butchery.

Bernard laughed. 'We do, unfortunately. Although, these days a full body CT scan is performed initially to determine most causes of death, including toxicology.'

I nodded. 'Postmortem Imaging.' It saved a lot of time and funding.

Bernard looked impressed. 'Correct. But it's often not enough.' He glanced at Mark's blank face. 'Especially with murder victims like this.'

I could appreciate that. The police needed to access every possible cause of death to build a potential case, nothing left to chance, nothing that could be missed. It was why bodies took so long to be released back to their families. It wasn't pleasant to watch. I didn't say anything about that.

'I assess any obvious wounds first, then check the brain, organs and anything else that might have contributed to death.' He was no longer looking at me, too busy doing his job. I automatically glanced at the poor guy's non-existent appendage. Bernard noticed. 'I already checked the exterior of the body before you arrived,' he added, giving me a sideways glance.

Bernard's gloved hands were already deep inside Mark's torso, his bloodied scalpel cutting into organs and tissue, his forceps clamped onto exposed flesh as he worked. He was talking into a recorder on the table next to us, my medical training ensuring I fully understood what he was saying. I now remembered why medical school wasn't for me. I'd already taken a couple of steps back.

'The organs look okay, no sign of disease or illness that could have contributed to his death.'

He didn't need to be a genius to work that out.

'It appears as if he was raped with an implement of some description.' Bernard was engrossed in his work, his findings just a normal part of his day. 'There is fresh tearing around his anus and bruising that confirms he was probably alive whilst this was happening and that it wasn't consensual.' Bernard glanced my way. 'Unless the guy enjoyed *pain*.'

## The Lost Raven

I winced, hoping Bernard wasn't going to turn him over and *show* me.

'How can you tell?' Bernard was good at his job, but even *I* didn't assume he was in any position (excuse the expression) to see those types of injuries. The guy was on his back, his buttocks facing the table.

'I checked before you arrived. Thought I'd spare you the indignity.'

I automatically shifted position, unaware how much investigation Bernard had already undertaken before my arrival, my presence here now purely as a joke concocted by him and Paul to make me suffer. If Bernard was smiling, I couldn't tell, his facemask covering any misdemeanour, although his eyes were crinkled at the corners, glinting with amusement. It wasn't funny.

'You might be interested to know that he was also drugged.' He glanced my way, an uncomfortable void between us. At least he was being serious again. Professional.

'Drugged? As in—?'

'Gamma butyrolactone. It's a cleaning solution found in paint stripper, cleaners, adhesives, nail polish remover, and such like. You'd know it better as GHB because it naturally converts into gamma hydroxybutyric acid in the blood. It would have made it easier for his attacker to do what they did.'

*Shit.* 'Does Paul know?' I moved closer to the body, despite my best intentions to stay well clear.

'You can give him *that* good news when you see him.' Bernard removed his gloves, washing his hands in a nearby sink.

'Anything else?'

'I found a couple of scratch marks on his cheek, as if someone dug their fingernails into him at some point. I managed to collect a couple of fibres from the wounds, including a hair.' He pointed to Mark's ashen features. Three gouge marks were positioned across his right cheek, bruising already formed beneath. I'd only just noticed.

'Fibres?'

'It's common to find whatever might have been behind fingernails inside open wounds. They're usually microscopic, unseen by the human eye. There was a tiny fragment of green thread inside one of the cuts. It might have been from something he was wearing—'

'Or something the *killer* was?'

'Indeed.'

Bernard dried his hands and removed his mask. He was still smiling, his beard showing his age, streaked with grey in places. 'I haven't checked yet, but I assume the brain will be healthy. Want to stick around while I cut off the top of his head?'

'No!' I didn't mean to sound so blunt, didn't mean to pull such a grim face. I'm sure he and Paul would have a huge laugh about that later.

Bernard chuckled. 'His heart, kidneys, and liver are healthy, no sign of diabetes in his blood, no cancer in his tissues.'

The conclusion was, of course, that Mark had been drugged, raped, his throat cut and penis removed before being set on fire. Judging by the bruising around his genitals, his penis was probably removed whilst he was still alive. Several fingerprints were found on the feather but no matches were on the system, so it didn't help. The amount of GHB was enough to kill a horse, apparently. If his throat hadn't been cut, he would have died anyway. I closed my eyes. I honestly couldn't think of a more terrible way to end a life.

# Twenty-Seven

## *Newton*

I left Bernard's pathology lab needing a strong coffee to steady my nerves, Stephanie on my mind. The image of my brother's cold body was something I'd never openly shared with her. Probably never would. She didn't need the image in her mind like the one I'd lived with. I dialled her number, needing to hear a friendly voice.

'You still coming over at the weekend?' Steph asked. My sister-in-law sounded tired. Having pubescent boys will do that to you.

'Can't wait.' What I really couldn't wait for is to hug my nephews. I had Angela on my mind, too, Mark Jenkins, Andy.

'You okay?' Steph always knew when something was on my mind.

'Just been a stressful week.' I considered telling her about Andy but thought better of it. She knew him, knew *all* the friends I'd had since university, which weren't many.

She would have asked about him, wanting to know how he was, how life was treating him. I didn't have the energy for such a conversation.

'Why don't I make lasagna and an apple pie?' I couldn't see her but I could tell she was smiling.

'Sounds perfect.' How could I refuse? Just the thought of a home-cooked meal was making me emotional.

'And Newt?'

'Yeah?'

'Don't stress. You look old when you stress.'

I raised my eyebrows—nothing like good old-fashioned honesty to cheer a man up.

\*\*\*

When Paul and his team walked into the station, their faces told me all I needed to know, their mannerisms confirming yet another brutal murder I didn't want to consider. I was standing next to another dead body, metaphorically speaking, watching Paul pin the latest collection of photographs to a board already brimming with information, the second apparent victim of *The Raven Rapist*, according to preliminary findings.

'How do you know it's connected to The Raven Rapist?'

'Because of the raven feather lodged at the back of his throat.'

I stared at the images in front of me, the body mostly burned and mutilated, similar to the last one, only this guy looked as if the killer was growing increasingly angry. I didn't want to but I looked at the dead man's penis, shocked to find it intact.

'They didn't cut off his...' I couldn't finish my sentence.

'No. Only partially severed this time, from what we can tell.'

## The Lost Raven

'Why?' I needed to know, despite the shudder my body automatically performed.

'Not sure. He might have been disturbed. We'll know more once Bernard has taken a look.' Paul glanced at me as if trying to ascertain the type of person who could gladly kill someone in this manner. I didn't envy Bernard's job.

'What's that?' I pointed to what looked like a pile of sick.

'What do you think it is?' Paul rolled his eyes.

I almost stepped in vomit at the last scene, too. I hadn't considered until now that it might have been the killer's. I didn't share my thoughts, had nothing to go on, yet the idea niggled me that we were dealing with more than a cold-blooded killer. You don't vomit unless something has troubled you. My mind was whirring. I glanced at the new victim's throat, a gaping wound causing massive blood loss, charred skin damaged but not completely unrecognisable.

'The killer is probably local, judging by his ability to disappear into thin air. He must know where the CCTV cameras are, how to avoid them.' Paul was checking his notebook, transferring his earlier findings onto the whiteboard. 'He was found at the back of Freeman House car park. There are no cameras there.' Paul didn't look comfortable confirming that. It was a short walk from my flat, the location still embedded in my brain. I couldn't tell from the photos, the place in relative darkness, the ground around the body scarred black, thick patches of blood spreading across the tarmac. I was glad I didn't have to witness that.

'Or it could be a coincidence?' Just plain luck. I couldn't imagine the perpetrator getting away without *something* being caught on camera, somewhere.

'Feel free to go through the footage with DS Baker if you like, Newt? She's going to need all the help she can get.'

Paul was grinning.

I narrowed my eyes. I might just do that, as long as I had plenty of coffee.

'By the way, how did you get on with Bernard?' Paul's face was full of lines, stress taking a toll neither of us wanted to address. I didn't need the reminder, still had the smell of the lab wedged up my nose.

'Mark Jenkins was drugged.' It was the first time I'd been able to confirm it, my turn now to share vital information.

'Drugged?' Paul looked surprised but not shocked. He'd seen it all before.

'Yeah. GHB. Enough in his system to kill a horse, apparently.'

'Well, that explains how he was attacked without any sign of a fight.'

I nodded, glancing at the board again. 'I assume *he* was drugged too.' I pointed a finger towards the latest body, convinced it wouldn't have been a one-off.

Paul nodded. He didn't smile, merely pressed silent lips together in response. His body wasn't found until first light, the police called this morning by a passing dog walker, the unwitting location keeping him hidden. Despite his obvious injuries, I could tell he was well-built, muscular, toned. Someone was targeting a specific type. A new body was now waiting to be dissected and assessed.

'We're obviously dealing with a psychopath,' my friend called out as he headed into his office, the door purposefully left open. 'And, to top it all, there was a fatal stabbing outside Billy's during the early hours of Saturday morning. This town is going down the toilet, Newt.' Billy's Bar was a favourite of Paul's, daytime trade far less intimidating, it seemed, than what goes on after dark. We'd enjoyed coffee and beer there many times, putting the world to rights, passing the time. 'DS Baker dealt with it, of course, whilst I was dealing with you and that jumper, but it was a brutal attack.'

Paul had made it sound as if Angela and I had concocted the event for fun. 'Any connection to The Raven Rapist?'

He popped his head around his office door. 'Don't think so. It was put down to a brawl that got out of hand, but no one saw what happened. Someone heard the victim screaming in pain and found him with a kitchen knife sticking out of his belly.'

'Is the guy okay?'

'No. He's dead. That's what *fatal* means.' Paul shook his head sarcastically, rolling his eyes.

I ignored him.

\*\*\*

I got home to an empty flat, still unable to fathom how tidy it was, almost as if I no longer lived there. Everything I owned had been cleared away, mugs placed inside the dishwasher instead of abandoned, growing mould. I was almost nervous about spreading police files across my lounge rug in case I created a mess. I should have been grateful, but Andy's presence was making mine disappear. I made myself a coffee, noticing a message pinned to the fridge confirming he'd replace the bacon later. *Whatever.*

I sat on my freshly plumped sofa, careful not to flatten the cushions, sipping my coffee, needing to assess the type of killer fitting a profile of misandristic rapist. To me, he would be angry, disturbed, no concept for the suffering of others, Bernard's recent *uncomfortable* analogy in my head that the killer probably used some kind of dildo. He didn't assume either man had consented, the sheer force applied enough to bring tears to anyone's eyes.

I'd seen this type of attack before, of course, men becoming unwitting victims of unhinged psychopaths, the so-called *stronger* sex no safer from sexual assault than women. I'd witnessed plenty of mutilations, too, a personal lingering pain becoming the hellish reason behind such brutal attacks, the killer acting out an intense trauma because he had nowhere else to aim it.

I stared at the bodies for an hour before I relented and ordered a takeaway. I couldn't be bothered to clear the mess I'd probably create by cooking. I ignored the fact that I rarely cleaned unless provoked, Andy no doubt assuming I didn't care. I did. I just didn't always have time to acknowledge the shit I classed as my life. And now, to make matters worse, my flat no longer felt like home. My day was concluded with a headache and two severed male organs to keep me awake tonight. *Perfect.*

# Twenty-Eight

## *Angela*

Euphoria has crept over me. I like it. For the first time in my life I have gained control over something far more powerful than me. I'm sitting cross-legged on my lounge carpet, a grin on my face and uncensored knowledge of The Raven Rapist that no one else has. The police assume they are looking for a man, of course, sending out immediate warnings to all local males to *not* travel by themselves after dark. It's very amusing. After all, it's usually women told to be careful. It makes me smile to think of typical male attitudes, a far cry from the presumed safety they believe they've earned. *No* woman is safe alone after dark these days and I've single-handedly changed the status quo, my latest manic episode ensuring I've spent the last hour dancing around my flat, loving the notoriety I've been given, collapsing into a sobbing stupor only once my mania wears off.

I'm still dressed in the clothes I wore for my rampage,

still covered in my latest victim's blood. I'm currently waiting to catch a glimpse of the next breaking story, nothing more, the fact that I've left a second raven feather purposefully with the body certain to confirm The Raven Rapist has struck again. The sun is already creeping around my curtains before the news comes in, forced to wait for hours in the dark, alone. Then those eagerly awaited images begin to show up on TV about a *second* victim found in the Eastcliff area.

I can't go back to work today, can't bring myself to fake the virus I need to pretend still lingers. I'm too hyped, one sideways glance surely giving me away.

'How are you feeling, honey?' Claire's bright tone greets me as I cough into the telephone. She usually has the ability to perk me up, but not today. Today my thoughts are set only on my latest victim and my colleague's unfiltered thoughts about The Raven Rapist. I want to collect raven feathers, run through the woods naked, shouting, laughing.

'Morning Claire,' I choke out my greeting as if I'm still not well, still not part of functioning humanity. As far as she's concerned, I have *no* idea about the recent events in our local community, my duvet the only company I've had for days. I'm keen to learn what's happened in my absence, any *murders* I haven't yet heard about?

'You sound terrible,' she says as I feign a sniffle.

I smile, glad I'm able to keep up the pretence, the last few days important for my health, my recent time off *vital*. I still haven't taken my medication, worried now that if I do, I'll slip back into old patterns, my confidence disappearing the moment I swallow a pill. My mania is keeping the ravens close, ensuring they speak to me, guiding my purposeful mission.

'Have you heard the news?' Claire's voice is sparkling with intent, gossip something she loves to share.

## The Lost Raven

'No. What have I missed?' I try to sound normal. Sane. I'm merely waiting to hear chatter about The Raven Rapist.

'I don't know where to begin.' Claire spends the next ten minutes filling me in on the gruesome details, most of which she makes up, nothing the media yet know about the real state of the bodies left behind. 'I heard the killer cut off those men's *dicks*,' she laughs. 'Before he *ate* them.' I suppress a smile.

No. It was just the *one* dick and I was never going to eat it. *Jesus*. What the hell? Touching the first one gave me the creeps. I wasn't thinking straight. It just happened, triggering a chain reaction I now have to maintain. My second victim has been identified as Michael Lawson, Claire confirms, as if she *knows* him, yet no one is aware that I also left another guy bleeding to death outside a nearby location a few days earlier. I still don't know if Lee is dead or alive, although if he *is* dead it would now make me a serial killer. I'm not sure how I feel about that. I hate that I remember his name. I don't think it will be appropriate for me to ask after him. I can't get Liam out of my head, a pain tugging at my chest that I want him dead, too. I *need* him dead. It's the only way this thing will end.

Andrew Hansley has asked after me, apparently, checking I'm okay, concerned about what happened the other morning, memories of the party still lingering, still painful. I've practically forgotten about that now, my attempted suicide not really the cry for help I was looking for. I want to ask Claire if he saw anything suspicious with Liam at the party, but I refrain. There's something about Hansley I don't like. I'm not sure what. He's a bit sleazy, actually, if I take the time to think about it.

Rosie has also taken a few days off. I can't think why. Maybe she has developed my virus, too. Claire tells me she's been trying to contact me, yet when I ask why, she falls silent. What else have I missed? It's not her place to say, apparently, but I should give my friend a call.

***

I spend much of my evening curled in front of the TV, a mug of hot chocolate on my lap and dark thoughts on my mind. I don't call Rosie. Instead, I have a weird compulsion to head into the night again, my raven feathers calling loudly from a shoe box under my bed. The police will be on high alert now, of course, extra security posted around the local nightclubs, restaurants, bars. I'll need to be careful, though I'm unexpectedly growing in confidence, my newly found fame made all the more prolific by words confirmed by strangers. I longer not care about the DNA evidence I've left behind, or the request made by the police to provide a sample. My details are *not* on any UK database. The police are *not* looking for a five-foot four inch tall, dress size eight blonde woman who couldn't *possibly* overpower a man. I sigh. That's the problem. It's always been my problem. I'm weak. *Pathetic.*

I get up and pace my flat, frustration increasing, irritation stinging my skin for things I can never change. I want to venture into the night, hide in plain sight and watch the increasing panic. I wet my lips. I'll be okay if I stay out of sight. I'm already out of my mind. Everyone believes I'm currently sick, unfit for visitors, unworthy of attention. What's the worst that can happen? I smile, dressing in a dark grey trouser suit I usually keep for funerals or job interviews, my outfit teamed with a little makeup, my hair tied back, Newton's jacket already an odd protector. I need to look nice, as if I've made an effort, but not too much, just an innocent evening out. If anyone asks, I'm attending a party. A birthday party. Mine.

## The Lost Raven

By the time I leave my flat, I've unintentionally filled a rucksack with vindicating items in case I should meet someone who takes my fancy, my newly found arrogance boundless. I take a taxi across town because I'm too nervous to drive, innocent in my mannerisms, not so innocent in thought, the driver friendly, relaxed. He chats about the weather, the state of the economy, The Raven Rapist. And then I head into the night, looking for trouble, knowing I'll find it soon enough.

The atmosphere is different this evening. People seem guarded, men watching each other, women unwilling to let their partners out of their sight. It eggs me on, provoking something deep inside to *show* them all who's boss. I amble around, watching, nothing more, nothing to provoke unwanted attention. I find myself walking the promenade, the ocean and the ravens calling, enough bars and restaurants here to placate my savage requirements. My last two victims were hidden in unassuming locations, discarded like trash, isolated areas chosen purposefully to disguise my presence and theirs, my hideous actions done out of pure, unadulterated hatred. Scum. That's all they are. *Were.*

I apply lip-gloss, bored now of observing, ready to make my obvious move. It won't take long to attract attention. Men can be so *fucking* predictable.

'You out by yourself?' someone asks. I turn to the sight of a relatively small guy with shoulder-length hair hovering behind me, two equally nerdy males giggling like drunken schoolgirls behind him.

'I take it this is a wind-up?' I reply, focusing more on his friends than him. I can't imagine any of these men would know *what* to do with a woman, let alone how to speak to one. They look like boys, barely out of school.

He turns, lowering his eyes, his embarrassment obvious.

'Ignore them,' he chides. 'They think I can't pull.'

'They're right,' I snap, briskly walking away. He isn't bad looking, I guess. A bit weedy maybe and my drugs will probably kill him before I have a chance to do much else. I'm looking for men who, under normal circumstances, can look after themselves, can put up a fight if needed. Besides, if I attack *him*, I leave two potential witnesses to identify me when their friend turns up dead. I don't need that kind of shit in my day.

It's frustrating. I don't think he fully appreciates just how narrow his escape has been. He can go home. Live another day. As it is, I amble around for a further hour, the warmth of each bar alien to the cold air outside. I leave each location unfulfilled, heading to the next, frustrated, bored, venturing along the seafront, considering giving up. Maybe I should go home, something not right with tonight's ambience, my instincts nagging. I can try again another evening, plenty of time for The Raven Rapist to make her mark.

Yet, my bag is heavy with ideas I haven't yet put into practice, the effort I've made causing me to falter. I watch a couple walk past me, their arms wrapped tightly around each other, their attention aimed everywhere but on me. They don't look happy, more worried than anything. I smile, knowing why, and it gives me a newly found air of confidence. People in Eastcliff are afraid, and I'm the reason.

My belly rumbles. I haven't eaten much today, too eager, too excited, my mania to blame for everything I'm unwittingly becoming.

'Hungry?' someone yells.

I turn around to the sight of a male, around forty, dressed in tight clothing he believes make him look cool but really just appear foolish, as if he's trying too hard, trying to maintain a lost youth. I'm surprised he still has hair. I glance around. I don't see anyone with him.

'Why? You want to buy me some chips?' I don't mean to sound sarcastic. A free dinner is *not* to be sniffed at.

He smiles and offers me his arm and, just like that, we head into the night. My heart is pounding. I hope he doesn't notice. He probably assumes I fancy him. *How stupid can one person be?*

# Twenty-Nine

## *Angela*

The two of us head arm in arm towards the nearest chip shop, a heavy smell of sweat making me feel sick, hot oil and vinegar making my belly growl.

'What are you doing out here, by yourself?' my companion asks, nothing on his mind other than my uninterrupted company.

'Supposed to be meeting friends,' I lie.

'They stood you up, hey?'

'Something like that.' I glance around. I don't care, don't want to continue this conversation.

He laughs. 'I'm Carl.'

I do *not* want to know his name, do not need another man in my head. I feign a laugh, nodding vaguely as he steps ahead of me, stepping inside a brightly lit building to order a bag of chips for us to share. I hover by the door, insisting he buy a can of cola to go with them, wondering if I can be cheeky and ask for a fish. I have no idea how this is

## The Lost Raven

going to work, used to dealing with men already drunk or seeking attention, already stumbling around like idiots by the time their focus is on me.

'Fancy a stroll?' I ask, nodding towards the sand, my chaperone's fingers already deep inside a greasy tray as he lifts an elbow for me to hook my arm into. It's dark along the beach, very few people here at this time of night, high tide already preventing unwanted trespassers. We won't be disturbed. I maintain a forceful grip on Carl, an icy canned drink balanced in one hand as we head steadily towards the beachfront, a chilling wind biting temptation into my overburdened thoughts.

Carl smiles and glances around, probably assuming I want him alone for sex. We head down a set of steep steps to the cool sand below, the tide already washing against the seawall in places. It's quiet here, dog walkers long gone, everyone else too drunk to notice my plan.

'Hold these will you, I need a piss,' Carl laughs, handing me a hot tray. What a lovely vision he's provided. I smile, knowing how perfectly timed this moment has become. Carl heads towards the shoreline to relieve himself whilst I stand and watch, offering a smile whenever he turns to check I'm still here. I wait until his back is turned, preoccupied with his mission before reaching silently into my bag to conclude my own. I'm on autopilot, terrifyingly focused, peeling open the can of cola I've already propped against the seawall. I still don't know how much GHB is required to *drug* a person and it's becoming costly to use the entire bottle. Still, I can't take the risk of it not working, can't risk being caught. I pour the contents inside the can, giving it a swirl before my victim returns, the guy busy wiping urine infused hands down the front of his jacket. *Nice*.

'That's better,' he jokes as I hand him the cola. He takes a long gulp, still zipping his trousers. I can't help but stare at his throat as the liquid slides steadily towards his belly. It's only a matter of waiting patiently now. 'What's your name?' he asks between swigs, assuming I'm staring at him because of lustful thoughts. Yeah. *In his dreams.*

'Jessica,' I lie, uncomfortable with the name I've given myself, recalling a doll I once owned as a child. I can hardly tell him I'm *The Raven Rapist*.

Instead, I eat most of the chips to myself whilst he finishes the cola, his constant requests for me to share some hitting deaf ears. We then head along the damp sand, arm in arm, a few hundred steps all it takes for him to feel the effects of my drug. I'm laughing, flirting, pretending I like the attention, laying him down on the sand in anticipation of something he can't possibly see coming. I almost laugh when he opens his trousers and takes out his penis, his assumption of what is about to happen, *sickening.* I grin when I look at it. I can't help it. It's not *that* small. He doesn't notice, instead begins to masturbate, asking for my assistance, at which point I reach into my bag and take out the knife.

'With pleasure,' I confirm savagely, grabbing the obnoxious thing with my steel grip whilst slicing my steel blade through his pale flesh, my eyes set on his, my demented grin the last thing he'll ever see.

He screams. I laugh. I've never done this while a man is awake and it makes me feel overwhelmingly powerful. He's stuttering, crying in agony, attempting to get to his feet as blood pumps onto the sand around us. I promised myself I'd never do *that* again, yet I can't help what I automatically do now, a smile on my lips as I do it.

'Shush,' I soothe, pressing his convulsing body into the tainted sand. 'There, there, now. Hush little man.' I can't have him draw attention before I'm finished.

'What the *fuck?*' is the only reply he gives me before

succumbing to his fate, passing out in response to his unexpected condition.

I don't want this moment to end, the evening more fun than expected. I roll tired eyes towards the heavens as I slice open his throat, forcing his flaccid penis into his chip-infused mouth along with a single, black raven feather. He looks pathetic, face set in shock, his own manhood jammed between his bloodied teeth. I almost can't be bothered to rape him, yet I must, it's my duty. The public have come to *expect* it.

My heart is still pounding when I leave him, heading along the beach, my deed complete, the unassuming lights of Eastcliff far enough away to hide my despicable crime. I haven't set his body on fire, the area too exposed, the idea that I might be identified too much. I stop, take a breath, the aftermath hitting me hard. By the time I get back to the promenade I'm trembling, adrenaline pumping, my unsteady legs uncontrollable. I can't believe he was awake when I mutilated him, yet it felt good. I held *all* the power, those drugs barely assisting, barely in his system. I unashamedly begin to feel almighty, the need for a second victim suddenly unmoving in my head.

I don't have long to wait, less than a hundred metres all it takes to hear someone calling Carl's name. I've carefully remained below the seawall until now, walking softly along a shelf of damp sand not yet covered by the sea. I'm hidden in the darkness, this location offering a moment of perfect contemplation.

'He's not answering his phone,' someone is yelling into a mobile phone above me. 'Yeah, I know. What a dickhead. He knows we should be keeping together.'

'Excuse me?' I ask, making my way gingerly up a set of sand-covered steps, my newly found confidence unwavering. I don't even check my clothes for blood, my murderous bag still clutched in my hands. I still have my knife in my grasp, swiftly disguising it behind my back.

The guy turns around. He looks worried. 'You okay, miss?' he asks politely. In the darkness, he can't see me clearly. It's probably a good thing.

'Are you looking for someone called Carl?' I'm grateful he told me his name now, this opportunity *perfect*.

'Yeah. Why? How do you know Carl?' The guy looks surprised, suspicious.

I *don't* know him, can't even be certain we're talking about the same person. It doesn't matter. 'It's probably none of my business but I was just speaking to someone called Carl a few minutes ago who claims to have mislaid his mates.' I'm making it up as I go, of course, no idea where I'm going with this.

'Where *is* he?' The guy glances along the street, the dim lampposts barely lighting the way.

I laugh, my supposed innocent female charm thankfully coming into play. 'Back there, down on the beach.' I point towards where I left Carl's body, in the dark, dead. 'I'll be happy to walk back with you if you like?' I can't imagine he'd want me to, yet I'm smiling anyway, my query merely a helpful gesture, cleavage thankfully on display beneath Newton's jacket that in this light should aid my impossible mission.

'Thank you,' comes his reply, along with a heavy sigh I try to ignore. 'Comes to something when *men* aren't able to walk the bloody streets alone.'

I narrow my eyes. He doesn't notice.

'Surely you're not out here by yourself?' he asks, stepping onto the sand ahead of me.

'Of course not. I just needed a bit of air. Your friend was heading towards the shore when I saw him. Said he couldn't get a phone signal. Didn't sound happy.'

## The Lost Raven

'That sounds about right. He needs a new phone. Bloody thing's older than my kid.'

I'm no longer listening, can see nothing beyond a red mist that blinds me. We head along the beach together, nothing he can say now able to save his life.

I stop walking. 'Hey, look at that,' I call out.

He turns around and I slash his throat, forcing the guy to drop to his knees. I haven't even *needed* drugs this time. Fucking hell, I'm getting good at this. I shouldn't, but I feel elated, my body infused with rushing blood and euphoria that threatens to overwhelm me. He stares at me, confused, a gaping wound shortly to witness his swift end. I can't help offering a sarcastic wave as he succumbs to his fate, falling face down at my feet. *Shit.* That was too easy.

I kneel by his side and wipe my blade across the back of his shirt sleeve before pulling down his trousers and positioning a raven feather between his upended buttocks. He's still choking, still dying, still trying to figure out what just happened. I almost consider leaving my dildo in a painful position too, but it's covered in his friend's recently spilled blood and I'll need it again soon. I don't feel compelled to cut off his penis either. I can still feel the last one in my hand. It doesn't matter. The Raven Rapist is tired. She needs to go home. It's been a very busy night.

# Thirty

## *Newton*

Another crime scene, another act of senseless violence. Two attacks this time, each occurring within a few hundred feet of the other, each with a direct view of the promenade. I stood on the beach, unsure how to react, Paul's focus set between *two* unwitting murder scenes, frantic panic setting in amongst the locals. Two separate areas had already been cordoned off, white tents erected around each. Many police officers were in attendance, many stressed faces preventing unwanted attention. It looked like a movie scene, the seafront swamped with on-lookers, everyone hoping for a closer inspection.

'Newt!' Paul was jogging along the sand towards me, his hair brushed back, cheeks flushed. It had started raining, the tide still rising, any evidence soon to evaporate if the police didn't act fast.

'What do we have?' I asked, already knowing the answer.

## The Lost Raven

'Two frenzied attacks by the looks of it.' Paul pointed towards the tents some distance away, several gulls already circling the area, hoping for a free meal.

'Any witnesses?'

Paul nodded towards a middle-aged male currently sitting on a bench speaking to DI Tony Avery, a foil blanket around his trembling shoulders. The guy was mid-fifties, smartly dressed, either out for a drink or on his way home. I thanked my friend and headed towards our unwitting witness. The guy gave me a blank look when I introduced myself, his cheeks pale, lips quivering.

'I already told the other copper everything I know,' he muttered flatly, tired of questions rapidly aimed his way.

'I'm not a police officer,' I reassured him, taking a seat next to him.

'Oh?'

'I'm a doctor.' I shouldn't have confirmed that as if I was an expert in anything medical, my training confined to four years out of the required seven.

'I don't need a bloody doctor.' The man attempted to get to his feet, wavered, sinking to the bench with a thud.

I smiled, retaining a calmness he couldn't. 'I'm here to check you're okay. Can you tell me what you saw?' Tony had already asked, of course, a formal statement requested. The detective rolled frustrated eyes my way.

The witness cleared his throat. 'As I told the other guy, I was just walking past Aubrey Point.' He nodded towards the promenade where Paul was now speaking with Bernard. 'I heard someone screaming so I raced down onto the beach. That's when I saw him.'

'Who?'

'The guy, holding his crotch as if someone had kicked him in the bollocks.' He shuddered. 'I didn't notice the blood at first but when someone slit his throat, I didn't hang around.'

'You *saw* someone cut his throat?'

'Yeah. But they didn't see me, thank Christ. Too dark.'

'So, you ran?'

'I bloody well did. I wasn't about to hang around to get caught up in *that* shit.'

'You didn't try to stop them?'

'Would *you*?' He looked at me as if I was mad. He had a point. 'I know about that raven person. I didn't want to become one of *them*.' He nodded towards the carnage behind us, shaking his head in protest of his own memories.

'Where were you heading?'

'Home. I work as an accountant. Long hours.' He didn't sound happy about that, no doubt wishing he could be anywhere but here.

'Did you get a good look at the killer?'

He shook his head. 'Not really. It was too dark.'

'Male?'

'I couldn't see very well.' He hesitated. 'Yeah… I think so.'

'Did they see you?'

'I don't know. I was too busy shitting myself to notice.'

'What happened then?'

'I called the police before going back to the beach.'

'Why did you go back?' His declaration surprised me. I don't know why. Despite the real possibility of being killed, I'd probably have done the same—curiosity and all that.

'No idea. Curiosity, stupidity. Call it what you like. But by then the guy was already dead.'

'Did you touch him?'

*'Fuck off did I.'*

'Sorry.'

'That's when I heard the commotion further along the beach.' He nodded towards the second white tent, closing

## The Lost Raven

his eyes tightly against the night air. 'Christ. What a night.'

It was indeed. Tony was currently gathering information from anyone else who might have witnessed the chaos, turning his attention to the gathering crowd.

'Did you see anything else?' I'm not sure what I was hoping for.

'No. Sorry. I don't know anything more than what I told that other copper.'

I thanked the witness and left him in Tony's capable hands, heading towards Paul's perpetually blank face, his stress levels through the roof.

'This is getting out of control, Newt. *Two* dead in the space of fifteen minutes according to early reports. What the *hell* is going on?' Paul looked around as if hoping someone would step in and provide the answer.

'Same M.O. as before?'

'Looks that way. Both victims' throats were cut.' He pointed to tent number one. '*That* guy's penis was jammed in the back of his mouth and was brutally raped judging by the amount of blood around his anus.' I shuddered as Paul pointed to tent number two. '*That* guy got away with just a slashed throat.'

*Just?* 'He wasn't raped?' The Raven Rapist was slipping.

Paul shook his head, his outraged fingers pointing wildly. 'Maybe *that one* witnessed *that one* being murdered and the killer needed to shut him up, fast.' Made sense. The killer wouldn't have wanted to leave a witness behind, the unseen accountant luckier than he realised.

'Feathers?'

'Yep. The first victim had one in his mouth, the other between his buttocks.'

*Nice.*

'There's something else you should know.' Paul didn't look happy, could barely look at me.

'What?' I don't know why I suddenly felt nervous.

'We found a jacket next to the second body.'

'And?'

'You might want to come and take a look.' Paul walked away, turning around briefly to make sure I followed. He stopped next to a marked police car, several evidence bags already laid out in the boot, sealed and labelled.

Paul picked one up. 'Recognise this?'

I went to take the bag from my friend but Paul pulled it away, oddly unwilling to allow me near it. I narrowed my eyes. 'It looks like my jacket.' I glanced at Paul, his features tighter than mine.

'It *is*.'

'How do you know? It could be anyone's.'

'We found several of your business cards in one of the inside pockets along with your notebook, a few unsavoury looking toffees, and your favourite pencil.' *Shit*. I hadn't even noticed, hadn't thought about my pencil for a few days. It was around two inches long now, chewed to within an inch of its life. I'd had it for years. It belonged to Isaac, my brother's teeth marks something I didn't want to relinquish. I didn't use it, of course, merely kept it with me for sentimental purposes.

I glanced around, unsure what this all meant. I hadn't seen my jacket for a few days, not since Angela had hastily stuffed it behind a plant pot. She was the last person to wear it—had been vulnerable, scared.

'Any idea why *your* jacket would be at a murder scene, covered in a dead man's blood?'

'Surely you're not suggesting—'

'*No*. Of, course not. As if.' Paul rolled his eyes, a shake of his head saying more than he meant to share. 'But I *will* need you to verify your movements for tonight. I'm sure you understand.'

## The Lost Raven

I nodded. I did. I knew how this worked, how apparent evidence could stack up against you. I glanced around. 'Any CCTV we can check?' Surely there were enough cameras in the area to highlight the fact that I *wasn't*. I couldn't imagine how my jacket had found its way to a crime scene.

'I've already assigned DS Baker to take a look. Want to help her? I can meet you back at the station and take your statement later.' Paul offered a strained grin, knowing I wouldn't resist an hour or two in Alice's unwavering company, the idea of providing an alibi for my whereabouts something neither of us expected.

***

Searching through surveillance footage with Alice wasn't exactly how I'd planned to spend my evening, yet I couldn't complain. She ensured the conversation and coffee flowed as we flicked relentlessly through hours of recordings, trying to get a feel for the victims last known movements. I ignored her lingering perfume and distracting presence, unwilling to expose a deep affection I'd shared with no one other than Paul. Besides, she might turn me down. I didn't know if I could take that kind of rejection.

It didn't take long for us to spot the two dead men. They were walking along the seafront around nine o'clock, a third male with them.

'So, they *did* know each other.' I wasn't relieved to confirm it, prodding the screen with my finger. It made sense. The idea that the second murdered male probably witnessed the first's was something none of us needed in our heads.

We traced their movements until one became separated, the other two searching the streets, frantic, worried. Eventually the missing male — our first victim — was seen emerging from a chip shop. There was someone with him. Unfortunately, whoever it was had their backs to the camera so we couldn't get a clear look, the image fuzzy, grainy, dark.

'Where is that?' I leant forward, hoping to get a better look, refraining from positioning my head at a different angle to potentially improve the view. I didn't need to provoke Alice's amusement.

'Chappy's Chippy, by the looks of it,' she confirmed, instantly recognising the location. She'd probably been there many times. We *all* had.

'Does the place have CCTV?'

Alice called Paul. I could hear him on the other end of the phone, pleased with our findings, assigning an officer to go to the location and ask, thanking Alice for her superb work. *Typical.* I didn't say anything. Instead, I watched the dead man cross the road, arm in arm with someone dressed in dark clothing. I couldn't tell if they were male or female, their hair either short or tied back, the reason for their close interaction unknown. I was unable to take my eyes off the couple in case I missed something.

'Is that a man?' I asked, once Alice was off the phone. I didn't confirm that whoever it was also appeared to be wearing my jacket, didn't want my imagination to run away with me.

Alice leant forward, her hand accidentally grazing mine. She didn't notice. 'Actually, I think it might be a woman.'

My heart lunged. I didn't want to confirm what I was thinking, the fact that Angela Healy's dress had turned up in a skip something I was still hoping was coincidental. I didn't want to believe what I was now mulling over, the person on screen unassuming, innocent. The couple disappeared behind the seawall. We waited. Neither reappeared.

## The Lost Raven

'What time did the witness call the police?' I was staring at the little clock on the screen, the seconds ticking away.

Alice tapped her keyboard. 'The 999 came in at seventeen minutes past ten.' The time frame fitted. *Shit.*

'I think we just found the moment of the first murder,' I confirmed. It didn't help, didn't bear thinking about. 'Can we get footage from any other cameras?'

Alice nodded, bringing up two more darkened images, both cameras pointing towards the beach, an imposing seawall in the way.

'What's that?' A dark figure was racing up the steps, a rucksack over one shoulder, something in their outstretched hand.

Alice zoomed in, the features barely visible. 'Looks like a knife.'

'Are we looking at the murder weapon?' I didn't mean to ask. It wasn't a comfort. A little detective work on Alice's part confirmed the figure was dressed in dark grey, approximately five foot four, slim build, small hands.

'*Definitely* a woman,' she confirmed sullenly, poking the screen with a finger. The image remained frozen. Surely we couldn't be looking at the killer? It didn't help that they no longer wore my jacket, a baseball cap now firmly pulled over their head. I didn't say anything about that, didn't confirm what I was thinking. 'You okay, Newt?' Alice smiled, tilting her head, noticing me staring at the screen with a blank expression.

'Yeah, just been a long night.' I glanced at the clock. It had already turned one. I couldn't bring myself to look at Alice. She might see my concerns, read my thoughts.

'Does your partner mind you working such late hours?'

I wasn't expecting the question. I hesitated, unsure how to reply.

'Sorry. *Jesus.* Where are my manners.' Alice blushed,

taking a long swig of lukewarm coffee, obviously embarrassed. I didn't know how to respond. We'd never spoken of such things, never shared anything of our personal lives beyond the requirements of police work and formal duties.

'I'm single,' I confessed, the wobble in my voice unexpected. 'I *was* married, but not anymore.' I wasn't happy to confirm I had a failed marriage behind me. Nobody wants to admit that, do they? Besides, it was unimportant. It had been fifteen years since Kate and I separated. Hardly breaking news.

Alice glanced my way, her plump lips pressed together, her cheeks glowing. 'It's none of my business. Sorry.' For all she knew, I might have been gay. I glanced at my clothes. Did I *look* gay? How *do* gay people look? I was probably overthinking. I took a breath, got to my feet. I needed a coffee and a change of subject.

'How long did Paul say it would take to get the footage from the chip shop?'

Alice looked equally glad to be given something to think of other than my failed love life. 'He didn't.'

Her response wasn't comforting.

We spent the next twenty minutes reviewing cameras, the shocked expression of our witness as he noticed the victim on the beach, a separate incident showing the killer meeting his second. By the time Paul walked through the door, I'm not sure which of us was more exhausted. I imagined Bernard working deep into the night, two more dead men to assess and dissect before their bodies could be released back to their families.

Paul handed Alice a USB stick.

'Is that—'

'Let's hope so.' Paul was standing behind me, arms folded, his features a collection of stress and exhaustion. His stomach growled. We all ignored it.

Chappy's Chippy was well lit, the image much clearer. I was surprised by how improved the quality was.

'Do we have names for the victims yet?' Alice asked, watching as the first one entered the building and stood in a queue.

Paul nodded. 'Yeah. Confirmed by their *very* shaken friend as Carl Grealy and Thomas Blackmore. Their families are being told as I speak.' It wasn't an image I needed in my head, early morning visits from the police never ideal. Their friend was a lucky man.

Something caught my attention and I pointed to the screen, unable to believe what I was seeing. 'Is that Angela Healy?' I watched as Carl Grealy turned to address a second person who had entered the building behind him. My mouth had fallen open.

Alice paused the image, zooming in on a small shape in the doorway.

It had to be a joke, a wind-up, or at least someone who looked like Angela. I thought about the raven feather she had the day we met, the green fibres found in the wound on Mark Jenkins cheek. My jacket. *Shit*. My heart sank. I didn't want my imagination to run away with me, didn't want to think the worst. Angela might have given my jacket to a charity shop, might have forgotten it wasn't hers to give away. Yet, I couldn't ignore what we were now looking at, her blonde hair tucked neatly into a bun, a rucksack slung over her shoulder, her face as clear as day.

'Could she be a witness?' I couldn't help asking. I'd spent an entire week worrying about the girl, trying to help her. I was clutching at straws, hoping, praying. I didn't want to believe anything else. Everyone assumed The Raven Rapist was a *man*.

Paul looked at me. 'She's five foot four inches tall and

her description matches the person holding a bloodied knife. I *doubt* it.' He shook his head, glaring at the computer screen. 'Okay, let's bring her in.'

***

I shouldn't have, but I called Angela's number, unsurprised when it went straight to voicemail, unable to leave a message in case I gave myself away.

'What the hell are you doing?' Paul snapped, his car moving swiftly through the darkened streets, two marked police cars following silently behind. He reached over to grab my phone, missed, swore.

'She's *vulnerable*. You lot will terrify her.' I was leaning away from my friend, preventing his intrusion, recalling the last time we'd arrived unannounced outside Angela's flat. She looked terrified then, too, and we only wanted to ask questions. I couldn't escape the fact that she'd moved my jacket, hid it, the potential reasons now painfully worrying. I called her again, shocked when she actually answered.

'I can't speak now, Dr Newton.' Her voice was tiny. I couldn't imagine her hurting *anyone*.

Flanigan. It's Dr *Flanigan*. I didn't correct her.

'I just wanted to see how you're doing, Angela.' I sounded fake, stumbling over my own words as Paul glared at me, one eye twitching violently. He couldn't speak, couldn't tell me off, one hint of his voice provoking all out chaos. Even *he* could hear the wobble in my tone, the nervousness in my query. 'Are you at home?'

'Why?' Her mannerism had changed.

I had to think fast, needing to keep her on the phone long enough for us to reach her, psychically if not *emotionally*. I wanted to know she was safe, wanted to believe her innocence.

'Because I spoke to Rosie earlier.' I paused. 'I've been trying to contact you all day.'

'Why?' Again the same question, irritation lingering.

'Do you know she was *raped* on Friday night?' It wasn't ideal, hardly the right time to confirm it, but I needed to create maximum impact, keep the girl talking. Paul shook his head.

'*What?*' Angela sounded panicked. 'Where is she?' I could hear rummaging, as if she was grabbing random items.

'I'm so sorry to have to tell you this over the telephone,' I continued, merely needing a captive audience for a few more minutes. We were heading along the high street in a hurry, past the very car park I'd recently talked her down from, past the university, my street. 'She's been trying to contact you for a few days.'

Angela went quiet.

'Angela? You okay?'

'I'm so sorry,' she muttered, before hanging up.

I glanced at Paul. *Double shit.*

# Thirty-One

## *Angela*

I call Rosie several times but it goes to voicemail, screaming into my bathroom sink because I have nowhere else to yell. I'm angry for ignoring her needs, my own selfishly factoring far higher than I deserve. Why didn't she tell me about *Liam?* We have a shared problem we must deal with, and yet until now, I haven't realised how much she *needs* me. I can't believe Newton knew before I did. Why he called so late, I don't know, but I'm sure I heard a car in the background, sirens, someone talking on a radio.

My limbs are numb, my eyes on stalks, my head throbbing as I turn on the TV in anticipation of recent actions I'm not entirely convinced are real. I don't have to wait long to hear that The Raven Rapist has struck again, of course, this time killing *two* men, both within a few hundred feet of each other. I sit down, unable to steady my faltering legs, hoping this night was my unfathomable imagination, a dream I can laugh about later. As it is, this is real, the police

*The Lost Raven*

looking for witnesses, anyone who can aid with enquiries. I can't recall much, don't know *who* might have witnessed the chaos I've unwittingly left behind.

I head into my kitchen feeling as if my body has been crushed, the evening taking a toll I can't yet assess. I always come crashing to earth after a manic episode, the comedown often worse than death, but I've never felt anything quite like this. Even my clothes feel heavy, as if I'm being pinned to the floor. Maybe I am. Maybe an unseen force is punishing me for what I've done, forcing me towards the darkness below. I've *killed* people. Four in total now, I think, although the details are hazy and I'm no longer sure *what* the number is. Five, if Lee is dead.

I make tea I know I won't drink, desperate to tell someone about the agony I'm in, terrified of the repercussions heading my way. Tears are falling. I can't stop them. Everything has reached a bottleneck, this night an accumulation of pain and suffering I don't know how to appease, my emotions ready to kill me for what I've become. My hatred for men has increased, understandably, therapy and medication of no real help. It was bad enough when I believed I was Liam's *only* victim, just another day in the life of Angela Healy. To now know he hurt my friend, too, a lady who, under normal circumstances, I might consider a mother figure, is something I cannot abide. *Liam* is the reason I've been tipped over the edge, the reason at least four men are *dead*.

I pick up my mug and throw it across the kitchen, milk and sugar spilling into the air along with a spoon that clatters to the floor. The mug smashes against the wall, dislodging a large glass jar from a shelf, shattering it into pieces, rice spilling everywhere. *Shit.* I liked that jar. It doesn't matter. What I really want is for Liam to suffer. He's conveniently avoided me, avoided Rosie, the guise of some hospital conference not enough to convince me it's a coincidence. *What a bastard.*

I reach for Newton's jacket but it isn't on the hook I've allocated, my hallway seemingly lost now without it. I can't remember the last time I saw it, can't remember taking it off. Unfortunately, I have no time to worry as I grab an oversized hoodie from the floor, heading outside into the darkness, no time to turn off my lights or lock the door. I don't stop until I reach my car, my feet aching, climbing into the driving seat in a state of shock. I sit in silence for a moment, lost, forgotten, just a lost raven with nowhere to go. I wonder how Liam will react when he sees me, finally forced to face what he's done. I need to track him down because this thing is *never* going to end until I do.

I check his social media accounts for updates whilst continually leaving Rosie increasingly panicked messages, my anger rising with every image I see staring mockingly back—smiling faces taken with colleagues who can't possibly appreciate the monster he is. I hate him. *Hate* what he stands for. I think about my flat, spilt milk that will smell terrible by the time I get home, a dent in my wall I'll now have to fix. I'll be picking up fragments of glass and rice for weeks, much of it already lodged in the crevices of my skirting board. I don't even know if I turned off the TV.

The cold is already creeping around the edges of clothing doing nothing to keep me warm, my hood pulled over a baseball cap I've become oddly attached to. My car heater doesn't work and I am grateful for the warmth of my hooded top, staring out of the windscreen ahead, not daring to look at anyone around me in case I'm noticed, identified, The Raven *fucking* Rapist out for an early morning jolly. Luckily London is only a short trip away, those seventy-something miles achieved in around an hour if I put my foot down. The police are still convinced the killer is a *man*, although it doesn't help, doesn't aid my faltering mood that I still can't get in touch with my friend. *Where the hell is she?*

Today has unwittingly become one of those days where I wish I could fly, avoiding the male population and the poison they eject, spitting acid into the lives of every woman they meet. I glance skyward through a panel of fast-moving glass, hoping to spot a raven, wishing beyond rational reason that my beloved friends will swoop down and carry me to safety. Yet, I see nothing but a black sky fading to grey, the incoming dawn awash with low clouds that threaten to suffocate me where I sit. They protect the ravens from my desperate stare, from uncensored thoughts that can't be mine. I honestly don't care. I'm *still* Angela Healy, still *The Raven Rapist*. I'm almost loathed to admit that I feel stronger with each life I take, becoming more powerful with each male heartbeat I stop in their cold, dead chests. I'm doing this for all women out there, no matter what walk of life they tread, their background, history, culture. It doesn't matter that they will never know my reasons, only that I'm keeping them *safe*.

I glance at my hands, nothing to see but pale palms trembling with each undeserved breath I take, metaphoric blood seeping through my fingertips, lodged behind my fingernails. The blood isn't *really* there, of course. I've already scrubbed most of it away. Yet my hands are sore, red, angry, mocking my actions, my emotions. I bring them to my face and sob so hard I genuinely believe my lungs will burst. I no longer care who's watching or my questionable driving. How can I keep going like this? *Where on earth do I go from here?*

# Thirty-Two

## *Newton*

This was the second time we'd arrived unannounced outside Angela's flat, a lump forming in the back of my throat. I no longer deluded myself the woman was an innocent bystander in events that placed the entire town on alert. What was she doing with Carl Grealy? I wasn't yet willing to assume any unfeigned connection to the crimes committed, keen only to get her side of the story. Besides, I needed to relieve my mind of unwanted ideas I couldn't now help having in private. It was still dark, still early, none of us yet able to find the sleep we desperately needed. It was the least of our worries, considering there were two new bodies in the mortuary, more paperwork and evidence to process.

Angela's flat was in darkness, although a flickering light through her top floor window suggested the television was on, that she was probably still awake. It didn't help that Paul's consistent ringing of her door buzzer returned no

## The Lost Raven

results, pressing every button on the intercom in the hope that a resident would, at some point, let us in. Uniformed police were in attendance, my presence required to assess Angela's state of mind, keep her calm, an unavoidable arrest pending. They'd batter the door down it they deemed it necessary.

Someone eventually appeared in the darkened hallway, unclicking the door, a flashing amber light from his bicycle highlighting his shocked face. He muttered a vague good morning as several officers stepped aside, his exit undeterred. Paul didn't say anything, merely displayed his identity badge before leaving the guy to cycle along the street. He looked relieved. We hadn't come for him.

Angela's front door was open when we stepped onto the landing, sending Paul's already tattered nerves into overdrive. He pushed it with a free hand, stepping hastily inside the flat, several officers behind us expecting trouble.

'Hello? Angela? It's DCI Mannering,' he called into the empty space, knocking a closed fist against her creaking door to confirm our presence.

No answer.

If he had a gun, it would be cocked by now, aimed towards anything that moved, anyone who didn't belong in this space soon to regret being on the receiving end of Paul's professional wrath. As it was, he wasn't armed, the officers behind us carrying taser guns, nothing more. The place was a mess. I initially wondered if she had been burgled but upon further inspection, nothing seemed amiss. Her laptop was open on a coffee table, discarded clothing scattered across the carpet, shoes everywhere, mugs of tea left half-consumed. The kitchen was peppered with pieces of broken glass and rice grains that crunched underfoot, the entire place subjected to someone's undeniable anguish.

'In here!' Just then a shrill voice cut into the otherwise

stillness of the building, the low buzz from the television barely noticeable in the background.

Paul headed into the lounge where he was greeted with an outstretched finger pointing towards a dark coloured trouser suit. It was covered in blood. Several raven feathers were lined up across the sofa, my business card sitting amid a pile of unopened envelopes that looked urgent, as if she hadn't paid her bills in a while.

'Okay, get this place secured,' Paul muttered flatly, glancing my way from the corner of his eyes, unwilling to confirm what we were both thinking. 'Looks like we'll be doing a full search.' He didn't have a warrant but it didn't matter, reason enough to believe a serious crime had been committed, enough evidence here to secure Angela Healy in custody for at least twenty-four hours.

My phone rang. Alice. She sounded flustered, frustrated, unable to get hold of Paul, calling me because she knew I'd answer. Under normal circumstances, I'd have been flattered. As it was, I was stressed, concerned for a woman I couldn't believe capable of hurting anyone other than herself. I glanced towards Paul, my friend knee-deep now in forensics, Bernard already on his way.

'Everything okay?' I asked, stepping onto the landing for some much-needed distance from the claustrophobic atmosphere behind me. I wasn't expecting Alice's voice to sound so calming, didn't realise how much I needed to hear it.

'I did some digging and found CCTV footage from the inside of a bus on the night Mark Jenkins was murdered,' she confirmed. 'It shows Angela Healy getting onto the number 76 bus outside The Bulls Head in Shelby at just before twelve thirty, getting off in Eastcliff at around one fifteen.'

'Am I missing something?' Alice sounded vague, as if

what she was seeing on screen wasn't matching what she was telling me.

'From what I can make out, she had blood on her arm and was carrying a bag that looks a bit suspicious. If she was on a night out, I'd expect her to have been dressed up, but she was wearing old jeans and a scruffy t-shirt that looked too big, almost as if she changed her clothing at some point. She looked flustered too. As if she'd just witnessed something she didn't want to acknowledge.'

I thought about the green dress found in a skip the very same night. *Angela's* green dress. I swallowed. 'Do we have anything from the lab yet regarding the dress?'

'Yeah. The blood was confirmed as Mark's.'

'So, I guess we just need to locate the person who was *wearing* it.' I knew what Alice was thinking. We merely needed to find Angela to confirm that. It wasn't a comfort.

The next hour passed in a blur, the police recovering a blood-soaked knife, a bloodied stiletto, several articles on how to source GHB, unsavoury messages on Facebook, information about Liam Goodman. Nothing was left untouched, no area of Angela Healy's home or life undisturbed. The police needed verification that the blood matched the victims, of course, yet they assumed they'd already found the murder weapon, all this mere routine now. There was plenty of evidence, enough to conclude that, without warning, we'd found The Raven Rapist.

'You may as well go home and get some rest.' Paul was standing in Angela's kitchen, lifting random items with the end of a pen, trying not to contaminate the scene and annoy Bernard.

'I'd rather we find Angela first.' I still couldn't imagine she'd do something like that. She seemed too vulnerable, too weak. I couldn't think about my needs. The entire place was a hive of activity, cameras flashing from every room, evidence bags steadily piling up.

'Yeah and that could take a while. We don't know where she is or where she'd go. There's nothing more you can do for now. When we find her, I'll let you know.' Paul glanced towards the chaos behind me. 'You can come to the station later to discuss your jacket.'

Paul didn't look my way. He knew I wasn't involved, of course, yet needed my statement anyway, my alibi eliminating me from enquiries soon enough. They just needed it on record. The fact that several of my business cards were found in one of the inside pockets *and* amongst incriminating items here, didn't matter. I gave a card to *everyone*. It was all just paperwork, bureaucracy, files that needed stamping, confirmations requiring verification, the CPS satisfied.

I didn't want to but I headed home. It was getting light now anyway, a new day dawning. I needed sustenance, a lie-down. Preferably before I fell down.

***

I was grateful my flat was empty, Andy on another early shift, already gone. He'd left a message that was, once again, pinned to my fridge.

*Ran out of coffee again. Sorry. A.*

I shook my head. How on earth did he drink the stuff so fast? I took a shower, already in a bad mood, a good night's sleep and lack of caffeine something I didn't fair well without. I needed to relax, yet Angela was on my mind, plans to visit Steph and the kids today still hanging over me. I couldn't let them down. They needed me. I lay on my bed, hoping for an hour's sleep, if I could, yet I was still staring at the ceiling forty minutes later so I got up and went into the kitchen, making a mental note to buy coffee, sort out my life, make an effort. I didn't assume I was any different to Angela, living from day to day in some vague hope that things would miraculously figure themselves out on their own.

I messaged Steph to confirm the time of my arrival, receiving a thumbs-up emoji and three love hearts in response. She was never big on expression and it usually made me laugh. Today, however, I could have done with something more solid. I didn't assume Paul would mind waiting for my wandering jacket explanation. It was just a box that needed ticking, nothing more.

# Thirty-Three

## *Newton*

I sat in the train station staring at a poster for life insurance, not interested in the contents, merely lost in the moment. My train was late, as always, nothing to do but sit in silence with untethered thoughts and an empty belly. Eventually, I relented and called Paul.

'Any news?'

'I thought you were meant to be getting some rest?'

'I couldn't sleep. Do I need to ask if *you've* been home yet?'

'I'm irrelevant.' I'm sure Paul's wife would be *pleased* to hear that. 'Where are you anyway?'

'I'm heading off to see Steph and the kids for a couple of hours.' I needed the distraction. Paul would understand.

'Good. It'll do you good to do something normal for a change. Go and spend time with your family, Newt. I've got this.' He laughed, sounding exhausted.

'Are *you* planning on getting any rest today?'

## The Lost Raven

'Yeah, I'm heading home in a bit. Adele isn't happy that she hasn't seen me since yesterday.'

I could appreciate that. I'd only met Paul's wife once, but she seemed nice. She deserved a husband who showed up from time to time, someone who was present. 'I'm sure you'll be the *first* to know when they have Angela in custody.' I attempted a smile that didn't quite reach my face, glad Paul couldn't see the weird shape it had oddly formed.

'Likewise, my friend,' Paul chided. 'Now *do one* before I arrest you for wasting police time.' He laughed. I laughed. I hung up just as my train arrived, the platform filling with screeching brakes, the muffled voice over a loudspeaker barely audible.

I boarded the train and sat by a window, watching Eastcliff give way to open countryside and unexpected freedom beyond. I was convinced The Raven Rapist was a man. We all did. Yet, why I'd jumped to such a conclusion, I wasn't sure. What gave *me* the right to assume that women were incapable of the same cold brutality seemingly reserved for the male species? I opened my laptop to check every piece of evidence I could, going over *anything* I might have missed. I assumed Angela was depressed, nothing more, therapy and medication all she'd need to settle her mood. The fact that I knew little about her made me uncomfortable. I should have seen this coming, should have noticed the warnings.

By the time I disembarked at the other end, I was stressed. A taxi ride to Steph's house seeing me unusually quiet, the driver chatting to himself rather than me, my disgruntled responses uncharacteristically frustrating. London felt so busy compared to the life I'd made in Eastcliff. It's amazing what you get used to. The bustle here used to thrill me, excite me, my university days packed with boozy late-nights and overdue assignments. These days I needed calm and tranquillity to rationalise my brain into some kind of valid order. And coffee. I *always* needed coffee. Maybe I was getting old. I climbed out of the taxi, paid the driver, almost leaving my laptop on the back seat.

Stephanie's home was a four-storey Edwardian property set close to the Thames, sandwiched in a tight row of what used to be thriving boutique shops before recession and deprivation took over. The ground floor windows had long since been covered in brown paper, the only reminder left of the florist shop my sister-in-law once dreamed of opening. That was until she lost Isaac, losing her way, her focus. She had the money to move away, of course, start a fresh life elsewhere, the only reason she didn't because she wanted to remain where she and my brother were happy, where her treasured memories lingered. She had a perfect view of London on a clear day, although not today, unfortunately, a dense mist making navigation impossible — although, in fairness, that might have been *me*.

'Uncle Newton!' Timothy raced out of the front door and slammed himself full force into my body, almost dislodging my feet from the ground in the process. He was laughing, jumping up and down, desperate to be picked up. He was eleven, too old for such affection, too heavy for such attention, yet his autism ensured a childlike personality he'd no doubt retain his whole life. Peter used to show me the same affection, yet he was at the age now where even an acknowledgement was too much, teenage years encroaching, the kid growing up fast. I missed those earlier times.

'Hey, kiddo,' I returned Tim's enthusiasm. 'How're you doing?'

'Mum's made a cake,' he stated excitedly, grabbing my hand and dragging me towards the open front door.

'Only because I forgot to buy apples,' came Stephanie's

## The Lost Raven

bright, apologetic voice, jolting me from my daydream. She pulled a "sorry" face behind her son, knowing how much I loved apple pie.

'Hey sis,' I leaned in and kissed her cheek, glad for this brief moment of normality after the week I'd had. I wished I could visit more often, my sister-in-law and nephews the only family I had left now. Our dad died when we were kids and Isaac and I leant on each other for the support we couldn't find elsewhere, our mum doing the best she could until dementia took her from us, too. When my brother was gone, I couldn't abide the idea of being in London without him, so I ran away, Eastcliff subsequently becoming my home.

'You look like *shit*.' Stephanie stepped into her hallway, already halfway up the narrow staircase that led to a first-floor landing, the smile on her face something I'd sorely missed. The house smelled of lemon and freshly chopped parsley, the high ceilings and narrow rooms telling of a time long past, of residents long dead, my brother included. I missed her home cooking, missed spending time with Isaac's family, laughing late into the evening, annoying the neighbours. I couldn't remember the last time I'd had a good laugh.

'Say it like it is, why don't you?' I smiled despite myself, knowing she was only joking.

'You just look as if you haven't been sleeping.' Steph took my jacket and hung it on a peg, the thing lurking at the back of my wardrobe until this morning, a musty smell lingering that I'd only just noticed. I kept a tight hold of my laptop bag. It was filled with incriminating evidence of a case not yet fully confirmed to anyone.

'Well, you know me.'

'Yes I do, unfortunately.' She smiled, heading into a brightly lit kitchen and an inviting aroma. I followed. Peter was on his mobile, seated at a large table that flanked the room, a giant wall of glass behind him opening onto a private decked area. In the summer those bi-fold doors would be thrown open, allowing nature inside, Steph's beautiful but small London courtyard garden vaguely visible through the morning mist. I glanced down, Timothy still beside me, his arms still wrapped around my waist. I missed this house. Missed the laughter.

'Sup, Uncle Newt?' Peter called out. He didn't look up, busy elsewhere, earbuds buried in his ears, better things on his mind. The teenage phase had well and truly entered the building. When did he begin calling me *Uncle Newt?*

Stephanie smiled, giving me a sideways glance. 'Say hello to your uncle *properly* please, Peter,' she instructed.

Peter sighed, turning my way briefly with a sarcastic grin on his face. 'Good morning, Uncle Newton. How are you this *fine* morning?'

'Less of the sarcasm please young man,' Stephanie chastised, trying and failing to hide her amusement. I couldn't help but grin. He reminded me of Isaac.

'How're you doing mate?' I replied. The thing I've learned about teenagers is that they rarely want to engage with the grown-ups, far too *cool* to be seen instigating a conversation with the "oldies".

'Yeah, buzzin. You?'

Jesus, I couldn't believe how grown up he was beginning to sound. He looked just like his dad, his voice already deepening, his facial features changing with every visit I made. I pressed my lips together, emotion something I'd always tried to control whilst in the presence of my brother's family.

'You know. The usual.' I was trying to sound blasé, failing.

Stephanie handed me a mug of steaming black coffee

## The Lost Raven

that I took with a wink and a generous sigh I couldn't help expelling into the room. She had no idea how much I needed this distraction.

'You boys go and tidy your rooms please,' she instructed.

Several grunts emerged as both boys headed upstairs, thunderous feet and mistimed irritation making me smile, the warmth of this family home making me envious. I'd only just noticed how tired I was, the last few days too hectic for me to stop and appreciate my own impossible failings.

'So, how are you?' Steph took a seat at the kitchen table, sliding Peter's now discarded mobile phone to one side. I joined her. Stephanie always asked me the same question and I always gave her the same answer. Fine. Everything was always fine. Today, however, I knew she would see right through *that* lie.

'Been a bit of a week, to be honest,' I sighed deeply into my coffee, wishing I lived closer. It didn't seem fair that I expected others to unload their problems onto me, yet I had nowhere to aim mine. My sister-in-law didn't comment, didn't need to know my feelings. I had Angela Healy on my mind, the growing reputation of The Raven Rapist certain to have reached London by now. 'The police think they might know who The Raven Rapist is.' I wasn't sure how much I should be revealing at this stage.

'Shit! No way.' Steph's eyes widened. 'I've been watching on the news about him. Sick pig.'

*Him?* Should I tell her? I didn't even have confirmation myself yet that The Raven Rapist might be a woman. 'Yeah. He is,' I confirmed instead.

'So, who *is* it?'

'You know I can't divulge that kind of information.' Steph knew. She was always trying to glean information where she could, uncover gossip to share with her superficial friends and neighbours.

'Worth a try.' She grinned, picking up her own mug, taking a long-needed sip of hot liquid. 'It's always good to see you. The boys miss you.'

I could see that Timothy did, but Peter was becoming a man, too old to be seen conversing with his boring old uncle. I smiled anyway.

'Do you ever feel that no matter how much you try to help someone, it's never enough?' I was speaking about Angela, of course, the idea that she could be on the roof of a building one moment, then raping and murdering innocent men the next, was not something I wanted to think about.

'A patient?'

I didn't exactly have *patients*, but it was an old joke, told because of my doctorate status, something that had stuck. It probably sounded better than saying *mentally ill criminals, murderers, psychopaths.*

'Yeah, something like that.'

'You really shouldn't get so involved with them, Newt. It's not healthy.'

Steph was right, it wasn't healthy, but how was I meant to do my job if I didn't get inside the heads of those I was trying to help?

'I get the impression there's something else on your mind.' She was tapping the side of her mug, waiting.

It never fails to amaze me how well she knows me, how clearly she can see through my moods, even when I'm unaware I'm in one. I sighed. 'An old friend turned up, needing a place to stay.'

'Ouch.' Stephanie knew how much my private space meant to me, *alone time* something I required in order to process my thoughts, dissect case files, muddle through my day. That might explain why I'd been feeling so stressed and out of balance all week.

'Ouch indeed.' I sighed again. I took a long swig of coffee, momentarily glad for the soothing texture.

'So, who's the *friend?*' Steph grinned as if hoping it might be a woman, a potential romantic interest in the pipeline. I thought of Alice. *If only.*

'Just an old uni mate.'

Steph gave me a blank look.

'Andrew Hansley.' I never expected to see him again, the fact that he was currently living under my roof seemed highly bizarre considering he'd talked of nothing but big cities and bigger ambitions for years.

'Andy?' Steph sat upright, something in her tone shifting dramatically, her brow furrowing frantically. Her eyes had darkened, a shocked look spreading across her now flushed face.

'Yes, why?' I narrowed my eyes.

'It's nothing. I just haven't heard that name for a few years, that's all.' She shifted in her seat, looking uncomfortable.

'What is it?'

Stephanie didn't reply.

'Steph? What's wrong?' I knew her too well, knew she was holding something back.

'Nothing.'

'Tell me.'

'It doesn't matter.'

'Clearly, it does.' I placed my mug on the table.

Steph took a breath. 'I never thought I'd ever hear that name again, that's all.'

'Why? What did Andy ever do to *you?*' I almost laughed but refrained just in time, the look on her face telling me I didn't want to know.

Steph closed her eyes. 'I'm *so* sorry, Newt. I never

expected to have to tell you like *this*.' A wobble had formed in her bottom lip that wasn't there a moment ago.

'Tell me what?' I was beginning to panic, worried by what I was about to hear.

A pause. I could hear the kids upstairs arguing, just a typical day in the lives of two brothers.

'Not long before you guys split up, Kate had a brief affair with *Andrew Hansley*.' Steph spat Andy's name as if it was poison, barely able to look at me, unable to acknowledge the response she knew I was about to offer.

'I beg your pardon?' What the *hell?*

Steph shook her head. 'I'm so sorry I didn't tell you before. She made me promise it was over. Promised it meant *nothing*.'

I couldn't believe what I was hearing. 'When?' I could barely speak, my coffee threatening to spill, the liquid suddenly uninviting, bitter.

Even though Kate and I had separated almost fifteen years ago, it still hurt. It wasn't something I admitted, had never spoken openly about my marriage to anyone. As far as the rest of the world was concerned (my sister-in-law included) I was over her. The truth was, I wasn't, a tiny piece of me still feeling the pain I'd experienced the day she told me she was leaving. She blamed her job, my job, stress, coffee. Anything other than the truth. The truth that she was seeing someone else.

'I always thought you were too young to get married.' Steph could no longer retain her frustration, her casual remark made purely to soften the blow.

'That's irrelevant.' It was, even though it was probably true. I was twenty-two years old. What the hell did I know about love back then? I didn't know much now.

'She wasn't right for you,' Steph muttered into her mug, barely able to look at me.

## The Lost Raven

I didn't contradict her.

'She wasn't exactly the settling down type, was she?' Steph continued, glancing sideways, attempting to convince me that something outside had caught her attention. 'She was bound to stray.' We both knew what Steph meant. Kate was a party girl, university a place she saw as a way to freeload, have fun. I was drawn to the rebel in her, initially, knowing that carefree misfit was someone I could never be.

'Why? Because she liked to enjoy herself?' I didn't mean to sound sarcastic, bitter. This was too much to take in. It seemed she had indeed enjoyed herself. With my best friend.

Steph shook her head. 'I never liked what they did to you, but when Andy—' She paused, an obvious attempt to change the subject now threatening to make things worse.

'When he *what*?' What the hell was I missing now? My voice had elevated. I didn't want the kids to overhear. I attempted to get to my feet, changed my mind.

'He made some unwanted advances towards me a few days before he left London.'

'*You?*'

Steph nodded.

'*When?*'

'I can't remember exactly. Isaac came in before anything happened luckily, but they had words. Isaac punched him. He moved away not long after that so I didn't think it was important to tell you.' She was finally looking at me, her embarrassment obvious. 'I didn't find out that Kate was seeing him until a couple of weeks later, I swear, although by that time she'd already confirmed you guys were over and I didn't want to make things worse.' Steph looked at me as if she couldn't believe she was reliving such events, something in her eyes confirming her own unforgotten pain.

'When you say *advances*, what do you mean?' I suddenly

felt nervous by her potential answer, the last few days still strong in my mind.

'He attacked me. He was drunk.'

'Are you serious?'

Steph nodded.

'Why didn't you tell me?' Didn't she assume I'd want to know? Andy's abrupt departure all those years ago now made sense.

'Isaac said it wouldn't help.'

I couldn't imagine my brother keeping something like that from me, unwittingly taking the knowledge of my best friend's betrayal to his grave. Andy was in my house right now, eating *my* food, drinking *my* coffee.

I stood up, needing to leave, or vomit, whichever came first, this place suddenly too small and oppressive.

'I'm so sorry, Newt,' Steph's voice rang after me as I stumbled across the kitchen and down the staircase, leaving my laptop behind, the front door left open because I was in no condition to close it. I couldn't be inside that house. Not today. I couldn't process how she was able to keep such secrets from me for all these years. Andy was meant to be my *friend*. I didn't know who I felt more sorry for—myself, my brother, or my unwitting nephews currently oblivious to *my* unexpected departure.

# Thirty-Four

## *Angela*

It's a sign, I swear. Liam is staying at *The Northern Raven Hotel*. Of all the places in the city he could be, I can't believe *this* is the one I've found myself standing outside, a recent posting on Facebook concluding my journey. I close my eyes, needing a moment, knowing I'm exactly where I need to be, the ravens forever guiding me, spurring me on. I've been here a while, waiting, watching. It's cold but I have a hot drink and a sandwich courtesy of a kiosk on the corner, enough money to prevent any unfortunate impression that I might be homeless. I look a mess, I know. My hair hasn't been brushed for a while, my panda eyes reduced to puffy pink dots that emphasise my traumatised face. I don't care. I don't want to look attractive. *Ever*.

I consider entering the hotel, demanding attention, answers, but judging by the mood I'm in I don't assume it will aid my mission. I don't expect to feel any better for seeing his face, unsure how I'm going to react when I do.

This last week has taken a toll, leading me to a place I never assumed possible, nothing left to do but take this to its bitter conclusion, to confront him — *to kill him*. I don't know what I'm expecting. Fireworks? A down-on-one-knee apology whilst crying into the surrounding London air at just how *sorry* he is? What do I want him to do? Throw himself into the path of an oncoming bus?

I'm almost surprised when he emerges from the hotel, looking the same as always, his facial features a focused set of twitching muscles he directs absentmindedly along the street. I can't help the anger that rises in my belly, nothing on his face confirming he cares what he's done. My feet automatically take control, forcing me to race up behind him, my hands grabbing his jacket, my overworked lungs far more ready to express provocation than I realise.

'You *raped* me!' I yell into the street. I don't care who's listening or how I sound, my entire body shivering in the damp air. I still can't believe he attacked my friend on the same evening, poor Rosie left to deal with her trauma alone. How can I let that lie?

Liam turns around sharply, no doubt wondering what's happening, not expecting his recent victim to be standing directly behind him.

'Angela?' He looks shocked, my existence unwanted. 'What are *you* doing here?' He has ignored my statement. How convenient.

'You *raped* me!' I repeat, louder, practically screaming in his face. I don't care who can hear, how I look, my entire body convulsing.

He stares at me, nothing in his eyes confirming his regret, no shame, no emotion. *'What?'* He seems surprised, his cheeks flushed with confusion. He's a good liar, I'll give him that.

'Do you want me to repeat it?' I place furious hands on

my hips, barely able to keep them steady. It doesn't matter that I'm in no position to take the moral high road, my own recent actions far worse.

'I did no such thing.' Liam's face is contorting as if he assumes me mad. He glances around, no doubt wondering how he can escape.

'Then what would *you* call it?'

'I have no idea what you're talking about.' He attempts to walk away, already bored of unwanted accusations.

'Don't you dare walk away from me,' I scream, still in his face, merely wanting to confront my attacker head-on. It is the first time in days I've felt such clarity over my mixed emotions. I push him hard in the back, causing him to stumble forward.

Liam turns around and swears, grabbing my arms as if I've lost the plot. Maybe I have. He doesn't need to confirm it. 'What the hell is wrong with you?' he asks, still unwilling to admit what he's done.

I should have done this a week ago, of course, before those other poor bastards died, before I became something I never assumed possible. Liam has spent the entire week avoiding me, ignoring my wrath, my existence. I wonder if he has ignored Rosie too, the fact that she already confirmed she'd spoken to him, bringing bile to the back of my throat. I'm crying, furious, yanking my flailing arms from his poisonous grasp as if he's an alien about to dissect me.

'Just tell me why you did it.'

'I didn't do *anything*.'

'At least say you're sorry.'

'For *what*?'

'For raping me!' And Rosie. I feel terrible I've ignored my friend all week. I can barely contemplate he'd do something so disgusting to a middle-aged woman, her own marriage a failure, her life unbalanced.

'Will you stop saying that?' He glances briefly towards a woman walking past, offering a mistimed apology that looks ridiculous. 'Why don't you calm down and talk to me?' He looks the same, sounds the same, the colleague I thought I once knew well, nothing to me now but an infestation I need to quash.

'I want you to admit it. Say you're sorry.' My fists and teeth are clenched so tightly I assume my jaw might break. If I could just hear that word, it might make me feel better.

'I swear, I haven't done anything.' He raises his hands. I assume to attack.

'Get away from me,' I scream, unable to do anything else. I can't help it, can't prevent my reaction.

'I don't know what you want me to say.' Liam's eyes are wide, his response one of shock. He turns around, needing to leave.

'How dare you!' I'm crying, sobbing, everything I am exposed and raw. I want to use my knife, stab him to death in the street, unconcerned by witnesses or consequence. But it's still in my flat, unfortunately, still covered in blood from the last idiot who crossed my path.

'Fuck off, Angela.' Liam must think I'm insane, nothing of my company wanted today. He's already walking away.

'You need to be careful, Liam,' I call after him, threatening to spill a secret I'm sure is about to finish me soon anyway.

'Why?' He stops. Looks blankly at me.

'Because you don't know what I'm capable of.' It's true. He has no idea.

'Oh, but you think *I'm* capable of rape?' He whispers the word "rape" so no further people will overhear. He doesn't want anyone to see him for the monster he is.

Something inside snaps and I rush towards him, my arms outstretched, my teeth gritted. I can't help it. I can't listen to his lies a moment longer, can't look at his face anymore. I scratch his cheeks, his neck, unconcerned by how manic I look, my throat a savage collection of screams I aim into the air. Several onlookers have already stopped to witness the commotion, already on their phones recording this moment, sharing my antics online. Some might even call me a "Karen". That's what they call *angry* people these days, apparently. I don't have my knife but I draw blood anyway, his face red, sore. He flinches, crying out, attempting to back away.

'Jesus Christ, you fucking *bitch*,' he spits, his true nature shining through. And there we are. There's the real Liam Goodman, everyone.

I smile, my facial muscles a grotesque display of hatred, my nails long enough to cause permanent injury, leaving a scar like the ones he's already left me with. I go in for a second attack, yet Liam steps to one side, anticipating my wrath, almost tripping over his feet as he jogs along the street, his intention simple—to get as far away from the crazy woman as he can.

I'm yelling but I can no longer understand my words, let alone my emotions, my head in a dark place no one could dare imagine. I'm lucky. In London, no one cares. No one wants to get involved with issues that don't concern them. I watch as several bystanders move on, already bored, better things to do. The only thing I care about now is revenge.

# Thirty-Five

## *Newton*

I needed some air, no idea where I was going, tracing swift footsteps along the pavement for an escape I didn't anticipate I'd need. I couldn't believe what Steph had told me, couldn't condone the fact that she'd kept such vile secrets so long. I couldn't stop thinking about my wife and so-called best friend. Together. *Having sex*. The very thought made me nauseous, my fists tightening in response that made me want to scream. Why didn't Stephanie tell me? Why didn't Isaac? Thoughts I didn't need to dwell on swamped my head, creating havoc, building panic. How long was it going on? When did it end? *Did it end at all?*

I had visions of Andy secretly married now to my exwife, the man I assumed a friend nothing more than an enemy in disguise. Maybe he'd come to gloat, our chance meeting at the hospital not by chance at all, instead orchestrated for some unseen confession I was yet to appreciate. I knew there was something on his mind, I knew

## The Lost Raven

him too well, but I didn't anticipate *this*. I considered calling him, confronting him, but saying something like that over the telephone wasn't right for such a momentous accusation. I needed to see his face. I still wanted to believe Steph had it wrong.

Paul still hadn't called regarding Angela Healy, hadn't reminded me of the statement I was meant to be providing about my wandering jacket. I assumed they didn't yet have her in custody, her whereabouts still unknown. I tried calling her but it went to voicemail, every message left unreturned. I stood in the street, nothing else to do, my lungs a struggling mass of air failing to do their job, my brain a knot of confusion from events I couldn't imagine real. I wasn't confident I could support Angela right now, anyway. I could barely support my own weight.

Another uncomfortable message, another missed call. I was convinced that if I could speak to her, I could better assess the situation, calm things before the police stepped in and tipped her over the edge completely. It wouldn't take much. She was volatile, suicidal and, although the evidence against her seemed overwhelming, I still wasn't convinced of her guilt. What triggers someone so violently that they'd be willing to kill? I was furious with Andy, irritated by Steph, but not enough to *kill* them. Yes, they'd hurt me, badly, my sister-in-law someone I thought I knew better, deserved better from. It didn't matter that I hadn't yet allowed her an explanation, far too incensed to listen. I wondered who had hurt Angela so badly that she was prepared to kill four grown men in such a violent way.

Steph was calling me, my mobile vibrating angrily against my leg. I considered answering but I was too annoyed, needing to calm down before I could speak, nothing of value in my head. I didn't want to fall out with the only family I had left. I rejected the call, resisting the urge to throw my phone into the street. My sister-in-law could wait. For now.

Steph's home was positioned between Whitechapel and Canary Wharf, the river a stone's throw from her front door. I didn't realise how much I missed this part of the city, joggers and dog walkers out in force, shoppers, tourists, locals. I should have been glad for the distraction, the oblivion, a chance to lose myself, to think. As it was, I felt sick, nothing on my mind but betrayal and mistrust. I'd opened my home to Andy, welcomed him into my space — had been a friend when he needed one.

I paused outside a riverside restaurant, the place positioned perfectly to steal your thoughts whilst the owners stole your money for coffee worth a fraction of the price. Despite this knowledge, my feet automatically led me inside, directing me to a seat by the window. A wrap-around terrace hid me from customers equally hidden behind newspapers — expensive coffee waking them up, their frustrated faces aimed nowhere in particular. None of them noticed me or appreciated the view, iconic buildings visible on a clear day, The Shard, Tower Bridge. I'd forgotten how beautiful it was.

I wasn't planning on staying long, a strong coffee enough to ease my cluttered thoughts and place much-needed clarity over this impossible day. I should have gone back to the house, of course, spoken to Steph, asked the questions I assumed too painful to acknowledge. Instead, I drank my coffee in silence, staring at the view, the whole of London unaware of my thoughts. I eventually found myself walking the riverbank, several quid poorer, oblivion threatening to drown me for my efforts. I wasn't exactly paying much attention. I certainly didn't expect to see Angela Healy, her familiar voice something I assumed had developed from my overworked imagination. Yet, a woman

## The Lost Raven

who looked remarkably *like* Angela crossed my path, yelling, fists clenched, jaw tight.

'Angela?' I called her way, assuming I was dreaming, my recent indignation creating images that didn't exist, my current anguish creating hallucinations I wasn't prepared to accept.

The woman turned around and glared at me, the distance between us not enough to retain anonymity. 'My God, are you stalking me?' It *was* Angela. She shook her head as if my presence was a set-up, my existence meant purely to infuriate her. I must have looked just as surprised, of course, unsure how I should react, my mind no longer in a good enough place to judge.

'I'm visiting family.' It was true, the concept raw, uncomfortable. 'Are you okay?'

'What do *you* care?' She was crying, snot and tears smeared across a reddened face, mascara streaming down both cheeks. She was yelling at a male some distance away, the guy already taking his chance to escape, heading hastily along the street. Angela followed, prompting me to do the same.

'Angela?' I called into the air, wanting her to stop, to talk to me. I needed to call Paul too, explain what was happening.

'Leave me alone.' She was running, uninterested in anything I had to say.

'The police are looking for you.' I was yelling, needing her to know the urgency of the situation. If I could step in first, I owed it to the poor woman to at least try and help. The last thing I wanted was to frighten her. I pulled my mobile phone from my trouser pocket, ready to alert the police to her whereabouts, one eye kept on her rapidly moving body, the other on locating my contacts. Angela didn't acknowledge me, didn't turn around, instead continually screamed towards the escaping male who was busy flagging a taxi.

I knew she saw me as a threat, so I hung back, waiting for my chance to accost her, continued obscenities leaving her mouth that made several by-passers glare in disgust. I didn't know who she was yelling at or why, only that her intended target eventually climbed into a taxi after several irate horns almost saw his unwitting downfall. He didn't look impressed, flushed cheeks confirming he didn't want Angela's attention. She yelled in frustration before turning around, racing right past me, disappearing from view several times and forcing unwanted expletives to leave my already frustrated mouth.

Eventually, we arrived outside a hotel where she continued to argue with herself for a few moments, seemingly talking to something in the sky. I couldn't hear what she was saying. I had no choice but to step in, explain why I was there, calm her down. She looked exhausted, glaring at me as if she no longer recognised my face. She didn't retaliate, didn't react, simply raced inside the entrance, nothing more to add.

I called Paul's number, out of breath, glad for a moment to rest.

'Still no news, Newt,' he chided sarcastically into the phone, knowing I'd be ringing about Angela. *Again.*

'I know where she is.'

'How? Where are you?' I'd caught his attention, the sound of several sheets of paper and a stapler falling to the floor momentarily calming my mood.

'Threadneedle Street.' I glanced towards a large Victorian building with a cream façade and impactful double-fronted entrance. 'Send the police to The Northern Raven Hotel. Angela Healy is in London.'

# Thirty-Six

## *Angela*

I find myself racing into the hotel, Newton close behind me, nothing on my mind other than revenge and the justice I plan to serve cold. Liam openly rejected me in public, what he did to me in private seemingly of no concern. I don't know why Newton is here, the idea of being followed to London not something I've anticipated. My cheeks are flush, my lungs struggling to absorb the fact that, even now, Liam is hell-bent on destroying everything. I have no choice but to confront him when he returns. He won't be expecting it, will assume I've given up, gone home, turned my attention to something else.

I head to the reception desk, my tears as real as they get, apologising inwardly to the hotel staff unavoidably met with my impossible anguish. I can't stay, they tell me, yet I can't leave. Not without the answers I need. Not before I *end* this.

'I'm sorry,' I tell the poor receptionist behind the

counter as calmly as my failing body will allow, security staff already called to remove me from the building. She gives me a narrow look. 'My husband is Liam Goodman. We argued this morning and now he won't allow me back into our hotel room to collect my things.' I swallow, taking in as much air as my lungs will allow. I'm weak, shattered, my tiny hands trembling with desperate anticipation. It's hardly an act. I need her to believe me, feel sorry for me. *Help me.*

'Are you okay?' The question sounds genuine.

'I forgot the key to our room. Liam can be *very* controlling.' It's true. I force a quivering smile, attempting to gain her favour, a tear falling I can't prevent. I'm only telling *little* lies. 'He'll be back soon. Please, you *have* to help me.' I glance over my shoulder towards two approaching security guards, the receptionist giving me a sideways look, holding a hand in the air that slows their approach. It prompts me to burst into tears that free fall down my cheeks. She offers a smile, handing me a keycard to Liam's room, a sympathetic look on her face I'm not ready to deal with.

I thank her and head to the lift, nervous, my heart pounding, palms sweaty. All I need is a few moments alone with him, a moment to end this. He doesn't appreciate what's coming, the person I've become this week nothing compared to the person I'm about to unleash. I've confronted him today already and the bastard rejected me. I'm not leaving things like that. He can't treat women as if they don't matter.

Room 107 is on the top floor, away from the bustle of other guests and potential prying ears. I unlock the room with a swipe of the card, stepping inside. I don't know how long Liam will be or if the receptionist plans to confirm my presence, although if she tips him off, it's over. I stand by the window watching the street for what feels like an eternity, Newton hovering some distance below, on his phone, looking panicked.

My own mobile rings and I assume it's him, believing he's once more trying to corner me. Thankfully, it's Rosie. I can't ignore her, knowing what I know, knowing I've been a terrible friend when she needed me.

'Thank God,' I breathe. 'Are you okay?' I sound deranged, my battery-depleted phone pressed firmly against my ear. This is the first time in days I've genuinely wanted to hear her voice. 'I've been calling you.' I'm whispering. In fairness, *I'm* the one who's not okay, hoping that someone, somewhere, might step in and save me.

'Sorry, I've been with the police.' Her voice sounds so small, so fragile. I want to cry again.

'I know what he did to you.' I close my eyes, lowering my voice, unwanted images littering my memory, choking my thoughts. 'I'm sorry. I should have gone to the police myself, prevented everything that has happened since.' She can't yet appreciate what I mean.

'Do you know the police are looking for you?' Rosie sounds so quiet, almost as if she's speaking on the opposite side of the room to her phone.

*What?* 'What do you mean?' I falter, automatically looking through the window to check that Newton isn't still out there.

'They were at your flat this morning.'

'How do you know that?'

'That detective came to my house, looking for you.'

'Why?' I'm trying to think, unconvinced that in my haste I didn't accidentally leave my front door unlocked. If the police gained access they will have found the knife by now, my clothing, my raven feathers.

'Only that it was vital I contact them if I hear from you.'

*Shit. SHIT!!* Is that why she's calling me? To confirm my

whereabouts so the police can arrest me? I start to panic. I can't help it, my legs suddenly juddery, weak, Newton's unexpected appearance now making sense.

'Do they know where I am?' I automatically hide behind a curtain, ready to throw myself into the street, if I must, no rational ideas left to placate my emotions.

'I don't think so. *I* don't even know where you are. Where are you?'

I can't tell her. The police might be with her right now, recording this call, waiting for me to slip up. This might be a setup, a story concocted to lure me in, help they claim I need, support they pretend to offer. I have to think fast. I can't let Liam slip away. Not again. I'll never get another chance like this.

'I have to go,' I mutter, unable to speak to my friend now about the rape we've both endured at the hand of a man we both assumed a friend. 'I'm *so* sorry. For everything.' I hang up and immediately turn off my phone. The police can trace it. I can't assume they already haven't.

Footsteps, no time for me to think, the hotel room door opening, forcing me to hold my breath behind this curtain. I pray it's Liam, hope he doesn't notice me, grateful when the first thing he does is turn on the shower. *Perfect.* He's muttering, talking to himself about me, nothing I haven't heard before, of course, yet I step gingerly around the bed, terrified, almost ready to give up and leave. I take a breath. I'm The Raven Rapist. I hold all the power and I'm done being nice.

When the bathroom door opens, I'm ready, slamming Liam over the back of the head with the bedside lamp as he enters the room. He doesn't see it coming, hitting the carpet with a thud, the anticipation of the incoming noise muffled by bedding I've already laid on the floor. I've visualised this moment for so long, those other men merely a warm-up act,

## The Lost Raven

a way to practice a craft I now plan to use on him. He looks pathetic, lying on his front, his naked skin damp and glistening, his towel no protection to the pain I'm about to inflict. I smile, momentarily grateful for the control I've taken. After today, Liam Goodman will know the true wrath of Angela Healy. After today, this *will* be over.

\*\*\*

My breathing struggles to keep up with the demands of my mind as I gag a man I now hate as much as my father, fastening his wrists to the legs of the bedframe, his ankles tied roughly to the radiator pipes with sheets torn from the bed. I haven't touched him. Not yet. I need him to witness what's coming his way, need to look in his eyes when I kill him. I kick him hard, jolting him awake, the man unable to speak through the sock I've jammed in the back of his throat. I temporarily relieve him of his suffocating prison, a smile on my face confirming my enjoyment.

'Jesus Christ Angela, what the *hell* are you doing?' He's trying to wriggle free, untwisting pale limbs from cheap cotton I've torn to shreds in a hurry. He isn't going anywhere.

'I want you to know what it feels like when someone rapes you.' I'm speaking, yet I can't understand my words, my voice bizarre, unreal.

He's afraid, can't move, nothing for him to do but lie still and wait. I haven't got any drugs with me today, no time to order any, no time to wait. It doesn't matter. I need him awake and aware of what I'm doing. I have my dildo. This is going to hurt him far more than he ever assumed he could hurt me. It's almost poetic how this moment is making me feel, justice mine to serve on a painful platter.

I feel invigorated as I crouch by his side, potentially

facing a prison sentence for what I've done, what I'm about to do set to seal my fate forever. I don't care. I've accomplished far worse, several corpses left to confirm that unfailing truth.

'Why are you doing this?' Liam is still speaking, still assuming he has any influence over his position, any power over me, still hell-bent on believing he's in control despite being unable to move anything other than his pathetic mouth. I slam my palm hard across the side of his jaw, blood spitting across the floor, nothing else emerging from his lips.

'Because I can.' I reply, fully aware of the power I hold, trembling with excitement I never expected to possess. I lean towards his cheek, whispering into his ear. 'People like you make me sick. You don't understand what it's like to feel the pain of rape. You don't deserve to live.'

I get to my feet, the air momentarily thin, my legs struggling to comply. I will rape Liam Goodman today as if I mean it, power the reason behind every rape committed anyway. I've never felt so hyped in my life, nothing dislodging this moment from my memory now. If this is my last day on earth, I'll go out with a bang, taking this bastard with me.

Liam grunts when I retrieve the dildo from my bag, firm silicone shortly to be inserted where nothing this large ever should. I've planned everything in detail, from the raven feather now laid in anticipation across his back, to the sharp knife retrieved from his breakfast tray that I trace across his trembling arms and legs. I cut deep enough to draw blood, yet not enough to end things. Not yet. I'm not ready. He's begging, crying out in pain, asking what I'm doing, but he already knows, subjected to agonising wounds that snake across his body. Liam can't move, can't stop me. He's weak, pathetic. I love the justice I'm inflicting, Rosie on my mind,

## *The Lost Raven*

Liam Goodman no good man at all.

Sex disgusts me, always has, my childhood taken too soon yet, standing here in front of him, his backside facing the ceiling, my mission is clear. I'll turn him over when I'm done, make him watch as I slice his pathetic penis from his puny body. He'll bleed out where he lies, some unfortunate hotel employee finding him dead before this day is complete. I can't help that, can't say in advance how sorry I am for such a discovery. I stuff his sock back inside his mouth, a grin on my face as he splutters and gags. He has brought this entirely on himself. This ends now. This ends with us.

# Thirty-Seven

## *Newton*

According to Paul, my presence outside The Northern Raven Hotel held the potential to cause more chaos, the police able to deal with this situation far better than I. I was subsequently told to wait, stay clear, *behave*. But for how long? I didn't want to think of Angela as The Raven Rapist but the evidence was everywhere, the inside of her flat confirming all we needed to know. If recent events were to be believed, she wouldn't be now planning anything good. When the male she'd earlier argued with returned, he ignored my pleas for attention as he made his way into the hotel, a sideways glare the only thing I was getting from him. I begrudgingly hovered in the street for as long as I could, eventually succumbing to my instincts, ignoring my friend's warnings as I headed inside.

'Can I help you?' The receptionist gave me a cold look. I didn't appreciate it.

'Do you have a woman called Angela Healy staying

## The Lost Raven

here?' I glanced around, no time for niceties, hoping this day would end with nothing more than a cup of coffee.

'I'm sorry, sir, guest details are confidential,' she confirmed, tracing unappreciative eyes over my flustered attire.

'I work with the police,' I confirmed. 'My name is Doctor Flanigan, clinical psychologist and forensics investigator.' I invented that last part to impress, my intentions merely to locate Angela, preferably before she located her intended target and ruined my day. I could only imagine the lies she had already invented. I needed to intervene before it was too late. I displayed my identity badge so she'd know I wasn't some idiot that had wandered in off the street.

She didn't look impressed, instead glared at me as if I was insane, sizing me up and down in anticipation of something the hotel did not condone. 'Was she small framed, gaunt looking, blonde hair, scruffily dressed, quite anxious?'

I nodded, unsure what else to do.

The receptionist frowned, biting her lip, realising with a nod of her own who I was talking about. 'Wearing a baseball cap?'

Another nod. Yep. That sounded like Angela.

The reception sighed. 'She said her husband was stopping her getting into their room. The poor thing looked terrified.'

'Who did she say her husband was?'

The receptionist didn't reply.

'Please. She was arguing with a male a short while ago. It's imperative that we find him.' We were wasting time with this nonsensical chatter. 'He came in here not long ago, tall, slim built, fair hair, dressed in a suit.' I didn't know his name, could have been describing anyone. 'We believe he might be in very real danger.' I was impressed by how authoritative I sounded. I didn't usually hold such a commanding presence. I considered calling Paul again, request his assistance, but wasn't confident what he would say. Stay the hell out of it, probably.

The receptionist looked momentarily horrified, her face contorting into a collection of spiderlike wrinkles confirming she didn't need that kind of stress in her day. She checked her computer system. 'Liam Goodman. Room 107.' She smiled. I smiled.

'Thank you.' Goodman. Of course. I should have realised. I couldn't assume Angela wasn't here to kill him, could only imagine what was going through her mind. If she *was* The Raven Rapist, the poor sod could already be dead.

I was shown to the lifts, entry granted to a part of the hotel reserved only for guests. I should have called Paul, told him my plan, but I was running out of time. I held my breath, hoping I had this wrong, hoping the items found at Angela's flat were a coincidence, nothing more. Everything had already been taken away for a forensic evaluation, the knife, the clothing, the feathers. I didn't want to know what she'd done with the dildo.

I stood quietly outside Liam's hotel room and listened.

'Beg!' A woman's voice filtered through the door, the request provoking a groan, something that sounded like laughter. Angela's laughter.

A grunt. It sounded like 'please' but I couldn't exactly tell. Liam Goodman, I presume. I swiped the keycard and headed inside, no time to think, no chance to change my mind. I didn't know what I was about to walk in on, didn't know what I'd find. It was fairly dark inside the room, the curtains closed, a heavy smell of aftershave lingering in the air. Angela was standing at the foot of the bed, a bloodied knife in her hand. From the doorway, all I could see were a pair of blood-soaked legs on the floor. She turned when she saw my approach, automatically pointing the knife my way.

'What the *fuck?*' she yelled, uncertain of my intentions.

I raised my hands. 'Is everything okay?' I knew it wasn't, but I was in no position to comment.

'What do you want?' Angela's confusion was evident. She blinked several times, shocked to have been disturbed, something in her eyes telling me she was more afraid than I was.

'I could ask you the same question.' I needed an explanation, confirmation of The Raven Rapist already noted. I glanced towards Liam. He was naked, tied to the bed by his wrists, his ankles secured to a radiator, deep snaking cuts over his arms, back, legs. He was spread flat on a ruffled duvet, most of it soaking up blood, face down, tears streaming down a reddened face he turned gingerly my way. There was a dildo next to him, a raven feather on the bed, more blood on the carpet.

'Go away. This is none of your business.' Angela was crying.

'The police are on their way. Whatever you think you're doing, Angela, you don't need to hurt anyone.'

She laughed. 'Too late,' she spat, salty tears blurring the line between sanity and confusion.

'Why don't you put the knife down?'

'Why don't you fuck off?'

Liam was trying to speak through the gag in his mouth, failing, his restraints too tight for him to move. I hoped she hadn't done anything stupid. I couldn't bring myself to look too closely, the condition in which The Raven Rapist had left her last victims too much for me to deal with.

'Whatever this is, we can talk about it. I've already told you, I'm always here.' I was trying to win her over, calm her down, expressing a genuine desire to help.

Angela began to sob, as if the last few days had broken her, something deep inside reduced to nothing now but dust. 'What do *you* know about it?' she asked me, genuinely assuming I didn't know anything.

'I'll never judge.' It was true. I needed to confirm that the police would be here any moment, very little time left for her to say anything that might be given in evidence against her. I glanced towards Liam, acknowledging his presence, silently confirming my pending assistance.

'Do you know what he did?' Angela spat, noticing my acknowledgement as she kicked him between the legs, making him cry out in muffled agony. Tears streamed down his sweat-infused cheeks. He couldn't react, couldn't stop her, forced instead to accept whatever she chose to do.

'Why don't you tell me?' I wanted to untie him, give him his clothes, his dignity, call an ambulance. I didn't know how much blood he'd lost but it looked as if Angela had been torturing him, enjoying the moment. At least he was alive.

'Men are scum,' she whispered, a false grin making her look insane. I assumed it was her mania, psychosis. She glanced my way as if I was part of the problem, no better than anyone else. I couldn't help staring at the raven feather. Angela noticed. 'You *know*, don't you?'

It was a simple question. We both knew the answer.

'Know what?'

She picked it up, the knife still in her grasp, Liam's blood dripping freely along her arm. 'You know who I am, don't you?'

I couldn't reply, couldn't think of anything that would have helped me if I confirmed she was The Raven Rapist. I swallowed.

'I'm curious to know where the name came from?'

## The Lost Raven

Angela spoke as if my silence was irrelevant. She turned the feather around in her hand, intrigued by a nickname meant only as a passing joke between three exhausted investigators at one o'clock in the morning.

'What name?'

'Do you know that ravens are highly intelligent birds who use their beaks and talons to rip open objects for food and shelter? They don't need anything other than what was given to them at birth, able to defend their territories, protecting themselves against unwanted attacks. They can talk, sing, and have a repertoire of more than a hundred vocalisations.'

I recalled a much earlier conversation on the roof of a car park, Timothy on my mind, as always. 'Why a raven feather?' I wanted to understand why she would leave such an item at the murder scenes. We no longer needed false conversation.

'It was an *accident*.' Angela laughed at some memory she hadn't yet shared, looking at me, amused by something I couldn't see. 'That first feather wasn't even meant to be there.' She closed her eyes briefly, trailing off, her thoughts left to wander silently. 'It must have fallen from my bag. I wasn't aware until I saw the news, the nickname they'd given me by then quite beautiful. Poetic.' I considered rushing in, grabbing the knife, but she snatched her head towards me before I had time to react. 'Do you know why I stabbed that guy?'

'You did far more than stab him, Angela.'

She looked up, seemingly surprised by something I wasn't yet aware of. 'Not *Mark*. I stabbed some idiot called Lee outside Billy's Bar in the early hours of last Saturday morning.' She scoffed. 'I didn't mean it. It just happened. He was in the wrong place.'

'*You* stabbed Lee Fellows?'

'Did he die?' Her eyes widened, as if the sound of his name was alien to her, her query unanticipated. She didn't sound sorry.

I nodded.

Angela looked as if she was about to faint, her legs wavering. I was waiting for the opportunity to race in, grab the knife, end this.

'I was four years old when I was raped. I should have been playing with teddy bears not a grown man's cock. No kid should suffer that, should they?' She glared at me, her earlier smile turning to a grimace, her eyes dancing with pain she was obviously still dealing with.

I wanted to ask who she was talking about but didn't dare speak in case she turned her anger on me. Instead, I shook my head.

'I got pregnant at twelve. He blamed a local boy who'd shown me nothing but kindness, telling the authorities the kid had attacked me. The poor sod wasn't able to defend himself against the accusation, couldn't deny or confirm his involvement. His autism saw to that. They sent him to a special school and I was forced to have a termination. I can't even remember his name. My father beat me for weeks, telling me it was my fault for getting my period. That he could have taken precautions if he knew we were at that *stage* in our relationship.'

I swallowed, not needing that kind of image in my head. What Angela was telling me now was old news, nothing she hadn't already processed in the darkness of every single unforgiving day since. *Her father?* I took a breath, unconvinced I wanted to hear any more.

Angela was pacing the room, keeping her distance, Liam on the floor, still bleeding, still in pain. 'It was an accident they caught him at all. God knows how long it might have continued if my mother hadn't walked into my

## The Lost Raven

bedroom and found him on top of me. She was meant to be at work but forgot her mobile phone so came home to get it.' Angela scoffed. 'She killed herself before my father's trial. She didn't want to accept that she'd missed something *that* terrible, didn't want to acknowledge what he'd done. She never looked at me again.'

'That's awful.'

Angela nodded. 'And then this bastard raped me at the party the other night and brought it all back.' She glared at the man at her feet, looking as if she wanted to kick the life out of him, stab him to death, whichever came first. She slumped onto the bed, dropping the raven feather to the floor, nothing on her mind other than pain.

I glanced towards the trembling wretch on the carpet, Liam Goodman in no position to do anything other than beg for his life. He glanced my way to make sure I was still in the room. I couldn't tell what he was thinking.

Angela looked broken. She laughed, something new jumping into her thoughts. 'You put the idea into my head, Mr Newton.'

'*What?* What idea?' What the hell was she talking about? I didn't like where this was going.

'To kill the bastards.'

'You're blaming me?' By bastards, I assumed she meant *men*.

A nod.

'What did *I* do?' Bloody hell, as if I didn't have enough to deal with.

'You told me to take back control.'

I recalled the precise moment I said those exact words. 'I didn't mean like *that*. I was talking about your life, Angela. I told you to take control of your life.' *Christ.* I glared at her, knowing the poor girl would have taken my words the wrong way, her failed state of mind and bipolar seeing to that. *Well done, Newton. Well done, indeed.* Angela had misconstrued my innocent concern as an instruction to kill, my attempts to reach out making things worse. I could hear Paul now, tutting loudly.

'And that's exactly what I did.'

I glanced towards Liam. 'Are you planning on killing him, too?'

Angela nodded.

'And what will that achieve?'

'It will make me feel better?'

'Why? Because you think he raped you?' Although nobody would ever want to go through something like that, rape alone wouldn't produce a killer.

'He *did* rape me and yes.'

'Why didn't you call the police?'

'Because the police never helped me. They failed to protect me from a monster who was meant to love me. I was angry.' I could see she still was. She was crying again. 'They didn't even help me when I tried to kill myself. Just locked me away, forgot I existed.'

'It's over, Angela.' I raised my hands, needing her to hand me the knife. I could already hear sirens in the background. I was hoping to have this under control before the police arrived, before things turned nastier than was necessary. I couldn't imagine what she'd been through, her young life destroyed because of someone meant to protect her, her adult life becoming a living pattern of hell. 'Give me the knife. Please.'

'I can't.'

'Why?'

'Because for me, it will *never* be over.' I could understand that. Something had shifted. Something she could never get back. Angela took a deep breath. She was gripping the knife to her chest. I couldn't imagine she

## The Lost Raven

wasn't about to use it on one of us, or herself.

'You can trust me.'

'I can't. You're all the same.' She sprang forward, I assumed to stab me, but she grabbed a lamp from a bedside table and swung it at my head. I didn't see it coming, too busy focusing on the blade in her hand. Although it didn't knock me out, it still hurt and I fell to the floor, allowing Angela to race into the hallway. She wouldn't get far, although I didn't want to know what Paul would think of this.

# Thirty-Eight

## *Newton*

Angela escaped whilst I helped Liam. It was unfortunate, but I could do nothing about that. I needed to prioritise a potentially dying man, help him reclaim his dignity, his safety. He was trembling, in pain, unable to look at me in case I saw something he didn't want me to see. Neither of us wanted to acknowledge his trauma, his embarrassment.

'Are you okay?' I wasn't sure if I was speaking to an innocent victim or a sexual predator. I handed him a bathrobe, allowing him to cover his lost modesty.

Liam winced, nodded. We both knew he wasn't.

'What was all that about?' The only thing I wanted was to lighten the mood, our current situation something neither of us assumed we'd find ourselves in. As it was, things couldn't have been more serious.

'I wish I knew.' Liam sounded lost, as if he wished the last couple of hours had never happened. I knew the feeling.

It wasn't my place to question him about Angela's

## The Lost Raven

accusation, the authorities' job to do that. Instead, we waited for the police, grateful his injuries would be shortly assessed by a doctor. He looked as if he needed one. I didn't dare ask what Angela had done to him, rape not something men talked about, especially in circumstances like these. I didn't assume he'd get over it easily. Who would?

I was relieved when he was taken to the hospital, taken out of my hands, my arrival well-timed, apparently. Left much longer and he would have bled to death, his cuts deep enough to kill, slowly, painfully. He would be left with scars, of course, a permanent reminder, several potential months of therapy ahead. The police would need to question him, rape allegations always taken seriously, nothing he could do about that.

I stood outside the hospital watching ambulances come and go, Liam's hotel room already subjected to a full forensics assessment whilst they hunted for Angela. He had barely acknowledged me, our shared hotel room encounter something neither of us would forget in a hurry.

'Newt?' I turned around to see Paul striding across the car park, Alice and Tony behind him, their faces as blank and unassuming as mine. 'What the hell happened?'

'I'm sorry.' I wasn't. 'I couldn't hang around and wait for her to kill him.'

'But you still let her go.'

'I didn't exactly *let her go*.' My head was aching, the impact of a bedside lamp still lingering, a dressing on my head confirming my ordeal.

'You should have waited, like I told you.' Paul glared at me as if I should have known better, his requirements firmly expressed, his authority confirmed.

He was right, but I couldn't stand by whilst someone was being murdered. 'Liam Goodman would probably be dead now if I had.'

Paul sighed. He couldn't argue with that.

'Angela accused him of rape.'

Paul raised his eyebrows. 'Fitting.'

'I believe her.'

Paul scoffed. 'You always like to see the best in people.'

'Everything we do is driven by circumstance, consequence, our past. None of us live in a bubble, Paul. Besides, it's my job.' It wasn't my fault that I saw beyond the behaviour of a person to their innermost, darkest emotions. Paul looked for the *who*. I looked for the *why*.

'Did she say anything that might be useful?' Paul was chewing a piece of gum he'd found in his coat pocket, offering the packet to each of us. We declined.

Angela Healy had said too much. I doubted therapy would ever dissect it all. 'She confirmed she's The Raven Rapist, if that's what you mean?' I couldn't believe I was saying it aloud, didn't want to seal the poor girl's fate. *Poor girl?* I needed to stop seeing her as a victim.

'She actually *told* you that?' Paul's eyes had widened. He'd stopped chewing, his gum left dangling between his teeth.

I nodded. In as many words. I doubted anyone would appreciate the reasons for such heinous actions, the emotions driving such hideous crimes buried too deeply. I recalled Angela's confession, nothing she said willing to settle my turbulent mindset.

'She say anything else?'

'She claimed Liam Goodman raped her.' For now, that was enough. It wasn't my place to highlight her historic traumas.

'Plenty of people are, Newt. It doesn't turn them into killers.'

I looked at Paul. He was right, of course, I couldn't argue with that. If that were the case we would be knee-

## The Lost Raven

deep in bodies, wading through a forever-expanding swathe of murdered sexual deviants. Yet Angela saw her trauma as a symbol of everything she hated in men, despising what they stood for, who they were, the unassuming appendage between the legs of all males nothing but a weapon used freely against women. I felt sick, the idea of what she'd been subjected to, too much to express. It wasn't helpful that she was right.

'Apparently, Liam's actions tipped her over the edge.'

'Why?'

It was a simple question, yet I didn't want to confirm Angela's past. It wasn't mine to share. I didn't assume she'd appreciate further interference from me. I'd done enough already. 'It sounded as if she's been through a lot. Once you check her records you'll understand more.'

Paul sighed. 'Well, for now, we can at least question Goodman.' He turned, heading into the hospital.

'What about Angela?' I jogged after him.

'There's a nationwide alert out for her arrest and every copper in London has a full description. She won't get far.' Paul glanced around, knowing there were enough cameras in the city for the net to close in soon enough, simple mistakes already made seeing us hone in on her, guiding us to her flat. She wasn't good at covering her tracks. I could appreciate why. She was a suffering young woman, not a calculated psychopath.

'I could do with a coffee, actually,' I chided, hoping someone would feel sorry for my injuries and get me one, glancing towards Alice. I couldn't help it. I'd been through a *traumatic* time. I hoped she'd notice. She glanced my way, offering a brief smile. It was probably more than I deserved. I hadn't spoken to Steph since I stormed out of her house, the kids no doubt upset that I'd left without saying goodbye. I needed to face her at some point, apologise, hug my nephews. I hated leaving things unsaid between us. I needed my family. It wasn't helpful.

\*\*\*

Liam Goodman looked worse now than when we'd met just a couple of hours earlier, if that was possible. He was lying on his front, his back, arms and legs covered with thick, white dressings, still in obvious pain. He didn't look happy to see us, Angela's whereabouts now a priority. Paul still needed to take my statement, several cups of coffee needed to placate my emotions before I could achieve that, my alibi required by law. The unfamiliar hospital we found ourselves in felt slightly alien, the London police only allowing him to conduct the interview because The Raven Rapist case was his.

'I didn't rape her.' Liam was attempting to turn his head our way, staring at the door, my thoughts left to wander silently behind Paul. At least I had coffee.

'Are you sure about that?'

'Yes. She's a friend.' Liam didn't look at the officers in attendance, probably couldn't, the very word conjuring painful memories. 'Or at least, I thought she was.'

'Do you always treat your friends like that?'

'Like *what?* Look at what the crazy bitch did to me.' Liam attempted to lift his bandaged arms towards Paul, wincing at the obvious pain he was in. 'You should be out there looking for her.'

'Don't worry, when we find her we'll be asking her the same questions we're asking you.'

'Such as?'

'Such as why were you in that hotel room together?'

'It was *my* hotel room and she wasn't invited.'

'You were seen arguing outside.'

'By who?'

'Several witnesses, including the hotel staff.' I was glad Paul didn't confirm my involvement, such questions only aimed his way now because of what I'd already told them.

'What's going on between you and Angela Healy?'

'Nothing.' Liam shifted uncomfortably, his wounds as painful as the constant flow of questions.

'That isn't what she's saying, according to our sources.'

'What sources?' Liam looked shocked that such sources existed. 'You mean that bloke who talked her out of practically murdering me?' He scoffed, unaware he should be grateful, unaware I was in the room. 'What does *he* know? He only got her side of the fucking story.'

'And now you get to tell yours.' Paul's tone was becoming more impatient with every word he spoke. I took a breath, pressed my lips together.

'I didn't hurt her. I wouldn't.' Liam was fiddling with the bed sheets as if he didn't know what else to do with them.

'What were you arguing about?'

'Nothing.'

'You argued for the sake of it? Nothing else to do with your day?'

'She made an accusation.'

'Of rape?'

Liam raised his chin, the very reason he was in this situation now because of that exact accusation. 'Yeah.'

'And, of course, it wasn't you?'

'No. What do you take me for?'

'I don't know, Liam. I don't know what you're capable of.'

'*Not that!*' Liam was almost shouting, almost ready to race from the room, if he could.

'Well somebody obviously raped her.'

Something flashed across his face that none of us could ignore, an acknowledgement he knew more than he'd confirmed.

'I know,' he muttered, shifting position, trying to get a better view of Paul, his previous defensiveness softening, his words emerging almost as a whisper.

'Why would Angela Healy accuse you of rape?'

'I don't know.'

'I don't believe you.'

'I don't care.'

'You will when we charge you.'

'I didn't *do* anything.' He was fidgeting, chewing his lip. So was I.

'You need to start talking.'

'I can't.'

Paul narrowed his eyes. 'So you do know *something*?'

Liam looked as if he was considering getting up, changing his mind when he realised he couldn't.

'Who raped Angela Healy, Liam?' Paul pulled a chair to the side of the bed, sat down, leaning his face towards Liam's, needing him to appreciate his next statement.

'No idea.'

'You said a moment ago you did. That girl is in a terrible state. If you know *anything* about what she's been through, it will help your case to help us.' Paul took a breath. 'I thought you liked her. I thought you said she was a friend.' I appreciated how Paul was using the accusation of rape in order to gain a better insight into the type of person who would willingly murder men. He hadn't confirmed who Angela Healy really was. Not yet.

'She is. I do. Or at least I did until today.' Liam was picking at the edge of a sheet, obviously unsure what he should do.

'If you know something, it is in your best interests to tell

*The Lost Raven*

us.'

Liam glanced at Paul, closing his eyes, his injuries causing him to continually flinch.

'I think I might know who raped her.' He was muttering. I could barely hear him.

'Who?'

Liam shook his head. 'Please don't ask me.'

'Who?' Paul's voice had raised, his interest piqued. So was mine. Was this Liam's way of deflecting the blame? Paul shifted position, writing something in his notebook with a scratchy pen.

No response.

'You'll get the protection you need. If you're worried.'

'From the police?'

Paul nodded. Liam scoffed. No one acknowledged it.

'I think it might be the same guy who attacked Rosie.'

There was a moment of silence, a knowing glance exchanged between Paul and Alice.

'You know about Rosie O'Connor?' It was Alice's turn now to ask the questions. She stepped forward, her brow furrowed.

Liam nodded. 'Rosie and I work together. We are friends, nothing more. I'm not into girls in that way.' He pressed his lips together, his cheeks flushing. He didn't need to explain. 'I didn't know that Angela had been attacked until today, I swear. If I had, I'd have tried to help her. She's a good girl. They both are.'

'What makes you think the same guy attacked them both?' Alice again. Paul nodded his agreement.

Silence.

'The more you tell us, the quicker we can leave you to get some rest.'

'Because he was acting strange.' Liam was tapping his teeth over his lips, his voice strangely high-pitched.

'Who was?' Paul was becoming irritated, tapping his hand on the side of the chair, tapping his foot on the floor.

Liam sighed, taking a lingering moment before responding. He glanced my way, noticing my presence, seemingly pleading for advice. None came. 'He's a doctor who works at the hospital.'

'Name?' There were plenty to choose from.

'Andrew Hansley.'

I couldn't breathe. *What the hell?* I took a sharp breath, glad that from my position no one could see the panic rising in my chest. Why would Liam implicate Andy? I wanted to demand answers but it wasn't my place. I was currently waiting to provide a statement about evidence found in The Raven Rapist case, still wanted for questioning. I couldn't speak, didn't want to cause any more unrequired shit. It was just as well Paul's team knew me, understood my jacket was a coincidence, nothing more, its ultimate location nothing to do with me. For now, all I could do was hold my breath and wait for whatever else emerged from Liam Goodman's mouth. Paul glanced my way, probably glad I was keeping my mouth shut, liable to make things worse if I didn't. Andy was my friend. I thought about Steph's recent revelation. Well, he used to be.

'Why don't you tell us what happened?' Paul was growing tired of Liam's games. So was I.

Liam sighed, knowing he had no choice now but to talk, his own arse on the line if he didn't. 'Andy was drunk, complaining about some neighbour who'd accused him of sexual harassment. He was acting odd all night, flustered, constantly telling me how much he wanted revenge on women, to show them all who's boss.'

'When was this?'

'My party.' Liam glanced at Paul. 'Last Friday night.'

I thought back to Saturday evening when Andy had

turned up at my home with a bottle of wine and a request, declaring his drunken unsubstantiated love for Angela. He looked flustered then, too.

Paul waited for Liam to continue.

'He was wild, ranting about how women have ruined his life. That he only ever wanted a bit of fun, that his neighbour should have been less flirtatious if she didn't want the attention.'

'What makes you think Andrew Hansley attacked Rosie O'Connor?' Paul continued.

'I don't know. A hunch.'

Paul sighed. He was in no mood for games.

'Andy barely left her alone all evening, kept touching her, flirting with her, plying her with alcohol. When she complained about feeling unwell he offered to drive her home, seemed keen, but he disappeared for around half an hour, asking about Angela's welfare, and so Claire drove her home instead.' That fitted with Rosie's statement.

'And what about Angela?'

'Andy likes her. Has done for a while. He hasn't told her though. Just stares at her when she's not looking.' I swallowed, knowing I did the same thing with Alice, recalling what Andy had told me last week. It didn't make us predators. I couldn't even look at Alice now.

'So what makes you think he attacked her?'

Liam sighed. 'I didn't, until today. Not until I saw the look on Angela's face. You can't fake something like that.'

'Then why does she think it's you?'

'I have absolutely no idea.' Liam closed his eyes. 'As soon as I found out what had happened to Rosie I went to Andy's place to confront him.'

'When was this?'

'Late Saturday afternoon.'

'You *knew* what had happened to Rosie before she

reported it to the police?'

'She called me. She was in a right state. She'd been trying to get hold of Angela but she was busy, apparently. It was *me* who persuaded her to go to the police.' Liam scoffed. 'Some good that's done me.'

'And what happened at Andrew's property?'

'He got angry. Told me he'd get my promotion revoked if I spread shit like that around. That's why I decided to come to London early. I needed some headspace, assumed I was getting away at the right time. I didn't know about Angela until today, I swear.' Liam shook his head. I believed him. 'I took some extra time off, used it as annual leave ahead of starting my new job. No one questioned it.'

'So Andrew Hansley denied your accusation?'

'Of course. He was hardly going to admit it, was he?'

'But you're convinced he was involved?'

Liam nodded.

Paul glanced vaguely my way, knowing what would need to happen next.

\*\*\*

'Andy? Seriously?' I was beyond furious, pacing up and down, my feet unwilling to remain still. We were standing outside the hospital, the icy air doing nothing to cool my mood.

'Why would he drop someone else in the frame?' Paul was clicking his tongue across his teeth in frustration. I wanted to tap his cheek, tell him to calm down. I needed to take my own advice.

'Obviously to defer the blame from himself.' I rolled my eyes. I couldn't help it. Andy might be a lot of things but he wasn't a rapist.

'Gov?' DI Tony Avery was heading our way, his mobile

phone in his outstretched hand. 'The station just sent this over. Goodman's DNA and fingerprints are on file for an unrelated assault at a football match last year.'

'Do they match anything from the dress found in the skip or samples taken from Rosie O'Connor?' Paul asked.

I almost held my breath, hoping that if Liam *was* guilty, Andy wasn't.

Tony shook his head. 'No.'

Liam was innocent. I didn't know whether to laugh or cry.

Paul glanced at me, unable to confirm what he was thinking, a potential rapist living in my home, the two of us connected to Angela Healy for reasons not yet confirmed. I didn't know how to process that.

'We'll need to bring Hansley in, take DNA samples if nothing is already on the system, either prove or disprove his involvement and get back to the important stuff.'

'Which is?'

'Finding Angela Healy.'

# Thirty-Nine

## *Angela*

I don't know where I'm heading, yet I find myself running, as far as I can go, away from Newton and the police he claimed were coming for me. I hear distant sirens, yet until now I did *not* assume they were on my trail, London always alive with criminal activity, danger and delusions around every corner. I didn't mean to hit him, my only intention to escape, get away, my mind a torrid explosion of infoxication I can't assume won't end me at some point. I hope he's okay.

Most people assume I ran away from my previous life because I have something to hide, believing it's the reason I speak very little of my past. The truth is I ran away from *myself.* From the person I didn't want to become. At four, I didn't understand. At sixteen, I knew better. Yet, I retained a secret brainwashed into my damaged skull, keeping quiet when I should have spoken up, hiding under my bed when I should have ran. I've now been hiding behind a dustbin for almost an hour, unable to move in case they find me, unable to think for fear of losing my sanity to a rapidly failing society. Nothing has changed, still afraid of the shadows, still cowering beneath a façade of hatred I never should have been allowed to possess in the first place.

I've no idea how the police ended up at my flat, still struggling to comprehend Rosie's earlier confirmation. The sheer volume of evidence I've left along my unwitting path of destruction is too much for me to consider. Does this mean I'm on the run, concealed amongst the rats, a common criminal awaiting her fate? It's only a matter of time before they find me, of course, lock me away, my fingerprints no doubt littering those discarded bodies, all the evidence they need to convict me peppering my home. I can't believe how foolish I've been.

I need to think, yet I'm unable to contemplate my fate, my downfall. I momentarily consider calling Rosie but change my mind, wanting to throw my recently damaged mobile phone in the nearest bin. I can't assume they're not already tracking me, tracing my movements, pondering my motives, waiting for me to do something *stupid*. I left Liam tied up, for God's sake, the guy more than capable of explaining what I did, what I was planning, his bitter words spilling readily, bringing me down.

I wish I had GHB. If I did I'd take it all and throw myself in the Thames. As it is, I have nothing on me aside from a mobile phone I've already turned off, the thing of no use to me now. My bag is still inside Liam's room, along with my identity, my cruel intentions. They will see me for what I am, what I'm capable of, plenty of witnesses left behind — the hotel staff, Newton, Liam. I shouldn't have made such a show of torturing him, should have killed him swiftly and ran. It doesn't matter that I wanted him to suffer, to feel a tiny piece of what I've been forced to deal with my entire life. It's too late now.

I was stupid to believe he was a decent guy. I take a breath, thin air catching my throat, causing me to inhale sharply. Do such men exist? I think back to the party, how he intermittently filled my glass, barely leaving my side. I was drunk, of course, but I can't help that now, can't help that I shouldn't drink, not on Lithium and Olanzapine. Alcohol drowns my feelings, takes away my pain. I have to deal with my life somehow. I wish I'd known his intentions, can't believe I allowed things to go that far. I can't recall giving consent, can't remember saying *yes*. Yet again, I can't remember saying *no*. Even now, almost a week later, I'm still sore and it burns when I pee. I flinch at the thought, a tear welling, Rosie on my mind again.

I rest my head against a cold metal railing, no words left for how my life has turned out. I am crying, desperate to disappear between the slots and be gone forever. It's taking all my strength not to scream, summoning everything I have inside to merely breathe. I don't want to acknowledge how weak I've become. Not yet. I want to remember The Raven Rapist a little longer, feel the power she once assumed she held over those unwitting bastards who deserved everything they got.

I glance skywards. My condition shouldn't define me. *It is what it is*, although it doesn't help that I can't easily snap myself out of deep depressions, get a grip, cheer up. That isn't how bipolar works. It's a label I've lived with most of my life. I can't help that now. If I could slink away to the once assumed safety of my pathetic existence, pretend this week never happened, I would. But I'll never now remove myself from the prying eyes of the police, will never be able to look at Liam the same way again.

Instead, I find myself heading absentmindedly along the Thames, searching blindly for the famous Tower of London ravens, nothing on my mind but an escape cruelly robbed

## The Lost Raven

from my thoughts. I cry as I walk, sobbing into the heavy air, ignoring blatant sniggers and sideways stares from strangers who will never understand who I am. I don't care what they think of me, don't mind what they are saying. The only thing I seek is approval of the ravens, those beautiful birds the only friends I need. I know their names, know them better than the millions of humans surrounding me. Jubilee, Harris, Gripp, Erin, Poppy, Georgie, Edgar, Branwen. We understand each other, share a connection.

*My name is Angela Healey and I am not defined by my actions.*

# Forty

## *Newton*

I stood outside, a cold breeze cutting into my body, calling Andy. Paul's instructions were plain. I was to find out where he was, nothing more, uncomfortably ignoring three calls from Stephanie, my heart in my throat, words not yet spoken ready to spill from my quivering lips. I couldn't share what my sister-in-law had confirmed, couldn't ask him about Kate. This wasn't about me. Police business came first, my needs factoring way down a list of encroaching priorities. I needed to know the truth, of course, but couldn't risk tipping him off. I felt angry. Betrayed.

'Everything okay?' Andy sounded flushed, as if his day was too much, his workload overbearing. He didn't seem the slightest bit guilty for past actions. I was having a hard time imagining my oldest friend as anything other than hardworking, caring, considerate, despite what had been said today to the contrary.

I licked my lips, unable to ponder past mistakes, query past actions. 'Are you still at work?' I sounded stressed, my

## The Lost Raven

voice reduced to a strangled whimper.

'Yeah, I'll be here for a few more hours, then I'm off home to sleep for a week.' Andy sounded calm, as if nothing was wrong, nothing able to spoil his day. *Home?* He meant my place. When did he make himself so comfortable? When did I fail to see what was in front of my eyes? He paused. 'Everything okay? You sound funny?'

'Yep. Just checking in with you to see that everything is all right at the flat.' Paul was behind me, burrowing a hole into the back of my head, waiting for me to slip up, tip him off. I could hear a cling of cutlery in the background, muffled chatter, Andy's much-needed break about to come to a rapid conclusion. I wanted to scream at him, demand an explanation.

'Are you sure you're okay, Newt?' Andy sounded concerned now, his words echoing along the distant phone line, my responses tense, robotic.

I glanced towards Paul whose face was a tightened ball of stress, his eyes reduced to narrow slits that glared at me between heavy spots of rain. 'Yeah. Why wouldn't I be?' *Why wouldn't I want to rip your face off for destroying my marriage and attacking my brother's wife, potentially raping a vulnerable young woman? Make that two.* I smiled, nothing else to do.

'Because you sound stressed. You worry too much.' Andy laughed, as if my troubles were unfounded—my doing, my fault.

He didn't know the police were coming for him, didn't know it was my job to now confirm his whereabouts so they could bring him in to answer questions about a crime I couldn't imagine he'd commit. It didn't matter that I had a personal score to settle, my sister-in-law unwittingly caught up in what he began fifteen years earlier. No wonder we'd lost contact. I assumed it was just part of life, the way of things, our circles moving in different directions, a coincidence that Kate's leaving matched Andy's. Now I wondered if they'd left *together*, still couldn't believe he'd slept with my wife. I felt sick, wanting to strangle him with his own stethoscope, scream, yell, ask him why. I innocently assumed he would be vindicated for the rape allegation soon enough, leaving me to ask the questions I desperately needed to understand.

I hung up, stress seemingly a normal part of my day now, unsure how I felt about anything. Tony and Alice had already left London without us, assigned to conduct Andy's interview in Eastcliff whilst Paul stayed here to tie up loose ends with me. He was hoping they'd locate Angela, of course. He didn't want to miss that.

\*\*\*

I stood in the rain, my mobile phone in my trembling hand, the silence more than I could stand. I couldn't look at Paul, nothing I could say able to sedate our increasing problems.

'The Metropolitan Police have kindly provided a space for us in one of their unused interview rooms. It's not ideal but it will have to do. I need your statement, Newt. I'm sorry to ask.' Paul was looking at me as if he couldn't understand the weird connection to everything that had happened, the fact that my jacket had turned up at a murder scene *nothing* compared to the rapist I had living under my roof. He needed me to set the record straight.

'I assumed you'd wait until we were back in Eastcliff?' I would have felt more comfortable on home territory. My heart lunged. I wasn't sure why.

Paul shook his head. 'Sorry. This can't wait.'

I nodded, wanting to get this thing over with, Andy on my mind, my stomach in knots. I was about to find myself on the wrong side of an interview table, the wrong side of a law I'd always upheld. Every single officer in that unfamiliar station would look at me as if I'd done something they couldn't appreciate, something I could never undo. Yet, they didn't know me.

We drove to the station in silence, Paul mostly discussing football and cars, filling the void, leaving me in a world of my own. There was much I wanted to say, of course, words I wished I could express. Instead, I spoke of the weather, thought about coffee. I was exhausted, our limited conversation overwhelming, Paul's consistent chatter overbearing. I was offered a duty solicitor. I refused. I had nothing to hide.

'Where were you last night between the hours of nine and eleven?'

I thought back, my memory spiralling. 'At home.' I was always at home. Unlike most people, I didn't have a social life.

'All evening?'

'Yes. Until you called me to Aubrey Point around eleven.'

'By yourself?'

'Unfortunately.' Andy was at the hospital, the fact that he had been staying with me since the attacks began and was now wanted in connection with rape himself, didn't make me feel any better. 'I ordered a takeaway and went through The Raven Rapist case files.' I could barely look at Paul sitting opposite me, knowing I was innocent, yet still needing to ask these uncomfortable questions anyway.

'Takeaway?'

'From the local Chinese.' Did it matter?

'What time was this?' Paul was writing, his tone flat, professional.

I shook my head. 'Around eight. I tidied my flat, fell

asleep, woke up just before eleven when you called me to join you down at the beach.' I was busy admiring the clean flat I now lived in. I didn't confirm that, couldn't appreciate how my thoughts had shifted since then. I was exhausted.

'So the takeaway staff will verify this?'

'Of course.'

'Do you know why your jacket was found with a dead body?'

I shook my head.

'For the record, Newton is shaking his head.' Paul attempted a smile that didn't reach his face.

I glanced at my friend. He only ever called me Newton when he was stressed. We'd been friends too long for such formalities. 'I gave my jacket to someone.' Now I really did sound guilty of something.

'Who?'

'Angela Healy.' I didn't want the reminder, didn't need the verification, couldn't imagine the confirmation now on record.

'When was this?'

'Last Saturday morning.'

Paul took a moment. 'The twentieth of November?'

Another nod.

'Why?'

'She was cold.' She was freezing, actually, the dress she wore hardly appropriate for an isolated rooftop, her mind in a terrible place. Paul knew this, was with me at the time, his connection to Angela Healy as inconsequential as mine. It wasn't helpful that the very same dress turned up just two days later, a dead man's blood all over it, my jacket joining the chaos soon after.

'And why didn't you get it back?'

'I don't know.' I wished I hadn't given it to her now. I felt like a criminal, a suspect, my innocent actions coming

## The Lost Raven

back to bite me where it hurt.

Further questions were aimed my way for what felt like an eternity, my jacket currently being expertly analysed, my involvement not yet substantiated. More CCTV footage was being scrolled through, confirming the moment it ended up in the hands of a murderer. I couldn't help it that she was innocent when we met, my aim only to help the poor thing when she needed support. Nothing that happened afterwards was my fault, no matter what Angela wrongly claimed.

I left the interview room feeling sick, nothing Paul said easing my increased nerves. He knew my involvement was circumstantial, a coincidence, my actions innocent. A stranger made me a coffee, a simple hand on my arm almost seeing me burst into tears. Luckily I held my emotions in check. I would never want anyone to see me like that, would never want to expose my weaknesses.

# Forty-One

## *Newton*

I did not expect my day to turn out like this, yet according to Alice's brief telephone confirmation when she finally called me, the look on Andy's face when they took him in for questioning said it all. It was nothing but a grotesque display of shock, apparently, his eyes telling their own story, the man battered, incensed. I was grateful for the update, thankful to have been spared the indignity. It was a misunderstanding, he claimed, glancing briefly over his shoulder towards several hospital colleagues as the police pressed him into an awaiting car, his reddened face bobbing like a nodding dog in the back. Like me, there was nothing he could do to change today's outcome other than go along with the relentless flow of drama.

However, because of my unfortunate involvement with the man, there was a conflict of interest, so I wasn't given much beyond a courteous confirmation that Alice would update me when she could. I was too angry to offer

## The Lost Raven

anything helpful anyway, ignoring Paul's insistence that I go for a walk, calm down. How could I? This was personal. Andy had made it so.

We were sitting inside a quiet coffee shop watching the world outside pass by, rain dotting the windows, keeping us company. Paul occasionally glanced my way to check I was okay. He didn't say anything. He didn't need to. I already knew what he was thinking. How does anyone comprehend a friend capable of such vile acts? I planned to ask the very question as soon as I could, of course, once the police had finished their enquiries. Right then, I was glad for the coffee, smiling blankly at Paul's sympathetic features because I could think of nothing else to do. Andy had betrayed me, had slept with my wife, yet beyond this I knew little about him, too many years passing for me to make any appropriate assumptions.

The way Kate had left me in the middle of the night, a taxi waiting at the bottom of our street, I couldn't now assume she hadn't left me for him. I might have forgiven a one-off, her mistake something we could have processed, eventually. Instead, she retained a false notion that she needed space, nothing I'd done wrong, merely something she had to work through, alone. It wasn't comforting to now consider it was another man's cock she was working her way through. I couldn't imagine the very same man capable of rape.

'Want to talk about it?' Paul was unusually quiet, waiting for me to enlighten him, blatantly feeling the cold by the way he continually shivered every time someone opened the coffee shop door. He noted the stern look on my face, no sarcasm required to lighten the mood. I couldn't feel a thing.

'He slept with my *wife*,' I sighed, unable to believe I was saying the words aloud. I'd held it in all day, more important things to deal with. Kate and I had divorced years ago, long enough for me to get over her, this new pain unexpected.

'Christ, Newt, I don't know what to say.'

Paul didn't have to say anything. I wasn't glad to confirm it. My nerves were in shreds, my heart permanently lodged in the back of my rapidly declining throat. I'd been with him only yesterday, shared a coffee, thought nothing of it. Now I had so much anger inside I didn't know where to aim it, didn't know how I could stop myself from punching him in the face the moment I saw him.

I shook my head. 'You might want to check with his landlord as to the reason he's currently living with me.'

'What are you thinking?'

Paul didn't want to know.

I swallowed, my coffee choking my thoughts, sideways glances from passing strangers doing nothing for Paul's unconfirmed street cred.

'Andy claims his neighbour made an accusation that wasn't true. Now I'm not so sure.' I was no longer sure about anything. I didn't want to believe what I was thinking, didn't want to imagine my friend attacking a woman. Yet, Steph had already confirmed the unwanted advances he'd made towards *her*, his neighbour in the process of getting him evicted for a similar offence.

I was shaking. I couldn't compromise the investigation, of course, but I wanted to scream at him, punch him, demand answers. I wanted to know why my friend would do something like that, why he would turn up at my flat and say nothing. He'd acted as if not a day had passed since our last encounter, those missing years unimportant. I was glad Paul's team had taken control of the situation, probably to spare my feelings, spare the embarrassment, the occasional glances he made towards me now, highly

## The Lost Raven

unhelpful.

***

It was three painful hours before I received the phone call I was dreading. I didn't know what to expect or if I should answer my mobile at all. I was standing outside the coffee shop, several coffees in my system, the rain lighter now.

'You're not going to like this,' Alice began, speaking softly to soften the blow.

I closed my eyes, swallowed, pressed my phone against my ear. 'What did he say?' I wasn't sure I wanted to know.

'The usual. Plenty of swearing and denial until we hit him with the evidence.' Alice paused. Paul was currently on his phone behind me, being told the same story, his reaction seemingly better than mine.

*'Evidence?'*

'He confirmed he *was* at the party, but assumed that gave him an alibi. However, when Mr Goodman was questioned this afternoon, we managed to obtain a warrant to gain access to his home and surveillance system.'

I held my breath, not wanting to know what they'd found, if anything, convinced they'd found nothing worth stressing over. Paul hadn't mentioned this to me. I assumed, for obvious reasons, he couldn't.

'And?'

'Due to a break-in at his property last year, Mr Goodman placed CCTV around his home, both outside and in, facing the exits, windows, hallway and upstairs landing.'

'So?'

'Not exactly something you'd do if you were planning to assault someone, is it?'

Alice had a point. I was momentarily glad I couldn't see her face.

'Imagine our surprise when, on one of those recordings, we spotted Andrew Hansley going into an upstairs bedroom on the evening of the party.'

'I don't see the relevance.' I wasn't prepared to put two and two together, not yet ready to believe the obvious.

A pause. 'It was literally a few moments *after* Liam Goodman had taken Angela Healy into the same room. He was only in there a few seconds, has already been ruled out of enquiries.'

'Are you serious?'

Alice sighed. 'Andrew can be clearly seen entering the bedroom at around ten-fifteen.'

I was staring into space, nothing around me of any relevance. 'That still doesn't prove anything.' It didn't. Alice knew this. I was getting annoyed now, my legs jolting up and down. I looked as if I needed the toilet.

'Unfortunately, he did not emerge from that room again until over thirty minutes later.'

'And what did Andy have to say about that?'

'Said he couldn't remember why he was there or what he was doing in the bedroom. That he was too drunk to remember. However, when he came out, he headed downstairs and left, getting into his car. Again, it was all caught on the external cameras. He didn't look drunk, Newt. We believe he raped Angela Healy in that bedroom and, dissatisfied, drove across town to the home of Rosie O'Connor where he broke into her house and raped *her*, too.'

'Where's your evidence?' Surely this was pure speculation, nothing more? I couldn't believe I was defending him.

'Semen was found on both Angela Healy's dress *and* samples collected from Rosie's body and clothing she wore at the party.' Alice went quiet. 'It matches Andrew's DNA

## The Lost Raven

profile.' I wasn't aware I was holding my breath until I realised I couldn't breathe. I couldn't even feel the rain anymore.

'You have Andy's DNA on *file?*' I couldn't imagine why.

'We do. He was accused of sexually assaulting a woman four years ago. He was brought in for questioning but at the time they didn't have any solid evidence to prove anything. The female who made the accusation did not come forward until almost two weeks after the incident. They were in a relationship at the time so, unfortunately, it was ruled as a domestic that got out of hand.'

'Who was the woman?'

Another pause. 'Kathryn Flanigan.'

I couldn't breathe, couldn't take in what she was saying. It was as if someone had sucked the air out of my lungs. I raised my eyebrows, glaring at Paul who was now equally looking at me, his shock matching mine. I needed to get off the phone, unwilling to listen to any more nonsense. I mumbled a half-hearted thanks for Alice's confirmation, almost dropping my mobile onto the pavement as I staggered forward. I can't even recall hanging up. I hovered uncomfortably, a coffee cup in one hand, incensed to confirm that for the first time in my life I was unable to drink a drop.

'Are you okay?'

I turned around to see Paul staring me. He looked irritated, cold, slightly concerned for my wellbeing.

'He *did* it didn't he?' I couldn't believe the man was living in my home, sleeping in my spare room, couldn't believe I was asking such a stupid question. I thought of Steph and Kate, women I should have protected left to suffer because of our friendship. I was struggling to accept that Kate and Andy were sleeping together, let alone in a relationship. It all now made sense.

'I can't speculate—'

'Cut the crap, Paul. You've known me long enough.'

Paul sighed. He didn't have to reply.

'Angela would have *killed* Liam Goodman without thinking twice. She's already killed five other men because of what *Andrew Hansley* did.' I didn't care who overheard me.

'Five?'

I sighed, confirmation that Angela had also stabbed Lee Fellows not yet provided. 'Yeah. The guy who was stabbed outside Billy's bar.'

'Shit. Really?'

I nodded.

'In that case, she *will* be held accountable.' Paul didn't add, *as will Andy*.

If the police didn't, I would, readily becoming a wanted man myself before this day was out. There was nothing else to say about that. I suddenly wanted to call Steph. She was always my first point of contact, the only family I had to lean on in times of crisis. Yet, what would I say? How could I confirm that Andy was a rapist, nothing to conclude from our earlier conversation that would help now? It wasn't Steph's fault. She was stuck in the middle, Kate a good friend to her, once upon a time. It didn't help me now though, unfortunately. I didn't know what to think, still unable to process the events of the day.

'Andrew's car has been impounded,' Paul confirmed sullenly, placing his mobile inside his pocket.

'And?' Why was that my problem? I was still shaking, still felt sick.

He took in a sharp breath. 'They found *your* DNA on the front seat and steering wheel.'

I shot my friend a blank look. What was I missing? I was growing tired of the accusations today, tired of fighting off

## The Lost Raven

Andy's shit. I couldn't reply.

'Along with traces of Rosie O'Connor's blood.'

'You *still* think I'm involved?' I honestly didn't know what to make of the situation.

'No. I know you better than that. But the CPS—'

'*Screw* the CPS. Paul, we've been friends for years. When have I *ever* given you cause to believe anything bad of me? When have I ever acted anything other than one hundred percent professional?' I couldn't believe I was saying such things aloud to a man I assumed a friend. I was trembling, my argument with Steph still fresh, still painful, Andy turning out to be no friend at all, in the end.

Paul shrugged, needing to question me anyway, despite my annoyance, just part of the process, the job. My whereabouts were once again required for the purposes of a little blue folder, boxes ticked to satisfy pen pushers who didn't even know who I was.

'Where is he now?'

'Locked in a cell.'

I knew at some point I would need to speak with him, look my *ex*-friend in the eye, punch him in the face. I ignored Paul's plea's to calm down and instead took my anger out on my coffee, the entire cup threatening to disintegrate in my grip. I needed to look Andy in the eyes. I needed to know the truth. Five men had died because of what his actions had triggered, a trail of damaged women left behind. I couldn't dwell on the fact that Angela was unstable anyway and therefore might have turned killer at some point, with or without Andy's help.

I hadn't seen Kate for years. I was getting over her, slowly getting my life back on track. Now, singlehandedly, Andrew Hansley had taken me back to that time, no explanation offered that I understood until now. I appreciated how Angela felt. Raped by her father, abused for years, only to then feel the same shame and repulsion at the hand of someone else, someone we thought we could trust, both of us scorned by the very same man.

'He's going down for what he did to those poor girls.' I was muttering, shaking, couldn't imagine him getting away with it, potentially more women out there who never came forward. Angela was one of them, prepared to take things into her own hands rather than face the shame of police interviews, court hearings, her friends. In fact, if it wasn't for Rosie O'Connor and the CCTV footage found on Liam Goodman's home security, a statement made by my ex, we wouldn't be in this position now. I had to find The Raven Rapist. I had to put right at least one thing that had happened this week. *This was my fault.* Lending her my jacket, letting Andy into my home. I didn't assume he would want to face me again. Neither of us would want that on our conscience.

# Forty-Two

## *Angela*

I am contemplating what might happen if I were to throw myself into the river. Would anyone notice? Would anyone care? I pull my phone from my pocket, its silence overbearing, my thoughts unravelling at a pace I can't sustain. I know, of course, that if I turn it on, my whereabouts will be highlighted immediately, my location pinging from several nearby masts. Yet, I need to say goodbye to Rosie, if I can. Apologise, tell her I'm sorry. The net is closing in and it won't be long before they find me. When they do, this will all be over. I don't think I can face a jail cell. I need to be free — like the ravens.

I hesitate before turning on my mobile, watching the logo flash across a black screen, several incoming notifications and messages highlighting my recent absence. I'm not expecting Rosie to answer so quickly, not anticipating the sound of her comforting voice.

'Angela! Where *are* you?' She sounds shocked, surprised

I'm giving her the time of day.

I don't know what to say. I'm standing next to the river's edge, my feet close to death, the dark water ready to claim me for its own. I can't speak, can't breathe, can't imagine life behind bars. I say nothing that will confirm my false innocence. I'm still crying. I can't help it.

'I wanted to tell you how sorry I am. For everything.' I no longer recognise my own voice.

'You've done nothing to be sorry for.'

I have. She obviously doesn't know yet, hasn't been told what I am.

'I never meant for any of this. I hope you will one day understand.' It's true. I will never get the justice I need now from Liam, the man no doubt already in the hospital, his injuries confirmed, his statement taken.

'Let me help you, Angela.' Rosie sounds as if she wants to, despite everything. She has a warming tone to her voice, like hot sugary tea, and I momentarily close my eyes, wishing I could be in a warm room somewhere with her, safe, well, wishing she could have been my *mum*.

'You already have.' In more ways than one. I almost end the call, my finger hovering.

'It *will* be okay.' My friend's voice sounds faint, as if the devil has snatched it away.

'Not for me.' I'm no longer convinced she can hear me. 'I can't go to prison.' It was never the plan. My phone is almost out of power and I'm almost out of time.

'Stay exactly where you are. Please.' I can't imagine she hasn't spoken to the police, isn't already with them, knows what I did—a confession in a darkened hotel room no longer private, closed curtains no longer protecting my secrets.

I don't want to think about what I've become, can't think about Liam. Should I kill myself now? It would be so

## The Lost Raven

easy. I *could* jump. They might never find my body. I'm losing all sense of time and place, the day slipping into a blur of confusion, my head along for an insane ride. The water is calling, waiting. I see demons down there, smiling at me, hyperventilating at the mere thought of my damaged soul, absorbing this moment, enjoying their power. It's all I deserve.

'Goodbye Rosie.' I hang up and throw my phone as firmly as I can into the water. It splashes loudly, sending several unsuspecting birds flying into the air, the solid object bouncing briefly before disappearing below the surface. I imagine a police scramble, plenty of panic ensuing as they race to my location. I stand on the waters edge for a while, my feet unable to move, my mind unwilling to accept my fate.

'Angela?'

I don't expect to hear my name being called behind me, yet I turn around anyway, barely recognising my own name. Newton is standing on the riverbank, several police cars already behind him, uniformed officers waiting. *Shit.* I take a breath, searching my surroundings, imagining the police triangulating my position whilst I was off in my own world. There is a helicopter overhead.

'Come with me.' He has an arm raised towards me.

'I can't.' My feet won't move, my legs set in place.

'I can help you.'

It's ironic. The only thing I *ever* wanted was help, someone to hear me, to understand. I thought I needed it. Now I'm a lost cause, *a lost raven*, forgotten by a world that has steadily devoured me. I glance skyward, knowing my real friends lie beyond the clouds, waiting for me to take that final leap of faith. I close my eyes. *I can fly*. I just need to believe it.

'I need to tell you something,' Newton declares, 'but I'd

rather we talk somewhere else.'

What could this man possibly tell me *now* that I want to hear? I shake my head, unwilling to comply.

A pause. 'I need to tell you that Liam Goodman did *not* rape you.'

What the hell is he talking about? I narrow my eyes. 'Yes he did. He was in his bedroom with me.' I can still feel him on me, *inside* me. I don't want to confirm it, hate that he's no doubt spent these last few hours trying to deny it.

'No, Angela, he didn't do it. *I promise.* The police have already ruled him out.' Newton is shouting over the breeze, unconcerned by prying ears, unwanted attention.

'On what basis?' The same wind is threatening to tip me into the water.

'On the basis that someone else's DNA was found on yours and Rosie's clothing.'

'Whose?' How dare he assume something like that? I imagine he lying in order to lure me into the open, keep me talking a little longer whilst they gather unwanted resources, making sure I can't escape when they arrest me. I glance around, police surrounding me now, armed officers poised, ready.

Another pause. I find it uncomfortable. 'Andrew Hansley.'

*What?* 'What are you talking about? How would you *know* that?' Surely he has this wrong. There's a wobble in my voice. It isn't ideal. How can it have been Andrew? I was prepared to *kill* Liam, had already murdered strangers because of the anger he provoked.

'Andrew's DNA matched semen found on Rosie O'Connor, her clothing, and *your* dress.' He doesn't confirm that if I hadn't showered and washed away vital evidence from my own body, they might have found Andrew on *me*, too. I feel sick, my legs faltering.

## The Lost Raven

I take a step forward, my foot raised ready, anticipating the icy water sucking me to my death. I can barely think beyond words I don't understand. I just want to die.

*'Angela?!'*

A yell, someone grabbing me, pulling me from the river's edge—the water no more my friend than the sky. I glance up. Newton is next to me now, his face ashen, worried. He looks genuinely concerned. I wish it were true.

'Tell Rosie I'm sorry,' I mutter, offering a smile that takes every effort to pull into a familiar shape. I can't live inside my head anymore, can't imagine another day like this. I wasn't there for my friend when she needed me and I've killed people. Innocent people. How can I ever live with that? 'She was a good friend.' And so, it seems, was Liam.

I pat Newton on the arm, a simple gesture, nothing more. Without hesitation, without thinking, I race into the street, no one to stop me, stepping directly into the path of an oncoming bus. Screaming brakes converge with a ravens call, loud, shrill, distinct. It's over. I feel nothing as I stare towards the sky, several black shapes looming overhead.

\*\*\*

I'm on my back, a tickle in my throat from escaping blood ready to jump from my collapsing lungs into my clammy hands, suffocate me where I lie, laugh in my face. I don't have long. Newton races forward, lowering his creaking body over mine, his knees cracking, the ground cold and damp, this week consisting of alien environments that have threatened to break my bones and mind to pieces. I stare into his shocked face, death already enveloping my weakened body. I try to smile but I don't think I can.

'Do you have a family?' I'm trying to speak through my bitten tongue, my broken ribs pressed into my punctured lungs.

He nods. I think he might be crying.

'Do they love you?'

Another nod.

'You're lucky.' I wished I could have had more time with Rosie. I can't dwell. My body is no longer willing to cope with the damage thrust upon it, my bones broken, my body irreparable. I reach a trembling hand towards his, pressing my icy fingers into his palm. Newton looks puzzled, as always, his face contorting, nothing left for him to say. 'Don't feel sorry for me,' I mutter, blood escaping my lips, making my words sound strange. Someone yells for an ambulance. I don't need one. I'm not going to the hospital.

'Try not to speak,' Newton whispers, nothing else to say, sitting now with my head in his lap, his warm hand holding mine.

I've been absorbing negative energies for so long it was bound to manifest as something evil in the end. I try to laugh, wondering why it has taken so long for me to realise this. It is hardly an appropriate time for jokes, I know. I don't confirm my thoughts.

'Help is coming.' He is yelling now, holding me in his arms, trying not to lose it, lose me.

'Do something for me?' I feel sorry that I tried to hate him. I don't. His jacket became my protection when I had nothing else to lean on. I feel bad that I lost it, can't give it back.

'Anything.' He attempts a smile, fails.

'Look after the ravens.'

I don't know why, but I feel them surrounding me, encasing my body beneath their beating wings, lifting me, taking me higher. *I can fly.* I find myself staring skyward, my body lighter than air, a powerful jolt from my failing heart sending the world into slow motion. I look into his kind eyes, nowhere else for me to be, watching how they widen in shock, mine glistening with more life than I ever felt when it mattered. I don't feel sad anymore. I can't even breathe. A flock of ravens are overhead. They have come for me.

'I will.'

Newton's words are the last I hear, my request the last I'll make, my journey in this life over. I embrace my fate as my body falls silent, my heart already stopped beating in the second it takes me to part my lips. It is the last thing I will ever do.

I'm home. I can finally let go.

*My name is Angela Healy and I will always be defined by my actions.*

# Forty-Three

## *Newton*

Angela was dead, yet the unfortunate scene that met my eyes took me back a decade, to my brother's body, a different London street seeing much-unanticipated panic, a different time still more painful than I wanted to admit. I glanced at my palms now covered in blood, the poor girl's fate once more in my hands. She was on the ground, her life over, the bus driver and several passengers mirroring my shock, my distress. Paul was yelling but I could hear nothing beyond a rush of pulsating blood through my ears, my heart pounding so violently I could barely think straight.

'Newt? Are you okay?' My friend's words were distant, barely audible above old memories I didn't expect to hurt so much after all these years, unable to process events I had no control over. Chaos surrounded us, people yelling, others screaming. A woman was dead, they said. Suicide. Only the police appreciated why.

'I'm fine,' I lied, getting to my feet, my legs trembling.

## The Lost Raven

I was grateful for the fast-paced car journey that had led us here, time saved, if not a life, The Raven Rapist enough of a priority to warrant the urgency. Angela's fate was sealed the moment she turned on her mobile phone. It was a shame that, in the end, we were too late to save her, too late to ask the questions nobody would ever now know about the girl behind the bravado.

'The police have apparently finished with your jacket,' Paul confirmed. 'You can have it back, when you're ready.'

I wasn't sure I wanted it, wasn't convinced I'd ever look at it the same way. Instead, I nodded, offering a smile I wasn't sure I achieved convincingly, ignoring the increasingly panic behind us. I watched my friend become absorbed once more in police business, needing only to see Steph, the kids, apologise, make things right. All I could see was Isaac lying on that road, not Angela, the last decade dissolving to dust, Kate included, Andy, the life I assumed I'd built. None of it mattered.

I climbed into a taxi, not so much as a glance behind me as I left Paul to deal with the fallout of today's events. The death of The Raven Rapist would soon make national news, the press and general public wanting their slice of information. It was too late for Angela but she'd unwittingly taught me something important, something fundamental. I needed to be with my family. Nothing else mattered. In a bid for normality I'd almost forgotten how much they loved me, taking for granted what wasn't always available to others. The only thing I knew now was that I would never again take *them* for granted.

I assumed I would confront Andy, at some point, demand answers, give him the respect he'd failed to give me. For now it didn't matter. I wasn't sure I needed his validation anyway. He didn't mean much in the scheme of things, didn't factor in the life I wanted to live. I glanced skyward through the damp taxi window, watching several ravens circling overhead. I genuinely hoped that, wherever she was, Angela had found her freedom. She deserved it. I guess, when all was said and done, it was down to the rest of us now to find ours.

# The Case of Angela Healy

## Bipolar Disorder Versus Victimisation and the Psychotic Mind

How do I describe Angela Healy in a way that can be adequately appreciated? On the surface she seemed just like any other young woman, relatively healthy, capable of maintaining a manageable existence. Yet, beneath the façade she was broken, no different to so many people, reaching out where there was nothing to find, searching for something that did not exist. She was on a rooftop when we met, contemplating suicide. It feels like a lifetime ago now however, and I did *not* anticipate we'd have a second conversation. Yet, despite knowing her for less than a week, I discovered more about humanity in those few days than I have during several years of prolonged therapy with many other damaged souls.

According to recent statistics, there are approximately one point three million people in the UK currently suffering with bipolar disorder. That equates to one in every fifty citizens, or two percent of the population. Unbelievably that's thirty percent more than those with dementia and twice of schizophrenia. Putting that in perspective assumes that, at some point in any given day, we will encounter at least one person privately living with this debilitating condition. How often do we stop to notice? How much do we care?

Angela displayed traits of classic bipolar, her symptoms synonymous with her behaviour, her emotional responses to both external and internal stimuli alternating wildly. Yet, I wonder how much of *The Raven Rapist* developed due to her mental health compared the inner trauma she'd suffered since childhood? What drove her to kill, believing murder was the ultimate way of escaping an otherwise impossible situation? What became the turning point that shifted suicidal tendencies to murderous rage, depression, and anger the driving force behind her repulsive crimes? What finally tipped her over the edge?

It is an unfortunate fact that criminals are caught by chance, not carefully planned policing, despite what television dramas and Hollywood movies will have you believe. After all, the police assumed, as did I, we were searching for a *man*. As it was, *The Raven Rapist* was no master criminal, her actions often outright chaotic, desperate, spiralling emotions an overriding factor for everything she did.

Despite knowing nothing about the girl until our fateful meeting on that freezing rooftop, from what I've since learned from friends and colleagues, she was a kind, loving, thoughtful young woman with a passion for music, dancing, and fun. She kept her bipolar under control for years, her condition not defining the person she was, only succumbing to her trauma after being raped a week before her death.

I've since learned her father died that same week, an event that ultimately spiralled her mood, tipping the balance of her once assumed stable life, bringing forward painful events from a past she'd worked hard to dislodge.

A single week was all it took for Angela Healy to kill *five* adult males, the brutality used beyond anything I'd seen from a female, anger an obvious overriding factor. Women usually kill in the heat of a moment, crimes of passion at the heart of most attacks. Yet, Angela's murderous streak ran far deeper than anything I've ever encountered. She was a damaged young woman, admittedly, off her medication because she believed drugs confused her mind. Yet, she saw herself as a victim, her earlier records concluding this truth along with a recommended reliance on antidepressants. It made for extremely painful reading. She was just sixteen years old when a request was granted to section her under the Mental Health Act, a failed suicide attempt behind her, her father already on trial because of twelve years of abuse. She subsequently spent six months in a psychiatric hospital before moving to a bedsit and beginning a potential new life. There was no record of ongoing support.

Stress, of course, is a trigger for bipolar, and Angela's moods swung wildly from suicide to extreme mania and psychosis. It affected her decision-making, rationalisation, judgment. Yet the *decision* to rape and mutilate four total strangers was neither conscious nor unconscious. The state in which she left her victims expressed savage desperation, as if she felt she had no choice but carry out deeds preordained by her past. She was along for the ride, nothing more, a *victim* of her own actions laid out by an unseen force, blaming her father, the man behind bars still very much in control of it all. She believed she was saving other females from men who'd scorned *her*, setting right the wrongs done all those years ago, healing old wounds by creating fresh ones. I assume that is why she loved ravens. They were free. Angela Healy only wanted the same outcome.

Of course, if every sufferer of bipolar turned killer, we would have a very serious problem, so it comes as no surprise that I must conclude her condition cannot be blamed for her actions. Yet, despite this, our brief interaction provided a clear appreciation of bipolar and how difficult it can be, if left untreated, including a higher regard for Angela Healy herself that I might not have otherwise understood.

Would Angela have become a murderer if she had taken her medication, sought help, remained calm? *Maybe*. After all, murderers are borne from their innermost emotions, deepest feelings, highest desires. No one has the right to dictate how another should feel, how they interpret their existence or view the world. Do I believe bipolar contributed to the killing of five men? *No*. Because if that were the case, every street in England would be littered with bodies, every newspaper overflowing with untold stories. I do, however, believe she used her illness as a weapon for unthinkable violence, twisting her innermost darkest thoughts into something far uglier than it needed to be. Did she *mean* to brutally murder those men? I really don't think so. Why? Because Angela Healy was nothing more than a lost girl in a world she believed needed changing—a lost raven, a suffering soul.

*N Flanigan*

# Acknowledgements

I want to thank a dear friend of mine for her valuable insight into what it's like to live with bipolar. If it wasn't for you Jade, this book might never have been written.

As always, a heartfelt thanks goes to SRL Publishing, their ceaseless support and hard work has, once again, ensured this novel exists. And to my husband who never fails to lend me a genuine ear when I need insight into my plotlines and ultimate aims.

Oh, and to my dog, who never leaves my side, no matter how long he must endure my inner chatter and typing fingers.

SRL Publishing don't just publish books, we also do our best in keeping this world sustainable. In the UK alone, over 77 million books are destroyed each year, unsold and unread, due to overproduction and bigger profit margins.

Our business model is inherently sustainable by only printing what we sell. While this means our cost price is much higher, it means we have minimum waste and zero returns. We made a public promise in 2020 to never overprint our books just for the sake of profit.

We give back to our planet by calculating the number of trees used for our products so we can then replace them. We also calculate our carbon emissions and support projects which reduce C02. These same projects also support the United Nations Sustainable Development Goals.

The way we operate means we knowingly waive our profit margins for the sake of the environment. Every book sold via the SRL website plants at least one tree.

To find out more, please visit
www.srlpublishing.co.uk/responsibility